Facets

Novels by Barbara Delinsky

*Facets**
*Commitments**
*Heart of the Night**
*Twilight Whispers**
Family Tree
Looking for Peyton Place
The Summer I Dared
Flirting with Pete
An Accidental Woman
The Woman Next Door
The Vineyard
Lake News
Coast Road
Three Wishes
A Woman's Place
Shades of Grace
Together Alone
For My Daughters
Suddenly
More Than Friends
The Passions of Chelsea Kane
A Woman Betrayed

Nonfiction by Barbara Delinsky
Uplift

*Published by
WARNER BOOKS

BARBARA DELINSKY

Facets

WARNER BOOKS

NEW YORK BOSTON

Copyright © 1990 by Barbara Delinsky

Warner Books
Hachette Book Group USA
237 Park Avenue
New York, NY 10169

Visit our Web site at www.HachetteBookGroupUSA.com.

Printed in the United States of America

First Warner Books Hardcover Edition: July 2007
10 9 8 7 6 5 4 3 2 1

Library of Congress Control Number: 2006934321
ISBN: 978-0-446-58027-4

Facets

Chapter 1

◈◈◈

New York, March 1990

O<small>F ALL THE THINGS HE'D DONE</small> to her in the past, of all the things he hadn't done or either might have or should have, his betrayal now was the cruelest. Hillary Cox stared at the television screen long after his image had faded. Her mind was nearly as blank, wiped clean by disbelief, shock, and pain.

Sweeping the long auburn waves from her face, she turned and stared at the carpet. But there were no answers to be found in the thick crimson pile.

Engaged? John was engaged?

She swallowed hard. The remote control fell from her thighs to the floor as she got up and wandered distractedly around the den. The room wasn't large. Nor was the rest of her apartment, but it was the best she could afford on Manhattan's Upper East Side, which was where she wanted to live, where she wanted to be with John. She had rented it as much to satisfy her own pride as to suit him. He was a man of means. Someplace shabby would never have appealed to him.

If he'd given her money, she might have had a bigger place. But then she would have felt more like a whore than she did now.

Her step faltered. She hadn't ever sold herself. Her feelings for John had always been deep, and whether they were of love, hate, respect,

or contempt, she had been faithful to him for many years. She was no whore. A fool, perhaps. But not a whore.

She moved from the back of one chintz-covered chair to another, and then to the front of a simple cherrywood table she used as a desk. Her fingertips skimmed the papers and magazines strewn haphazardly on its top. She knew exactly what was where. John had never been able to understand that. In his mind, organization was crucial and neatness its prerequisite.

At the bookshelf she paused to touch the CD player he had given her the Christmas before, then the Steuben owl of a couple of Christmases earlier, then the framed picture she had taken of him several Christmases before that. He was a handsome devil, dark-haired and dark-eyed with features that were aristocratic enough to foil the occasional primitive look. She had seen him mature over the years, had watched his shoulders broaden, his five o'clock shadow thicken, his sideburns don a silver lining. Twenty-seven years was a long time to know a man, but she hadn't counted until now. She'd just assumed there would be many years ahead for them.

A knot tightened inside her.

He couldn't be engaged, she told herself. John wasn't the marrying kind. He had reached fifty without speaking his vows, had attained extraordinary success without benefit of a wife. There was no earthly reason why he would choose to take one now—and John never did anything without reason.

Fallen in love? No, not John.

But he had said he was engaged. On nationwide television, he had said he was engaged.

Feeling a pang in the pit of her stomach, she turned from the imperious face in the picture and resumed her pacing. Moments later she found herself at the door of her bedroom, leaning weakly against the jamb, staring at the bed. It was carefully dressed in its white satin cover as it hadn't been the weekend before. There had been no point in making it up then. She and John hadn't left it for long.

Her breath came less evenly in the wake of memory. John was an incredible lover. He was demanding but rewarding, and if there

were times when he was a little rough, she liked that, too. It was a change from the civilized veneer he showed the world. She took pride in sparking that roughness. It was a sign of power, proof that she did things for John that no other woman could.

On Sunday afternoon he had headed back to Boston, *Facets'* home base. She hadn't heard from him since, but that was his style. She had adapted to it over the years by making the best out of a situation she couldn't change. John did what he wanted. He answered to no one.

Engaged? It wasn't possible.

Or was it?

She paced with growing agitation. She wouldn't have thought twice if she had read of his engagement in the *National Enquirer.* Lord knew the tabloid had announced the same before. But that had always been wild speculation, pairing him with women he hardly knew or could barely abide.

The interview on *20/20* was different. The show had credibility. So did Janet Curry. She was a mature, elegant woman, a fixture in Boston society, in her midforties, newly widowed and financially set. Hillary knew that John had dated her. He'd told her so. But he hadn't mentioned an engagement—not when she'd seen him at the time of the show's filming a month before, nor during last weekend.

As the meaning of that sank in, so did the hurt. If the engagement was for real, John had been making love to her well after he'd committed himself to Janet, which cheapened both their lovemaking and Hillary herself. Moreover, if he got married, there would be a steady woman by his side and in his bed. A steady, legitimate woman. And it wouldn't be Hillary.

Fighting off a wave of panic, she crossed to the nightstand, picked up the phone, and hastily punched out Pam's number. Pam would know the truth. After all, she was John's sister. Surely he'd have shared such news with her.

Then again, he might not have. Hillary pressed the disconnect button. Although Pam was deeply involved in the family business, she and John weren't close. It was no wonder. John was a bastard.

And who better to confirm his plans than the bastard himself.

Punching out the number of John's Beacon Hill townhouse, she waited through four long rings, growing more anxious with each.

"St. George residence." There was noise in the background.

"Christian, this is Hillary Cox." She spoke firmly, with as much authority as she could muster, given the probability that if she was a has-been in John's life, his houseboy would know it. "Is John there?"

During the few seconds it took him to answer, she identified the background noise. There were people there. Their voices blended into a single, cacophonous drone. "He's here, Miss Cox, but he's occupied at the moment." She heard a peal of laughter. "May I tell him you called?"

She had the disconcerting suspicion that there was a party going on. "Now," she insisted. "Tell him I'm on the phone and that I'd like to talk with him now."

"Perhaps it would be better—"

"Please, Christian. This is urgent."

Some of her desperation must have reached him. After a brief pause, then a short directive, Christian put her on hold.

The sudden silence was worse for the voices she'd heard before. They haunted her, making her feel shut out, and while she'd felt excluded from John's life many times in the past, this time was harder. It was one thing to be excluded when everyone else was, another thing to be shut out when others so clearly were not.

"Hillary?" His voice came as low and composed as ever. The background chatter was gone. She pictured him in the library, surrounded by walls of books he'd never read, his long lean fingers propped on the gleaming mahogany desk. He would have shut the door to ensure his privacy, a need that suddenly smacked of guilt.

"What's going on, John?"

He seemed oblivious to the strained tone of her voice. "How are you?"

"John—"

"Did you see the show?" He spoke slowly, deliberately.

"Of course. That's what—"

"What did you think?"

"I don't know. That's why—"

"It wasn't bad." His tone smoothly countered the under statement. "Those shows can be poison. As charming as the interviewer may seem in person, once the filming is done and the editing begins, the brightest man can sound moronic."

Hillary was losing what little composure she had. "John, what was—"

"I came across well, I think. I'm pleased."

"So are a lot of other people, from the way it sounded when Christian answered the phone." She hurried the words out before he cut her off again. "What's going on?"

He was silent for a moment. "A few friends dropped in to celebrate."

"They must have had great timing. The show hasn't been over for fifteen minutes." Which could mean only one thing. "They watched it with you, didn't they?"

"Several did."

"Several. Three? Eight? Twenty?" She made no attempt to hide her hurt. "John, I'd have come too, if I'd known you were having a party. But I wasn't invited. You didn't want me there. You rarely do. And you won't now." She took a quick breath. "Is it true? Are you and Janet engaged?"

He hesitated. "I'll call you back later, Hillary."

"No. Now. Are you engaged?" He didn't answer. "Are you marrying her?" Still there was no response. "Tell me, John."

"We'll discuss it later."

"I have to know now. It was bad enough hearing it on television. How could you do that to me?" she cried. Once the pain started tearing from her, it wouldn't stop. "How could you do it like that? After all the years, all the time we've been together, how could you let me find out along with millions of other people? Didn't you think I'd be hurt?"

"Not now, Hillary."

He sounded annoyed, but she didn't care. "You don't love her. I know you, John. You don't love her. You love yourself and those

damned stores. So why are you marrying her? You have the power you've always wanted. My God, after tonight you'll have newspapers and magazines banging down your door for interviews. You've got money. You've got fame. So why do you want her? She isn't gorgeous. My looks are better. And she can't give you what you need. I'm the one who does that. All these years, it's been *me*."

His voice was tight. "Hillary, this isn't the time or place—"

"And speaking of time and place, what was last weekend about? You were with me, John. For forty-eight hours you were with me, doing every intimate little thing we've been doing for years. If you were engaged to her, what in the hell were you doing with me?" She wrapped a trembling hand around her middle. "Tell me that, John. What was last weekend about?"

"Last weekend was about us," he answered, clearly angry that he'd been pushed. "It's what we've always been and done."

"But you're engaged to marry someone else!"

"So?"

Hillary's mouth fell open. "*So?* So you're two-timing her!"

"Janet will benefit from this marriage. She'll get the protection she lost when Turner died. She'll have someone to take control of her life again, which is what she's missed. I never promised her fidelity, and she hasn't asked for it."

"Then you think you're going to keep it up with me while you're married to her?"

"She won't mind."

"Well, I will!"

"I don't see why." He sounded totally serious. "We've been involved before, you and I, while I've been seeing other women."

"But you've never been married to any of them!"

"And you've suddenly turned righteous? Come off it, Hillary. What difference will my being married make?"

"A big difference."

"No, it won't change a thing between you and me. We'll see each other as often as we ever did. My relationship with Janet is a rational

thing. It's convenient. It gets hangers-on off both of our backs. It quiets skeptics. I'm not looking for passion from her. I get that from you."

"But you're marrying her!"

"And you refuse to carry on with a married man? Try again." His voice hardened. "What is it you want? Money? Jewels? Company stock?"

His words hit her like a slap in the face. He was so far off the mark, so far from understanding her, even after all the years they'd known each other. As long as she'd been mistress to a man who shunned marriage, she'd been able to abide the other women who had come and gone in his life. After all, she was the one who remained. John always returned to her, and that had been some solace for all else she might have wanted from him. Now, though, he was giving another woman his name, putting another on a pedestal that had previously been empty. The issue was self-respect. Hillary had too much pride to have her relationship with him finally and deliberately spelled out, reduced to its lowest common denominator.

His presence on the other end of the line suddenly grew grating. Given how raw she felt, it was too much. "Go to hell," she muttered and hung up, then stared at the phone, praying that it would ring, that he would call back.

But she knew he wouldn't. He wouldn't give her a sign that he cared, and he certainly wouldn't apologize. He was too arrogant for that. Instead, he would turn off the light in the library and return to his party, well aware that she would know he was doing just that as she sat alone in New York. He would let the pain of her imaginings be punishment for having hung up on him.

And so she felt punished. Picturing him with a parlor full of people, one of whom was certainly his fiancée, all no doubt in awe of him for having pulled off such a smashing publicity coup on network television, was torture. Hugging herself, she rocked back and forth on the edge of her bed, but the movement did little to ease her misery. Nor did prowling through the apartment. She felt odd, empty in a gut-wrenching kind of way, yet filled with emotions that all clamored

for her attention. Sadness, pain, anger, loneliness, fear—she didn't know which to address first.

She threw on a long coat and sought refuge in the March night. The air was cool and welcome. Clutching her coat closed, she strode quickly along the city sidewalk, past brownstones and storefronts and many people who were also strolling the streets at midnight. Just then she was glad that New York never slept. Seeing others who were alone, she didn't feel quite so lonely.

Then again, she had always prided herself on being a step above such urban isolation. No matter how much time she spent alone—and as a writer she spent plenty—there was always the knowledge that she had John. Even when months went by between visits, she knew he was there. They didn't talk on the phone. They didn't write letters. But he was there, and she knew that when he was ready he would come to her.

No more.

She walked on and on. At length, feeling chilled despite the exertion, she headed back to her apartment. Her answering machine showed a single message. Telling herself it had to be John, she felt a surge of pure happiness and activated the machine.

"Hi, Hillary." Her heart fell. "It's Pam. I really want to talk with you, but I'm not home, so you can't call me back. I'll try you again in the morning."

The machine beeped off. Had it been John, she might have saved the message in order to hear his voice again and again. Instead, she stood where she was, weighed down by disappointment. She loved Pam. But John's voice was the one she craved.

She wanted to talk with someone, wanted to shriek and cry on a sympathetic shoulder, but Pam wasn't home, and she couldn't bother friends at this late hour.

In truth, with the exception of Pam, Hillary wouldn't have dared call her friends. John was a touchy subject, one she had long ago learned to keep to herself. Few of her friends had met him. Several didn't even know his identity, only that she had a lover of long standing. None of them could understand why she put up with him. They

thought she was crazy to wait out the silence between visits, crazy to let him come and go without making any kind of formal commitment. Every woman had a right to protect her interests, they claimed, and though she had always argued that she was self-sufficient enough not to need that where John was concerned, maybe they were right. If she were to call now and complain about what he had done, she would be in for a string of I-told-you-so's. She wasn't up for that.

The night seemed endless. She was too wound up to sleep, too wound up even to sit still for long. No diversion worked. She played soft music, drank mellow wine, soaked in a bath that should have drained the tension from her limbs. But all the while she thought of John, and the pain inside gave no quarter.

With the coming of dawn she was a bundle of nerves. She watched the first needles of sunlight pierce the concrete canyons of her street, watched the delivery truck bring the newspapers. She went down for hers, carried it back upstairs, opened to the society page, and died a little. The article wasn't large. John wasn't royalty yet. But the mention was there, four full paragraphs on the imminent marriage of one of the East Coast's most eligible bachelors. With shaky desperation, she hid it under yesterday's paper on the kitchen counter.

She took a hot shower, dressed, looked at her watch. It was barely seven-thirty. Pam would be up. But she didn't want to call her. She was too upset to talk. So she went to her desk, determined to work, but she couldn't think of a thing to write.

She needed air. Grabbing her coat from where she'd thrown it the night before, she went out walking again. She took deep breaths. She made eye contact with the few other early Saturday morning walkers she passed. She held her head high. Inevitably, though, at each corner stand, her attention fell to the papers. Finally, unable to resist, she bought the one that she didn't have, tucked it under her arm, and went home.

There, too, was an article on John's engagement.

Disgusted, she pushed it aside, snatched up her briefcase, and went out again, this time to the library. She stayed there for most of the day, not because she was accomplishing much but simply because

she couldn't bear to be home alone with the bittersweet memories and the silence.

When she finally headed back, she found another message from Pam. This one was more pointed: "Hi, Hillary, it's me again. Listen, we have to meet. I'll be flying down on Wednesday to see a client. Let's do lunch. One o'clock. The Four Seasons. If you can't make it, call me back. Otherwise, I'll see you then."

The message was typically Pam, quiet and efficient, knowing what needed to be done and doing it. Beneath the quiet efficiency was insistence, but it was spawned not so much by arrogance as by a passionate conviction. That was one of the differences between Pam and her brother. Pam was an emotional being. She felt. She cared. She bled.

So did Hillary.

But not John.

That thought, more than any other, kept coming back to taunt her through the long, lonely hours of the weekend. Her emotions ricocheted between disbelief and hurt, confusion and despair. She struggled to see the future as it stretched before her, but the bleakness of it made her turn away. It didn't seem fair. For too long she had held back, orienting her life to John's. While she cursed him in one breath, in the next she had to curse herself. He had used her, and she had allowed it.

By the time the weekend was over, she was as angry as she was hurt, and the anger gave birth to an idea. She was finished with John's abuse. Life went on, and with it her potential for growth. She didn't care if her anger at John was the catalyst. She didn't care if he would be furious at what she planned. She had nothing more to lose.

It was time she made something big of her life. Using John to do so would be poetic justice.

Chapter 2

◈ ◈ ◈

PAMELA ST. GEORGE WAS the kind of woman who exuded class without knowing it. Self-confidence wasn't something she gave much thought to, nor was beauty, but she had both. She could catch her long dark hair in a single thick braid and pair it with an Armani suit, and the next week the socialites would be copying the look. Not that she would notice or care. She had priorities in life, and setting the style wasn't one of them.

Except when it came to jewelry. Jewelry mattered. Especially jewelry with her name on it. She was a live advertisement for Pamela St. George Originals, for as coveted as her designs already were, she could never overlook an opportunity to make them more so. From strength came power, she believed, and though Hillary wasn't entirely sure why Pam needed all that power, she didn't find fault. Pam had borne her share of crosses in life. She still did.

Now, watching her approach in the wake of the maître d', Hillary felt the familiar mix of jealousy and affection for the woman who was closer to her than her own sister. She wanted to hate her—for her looks, her grace, her success—but she couldn't. Pam was too good a person, too warm, too genuine, and she'd been too loyal a friend.

As always, she had an aura about her. With her hair caught over one ear in a silver clasp, she looked very much the artist. The bohemian effect was enhanced by a suede outfit whose ragged hemline dusted matching boots, but the closer she came, the more Hillary's

attention was drawn from her clothes to her throat. Like her hair clasp, her necklace was silver, encrusted with a mosaic of stones ranging from pale pink to purple. The semiprecious gems were tourmalines—Pamela's trademark.

Slipping an arm around Hillary's shoulders, Pam leaned down to hug her for a long, meaningful minute. Then, with a brief smile to the waiting maître d', she settled into her chair, resting her menu on the china place setting. Her eyes were on Hillary.

"Are you okay?" she asked softly.

They hadn't spoken since John's appearance on television. Even after four full days, Hillary still felt battered. "I'll survive. Pride has a way of keeping things in perspective."

Pam studied her for a minute longer before saying, still in her soft voice but with the glint of steel in her eyes, "I'm appalled. You do know that, don't you?"

"You're kind."

"Kindness has nothing to do with it. Common sense does. And compassion. And love. It should have been you." She rushed on when Hillary suddenly looked mutinous. "I'm saying that first thing, because it's what I believe, and I have to get it off my chest. If he had to marry anyone, it should have been you."

"But it wasn't."

"For which you should probably thank your lucky stars, though you won't. You've always been a sucker for John. God knows why. He's arrogant, self-centered, despotic, and sly, all of which spells lousy husband material. Think about it, and you'll know it's true." She touched her head. "Up here, at least." Her hand fell to her heart. "This is another story. We've never talked the word *love*—"

"I don't love him."

"No?"

"No."

"You've stuck by him for a mighty long time."

"Habit," Hillary said with a self-effacing smirk.

Pam gave her hand a squeeze. "You deserve better. John may be my brother, but I want far better than him for you. Maybe what he's

doing now is a blessing in disguise. Maybe it'll open your eyes to other men."

"I'm not looking for other men." There had been times when she had, but none had measured up to John. Not that she'd tell that to Pam. It would mean analyzing John's appeal beyond the physical level, and she didn't understand that herself. There was something beyond habit, something almost irrational that drew her back to him time and again. "I don't need a man to survive."

"I know. Still—"

"I'll be fine. This has been a shock. That's all."

"Yeah, but knowing you, you'll be back defending John within a week."

"I'm not defending him now. I agree with you, Pam. He's gone too far this time."

"He didn't tell you beforehand?"

Hillary shook her head.

"Bastard," Pam whispered viciously. "But that's nothing new. What's new is his engagement. After all this time, after everything he's achieved, it doesn't make sense." There was an urgency in her voice. "What is he after? I've been trying to figure it out, but nothing fits. John isn't the marrying kind. He's too much of a loner. Surrounded by people, yet alone—that's John in a nutshell. He could never abide having any one person around for long. So what's changed?"

Hillary had asked herself the same question dozens of times since the *20/20* airing. "Maybe he's going through the midlife crisis he didn't have time for ten years ago."

"Maybe. Maybe he's suddenly thinking of his own mortality, wanting his headstone to read 'beloved husband.' But if so, he's got the wrong woman. I know Janet Curry. Her credentials are impeccable. She's like one of the old marble buildings that line Commonwealth Avenue—smooth, stately, and cold. I can't image anything 'beloved' about a relationship between those two." She sighed. "John has never been known to do the unexpected, but this certainly was."

"Have you spoken with him?" Hillary asked, careful to keep her anxiety in check. Over the years she had often used Pam as a source

of information about John. Pam never minded, particularly since the information-sharing was mutual.

She nodded. "Saturday. Briefly. He accepted my congratulations like he does everything else—as though it's his due. Of course, he thought I was congratulating him on the show. The man is incredible." It wasn't a compliment, but then, nothing Pam said about John ever was. So easy with compliments to others, she found little to like about him. "His reflexes don't seem to work like other people's. We may have the same father, but I'm telling you, he comes from somewhere strange. No matter that he just popped the surprise announcement of the decade, all he wanted to talk about was the program."

"I can understand why."

Pam looked disgusted. "So can I. Have you ever seen anything so one-sided? He managed that interview the way he's managed things all his life. He's a master at manipulation. He never enters a situation where he doesn't have full control. He must have set certain ground rules that *20/20* had to follow if they wanted the interview."

"They must have wanted it badly."

"I'm sure they did. They had reason. We've been asked to provide pieces for the First Family's trip to Moscow."

That was the first Hillary had heard of it. "Exciting!" she said and meant it, though she felt another deep twinge of envy. Pam's star was rising, *always* rising—while Hillary was still waiting for hers to get off the ground.

"Coverage will be live," Pam explained, "which means that the reporters will have to fill the dead spots with trivia like clothes and jewelry."

"*Trivia.*" Even if Hillary had had no interest in jewelry, and even when she was at her most begrudging, she couldn't think of Pam's work as trivia. It was too beautiful. And too costly. She couldn't afford to buy it herself. The only reason she was wearing a Pamela St. George Original—a bold ring with a single green tourmaline set in ceramic—was that Pam had given it to her as a gift. Not John. Pam.

"Believe me, I'm thrilled to be considered trivia," Pam remarked. "Can you imagine the publicity we'll be getting? Free publicity? So

20/20 decided to scoop the *Facets* story before the reporters got it. Apparently the producers were willing to compromise."

"And go by John's rules."

"What else explains it? John has enemies. God only knows he has enemies. So why wasn't *20/20* able to find them?"

"He must have given them a list of who they could talk with."

"My name sure wasn't on it," Pam drawled.

"If it had been, would you have spilled the beans?"

"You bet!" she exclaimed with characteristic impulsiveness, then caught herself in the next breath and sat back in her chair looking torn.

Hillary wasn't surprised by Pam's ambivalence. On one hand, Pam's grievances against John were far from minor. She thought he was a rat and had called him just that many times, particularly in the days before she'd been sophisticated enough to have other words on the tip of her tongue in moments of her undisciplined fury. Hillary had been the one to defend John, to point out that he had doubled, then tripled and quadrupled the net worth of the business, that he paid every cent of the taxes he owed, that he gave handsomely to charity. She had been his champion in all but the most defenseless of his misdeeds, some of which had been directly aimed at Pam.

On the other hand, John was still the ultimate power behind the St. George Company and, hence, *Facets*. Pam could easily pick up her designs and go elsewhere, but Hillary doubted she would. Even if it weren't a matter of respect for the memory of her father and the company he'd started, there was the matter of John's wrath.

"You're afraid of him," she mused, more in sympathy than accusation.

"Not as much as I used to be."

"But you wouldn't have spoken with *20/20*. You're too good a person. If you'd agreed to be interviewed, you'd have had to choose between slandering John or lying through your teeth. You couldn't have done either." She paused, sat back in her chair, linked her fingers tightly, took a breath. "I can, Pam. And I'm going to. I'm going to write a book about him."

Pam was startled. "You've got to be kidding."

"I'm not."

Pam considered that for a minute. She was wary. "What kind of book?"

"A biography. I know him better than most. I'm in a perfect position to do it."

"But you're personally involved."

"Not anymore."

"So you say." Pam paused. "I don't know, Hillary." Her words were slow, hesitant. "I'm not sure it's such a good idea."

Hillary studied Pam's face and knew from its skeptical expression the direction of her thoughts. Writing a book on John meant writing a book on the St. George Company. It also meant, to some extent, writing a book on Pam, on Pam's mother, Patricia, and on Cutter.

"I wish you wouldn't," Pam said quietly.

"I have to. It's the only thing that can come out of this whole, horrendous experience. I have to in order to justify who I am."

Pam thought about that. She looked uneasy. "John will be furious."

"I know. But I have nothing to lose."

"I do. I have a husband, a daughter, and a reputation. My mother doesn't need the exposure. Neither does Cutter."

"None of you will be hurt. None of you did anything wrong."

"Still . . ." Pam began, only to be interrupted when a man appeared at their table. Looking up in surprise, she broke into a smile, at the same time extending a hand to be clasped and a cheek to be kissed.

"I saw you walk in and couldn't resist saying hello," the man said. "Damn but you look wonderful, Pamela. How have you been?"

"Just fine, Malcolm. It's so good to see you. Please, let me introduce my friend Hillary Cox. Hillary, Malcolm McCray. I've sold some of my favorite pieces to Malcolm's wife," she told Hillary, then turned back to Malcolm. "How is Lorraine?"

"Having a great time in Vermont, now that the crowds of skiers have left. I'm heading up there myself on Friday. It's the only place I can get any rest."

Hillary could understand it. She knew the man's name, if not his face. A transplant from San Francisco, Malcolm McCray owned several of the newest and most posh hotels in New York. He and his wife were also involved with the charity ball scene, if *W* was to be believed. Hillary wasn't surprised that Pam knew them; her circle had grown larger and more illustrious in the past few years. Rising stars had a way of generating tails like that.

"Will you give her my best?" Pam asked.

"Of course." Malcolm lowered his voice. "How about Brendan? Is he doing any better?"

Pam smiled sadly. "He has his ups and downs."

"Next time he's up, come see us. The country is a healing place."

The sad smile remained. "Thanks. We appreciate the thought."

With a final squeeze of her hand and a nod to Hillary, he left. Pam opened her menu, but Hillary could see that her thoughts were in Boston.

"How is he?"

"Brendan?" Closing the menu again, Pam wavered one hand. "The treatment can be worse than the disease. It's hard not to get discouraged."

"Are the doctors discouraged?"

"Who knows. We don't always get straight answers from them."

"Do you ask straight questions?"

"Of course not. Some things we don't want to hear."

"But you do keep smiling."

"I have to. For Brendan's sake, if nothing else. And it's not so bad. I'm busy with work. It's one escape. Ariana is another." Her face brightened at the mention of her daughter. "She is an angel. I honestly don't know what I'd do without her. She stands for so much—hope and love—all kinds of other things. She was—is—a gift."

After only the briefest of pauses, Hillary asked, "Are you in touch with Cutter?"

Pam studied the delicate sterling scrollwork at the end of her butter knife. "We talk. I haven't seen him for a while, what with Brendan being sick. But," her voice fell, "I don't know what I'd do if I were

completely cut off from him." She took a fast breath. "This conversation is getting maudlin. Let's order." She glanced at the waiter, who was quickly by her side.

But Hillary wasn't about to let the subject drop. As soon as the waiter left, she set down her wineglass. "You have a greater axe to grind than I do, you know."

"Against John?"

Hillary nodded. "Your life would be very different if it weren't for him."

After a moment's thought, Pam propped her elbows on the arms of her chair and looked Hillary in the eye. "True. He's not much better than scum, which is really pretty funny when you consider that he's spent his life trying to prove what an aristocrat he is."

"It's time someone pointed that out," Hillary said, thinking of her book.

Pam was thinking of it too, if her earnest tone was any indication. "But there are other ways. Less public, but more powerful ways. We'll get him, Hillary. We'll get him where it hurts."

Hillary saw the purposeful set of her jaw. She had seen it before and never pursued it, but, with John's defection, times had changed. "Is that wishful thinking on your part?"

"Believe me. He'll get his."

"Inside the business?"

"Inside—outside—whatever. It's coming, Hillary."

"What is?"

"Justice. Sweet, sweet justice."

Needing more than that, Hillary tried a teasing tone. "What's going on, Pam? You've hinted at things before. I've seen that same look on your face, and it's stronger each time I see it. You're doing something, aren't you? You and Cutter?"

"John's the one who's doing it."

"That's a platitude if I've ever heard one." When Pam didn't deny it, Hillary chided, "You wouldn't have gone on *20/20*. You wouldn't have stood up to him in public."

"Television was the wrong forum."

"So what's the right one?" Hillary thought her book was. Clearly, Pam disagreed.

"There's a right one. Trust me. He'll get his."

"When?" After several seconds of silence, Hillary asked, "How?"

Pam sighed. "I can't say more now. But think about it. It stands to reason that when a man like John goes through life hurting the people closest to him, at some point they'll strike back. You want to strike now—as many of us have wanted to for years—but there are ways and there are ways. Some are better than others. It may take time to do it right, but it will happen. So help me God, it will."

Hillary wasn't particularly reassured. She wanted to write her book. She didn't want to wait around while Pam and Cutter and whoever else they were in cahoots with plotted revenge against John. She had her own instrument of revenge, and she wanted to use it now.

"Don't worry," Pam said, misinterpreting her expression. "It won't be cheap. We're not talking a public smear here."

"A public smear mightn't be so awful," Hillary argued. "When a man goes public, he goes public. As of last Friday night, John is fair game. He wanted the good and took it, and now he has to risk the bad."

"I doubt he sees it that way."

"Probably not, the pompous ass."

Pam gave a dry smile. "Now I know he's in trouble. When you start calling him names, he's up the creek."

"That's for sure," Hillary said. "I know what I've felt these past few days. It has to be something like what you've spent years and years feeling."

Pam gave a sage nod. "The anger. The sense of injustice. The need to lash back. I've felt all of those things. But you know that. You've seen me kicking and screaming, banging my head against the wall because of things John's done."

The image of ladylike Pam banging her head against the wall made Hillary smile. "It's been a while since the kicking and screaming. I remember the first time I saw it, though. You couldn't have been more than eight. You were in Timiny Cove over school vacation. John

was having a go of it with your dad, and because of that, what was supposed to be a special time between you and Eugene was ruined."

Pam remembered well, if not the specific incident then dozens just like it. "Those two were like oil and water. Ten minutes in the same room with each other and there was trouble. If I was eight, John would have been twenty-four, so he'd have already been involved in the company. He thought he knew how to handle things, but his way was the antithesis of my dad's. He was arrogant even way back then. Twenty-four and wanting to run the ship. He was born arrogant."

"So were you, I thought. You looked like a spoiled child throwing a temper tantrum."

"Frustration. It was frustration."

"You were furious that anything or anyone should upset your plans."

"My relationship with Daddy was special," Pam argued in indulgent self-defense. "When school was in session, I was in Boston. He split his time between us and Maine, so I didn't see him much. But every vacation I went to Timiny Cove. Mom stayed behind in Boston, so it was just Eugene and me. He had John cover for him at the mines. It used to drive John nuts."

Hillary could understand that. "He didn't like Timiny Cove any more than your mom did."

"No. He wanted to be in the city. That's where everything was happening, he said. Nothing happened in the sticks."

Hillary reminisced with a chuckle. "The sticks."

"You hated it there too. You used to ask me all kinds of questions about life in the city. Remember?"

"Uh-huh. It must have seemed bizarre. I was ten years older than you were. But I was starving for information. John gave me some, but never enough. He always held back a little to keep me curious. You told me everything you knew."

"Which wasn't an awful lot."

"To me it was. Besides, I liked you."

"Because I was John's sister?"

"No. Well, yes, maybe at first, but I really did like you. You had a spark. You were fun. Happy."

"Except when I was throwing temper tantrums," Pam said with a droll look. Then the look grew pensive. "I loved the time I spent in Timiny Cove. The house was big and airy, the people friendly and interesting."

"Interesting?"

"They were colorful."

"Colorful."

"They were, Hillary. How else would you describe Phoebe Hanks or Rufus Hackett or Dwayne Wardwell? God," she sighed through a smile, "they were great. Phoebe with her crochet hook making those hideous slippers, one after another after another, Rufus with his chipmunk cheeks and his toothless grins and the jokes whose punchlines he always messed up, Dwayne looking so stern under his butch haircut—all of them with hearts of gold. Daddy and I used to play poker with Rufus and Dwayne. I remember it so clearly. . . ."

And so it began. Hillary hadn't asked for it, but it was easy to keep Pam going. A question here, a disbelieving look there, a teasing prod drew forth Pam's unique impressions of Timiny Cove. She accepted Hillary's curiosity about those impressions. Likewise, the questions Hillary asked about Eugene St. George and, of course, John seemed perfectly natural.

As Hillary listened closely, her interviewer's mind filing every detail, a distant part of her brain foresaw other lunches, other mornings, afternoons, or evenings spent with Pam or Patricia or Cutter. She would tell them what she was doing, because they meant the world to her, and if they had qualms, she would soft-pedal one private chapter or another. She would be compassionate, where they were concerned.

Where John was concerned, she would be merciless.

Chapter 3

Timiny Cove, 1964

Pam LEARNED TO BLUFF WHEN she was eight years old playing poker in the back room of Leroy Robichaud's general store. She didn't do it deliberately, at first. She was innocent and enthusiastic, and she dared risk her pennies on a hand that none of the others would have, because she had never known what it was like to have to count her pennies to survive.

The other men had. Rufus Hackett and Dwayne Wardwell still did, though nowhere near as much as before the big gem finds; and Eugene, well, Eugene remembered. He told Pam stories of the days when he had lived hand to mouth. She listened to those stories with a child's round eyes, but they were unreal to her. Nothing in her existence remotely resembled those hard times in the 1920s and '30s. By the 1940s, Eugene had already turned tourmaline mining into a lucrative venture, and by the '50s, when she was born, he owned the townhouse on Boston's Beacon Hill, the stately brick home in Timiny Cove, and the Cadillac. But she listened to the stories for hours, because her father was the teller, and she adored him.

"Raise ya, missy," Dwayne said, tossing two pennies into the pot after a somber study of the cards in his hand.

Pam studied hers. It wasn't a particularly good hand, had none of the picture cards that she liked, but she did have a pair of fours, and

a pair of anything was better than nothing. "I'll call," she decided. She pushed another penny toward the center of the table and grinned at Dwayne.

"You was s'posed to fold like your daddy and Rufus," he informed her.

When Eugene leaned close to take a peek at Pam's hand, she jerked the cards to her overalls. "I can do it, Daddy," she whispered.

"You know how?" he whispered back.

"Yes." Taking a two of clubs and a three of diamonds from her hand, she laid them delicately on the table and took the two cards that Eugene handed her. A nine of hearts and a three of spades—they didn't do a thing for her hand; still she widened her eyes just a little bit in mock excitement before composing herself and looking serenely at Dwayne.

He'd been watching her closely, which was just what she wanted. She knew Dwayne. He was the most easily fooled of the three, simply because he didn't have any children of his own who pretended. He knew that children liked candy, and he always had a barley pop in the pocket of his faded flannel shirt to give Pam before she left for home.

While he gravely studied his hand, Rufus leaned close. "I got a good one for you, Pammy. It's a traveling salesman joke."

"Okay," Pam said. Rufus sometimes tried to distract her with his jokes, but since Dwayne was the one concentrating at the moment, she wanted to hear. "Tell me."

"Y'see, once there was this traveling salesman, and he has this horse. Now, the two of them was down in Rumford when the old horse up and died."

"Hush," Dwayne grumbled. "I can't think."

Rufus talked softer. "Now, th' old horse died on Piscatawogue Street, y'see, and there's a whole crowd gatherin' round, and pretty soon a policeman comes up to make out a report. So he asks how to spell Piscatawogue, and everybody looks around. No one knows how to spell it, y'see."

"Rufus," Dwayne complained.

"So because no one knows how to spell Piscatawogue, the policeman

closes his book and says to the crowd, 'Okay, you guys, gimme me a hand and we'll carry this horse over to the next street.' "

Pam was silent, looking first to her father, then to Dwayne for help. Guarding his cards against his chest, Dwayne muttered, "No, no, no. You done it wrong. That ain't how it goes. You're s'posed to say, 'Okay, you guys, gimme a hand and we'll carry this horse over to Main Street.' "

Pam did laugh then, because even she could spell Main and because Eugene laughed, which was always a treat for her. He didn't laugh much in Boston.

Then Dwayne made his move. Tossing three cards face down on the table, he took three new ones from Eugene and slipped them into his hand. His expression instantly grew more grim. Aiming a look of disgust at Rufus, he folded, snapping a pair of sevens, a queen of hearts, a king of clubs, and a two of diamonds onto the table.

Fanning out her cards near his, Pam let the others look at her pair of fours while she gathered in the pennies with both small hands.

Eugene gave an even heartier laugh this time. "You're a wonder, Pammy girl!" he said as he collected the deck and shuffled before dealing another round.

Pam glowed. She loved her father. He was a man to please, a man whose voice could thunder through the house when something wasn't right, but he never thundered at her. He might yell at her mother, and he certainly yelled at John, but never at her. She was his special gem, he told her, and though she was too big now to ride on his shoulders the way she used to when he took her to the gem pits, he still said the words. Holding a newly unearthed piece of tourmaline in his hand, admiring its beauty in one breath, in the next he would say, "But you're my special gem, Pammy girl."

Through her mother's eyes, she saw him as a man. "Your father is the most handsome of all the handsome men in the world," Patricia told Pam when she was no more than three or four. "I'll never forget that first day he walked into the bank and I saw him. So broad-shouldered and sure of himself. He took my breath away."

"Your mother was barely nineteen at the time," Eugene teased.

"Most anything would take her breath away. She was a beauty then, as she's a beauty now, but she sure did look pretty with those cheeks of hers all pink."

"How old were you, Daddy?"

"I was an old man."

"He was not," Patricia argued, taking the insult personally. "He was forty-seven and younger of body and heart than many a twenty-five-year-old. When he walked into that bank, I knew he was the one I wanted, even if I didn't think I had a chance in the world of getting him."

"She loved my house," Eugene injected, mischief in his eyes, and Patricia was quick to say that it hadn't only been that, though even Pam knew how much she adored Beacon Hill. Patricia's pleasure was evident each time she returned home and walked up the stone steps while envious onlookers passed by.

It was a fairy-tale life, Pam thought, particularly when she watched her parents dress up for a ball. Her mother was as beautiful as her father said, small and willowy, with delicate features and blond hair that was long and flowing, as straight as Pam's, though Pam's was dark. Perhaps because of that color difference, Pam didn't make the usual kinds of comparisons between her looks and her mother's. She assumed that she was different but just as pretty, because her father always told her so, and she always believed what he said.

Her father was her hero. He was taller than most men she'd seen, had more hair than most—thick, silvery hair—and redder cheeks. Her mother used to say he was ruddy and robust, as he eyed himself in the mirrored door of the armoire. And when his bow tie was neatly knotted and his tuxedo jacket spread smoothly across his shoulders, Pam could see it for herself. He looked grand, like Wendy Darling's father in *Peter Pan*.

Pam knew her mother liked him best when he was all dressed up and they were going out. "To see and be seen," Patricia used to tell Pam. "It's very important. Your father's name is just becoming known. One day he'll be a very important man in this town."

"What do you mean?" Pam would ask, a little unsure because the

look in her mother's eyes suggested that things might change, and Pam didn't want that. She liked her life the way it was. She couldn't imagine how things could get better.

"He'll be wealthy, for one thing."

"Isn't he now?"

"Now we're comfortable."

"But we have two houses. Melissa Gentile said that makes us rich. She doesn't have two houses."

"But the one that she has is far nicer than ours."

"I like ours."

"Melissa's is bigger. Hers is an estate, with lots of land."

"We have lots of land in Timiny Cove, and our house there is the nicest one in the whole town."

Patricia grunted. "Timiny Cove is dirty. It's shabby and poor."

"I like Timiny Cove," Pam argued, though from an early age she learned that she wouldn't change her mother's mind on the matter of Timiny Cove. "What else is Daddy going to do?"

"Besides make lots of money? He's going to have an office that's even fancier than the one he has now. He may even own the building, and if he doesn't own that one, he'll own others. Real estate is a good investment. It's a good way to make money."

"But if he already has lots of money, why does he need more?"

"Security," Patricia said in a way that left no doubt about its importance. "You're a very lucky little girl, Pamela. You don't know what it's like to be without. I do. I remember when I had to wear the same pair of shoes for three years even though my feet had outgrown them after one. I remember when my mother used to send me to the butcher's shop for a small bit of stew meat, knowing that I didn't have enough money but hoping that the butcher would take pity on us and leave the extra piece or two in the bundle. I remember . . ."

Coming from her father, the "I remember" stories were warm and fun. In spite of the hardships he described, there was a fondness in his voice for the time in his life when he'd made the best of the low cards he'd been dealt. There was nothing warm or fun or fond in Patricia's voice when she spoke of the old days. Her tone was hard. Everything

about her was hard when she spoke of the old days, and if Pam had been leaning against her, that was the time when she would get up and move to sit on the floor or wander around the room. Her mother wasn't happy when she talked of the past. Sometimes she wasn't much happier when she talked of the present.

"I never had any security until I met your father. We have some now, but not enough. Real estate is the future. I'm going to have your father talk with Franklin Dowd at the symphony dinner on Thursday night. Franklin has done well for himself in the last few years."

Pam was too young to know who Franklin Dowd was, why real estate was the future, or what the necessity was for stockpiling assets. But she was sensitive to simple emotions, attuned to facial expressions and tones of voice. Just as she knew that her mother grew agitated when she talked business with her father, so she knew that Eugene was correspondingly complacent. He agreed with Pam. His life was just fine. He loved the things money could buy and availed himself of them as he pleased, but he was happiest and smiled the most when he was in Maine, wearing overalls, either checking on work at one of the mine sites or visiting with his friends, the men he'd known all his life.

Pam knew them all. Whenever she was in Maine, Eugene had her with him, showing her off, teaching her to love the men, the mine, the crisp, clean air on a cool Maine night. Some of the things they did, like sneaking out to swim in the stream at midnight, were secrets because Patricia wouldn't understand. Other things they did, like share a picnic lunch with the governor, were secrets because John wouldn't understand.

John didn't understand much, as far as Pam was concerned. He was sixteen years older than she, the product of Eugene's first marriage and a different world, and if he'd ever been a child, Pam couldn't see it. He didn't play games, tell jokes, or watch television. Moreover, he didn't like tourmaline, didn't like Timiny Cove, and didn't like Eugene or Patricia or Pam. "He's jealous," Eugene would sometimes say when John was at his worst around Pam, and in her innocent way she understood. The warmth that she shared with her father never

flowed between father and son. When Eugene and John stood side by side, they rarely touched. When they talked, they rarely smiled. They shared a temper, but then, Pam shared it too, and though in time she learned to control it, she hadn't managed it when she was eight and playing poker.

The game had gone on for little more than an hour when John burst into the back room. "We have a problem," he announced to Eugene without preamble. "Your foreman's stealing stones."

Eugene sent his son a dark look before shifting a slow gaze first to Rufus, then to Dwayne. "That's quite an accusation." Lips pursed, he looked back at his cards.

"I've been going over the books," John went on. He didn't bother to look at Rufus or Dwayne, and Pam was just as glad. The looks he usually gave them weren't the nicest. "They're a mess. When was the last time you went through them yourself?"

Eugene tossed a penny into the pot to match the one Dwayne had bet before him. "I don't have to go through the books. I have a bookkeeper to do that."

"Then your bookkeeper is as crooked as Blaise," was John's brash assessment. "We're taking more out of the ground than is reaching the vault."

"Another time, John. We'll deal with this another time."

"Simon knows he's been found out."

Eugene looked up. "You told him?"

"He was there. I didn't see the point in waffling."

"Did you fire him?"

"No. I thought you'd want to do that."

"Well, I don't. Simon Blaise has worked for me for twenty years, which is a damn sight longer than you have. What gives you the right to waltz in and start harassing my people?"

John did glance at the other men then, obviously resentful of being taken down by his father in their presence. Pam wasn't bothered by it at all. It was John's fault. He'd started it.

Apparently realizing that he had no escape, he turned on his father. "You were the one who wanted me here, when I'd rather have stayed

in Boston. There's plenty there to keep me busy. But you dragged me up so you could play hooky with her." He shot Pam a nasty look. "I have an interest in this company. You're the one who keeps reminding me of that. So I called a crooked employee to account. Blaise is stealing."

"Says you. We're making money hand over fist, and someone's stealing our stones, says you. The state gives us an award for fair service, and the books are messed up, says you. Well, I say that Simon Blaise is a good man."

Even if Pam had been deaf, she'd have known Eugene was angry from the set of his jaw. In turn, she got angry. This was her time with her father. She didn't want John spoiling it.

But John seemed determined to do just that. "He's waiting. I told him we'd be back. If we take much longer, he'll have skipped town."

All four at the table still held their cards, but none was paying attention to the game. The instant Eugene laid down his hand and stood, Pam was up on her knees on the chair, protesting, "We're playing, Daddy."

"This is more important than poker," John told her.

"Only because you've made it that way," Eugene said. Standing at his full height, he was an inch or two taller than John, but still the family resemblance was marked. The fiery eyes, the rigid square jaw, the belligerent stance—the two men were definitely father and son. "You shouldn'a said anything to Simon, John. I'm not in the habit of throwing accusations around, especially when it involves my men. If something strange is goin' on, there's a reason."

"Greed. How's that for a reason?"

"No good. Doesn't apply to Simon. You should'a known that, John. You've been working full-time for this company for two years, summers longer than that. You should know by now who you can trust and who you can't." Turning back to the others, he said, "Simon needs talking to. I have to make sure he don't quit on me. Pammy, Rufus'll walk you home."

"But we just started! I want to play longer!"

"It's past your bedtime," John told her.

Pam ignored him. "Why don't I wait here, Daddy, and you'll come back when you're done?"

"Because I don't know when I'll be done, thanks to your brother. So long as he's ruined the night, I might as well take a look at those books." Stooping down, he gave her a hug. "We'll play again tomorrow. Right, Rufus?"

"Yup."

Adding his own "Yup," Dwayne took the lollypop from his pocket, but Pam didn't want the sweet. She took it so as not to hurt his feelings, but she held it tightly in her hand, fully wrapped, all the way home.

Once there, she ran inside, but instead of finding Marcy, who would have been sympathetic to her cause, she found Hillary Cox. "John isn't here," she yelled and gave the stairs a kick. "He's making trouble for my father."

"Where's Marcy?" Rufus asked Hillary.

"She ran over to see her mother. She won't be long. I told her I'd keep an eye on things while she was gone." Pam coiled herself into a corner of the bottom stair and refused to say goodbye to Rufus. The instant he was down the walk, as though she'd held her temper in check as long as she possibly could, she cried, "I hate him. I hate him."

"Rufus?" Hillary asked.

"John. He's a rat. He spoils everything, and I hate him!"

She punctuated her claim with several more swift kicks to the stair riser. "He should have stayed in Boston. I don't like it when he's here. He takes the fun out of everything."

Hillary left her post against the parlor arch and sank onto the step above Pam's. "What did he do?"

"He got Daddy angry. He's always doing that." She turned blazing eyes on Hillary. "Know what I think? I think he was a mistake."

"What do you mean, a mistake?"

"I think he was the wrong baby. He isn't Daddy's."

"That doesn't happen."

"It does. My friend Sharon was telling me about a baby that hap-

pened to, and it makes sense. John and Daddy don't get along. They're always fighting."

"But they look exactly alike."

"They do not. Daddy smiles."

"That's external, like their clothes. Your father's are older and more worn, because he's been wearing them here for so long. John isn't here as much, so his are newer and stiffer. He wears a suit in the city. But if you look at their build and their features, they're definitely father and son."

"Poor Daddy." She rushed on when Hillary looked ready to defend John. "You like him, but that's because you think he's handsome. You came over here to see him, didn't you?"

"Do you know when he'll be back?"

"No, and I don't care! He's a rat!"

"I don't know about that."

"Are you his girlfriend now?"

"I don't know."

"I do," Pam cried. "He hates it up here. if you're his girlfriend now, you won't be for long, because he's leaving."

"Well, so am I," Hillary shot back.

That diverted Pam's attention for a minute, though it didn't surprise her. Everyone knew that Hillary Cox was different from most of the people in Timiny Cove. She looked different, for one thing, kind of exotic with her dark, curly hair and her light, light skin. For another thing, she kept to herself. Her whole family did. They were odd, Pam had long ago decided, because she couldn't imagine any family in Timiny Cove that wouldn't want to go to the annual spring picnic. Her father said that the Cox family was brilliant, but that still didn't explain to Pam why they kept to themselves.

"Where are you going?" she asked.

"To college in Boston. Maybe I'll see you more often."

If not brilliant, Pam was astute. "You're going there to be closer to John."

"I'm going there for an education."

"It's a dumb thing to do! John's a rat. He spoils everything he gets near, and if you get near him, he'll spoil you, too."

"I certainly hope so," Hillary said with a smile.

Pam was not old enough to understand Hillary's smile. Besides, with the mention of John, she remembered that she wanted to be playing poker with her father, that the game had been ruined, and why. "Well, if you're stupid enough to go looking for trouble, you can have him! Because that's all John is! He's a rat and a spoiler and I hate his guts!" Hurling Dwayne's candy against the far wall, she bolted to her feet and sped up the stairs to cry by herself.

Pam's tears were long dried by the following morning. She had kicked the anger out against her bed and was spent. John returned to Boston, and although Eugene didn't have as much free time because of that, calm once again returned to Pam's life in Timiny Cove. When the vacation ended and she returned to Boston, that peace was with her. She was glad to see her mother, and with the ease borne of practice she slipped back into the more formal life that Patricia dictated.

Pam liked that life, too—her school, her friends, shopping with her mother, going out to eat, going to parties. Her Boston life was busy and full, a fine counterpoint to the casual spontaneity of Timiny Cove.

What she wished for on the first star each night was that Eugene would come home soon. She missed him when he stayed in Maine, which he did more and more as time passed. He came home for everything important—Thanksgiving, Christmas, and Easter—and she went north during every vacation, but there were fewer times than ever when they did things as a family, just Patricia, Eugene, and her. Those were her favorite times, the times when she felt the happiest. She loved her birthdays, too, for that reason. When she turned nine, Eugene came home and took Patricia and her to a special dinner at the Ritz. When she turned ten, he came home and took them to New York. John usually managed to be away when Eugene was home, which was just as well. Pam decided she would hit him with the fireplace poker if he dared spoil her birthday.

Mercifully, he didn't do that, and for the most part he avoided her. He had his own friends. He worked at the headquarters of St. George Mining in Boston, but on weekends he went to places like Long Island

and Newport and Bar Harbor with the sons of judges and lawyers and bankers. Patricia encouraged him, and Pam didn't mind his absences because when he was around, and when he did talk to her, his words were often cruel.

Partly because Patricia liked John, and partly because a little voice inside told her not to, she never discussed that with Patricia. Marcy was the one she went to then.

Marcy Willow was reed-thin and pale, but for all her mousy looks, she seemed to know everything about life. When Pam asked Eugene how someone who was only sixteen could know so much, he explained that Marcy had seen life at its most bare, without any of the frills and cushions Pam had.

Even without that bid for compassion, Pam would have liked Marcy. For one thing, Marcy was from Timiny Cove, and though her home there wasn't much more than a broken-down tarpaper shack, Pam adored anything to do with the Cove. For another, Marcy was shy, unassuming, and undemanding, which made giving her little gifts and taking her places a treat for Pam. Although Marcy was in the St. George home to work as a maid, she was like a big sister to Pam. Marcy was the one to whom Pam could pour out her heart when she felt so inclined, the one Pam could count on to help understand John's mutterings.

"What does he mean by that?" she asked. She and Marcy were sitting at the edge of the frog pond on the Boston Common. They'd just come from grocery shopping on Charles Street and were eating the chocolate-covereds that Pam had bought from a nearby vendor. " 'A five-month baby.' He's said it before. What does it mean?"

Marcy was a while in answering, which was part of her charm, in Pam's eyes. She had the same slow way about her that most of the Mainers did, silently mulling over her answer before offering it up. "Has your mama talked to you about that?"

"She doesn't talk about babies at all, except to say that she won't have another one. Does that mean she *can't* have another one?"

Marcy took a slow lick of her cone. "Could be. Could be it means

she doesn't want another one b'cause she knows she'd never get another one so good as you."

"I'm not so good, not all the time. So what's a five-month baby?"

Marcy leaned against the cement rim of the pond and watched the people who passed. "Has your mama told you about making babies?"

"No. But I know."

"How do you know?"

"Melissa and I talk about it. She has a book that we've read." Pam scooted close to Marcy and lowered her voice. "And another one about periods. Janice Brooks just got hers. We thought we ought to know what it was."

"Janice Brooks is twelve. You're just ten."

"That doesn't mean anything. The book said that a girl can sometimes get it when she's ten or eleven."

"Not much. She can be sixteen, too. You may have to wait."

"Do you get one?"

Marcy thought about it, then nodded.

"So you could have a baby now if you wanted to?"

Again Marcy nodded.

"And it would take nine months to grow. But the book didn't say anything about five-month babies. John looks disgusted when he calls me one. So what does it mean?"

"You better ask your mama."

"I don't think she'll answer."

"Why not?"

"I don't know. I just don't think she will. She'll probably laugh at me. She doesn't think John's so awful. So I'm asking you, Marcy. Come on. You're my best friend, and you *know* about things. What's a five-month baby?"

Marcy took another lick of her cone before turning her slender body toward Pam. "A five-month baby is a baby born only five months after the parents get married."

It didn't take long for the meaning of that to register on Pam. She was good at math. "Then John is saying," she began slowly, "that my parents made me before they got married?"

"Could be."

"That they got married because they were going to have me?"

"Th' important thing," Marcy said, "is that they were married when you were born."

"Did they have to get married because of me?"

"No."

The conviction behind the word was some reassurance to Pam, but still she had to ask, "How do you know?"

"B'cause they love you. And they love each other. People who love like that get married whether there's a baby or not." When Pam continued to look skeptical, she added, "You know they love you."

"Sometimes I think they don't love each other. Daddy spends so much time in Maine."

"That's on account of the pits. He has to be there."

"No," Pam said, but distantly.

"Yes'm. If he didn't spend so much time in Maine, you wouldn't have all the nice things you do here. Your daddy is a fine man, about as fine as any that comes along. I'm sure that if he had his way he'd be here all the time with you. And your mama."

Pam didn't argue further, though it seemed to her that the last "mama" had been stuck on as an afterthought. She could understand why Marcy would insist that Patricia and Eugene were still deeply in love. Marcy's own parents had a volatile relationship, if the screaming Pam had heard the one time she'd gone with Marcy to visit was any indication. By comparison, anything was better.

Pam's point of comparison, though, was different. Increasingly she could look back on her earliest memories, and, even allowing for the innocence of those first years, she could see the change in the way her parents treated each other. The nice times were fewer and farther between. If Patricia and Eugene were in love, it wasn't as deep a love as it once had been.

Pam was convinced that something was wrong, and nothing in the course of the months that followed suggested otherwise. Eugene was in Maine more often than not, which irritated Patricia so much that she made several trips there herself.

"Do you blame me for wondering?" she asked in a huff one Friday night. She'd taken Pam straight from school and made the three-hour drive without forewarning Eugene.

In the eyes of a twelve-year-old, his welcome was one of unqualified pleasure, everything Pam had hoped for. The three of them went out for dinner at the nicest restaurant within twenty miles of the Cove, and when they returned they sat for a time in the den catching up on what each had been doing since last they'd been together. When the talk turned to business, Pam quietly left. But the conversation easily carried up the stairs to the hall, where she leaned against the wall papered with Queen Anne's lace and listened.

"Yes, I do blame you," Eugene argued. "When I say that I'm here because I have to be, that should be enough. There was no need for you to race on up just to make sure I was working."

"I raced on up because I missed you. It's been three weeks."

"It's often been three weeks."

"But it shouldn't be. It doesn't have to be. I need you there."

"You nag me there. You've got me dressed up and going out every night to some party or ball or art show."

"They're important."

"They're boring."

"Those parties and balls and exhibits are where you can make contacts to broaden your base. That's what you should be doing."

Pam heard the tension in her father's voice as he said, "My business is taking tourmaline from the earth and selling it, and I'm doin' pretty damn well."

"But you could be doing better. Don't you see? You're not making the most of your assets. You sell the stones, pay your crew, buy new equipment now and then, and put the rest of the money into the bank. It's piling up there, Gene, when it should be earning twice as much in another venture."

"This sounds familiar. Have you been talking to John?"

Pam flattened her back against the wall. She knew the answer to that one. She saw the way Patricia had begun to wait for John to

come home from work. She heard the discussions they often had over drinks before dinner.

"Who else do I have to talk with?" Patricia shot back. "You're never around."

"Why do you have to talk with anyone? Why can't you just trust me?"

"I *do* trust you, but I get nervous. We have all our eggs in one basket. What if something should happen up here? What if the mine caves in or there's a flood, or you take the last piece of tourmaline out of the ground and can't find any more? What will you do then?"

"If that happens," Eugene said with renewed patience, "which it won't, but if it does, I'll know that I've got all this wonderful money in the bank that I can use to keep from starving."

Pam pictured him grinning that broad, self-confident grin of his. Leaning against the wall, she smiled. But her smile soon faded, because Patricia wasn't as easily reassured.

"But why not invest it and make even more money? Why not diversify? If you branch into another field, you can be in Boston more. I need you there, Gene. When I'm alone, I start imagining things. I get very nervous." She was speaking more quickly. Even from the distance, Pam could hear the tremor in her voice.

Eugene must have heard it too and been touched. "Now, now, Patsy . . ." He went on, but his voice faded to a gentle murmur, too low for Pam to hear at the top of the stairs.

Telling herself that things were in hand now that her father knew her mother's fears, Pam went to bed. She heard no more voices, and if her parents slept together in the large master suite, she was asleep before they climbed the stairs.

She and Patricia stayed the weekend, and by the time they headed back to Boston on Sunday afternoon, Pam felt optimistic that her parents' differences had been ironed out. "You'll be down to see us soon?" she asked after giving Eugene a last hug and kiss.

"Soon, Pammy girl. Real soon."

He kept his word. He was back in Boston the following week, but it was for a single night. Then he was gone. Patricia was more disap-

pointed than usual and therefore more nervous. That added to Pam's disappointment, because when Patricia was nervous, she turned to John.

He was, without doubt, Pam decided, one of the coolest people she'd ever known. His hair was always combed, his tie always straight, his posture just so, with one hand in a pocket so that he'd look casual even if he felt tense.

She could forgive him that, she supposed. What she couldn't forgive was that he always seemed to know how to put Patricia's mind at ease, which wasn't right at all. That was Eugene's job.

But Eugene wasn't there, and the more John filled the gap, the more Patricia sought him out.

Pam didn't know what to do. Each time she talked with her father, she begged him to come home, but he always had an excuse. Then vacation came, and she went to Timiny Cove. Patricia joined them for several days, driving up with John when Eugene demanded he come. But when John returned to Boston, so did Patricia.

Watching her leave, Pam felt a sense of loss. She wasn't as close to her mother as she used to be. They didn't talk much. They didn't laugh together or daydream together or spend days together, just the two of them, the way they once did. Patricia seemed distanced from her, even when they were in the same room. She watched her mother drive away from her and she knew their relationship had changed.

Unable to blame Eugene, whom she adored, or Patricia, who seemed too distracted, Pam put the responsibility on John.

Chapter 4

◆ ◆ ◆

JOHN WASN'T SURE JUST WHEN his fear of his father hardened into contempt. It was a gradual process, starting in his early teen years when he formed an elite group of friends, continuing when puberty gave him the confidence of height and a physical par with Eugene, and culminating with his parents' divorce and his mother's subsequent death.

He wasn't sorry to see the fear go. Long after childhood, he could vividly remember the quaking he'd felt when Eugene's loud bellow told him that he'd disappointed his father again. Sometimes, it had been the way he looked: "Too new, for pity's sake." Sometimes it had been the way he acted: "Starchy, boy, where's your sense of adventure?" Sometimes it had to do with the business: "What do you mean you don't want to work in the mine?" It wasn't only the voice that made him tremble but the flashing eyes and the cheeks that grew red with temper. "You've got the whole summer lying out there ahead of you, with nothing better to do. Hell, by the time I was your age I'd been workin' for three years shovelin' manure at Grady's farm!"

John shrank back against the paneled wall of his bedroom, but the painted pine offered no protection from this man who didn't like him. "Why do I have to work?" his small, eight-year-old voice asked.

"To learn. And you won't be doing anything killing. You'll be helping out with little things like carrying water and running errands. I'm no slave driver, for pity's sake."

There was no solace in that, since John had no idea what a slave driver was. The word *work* was enough. But the words *Timiny Cove* were even worse. His very first memory of the place was of being lost in the woods, and lost was what he'd felt every time he'd been there since. Timiny Cove was filled with people who didn't dress like he did, didn't live like he did, didn't like what he did.

"I want to stay here," he protested, but his voice sounded feeble next to his father's full boom.

"And do what?"

"Play with Timmy and Doug."

"Timmy and Doug? What for?"

"I like Timmy and Doug."

"Well, that's just fine, since they're your cousins. But what they can teach you about business ain't worth a tinker's damn. With due respect for your mama's family, the Wrights have had their money since the Pilgrims landed. They don't work. We St. Georges do." Under his breath he mumbled, "You wanna play with Timmy and Doug." Then he thundered so loud that John jumped, "For pity's sake, you do enough of that here. Your mother's got you runnin' around with your cousins and a whole bunch of other little boys with fancy names. Well, enough! There are some fancy names up in Timiny Cove, too, and the boys there can teach you a whole lot more about living than any Saltonstall ever could. So this summer you can do your playin' with the Duffys and the Greenleafs and the Pelletiers, and you'll learn a thing or two along the way."

Given no choice in the matter, John tried. He worked for his father that summer and hated every minute of it. He didn't like the dirt, didn't like the smell, didn't like the men. Mostly he didn't like the way Eugene kept yelling at him. In his father's eyes, he could do no right. If he was sent for a tool, he brought the wrong one. If he was sent for the medical box, he brought it too slowly. If he was sent for water, he spilled too much along the way. John knew that Eugene yelled at other people, but never as loudly as at him.

He did learn, though. During that summer and the ones that followed, he learned what went into the mining operation, when to use

a hammer versus a chisel, how to blast open a new pocket, how to care for each crystal unearthed. He also learned that he didn't want to spend the rest of his life in the family business if it meant hanging around with the men at the mine, and he certainly didn't want it if it meant working with his father.

His father and the miners were alike. Eugene was one of them, a local. It didn't matter that he was the boss, that he lived in the biggest house in town, and that he had an even finer one in Boston. He could drink with the others, tell jokes with the others, spend his Saturday mornings on the bruised brown bench on the town green passing the time of day with the others. He fit into the Timiny Cove life as only a native could.

John never would. He'd been born in Boston and had spent his earliest years in a neat little house in Brookline before his father bought the Beacon Hill home. He loved the city. He found it stately and genteel, civilized in ways that Timiny Cove would never be. Of course, he viewed it through the eyes of a Wright, and a Wright was a person of status.

Eugene St. George had none of that status. He may have risen a little when he married John's mother, but when they went places as a family, even John could see that Sybil was the one who drew the respect. Not that Eugene didn't hold his own. He looked right and talked right. John had often wondered how he did it, coming from the backwoods and all, until he found a book of etiquette lying open in the library one day. So Eugene never embarrassed them. Neither, though, did he impress the Brahmans of Boston.

Early on, John felt the sting of being a St. George. More than once when he went to a friend's house, the shout from the door was, "It's that St. George boy," in a tone of voice that made him swallow hard and hold his chin high. The name should have been regal, he thought. On a blue-blood's tongue, it wasn't. Even then, he knew he had an uphill battle to wage.

What mystified him, given his mother's family, was why they had allowed the wedding. Sybil and Eugene were from different worlds.

Sybil was a lady, and while Eugene did his best to be a gentleman to match, he never quite seemed polished.

"Earthiness," his mother had once said, grinning at Eugene at the time. "Earthiness is very exciting in a man."

But John couldn't see it. He found nothing exciting in dirt or sweat. The Wright side of the family had nothing to do with either and lived an exciting enough life shuttling between Boston and Cape Cod. In time, his mother seemed to see that too, because she had terrible arguments with Eugene about buying a summer house and joining the club. Eugene didn't want either. He said that they had enough going for them between Boston and Timiny Cove, and that if Sybil wanted to summer on the Cape, she could just move in with her family.

She did that for a summer or two, while John suffered in Maine with Eugene. By the time he was old enough to understand what his mother meant by the appeal of earthiness in a man, his parents had split up.

It was inevitable. The way it happened, though, was wrong. Even at fifteen John knew that. Eugene announced one day that he wanted the divorce, that he would pay Sybil to file for it, pay for her to travel to a place where the divorce could be granted without delay. If she protested, he said, he would simply move to Maine and let her come along like a good wife or be branded the offending party. In either case, he would get his divorce. Whether it was sooner or later, more or less painful, depended on her.

She was devastated. She didn't want a divorce. It just wasn't done. It represented failure.

The Wrights, who had never cared for Eugene, argued otherwise. In their opinion, Sybil had married beneath her class and was now simply freeing herself from a man who would be nothing but a burden in the years to come.

Such was the story they passed among their friends. John heard it more than once. Living with his mother for all but the summers, he had even greater exposure to the Wright circle than before. He wasn't offended when people criticized Eugene. Eugene was of a lower class.

The fact that John had chosen to remain in Boston with his mother was proof that he was his mother's son, a Wright in all but name.

That was what he kept telling himself, though the mirror told him different. At sixteen, he was becoming quite a man, tall and broad, with eyes that flashed vividly when he was angry and a voice that sounded self-assured even when he wasn't. A handsome devil he was, and he knew it, but at sixteen he looked just like his father had at that age, if the observations of old-timers lounging on the porch of the post office in Timiny Cove were correct. John's saving grace, as far as he was concerned, was his skin, which was less ruddy, smoother than his father's, and his hair, which was darker, finer, and more easily groomed.

And, of course, he had class. Physical attributes alone meant nothing. Far more important in life, he told himself, was what he did with those attributes, which was where his Wright genes took over. He believed that he had more class at sixteen than Eugene St. George would ever have. He could go anywhere, do anything, and be sure of himself, because of the exposure he'd had. He knew the right people. If some of those right people still seemed wary of him, he assured himself, it would pass with time.

His life in Boston was rewarding. He attended the most prestigious prep school, wore the nattiest clothes, played a solid game of tennis on the clay courts at his grandparents' club, and partied to his heart's content. Eugene bought him a car to drive to Maine and back, but John took perverse delight in using it for all else but that. The car was shiny and new, everything Timiny Cove wasn't, and the girls loved it. Not for a minute did John feel guilty about showing it off. After all, he was one of the privileged.

The carefree carousing he did was some solace for the fact that, a week after Sybil obtained her divorce, Eugene remarried. It came as a surprise to John, whose mind was on his own sexuality, not on his father's. It hadn't occurred to him to associate Eugene with another woman.

Before he could respond one way or another to the marriage, he had to cope with his mother's reaction to it. She was stunned, then

appalled, then furious that she hadn't seen what was happening. Piecing things together, she realized that Eugene had been having an affair with Patricia for more than a year. The pain of that seemed her undoing more than the divorce itself. She lost something, became less enthusiastic about everything, including John.

He was furious. He had already decided that his father wasn't worth much, but with his remarriage, that assessment fell even lower. John was personally affronted by what his father had done. The pain his mother felt was nothing compared to his own humiliation, because word spread quickly. Within weeks, all of Boston knew that Eugene had taken a second wife, that that wife was a good deal younger than he was, and that she was noticeably pregnant. John took his share of ribbing from his friends at school, even some from their parents, and although he swallowed it all with the good humor of the aristocrat he was determined to be, inside he seethed.

Eugene must have seen it, because before he introduced John to Patricia he took him aside with a warning. "Don't say it, John. Don't say it if you know what's good for you. I don't mind if you feel loyalty to your mother. It'd be strange if you didn't. But I won't have you upsetting my wife. You'll show her respect, even if you choke on it."

"I well might," John mumbled.

"Come again, sonny?"

He should have known better, should have known that in the long run he couldn't win, but he'd bottled the anger inside for too long. "You knocked her up. You got her pregnant while you were still with my mother. Is that why you married her, because she's having your kid?"

Eugene glared at him, red-faced and rigid. "I married her because I love her."

"What about my mother? What happened to the love you were supposed to be feeling for her?"

"Things happen sometimes. Love fades."

"If it fades, what's it worth? Will you love this one till it fades, then dump her, too? Will she be feeling the same kind of pain that my mother is now? This one—"

"Her name," Eugene stated through clenched teeth, "is Patricia."

"—must be really dumb—"

"Watch it, boy!"

"You want me to respect her, when she takes a married man away from his wife? What kind of woman does that? My mother was there. She was your wife. Were you respecting *her*, while you were shacking up with Patricia?"

Man of passion and impulse though he was, Eugene had never resorted to violence as an outlet for anger. Somewhere in the back of his mind, John knew that, and it was confirmed by the fact that Eugene kept his fists locked tightly to his sides.

"You're treading on shaky ground, boy."

"What can you do to me that you haven't already done? Yell. Go ahead. Yell all you want. I'm used to that. Face it," he dared say, at his most rebellious, "what you are and what you've done don't concern me anymore. Two more years and I'll be eighteen. Then I won't even have to come when you call."

But John had underestimated his father, who said in that same dangerously slow, tight-jawed way, "Don't be so sure. I'm your future, John. St. George Mining is your future."

"Not if I don't want. it."

"You will," Eugene bellowed, "because the day you turn your back on it will be the day I write you off. That'll be the end of the money, sonny. And don't"—he raised a cautioning finger—"think you'll be supported by the Wrights in the style you like, because there's somethin' you don't know about people like that. You think they live high off the hog? Well, look close. The house on the Cape has been in the family for three generations and is shabby as hell. The membership in the country club was bought for perpetuity by the Wright who was a founding member. Do you see your aunt an' uncle buying fancy clothes? Or flyin' to New York for the weekend? Your cousins didn't get new cars when they turned sixteen. The fact is, sonny, that people like that have the pedigree and the history and the money, but they don't shell out. So if you think you're gonna turn to them to support

you while you piss away your time with your nose up in the air, you're wrong."

Seeing that he'd regained the upper hand, he took a breath. "You need my money, John. Think about it, and you'll know it's true."

John wanted to argue, but his rebelliousness wouldn't take him that far. He wasn't sure if he believed that the Wright side of the family was a dry well, but he did know that there was money in St. George Mining. He liked nice things, and nice things cost money. Until he knew his options, he couldn't risk disinheritance.

So he met Patricia, and it took every bit of the social skill he'd developed in his sixteen years to be civil. The gossip hadn't quite prepared him. Married, she was; the shining gold band on her finger confirmed that. Pregnant, she was; her protruding belly confirmed that. But John had imagined a husband stealer to be more sharp-edged. Patricia was pretty and soft, hatefully so.

She was also very, very young. Gossip had hinted at that, but John wasn't prepared for someone far closer to his own age than to Eugene's. She was, it turned out, twenty, to Eugene's forty-eight, which was the most bizarre, the most hateful turn of all.

John couldn't return to Boston fast enough, not so much to report on what he'd learned, since he was too disgusted to confess it, but because he needed to return to his own life and blot out his father and his father's very young, very pregnant wife.

He might have succeeded had Sybil not taken suddenly ill. The diagnosis was cancer. The prognosis was guarded. She had one operation, then another, and though the Wrights came often to visit, John was the one who stayed by her side. "You look so much like your father," she would say with a smile in fuzzy moments, just before she drifted into a drugged sleep, and although he hated the comparison, he knew he would bear it if it brought her some comfort. Nothing else seemed to. The lethargy that had set in after Eugene's marriage was magnified tenfold. The doctors told her to fight. The Wrights told her to fight. John told her to fight. But she wouldn't.

Seven months after the cancer was found, she died. John, at seventeen, was hit in the face with the facts of life and death. His grief

was intense and complex. He felt fear, confusion, anger, and a pride that kept him from sharing his feelings with others lest they think him weak. So he guarded his emotions well, pressing them into a deep, dark portion of his mind, covering them over with the practical concerns relevant to survival. Because that was the name of the game. Not only was Sybil gone, but no invitation had come from the Wrights for John to move in with any of them. They didn't have to respect Eugene St. George to fear him, John was dismayed to discover. They gave Eugene wide berth, which meant keeping well to themselves where the matter of John's well-being was concerned.

John was totally disillusioned. Wasn't blood thicker than water? he wondered. Wasn't the fact that he was his mother's son enough to keep him in the Wright fold? But they let him go. He had to accept that what his father had told him that night in Maine was true. When the chips were down, help wouldn't come from the Wrights, particularly now that Sybil was gone.

Within weeks of her death, Eugene moved Patricia and their newborn daughter into the Beacon Hill townhouse to which he had never relinquished the title. If he'd been able to think charitably, John might have thanked his father for maintaining the continuity of his senior year in high school, rather than forcing him to move up to Maine. But he was beyond gratitude. He saw the move as an insult to the memory of his mother. More than that, he saw it as an enemy occupation. They were the enemy, Eugene and Patricia. Sybil had given up on life, and they were to blame. Not even the baby was without guilt. Despite Eugene's denials, John was convinced that she was the one thing most instrumental in bringing about the marriage.

But he was over a barrel. He wanted to pack up and move out, but his father had the money. John's weekly allowance wasn't enough to carry him long. Turning eighteen wouldn't matter. Twenty-five was the magic number, and "modest sum" was the term Eugene used when describing what John would receive then if he didn't join St. George Mining. Otherwise, John's weekly allowance would continue until he graduated from college, when he would go on salary with the

company. That salary would be generous. John wouldn't have cause for complaint as long as he stayed with the business.

John would have screamed in frustration if it wouldn't have been uncouth. In the privacy of his thoughts, though, the curses went on. He had wealthy friends, friends with potential, friends to impress. Living with his father didn't help his image; Eugene was and always would be the miner from Maine, in the minds of those who mattered. John knew he'd have to work twice as hard to avoid that stigma and prove himself worthy of his city friends. He'd have to build on the image of self-confidence, wealth, and sophistication that he'd already established.

So he needed money. He was the proverbial beggar who couldn't be choosy, and he despised the role with a passion. His daily life was tormented. Although he spent as much time as possible out of the house, inevitably he encountered Patricia. More than Eugene and the baby, who did little more than sleep and eat, Patricia bothered him. He despised her—despised her for snaring Eugene, for having been poor and desperate and pregnant at the time of her marriage, and for clinging to Eugene ever since. He despised her for being surprisingly nice to him. Mostly, he despised her for being so young and so pretty.

With a deliberate effort at first, he was civil to her. In time, that civility became a way of life. It was easier, he decided, to shut off his emotions and do what had to be done than to challenge his father's power. Someday he would. He wasn't about to stand in Eugene's shadow for the rest of his life, any more than he was about to break off from the company with nothing more than a "modest sum." He figured he had more due him, and he intended to collect.

First he had to graduate from high school, which he did with his share of academic honors. Eugene couldn't appreciate that, he knew, any more than Eugene could appreciate the fact that he had been accepted at the University of Pennsylvania's Wharton School. As far as Eugene was concerned, any school that could give John the basics in business would be fine, since he had a job waiting for him.

But John had worked his tail off—with panache, of course, and

ease, in the eyes of his friends—to get into a top college for a purpose. The academic honors and acceptance at Penn were credentials to add to his name. They complemented the image of the aristocrat, the man who aimed for greatness and achieved it without noticeable effort. The Wharton School was prestigious. It was rich with contacts. It was also far from Boston.

Other than summers, when he commuted between Boston and Timiny Cove, he was rarely at home during his four years at Penn. He liked it that way. He didn't particularly care to see Eugene or Patricia, and he certainly didn't care to see the baby. The way they fawned over her disgusted him—though there were, he had to admit, some amusing moments. When Eugene tossed her high into the air, Patricia was furious, but no more so than Eugene was when Patricia dressed the little girl up like a doll. They were forever arguing about what was and wasn't right for her to do. John might have felt sorry for the kid had she not been such a charmer. From the earliest, she played up to both of her parents, sensing what each wanted from her and delivering. She could make them smile, which was something that, at least when it came to Eugene, John had never been able to do.

He wasn't jealous. One couldn't be jealous of a child, he reasoned. He had his own life, his own future. He could afford to let them all smile. His turn would come.

So he waited. When he graduated from college, he took over the office that Eugene had designated his at the St. George Mining headquarters in Boston. Given his druthers, he'd have been working for another company in another city, but other opportunities had been scarce. Neither the contacts he'd made at Wharton nor his own Boston connections—most of them were busy finding prestigious spots of their own—produced a better offer than Eugene's. Certain circles were tight, and he was, after all, a St. George. He might have taken an entry-level post somewhere, even managed to wangle something a little higher up the ladder, but nothing could compare with the title of vice president that awaited him in Boston.

Again, it was a matter of show. An impressive office and a title to match were valuable in and of themselves. They were part of the image

he cultivated and went hand in hand with dinners at Locke Ober's, rounds of tennis at the Cricket Club, and weekends in Newport.

He also happened to know more about the workings of St. George Mining than he did about anything else, and for the first time in his life he had clout. It wasn't a whole lot, but it was something, and the more he used it, and used it well, the more it worked for him. People within the company were eager to please him.

Clinging to that notion and the satisfaction that it brought to his everyday life, John spent the next few years refining his interests. Although he was intimate with no one friend, he was active with many, and that included women. He was good-looking, well-to-do, and had an impressive position and enough charm to please almost any woman he met. He took advantage of that. If he'd been into carving notches on his belt, it would have been covered.

Most of the women he dated were debutantes, firmly ensconced in the social scene within which he saw himself taking part. He wasn't wildly in love with any of them, but then, love wasn't something he valued. He wasn't looking for it and he didn't need it. What he needed was to be seen at the right times and places with the right people.

As he moved into his midtwenties, though, he needed something else. The women he bedded were pretty enough and accommodating enough. They were clever enough. But they weren't loose and exciting and aggressive. He found himself dreaming of women who were.

Women like Hillary Cox. John hated to admit it, since she was from Timiny Cove and he didn't want to give the town credit for much of anything, but Hillary, in bed, was something else.

He met her for the first time during the summer after his junior year in college. She was fifteen to his twenty-one, and she seemed to be hanging around the places he went—sitting outside the post office when he came out, standing by the magazines while he was buying cigarettes. She was always alone, and while other local girls eyed him when they thought he wasn't looking, she made no bones about meeting his gaze. She was different in other ways, too. Her clothes were

nicer, newer, not high fashion by a long shot, but interesting. She had darker hair, fairer skin, and looked gypsyish and smart.

Having nothing better to do until he finished his business in Timiny Cove, he approached her. She wasn't shy. No sooner had he introduced himself—a formality, since the whole town knew who he was, but it was the proper thing, and he prided himself on doing the proper thing even in as backward a place as Timiny Cove—than she began asking questions. She wanted to know about life in the city. She imagined it was very exciting.

Because she was different, and because she was interested, he talked with her. While the others in town made him feel like an outsider, she made him feel like the worldly sort he considered himself. She was good for his ego. He wanted to think he was good for hers, but he wasn't sure. She didn't seem to care much whether people saw them talking. Her main interest seemed to be in learning as much as she could about the life he led.

He gave her information to dream on, and she sought him out often after that, always with curious dark eyes and questions that only a person with a destination would ask. She was going to Boston, maybe even New York, she informed him, either for college or after. She wanted to be a writer. She was going to make a name for herself.

John humored her. He doubted that she'd ever attain her lofty goals, this young girl from Timiny Cove, but the fervor in her eyes when she spoke intrigued him. When she was accepted into Radcliffe, he was impressed. That fervor could do things. He began to wonder whether it went beyond her mind.

It was a simple enough matter to find out. She was clearly smitten with him. One night, not long after, he took her for a drive down the private lane behind Eugene's big brick house, parked the car on a rise overlooking the valley, and kissed her. She was hot, responding to him with an innocent hunger that he couldn't resist. He took her virginity in the backseat of his Olds, then made love to her twice more before driving her home. Each time she grew bolder. He taught her wildness even as he discovered it in himself. The release he found with her was potent.

He didn't see her often, even when she came to Boston the next year. His lifestyle didn't allow for a steady woman; his image didn't allow for one from Timiny Cove. But from time to time he needed the rowdy passion she offered. As an outlet for sexual aggression, she was second to none.

She also happened to be the only person with whom he could talk. Not that he said much; he was largely self-contained. But he was human. Some things had to come out. He might have been more guarded if Hillary had been from society, but she was from Timiny Cove. She already knew his family. Nothing he said about them could change her opinion of him.

So he sounded off about his father. Although Eugene pretty much let him handle the office end of the business on his own, the times they were together were more difficult than ever. John was learning the business well, noticing its strengths and weaknesses. While it was a steady, profit-making venture, he saw potential for far more. Eugene wasn't interested. He was perfectly comfortable with the status quo and saw no need to take unnecessary risks. John argued ad infinitum about the value of growth, but Eugene couldn't see it. He couldn't see much of anything John's way. He was too busy feeling pride in Pam.

John had no qualms about telling Hillary his opinion of Pam: "She's a regular bitch."

"Come on, John. She's only twelve."

"Try telling her that. She's spoiled as sin, and no wonder, the way he dotes. You'd think there was something special about her, but if there is, I can't see it. She isn't a genius. And she's not gorgeous."

"She's cute."

"She smiles a lot. That's all."

"Not at you. She's very careful with you."

"She knows I'm no fool. She can't wrap me around her finger the way she does him."

"I think you're jealous."

"Of what?"

"Their relationship."

But he didn't believe that. He'd go farther in life than either one of them. "Try again, Hillary."

"I think it's nice that they're close, she and her father. I wish I had half that closeness with mine."

"If you did, you wouldn't be as independent as you are. That's what I like about you. You think for yourself. You don't cling. You have your own life, and you let me lead mine."

"Am I supposed to be happier that way?"

"Definitely. Look at Patricia. She's just the opposite, and she's miserable."

"Is she jealous of the relationship between Pam and Eugene?"

"Not quite. She's relieved they're close. It takes the burden off her. She has a lot on her mind."

That was a whole other story, one that John chose not to relate to Hillary. In her own way, Patricia was bothering him even more than Pam and Eugene. From the start their relationship had been awkward. Their closeness in age, John's antagonism toward her, and her resultant deference all led to tension. For years they walked carefully around each other.

Then John joined the business, and it was as though Patricia had suddenly found a friend. The business concerned her. She wanted to know how it was doing and where it was headed. Not only was Eugene spending more and more of his time in Timiny Cove, but when he was in Boston he had less and less patience for her questions.

John could understand why she turned to him. He knew what was going on in the company, could give her the answers she wanted, and he was available. He also came to understand that there was a power to be had in possessing and sharing information, particularly when the power had to do with Patricia and Eugene. So he indulged Patricia her questions, and the more he did, the more she asked. Increasingly, he found her waiting for him to come home, upset by something Eugene had said or done, desperate for reassurance. He gave her that, and if it meant speaking out against Eugene, he did so.

Surprisingly often, Patricia was on John's side, particularly on the matter of expansion. She too wanted Eugene to broaden his base, but

he wouldn't listen to her either. Frustrated and upset, she argued with him, which promptly sent him running back to Maine, frustrating and upsetting her all the more.

And John was there.

It was totally spontaneous the first time, on a dark and rainy Friday night shortly after Eugene and she had argued. Eugene had swept Pam off in the car to spend the weekend in Maine, leaving Patricia behind to stew alone. Coming in from work, John had found her distraught. Gentleman that he was, when she slipped her arms around his waist and began to cry, he comforted her. Then, in the course of the comforting, something happened. His hands began to move over a body that was soft and lovely. His mouth touched hers once, then again and again. His body responded in the only way that an active twenty-eight-year-old man with a healthy appreciation of women could respond.

While the climax he reached that night wasn't as sweet as some he'd had or as fiery as others, it was unique. It satisfied the dark cravings of his mind, gave him the perverse pleasure of cuckolding his father.

Chapter 5

◆◆◆

MOM?" PAM BEGAN CALLING as soon as she opened the front door. "Mom?" Even before the door slammed shut, she had dropped her book bag and was darting into the living room, but there was no sign of Patricia. Nor was she in the parlor or the library. *"Mom?"* She poked her head into the kitchen. "Hettie, isn't my mother home?"

Hettie was a very large, very dark Jamaican who cooked like a dream. "Oo-yes, Miss Pamela. She be upstairs napping." She held out a plate. "Sand dollars. Made just for you."

Pam flashed her a grin, took one of the cookies from the plate, and pushed it into her mouth on the way out the door. She dashed back through the hall and was halfway up the front stairs when John came down from the top and blocked her way. He was the last person she wanted to see.

"What are you doing here?" she asked.

"I live here."

"You're supposed to be at work." She moved to the side to pass him, but he flattened a hand against the wall.

"I had to change clothes. There's a cocktail party at the Parker House."

She moved to the other side, but he gripped the mahogany banister. "Move, John. I have to go up."

"What's the rush?"

"I have to see my mother."

"She's resting."

Pam tried to duck under his arm, but she wasn't as short as she used to be. In the last few months she'd sprouted up. She might have minded, had Eugene not been so proud of her height, which he said she'd inherited from him. Since she had more friends than ever in seventh grade, she figured it was just fine to be tall and slim rather than voluptuous.

She wasn't anywhere near tall enough to be able to look John in the eye, though, and she wasn't about to physically butt him. He made her uneasy. Although he wore the trousers and shirt he'd worn to work that day, the shirt was unbuttoned, exposing his chest, and his hair was mussed. He didn't look as civilized as usual.

"I have to talk with her. Please, John. Let me by."

"What do you have to talk with her about?"

"Something."

"What is it?"

Pam wasn't about to share her excitement with him. "Nothing special."

"You're in a pretty big rush for nothing special. Couldn't you even stop to take off your coat?"

Her coat was the last thing on her mind. "Let me by, John!" She aimed her voice up the stairs. "Mom? Mom!"

"I said, she's resting."

"I just have to ask her something quick." She tried to move his arm, but it wouldn't budge. Taking another breath, she hollered, *"Mom?"*

"Shut up, Pam, and leave her be." Grasping her arm in one very large hand, he began to propel her back down the stairs.

"Let me go," she protested, squirming. Freed after a step or two, she turned on him. "Who do you think you are? You're not my father, and you're not my guard. She's *my* mother, not yours. If I want to see her, I have a right to!"

"Not when she has other things on her mind."

"She always has other things on her mind, because you come home and talk about work, work, work with her. Well, this is important. I have to speak to her now. It can't wait."

"It'll just have to, princess, because you're not going up there yet—"

"John?" Patricia called from the top of the stairs. She was wearing a silk robe and was combing her hair back with her fingers. "It's all right, John. What is it, Pamela?"

Pam heard the annoyance in her voice and blamed it on John. "I have to ask you something, and he won't let me." She tried to dodge him once again, but he deftly shifted his body and continued to block her way. There was no need for him to do it, since her mother was up, but he was enjoying himself, she realized. He was enjoying her frustration. So she promptly stopped fighting him and moved back down the stairs until she could look up at Patricia around his towering frame. "The Claflins asked me to go to North Conway with them this weekend. They're leaving right after dinner and will be back Sunday night. Can I go?"

"What's in North Conway?" Patricia asked.

"They have a house there. It's less than five minutes from the mountain, Laurie says."

"Skiing," John told Patricia. "You can't go," he said to Pam. "You've never been skiing before. You'll break a leg."

Ignoring him, Pam pleaded with her mother. "There's a ski school at the bottom of the mountain. I'll take lessons. That's what Laurie does. Please, Mom? I've always wanted to go skiing."

"You have not," John argued. "But you and every other little teen-ager is dreaming about bumping into Jean Claude Killy on the slopes. He won't be there, princess, and the boys who will be will laugh when you fall." The doorbell rang. "If you wanted to ski, you should have started when you were little." He scowled when she turned and ran toward the door. "For God's sake, Pam, we have a butler."

Not one to stand on ceremony, she opened the door herself. "Hillary," she breathed in relief. Despite their shaky start, she and Hillary had become friends. Hillary wasn't exactly a flower child like the ones on the Common, but she'd loosened up since she'd been at college. Pam thought she looked wonderful. Her eyes were lined in black, her hair was parted in the middle, worn long and loose, and her coat

was open over a dress that was far more mini than anything Patricia would allow Pam to wear. "Am I glad you're here. Have you ever been skiing?"

Hillary regarded her quizzically, then looked past her toward John. The quizzical look became one of interest when she saw his state of dishabille. "Skiing?" Then she caught sight of Patricia at the top of the stairs, and her eyes shot back to Pam. "Sure I have. It's fun."

"When did you first go?"

"Three years ago, when I was a freshman."

"And you didn't break a leg?"

"Of course not."

Pam turned a triumphant smile on John before transferring the smile, minus the triumph, to Patricia. "See? It's perfectly safe. Laurie says I can rent skis and stuff there. I already have a parka. All I have to do is buy ski pants and heavy socks and long underwear."

"But they're leaving tonight," Patricia protested.

"We have this afternoon."

"I can't take you shopping now. I have to get dressed. What time is the party, John?"

"Five-thirty."

"You're going too?" Pam asked, feeling the dismay she always felt when Patricia did things with John.

"Of course I'm going. I'm on the committee. There are cocktails and hors d'oeuvres at the Parker House, then we're all going down to the theater. After the show, there's a light buffet back at the hotel."

"Why isn't Daddy going?"

"Because he's in Maine," John answered.

Still Pam directed her questions to Patricia. "Does he know about the party?"

"Of course he does," she answered. "But he can't get in, so John has agreed to take me. Honestly, Pamela, this really doesn't concern you."

"It does. I want to go skiing, and I can't do it if we don't go shopping first. It won't take long to run down to Filene's."

"I *can't*, Pamela."

Hillary spoke up. "I'll take her shopping."

Looking back at her, Pam saw that her eyes were on John, which wasn't at all surprising. Hillary always looked at John. What was surprising was the edge Pam saw in the look.

"I have nothing to do until later tonight. I'd be glad to take Pam shopping. I've been skiing. I know just what she needs."

Pam looked more hesitantly at her mother. Much as she liked Hillary, she'd still rather shop with Patricia. They hadn't done it in such a long time.

But Patricia was already accepting Hillary's offer. "Are you sure you wouldn't mind—"

"Patricia," John cut in, "I don't think skiing is the best idea."

"It can't harm her. She'll be busy and happy for the weekend. Hillary, wait there. I'll get the charge card." And she was gone.

"Thanks a lot, Hillary," John said. His eyes were cold.

Passing Pam, she approached him. Her palm went flat against the bare flesh of his middle, fingers splaying wide. In a low, even tone, she said, "Pam shouldn't have to suffer because you have escort duty. Neither should I. I like your sister. She has the spunk in the family. We'll have a good time together, maybe even catch an early dinner before she leaves."

"And after that? Where are you going?"

Before she could answer, Patricia was back, leaning over the top railing. Hillary trotted up the few steps and took the charge card from her hand. "I'll get her something nice."

"Not too expensive. And not risque. Pamela, darling, be good for Hillary, and be good for the Claflins. It was sweet of them to invite you. Have Hettie pack up a box of cookies. Better still, stop at S.S. Pierce and pick up some jams. They make a nice gift."

"We'll be back before you leave," Pam started to say, but Patricia was already disappearing back down the hall toward her bedroom. John was once again an immobile force on the staircase, and this time it didn't seem worth the effort to fight him. She'd won on the issue of skiing. She wouldn't push her luck. "I have to call Laurie and tell her I can come," she told Hillary. "I'll be right back."

She took her time with the call, then stopped in the kitchen for another cookie. But when she returned to the hall, there was no sign of John.

"Where did he go?"

Hillary shot a despairing glance toward the second floor.

"I thought he'd stay and talk with you."

"Yeah. So did I."

"He's a rat."

Hillary slipped an arm around Pam's shoulder. "What else is new?"

"You should tell him to go to hell."

"Oh, my, such language from one so young."

"I mean it. Doesn't it bother you when he ignores you that way?"

She smiled. "Nah. That's just John."

Not for a minute, though, did Pam believe that Hillary wasn't bothered. She could see it in the sadness in her smile. Wanting to cheer her up, she said, "But you have plans for later, so John's the loser. Who are you seeing?"

Hillary collared her with a playful elbow and ushered her out the door before she handled that one. "A guy from school. Tom Rush is playing at a coffeehouse in the Square." Side by side, they trotted down the stairs.

"Who's Tom Rush?"

"A folksinger."

"Who's the guy?"

"No one special."

"Why not? You should be meeting someone special. You're at that age."

Hillary laughed as they started up Mt. Vernon Street. "Who told you that?"

"Marcy. You're a senior. You're supposed to get married soon."

"Not me. I'm not getting married."

"Never?"

"I wouldn't say that. Just not real soon."

"Because John won't get married? What's wrong with him,

Hillary? Everyone he knows is getting married. He goes to weddings all the time, and if it isn't weddings, it's christenings. So what's wrong with him?"

Hillary shrugged.

"Can't he at least find his own place to live?"

"Is he still giving you a hard time?"

"Yes. Why don't you propose to him? Maybe he needs a little push. Tell him that you're graduating and that it's time for you two to get married. Tell him that you're madly in love—"

"I will not. I don't want to get married. I have other plans."

"What are they?"

"I'm going to New York." She half-turned as they walked so that she faced Pam. "And don't breathe a word of this to John, because it isn't definite. I still have to find a job, but whether it's this year or the next or the next, I'm going to New York." Facing front again, she linked arms with Pam. "John doesn't know. I'll tell him when I'm sure."

"Why do you want to go to New York?"

"Because that's where big things happen."

"But you're a writer. You can write anywhere."

"I want to do it in New York."

"Then I won't see you. Then *John* won't see you. Then you won't see *him*." When Hillary didn't answer, she said, "That's a lousy idea, Hillary."

"That's what John will say. He'll say that I'll never make it in New York and that I'm silly to try. But he's not offering me anything better, is he?"

Turning down Joy Street, they walked on. When a chill wind whipped up from the Common, they leaned closer together.

"I'll miss you if you move to New York."

"I'm not moving yet."

"But you will, and what will I do then? Who'll stick up for me when John does his rat thing?"

"You'll stick up for yourself. You already do, Pam. I admire you for that."

"He wouldn't let me up those stairs today, and there wasn't anything I could do about it."

"Just wait. Before long, you'll be bigger and more grown-up. He won't be able to block stairways then. He's just taking advantage of your age. You'll see. Just wait."

It was going to be a long, painful wait, though. Pam knew that the instant Hillary dropped her at home and she ran inside to find a note for her from Patricia. She and John had already left.

"Darling, John is right," the note read. "You really shouldn't go skiing for the first time on such short notice. If you want to go that badly, John says he'll take you himself another time. I've called the Claflins and explained. They understand. Laurie says she'll call you when she gets home Sunday night. Don't worry about the things you bought. I'll have Marcy run down and return them next week. I hope you had fun with Hillary. Don't wait up. I'll be late. See you tomorrow."

Pam crushed the paper in her hand. "No. No! *No!*" She yelled it a few more times before storming through the house. Hettie had long since left, and Raymond, the butler, was nowhere in sight, which was just as well. She didn't want either of them. She wanted Marcy.

Following the smell of starch, she found her in the basement laundry room ironing shirts. "Do you know what he's done?" she cried without preamble. "He canceled my trip! He convinced Mom that I shouldn't go! Why did he do that, Marcy? What harm was it to him if I went? I don't tell him what to do with his life. Why does he have to tell me? He won't ever take me skiing. I don't care what he told Mom, or what she said in the letter. He won't ever take me skiing. He's never taken me anywhere, and anyway, I wouldn't want to go with him." She stood for several seconds with her feet braced wide, breathing hard as she struggled to find a reason for the change in her plans. "Know why he didn't want me to go today? Because he said no. That's all. He said no when I first mentioned it, and he wants his word to be law. There was no one here to argue when Hillary and I went shopping. He's a snake, Marcy! It isn't fair!"

Marcy moved the iron slowly over the white collar that lay flat on the padded board. "Life isn't, sometimes," she said at last.

"Well, it should be," Pam argued and turned back toward the stairs. "I'm calling my father. If he says I can go, I'm going."

"Pammy?"

Pam paused with her hand on the wood rail. "What?"

Marcy just looked at her in a sad, sage way.

Dropping her hand from the rail, Pam slowly came down again. "I should. It would serve John right."

"It would rile him."

"That's *his* problem."

"No, it's yours. If he gets angry, your mama will, too. Even if you go skiing, you got to be back here with them come Monday morning. You'll pay for the fun then."

But they both knew that was only one of the reasons Pam wouldn't call Eugene. The other had to do with a twelve-year-old's instincts about what would and would not help her parents' foundering marriage. As always, thoughts of that set Pam's stomach to churning, which in turn made her snappish.

"I don't care. I want to go skiing."

"Now you're being stubborn."

"So? If John can be, so can I!"

"But you're better than him."

"If that's so, why is my mother with him much more than she's with me?"

"B'cause he knows about the business. He's your daddy's assistant, kind of."

"But I'm her daughter. I need her sometimes, too." Her anger began to fade. In its place was worry. Slipping onto the stool by the ironing board, she said, "It's awful, Marcy. Sometimes I say things to her, and she smiles and nods but she doesn't hear me. I can be talking about school, and ten minutes later she'll ask me how school is."

"She loves you."

"Maybe, but something's happening." She looked bleakly at the shirtsleeves Marcy was straightening. "Maybe they'll get divorced."

"They won't."

"How do you know?"

"B'cause your mama likes being married to your daddy."

"You wouldn't know that to hear her talk. It used to be that she was upset when Daddy was angry. She isn't anymore."

"She got used to it."

But Pam had another reason. "She has John now. He probably convinces her that it's better for Daddy to be in Maine, just like he convinced her that I shouldn't go skiing. Why does she listen to him, Marcy?"

"B'cause he's got the answers for the things she's asking."

"But why doesn't she ask my father those things?"

"B'cause he's in Timiny Cove."

"She could call him. If she wanted to, she could. I think it's gotten so that she likes being with John more."

"But she loves your daddy. There's a difference."

"They're never together."

"But when they are, it's not so bad." Marcy paused, pulled a cuff straight, pressed the iron down hard. "I've seen bad. I know."

Pam remembered the screaming she'd heard. "At home?"

Marcy moved the iron back and forth over the cuff. Then she set it on its end and turned the cuff over.

"Marcy?" After another moment's pause, she said, "Is it really bad in your house?"

The iron began moving on the reverse side of the cuff. "It's bad."

"How? What happens?"

After a pause, Marcy said, "They fight. Mama goes back and forth to the factory—"

"Why doesn't she work at the mine?"

"B'cause that's men's work."

"I could do it. Daddy's shown me how. I could do it."

"But you won't, b'cause it's men's work."

"I don't believe that. If women can do what men do, they should be able to get the job. I'm going to be president of St. George Mining someday."

"Did your daddy tell you that?"

"He tells me I can be what I want, and that's what I want."

"What about John?"

"What about him?"

"He's already there. Won't the company be his?"

"I'll fire him. That's the first thing I'll do. The second will be to hire your mother. She can do sorting and matching."

But Marcy was insistent. "Mama won't do nothing different from what the other women do, and they don't work at the mine. B'sides, she doesn't mind the factory. She gets paid enough so there's food on the table, even if there isn't much left over for anything else."

She paused then, and Pam was quiet, too. She could see the sadness on Marcy's face, a face that didn't usually reveal too much. What it told Pam now made her wonder just what Eugene had meant when he'd said that Marcy had seen the bare side of life.

"Is that what makes things so bad?" she asked cautiously. "Not having money for things?"

Still ironing, Marcy tipped her head to the side. "It's one of the things."

"What's the other?"

"Him."

"Your father?"

"He's not my father. My father died in Korea. Mama married Jarvis a couple of years after that."

"Is he Tommy and Lizzie's father?"

She nodded. The iron hissed a breath of steam. "Wouldn't know it. He hits them, too."

"He spanks them?" Pam had never been spanked in her life. She'd been yelled at, but never spanked.

"Not spanks," Marcy clarified. "Hits. Sometimes he's drunk, sometimes he's not. But when he does it, he does it hard." She hauled back an arm in demonstration. *"Bam!"*

Pam flinched. "Did he ever hit you that way?"

"Lots. That's why your daddy took me to live here soon as I could leave school."

Pam hadn't known. She felt awful. "Oh, Marcy."

"It was worst for Mama. I could run away from him, but Mama,

she never did have so much strength after Lizzie was born. She's all tired after work, and he wants somethin' to eat. If she doesn't get it for him fast enough . . ."

"He hits her?"

Marcy nodded. "And yells. And throws things sometimes clear across the room." She snapped the shirt from the ironing board, shook it straight, and reached for a wire hanger. "That's what bad is."

So now Pam knew, and, as Marcy had intended, it made her feel less sorry for herself. Although there were arguments in her house, there wasn't any hitting, yelling, or throwing. Patricia wanted dignity and peace nearly as much as prosperity.

Thinking about it that night, curled up in her bed, Pam had a lot to be grateful for. True, she hated John. But she loved her mother. And she adored Eugene, who was kind and gentle and wasn't anything like Jarvis Willow. Maybe Marcy was right—maybe her parents weren't going to get a divorce; maybe they were comfortable just living apart like they did.

None of her friends' parents lived that way.

But there were some advantages to it. Like the tourmaline crystals Eugene had taught her to love, her life was dichroistic, glowing in one color, then the next as the light turned. When she was in Boston, she was the lady her mother wanted her to be. She went to a private school with her friends, took dancing lessons and piano lessons, went to Saturday morning classes at the museum, which she loved, ate at the best restaurants in town, and went to the ballet and the theater. There were times that she felt she was playing a game, but since she did it well, she didn't mind—especially since she could then turn around and go to Timiny Cove, take the satin ribbon from her hair, put on jeans and a long shirt, and do all the fun things Patricia might not like.

She couldn't imagine living in Timiny Cove without returning to Boston. Nor could she imagine it the other way around. Maine was her salvation. It was where Eugene was. It was where everyone knew her and liked her, and she knew and liked everyone. It was small, close, like family.

It was also where Cutter was.

Chapter 6

◈◈◈

THERE HAD NEVER BEEN A TIME when Cutter Reid hadn't known the name St. George. He'd been born and raised in Timiny Cove, and though his father had been kicked off the company payroll soon after Cutter's birth, St. George Mining was too visible a presence in town to be ignored. That wasn't to say that Cutter respected it. He didn't respect much of anything, and, being his father's son and his own worst enemy, not much of anything respected him.

In 1965 Cutter was sixteen going on twenty-eight, if being street-wise counted for anything. His father had drunk himself to death when Cutter was nine, and his mother had whored her way into an adjacent grave soon after. From the age of thirteen, Cutter had fended for himself. He had worked at odd jobs until he quit or was fired, had gone to school only when the truant officer came looking, and had committed enough petty crimes to firmly establish himself as one tough kid. He'd spent more than his share of nights in the local jail and had managed to avoid a serious conviction only by the skin of his teeth.

That was why, when Eugene St. George tackled him in the trash alley behind Paquette's Luncheonette, he wasn't expecting an ounce of mercy. Having helped himself to the contents of the cash drawer at the gas station in the center of town, he suddenly found himself being chased not only by the attendant Judd Stuckey but by Eugene St. George, who had stopped for gas.

Cutter cursed himself for not recognizing the large, dark blue Lincoln, but it was raining so hard that visibility was next to nil, which was one of the reasons he figured he could get away with the heist. Even when Eugene caught sight of him and jumped from the car, he wasn't concerned. He was younger and lighter than Eugene; he could outrun him. But one block into his escape he knew he was in trouble. March was mud season in Maine, and with the rain pouring down, footholds in the mired earth were precarious at best. Unable to stay on the pavement, which would have led him straight through the center of town and past dozens of pairs of curious eyes, he had to take the back paths. That was how he found himself sprawled face-down in the mud in the trash alley beneath Eugene's large frame. He barely had time to catch his breath when he was hauled up by the collar.

"What in the hell do you think you're doin', boy?" Eugene roared. He was panting from the run, but the exertion hadn't dulled his indignation.

Cutter wrenched his body to the right, a move that should have taken Eugene by surprise and secured his freedom, but it didn't. Eugene hung on tight.

"Got him," Judd gasped, coming around the corner at the fastest his gimpy left leg would allow. "Who—Cutter Reid, you no-good thug!"

Cutter wrenched to the left, but Eugene's hand was like steel around the collar of his drenched jacket and shirt. Still he struggled, trying to head-butt his way free, and when that didn't work, he kicked. But Eugene's superior size and bulk—and cunning, it seemed—had him down in the mud again before Cutter knew what had happened. This time, a knee was pressed sharply to his groin, holding him still. Eugene fished inside Cutter's soggy clothes and came up with the cash that Cutter would have denied he'd taken.

As if all that weren't bad enough, the trash alley was suddenly filled with more people than it had seen in days. Most notable among them was Verne Walker, Timiny Cove's police department.

One look at Cutter's muddy face and he said wearily, "What's he done this time?"

There was nothing weary in the way Judd held up the money Eugene had recovered. "He stole from me, the dirty rotten thief! You gotta do somethin', Verne. He's gettin' bolder 'n' bolder. Just walked in and took the money from the cash drawer. If it hadn't been for Eugene, he'd a got away."

Cutter wanted to argue, but his balls were hurting something fierce. It was all he could do to take one breath after another and make like he was fine, and he was determined to do just that. He wasn't about to let them think him a sissy on top of everything else.

"He been eyein' that gas station for a while," someone behind Verne said, calling out to be heard above the rap of rain on a rusted tin gutter nearby.

Someone else called, "Last time was the supply store. Couldn'a been more 'n two months ago."

A third voice said: "He's trouble. Been trouble since the day he was born. No wonder his daddy drunk so much."

Cutter turned a deaf ear to the talk. He'd heard it before. His eyes were on Eugene, whose eyes were on him. He was starting to feel dizzy.

Verne bent over at the waist, rain dripping off the visor of his cap. "So what you got to say for yourself, sonny? Just can't keep your nose clean, can ya? I'm gonna have to lock ya up again, and if Judd presses charges, you gotta go to Portland. Got yourself a lawyer? Ya may need one this time."

"He doesn't have any lawyer," Eugene muttered. He was looking closely at Cutter, who had broken out in a cold sweat and was ash white. "Doesn't have any parents, doesn't have any money, doesn't have any food from the looks of him." The knee came off his groin. In a helpless reflex, Cutter rolled to his side and curled up. Eugene's hand went to his shoulder, ostensibly restraining. "Deep breath," he murmured in a low voice.

Cutter took a deep breath, then a second when the first one was ragged. After a third the dizziness began to ease. In the next instant Eugene released the pressure on his shoulder and helped him sit up. With all eyes on him, Cutter shrugged off the helping hand.

"So what you got to say for yourself, sonny?" Verne repeated.

"To you, nuthin'," Cutter answered in a voice deliberately made deep.

"You want to say it to the judge?"

"It don't much matter. He ain't gonna give any more of a damn about me 'n you do."

"Then we might as well give it a try," Verne concluded and straightened. "Okay, folks. Back to what you was doin' before Cutter Reid got you out in the rain." He watched while the first of the onlookers turned to leave. "Judd, you gonna press charges?"

"Damn right I am. He got no right lookin' to wipe me out that way. I work hard for my money. He ought to try doin' that for a change."

Verne turned back to Cutter, who was gingerly pushing himself to his feet. Upright, he was taller than the police chief. He knew that from experience and wanted the advantage it gave.

"You hear that, sonny? You're in trouble this time. Judd's gonna press charges, an' what with everythin' else you done in the past, it ain't gonna be good."

"Nuthin's good," Cutter said, in the grip of a familiar bleakness. "Tell me somethin' I don't already know."

"You know what it's like in prison?" Eugene asked.

Cutter looked off in the opposite direction, not caring what he saw as long as it wasn't Eugene. He might have gained a physical superiority over Verne in the last year, but he had a way to go to catch up with the big man who owned half the town.

"It's mean," Eugene went on, "meaner than anything you ever known. Meaner than anything you ever dreamed. It's dark and hard and unforgiving, and once you're in there, you're a con, then an ex-con. You think it's tough goin' through life with your daddy's name? Well, tack ex-con after it, and see how that feels."

Cutter thought of Eugene's big house and his big car and his big bankbook, and made a disparaging sound. "How would you know?"

"I had a friend once. Born right here, just like you. Alvie Joplin, remember him, Verne? No, I guess he was before your time." He addressed Cutter again. "Car theft was his specialty, only he didn't do it

here, he did it down in Boston. After a time they caught him and put him away, and when he got out, he tried to find a job, only he was an ex-con, and people were nervous hiring an ex-con. Since he wasn't good at much of anything but stealin' cars, he tried it again, and they sent him away again. He was longer in gettin' out that time, and he wasn't a kid anymore, older and hardened, so when he needed money to eat, he took a job for some quick money. It was right down his alley, stealin' a car, only he used the car to help his two buddies get away after they robbed a bank."

"What happened to him?" Verne asked, fully taken with the tale.

But Eugene kept looking at Cutter, who was looking right back at him. "Cops got 'im. Shot 'im. I read that he was in serious condition, so I went to the hospital. Didn't even recognize him. It had been ten years since I'd seen him. He looked thirty years older. But that was as old as he got. He died the next day."

Cutter was used to people lecturing him, and there was always a moral to their stories that was tailor-made for him. It was too convenient. "Nice tale," he said.

"True tale," was Eugene's comeback.

"So you gonna learn somethin' from that, sonny?" Verne asked.

Coming in the breath after Eugene's vow, Verne's gloating voice was a rude abrasive to Cutter. "I ain't gonna learn nuthin' from you," he spat.

"Well, that's just fine," Verne said, "but you're comin' with me whether you like it or not." When he closed a hand around his prisoner's arm, Cutter knocked it away. "Watch it, sonny. I don't want to have to add resistin' arrest to the charges." This time, though, when he reached for Cutter, Eugene was the one who stopped him.

"I want him, Verne."

Cutter's eyes shot to Eugene while Verne said, "You what?"

"I want him. Let me have him for the rest of the day."

"You gone mad?"

"Do I look like I've gone mad?" Eugene asked, his tone dead serious.

"What are you gonna do with him?"

"That's between him and me. Any problem?"

"You want him, you got him. But I'd be careful if I was you. Turn your back on him and he'll be gone."

"I'm not turning my back." He took Cutter's arm. "Let's go."

Cutter didn't resist. He didn't know why, whether it had to do with the choice being between Eugene and Verne, memory of that hard knee in his groin, curiosity about what Eugene had in mind, or something else. But he went along, albeit uneasily. Eugene was more commanding than Verne any day. He was also stronger, quicker, and more wily. Making a break for it would be hard. Not that Cutter planned to do that, at least not right off. It might be worth sticking around if there was promise of a hot meal in it.

"Where you takin' me?" he asked.

"You'll see."

"I want to know."

"If you wanted to know where you were goin', you should'a gone with Verne."

Manacled to Eugene by a single strong hand, Cutter didn't have much choice but to march alongside him, through the rain and the mud, back to the scene of the crime.

They didn't talk. Cutter wasn't good at conversation in the best of circumstances. When they reached the car, Eugene opened the passenger's door and nudged him in.

He balked then. "I got mud all over me."

"So do I."

"Your car's new and clean."

"So? I don't plan on stayin' out in this rain forever, and I'm sure as hell not goin' to walk for miles in it. You may be young and insensitive, but I'm gettin' cold. Now get in."

He gave Cutter another push, a firmer one this time. Cutter got into the car.

Slamming the door, Eugene rounded the car and climbed in behind the wheel. He shot Cutter a glance. "You missed your chance. The keys were here in the car. You could'a taken off when I was goin' around."

But Cutter was cold and tired. It never occurred to him to take off. Not that he was about to tell Eugene that. "I don't know how to drive."

"No? So how do you get around?"

"Motorcycle." He snorted. "Got no gas for it now, thanks to you."

"You want gas, you can earn the money to buy it."

Cutter snorted again but didn't say another word. He thought it was fine and dandy for Eugene St. George to talk about earning money. He lived an easy life, had everything he needed, and if there was something he wanted, all he had to do was open the company till and help himself. No one would call him a thief. No one would come running after him, threatening to lock him up. Some people had it made in life, that was all there was to it, and Cutter wasn't one of them. He couldn't earn decent money because he wasn't trained for a damn thing. The only jobs he could get were ones any idiot could hold. They always bored him so he quit.

Eugene was heading out of town, not in the direction of the big brick home or the gem pits but in the opposite direction, the one that was familiar to Cutter. "Where are we goin'?"

"Your place." He peered through the windshield. "Is this the turn?"

Instantly Cutter was wary. Folks from town came to his place only when something was wrong, like when his daddy ran the old truck into a tree or when his mama died. "Why are we goin' to my place?"

"So you can change your clothes. Is this the turn?"

The reason was fair enough. "Yeah."

As soon as Eugene made the turn, the Lincoln began to bounce on the rutted road, and the deeper into the woods they went, the worse the bouncing became. Momentary relief came with the occasional spin of a wheel, but the tires were new, regaining their traction every time. So the jolting went on. "Jesus," Eugene breathed at one point, "and you do this on a cycle?"

"I got a hard butt."

"Must have a hard head. Why in the devil don't you live in town like everyone else?"

" 'Cause this place is mine. It's all I got."

"It's isolated."

"I like it like that."

"You ought to be with people."

"I don't like people."

Eugene snickered. "You picked the wrong planet, boy."

"I didn't pick a goddamned thing," Cutter blurted. "It was picked for me. I didn't have no say at all. Even this house"—which was coming into sight, looking pathetically ramshackle in the rain—"was forced on me, but it's the only one I got."

The car came to a stop. Yanking at the door handle, Cutter was quickly out and tramping through the sludge toward his front door. With a single push it was open. He went through without looking back and kicked it shut with a heel, just like he always did. In the next instant, Eugene threw it open again.

"Don't you have any manners?" he growled.

Cutter hadn't expected him to come in. He didn't need help changing his clothes. "What do you want in here?"

"I want to look around." He was scanning the room with a disapproving look on his face. "You live here?"

"Something wrong with that?" Cutter asked. He didn't love the place either, but it was the only home he had.

"Sure is. It's a mess," Eugene decided. From a battered table covered with dirty cardboard containers and plastic plates, he moved past an upholstered chair whose shabbiness was barely hidden beneath a pile of worn clothes. "It's filthy, and it smells. Don't you have any pride?"

"I wasn't expecting guests."

"What I'm talking about's got nothing to do with guests." He glanced into the shadows, of which there were many, and frowned. "Where do you sleep?"

"What's it to you?"

"Where do you sleep?"

Cutter hitched his head toward the darkest end of the room, where a narrow ladder led to a loft. In the barely discernible light, the loft

didn't look large enough to hold much. Eugene apparently thought the same thing. "You fit?"

"I manage." He watched Eugene stare at the loft for another minute before dropping his eyes. They fell on the old, grimy-topped potbelly stove that stood out from one wall.

"Is that for heat?"

"When I got wood."

"And when you don't?"

"I make do."

"You freeze."

"Hey, man, I'm not the only one. Lots of people around here don't have heat."

"Not if I can help it," Eugene muttered. He tugged at a lamp chain. Nothing happened. "And you didn't pay your bill."

"I *couldn't* pay my bill. Besides, what do I need lights for? When it gets dark, I go to sleep."

"So how do you read?" To Cutter's chagrin, Eugene had spotted the books that were sticking out from under the clothes on the chair. "Did you steal them?"

"They're from the library."

"Did you steal them?"

"No."

Eugene lifted one. "*Catcher in the Rye*. Any good?"

"It's okay."

"What's it about?"

"Some kids." He prayed Eugene wouldn't ask more. He liked the book, felt a kind of affinity for the rebelliousness of Holden Caulfield, but he had a feeling he'd missed a lot of what the author was trying to say. That was what his teachers had always told him, that he was missing things. Personally, he didn't care. He liked to read, but he didn't want to be forever taking apart every line. So he missed some hidden meaning. So what?

When Eugene tossed the book back to the chair, he was relieved, but his relief was short-lived. Folding his arms over his chest, Eugene

leaned back against the door. "Got anything clean and dry in this mess?"

Cutter knew he could find dry. Clean was another story. Sifting through a pile of clothes on the floor behind the ladder to the loft, he came up with the best of the lot, jeans and a shirt that would have to do. He looked up to find Eugene watching him. "I got some."

"Put them on."

"You just gonna stand there and watch?"

"Yup."

"Look who's talkin' about manners."

"The way I see it," Eugene said, "if you were in jail, you'd be doing this and more in front of a dozen guys. Now speed it up. I'm not getting any warmer standing around this shitbox."

Neither was Cutter. Peeling off his sodden jacket, then his shirt, he mopped mud spatters from his face and neck as best he could with the inside of the wet shirt, then put on the dry one. Without looking at Eugene, he went at his pants. When he had the dry jeans on, he found a pair of socks. But the wet work boots had to go back on. They were the only shoes he had. Grabbing a jacket that he'd snitched the month before from a hook in a soda shop two towns over, he approached Eugene.

"My place isn't so bad, y'know. Some are worse."

"Only if the people who live there are feeble-minded or infirm. So what's your excuse? That your folks are gone? That you're just a kid? That you don't know what a laundromat is? That you don't have time to go? Well, I say bullshit. You're a lazy bum without a stitch of pride." He pulled open the door and stomped out.

"I'm not lazy!" Cutter called after him. "And I got pride!"

"Get back in the car!" Eugene bellowed.

One part of Cutter was tempted to turn around and race into the woods. Given that he knew them like the back of his hand, he'd escape Eugene for sure. The other part, though, was thinking that Eugene had to be getting hungry.

He got back in the car.

Eugene started it up, and after some tricky maneuvering in the

mud he had it turned around and bouncing back over the ruts toward the main road. Cutter stared out the windshield, wondering where they were going next, darting Eugene the occasional glance in hopes of finding out. But the man's face told him nothing, and since Cutter wasn't about to ask again, he stayed silent. He definitely had pride.

After hitting the main road, Eugene drove straight back through the center of town. He pulled up at the large brick house that stood several blocks beyond the town green. "Get out."

"You want me to go in there?"

"Why not?"

"I'm a thief. I might just steal your silver."

Eugene shot him a smug look. "You won't." Without another word, he climbed out of the car.

Cutter followed, trotting up the brick steps, passing through the large oak door, taking in everything he could of the spacious front hall before Eugene's lead took him down a narrow hall to the kitchen. Minutes later, he was looking at the loaf of bread, container of ham, and wedge of cheese that Eugene had set on the counter.

"Make yourself a sandwich," Eugene told him, setting a knife next to the food. "You look to be half-starved. I'll be back." And he was gone.

For a minute, Cutter didn't move. He listened to the footsteps that went up the front staircase and receded, but his eyes were on the counter. He tried to think of what possible hitch there would be if he ate Eugene St. George's food. No one ever offered him food for free. There had to be a price.

But he was too hungry just then to try to figure it. Wasting no more time, he made himself the thickest sandwich he could and, standing right there at the counter, wolfed it down.

"Want another one?"

He spun around. He hadn't heard Eugene come back down the stairs, but there he was, standing at the door wearing fresh clothes and a somber expression.

"You've been growing tall, boy, but you're thin as a rail. I can't remember the last time I seen so many ribs." He tossed his chin toward the counter. "Take another. Go on. It's free."

Cutter didn't care if it was or it wasn't. If anything, the sandwich he'd eaten had made him more hungry. So he turned his back and fixed another one. He ate more slowly this time. Halfway through, he faced Eugene. "Where is everyone?"

"Who?"

"Your family. I know you got a family."

"They're down in Boston."

"Why are they there when you're here?"

Eugene pondered that and finally said simply, " 'Cause that's the way it works."

Cutter wasn't about to ask what he meant. There was something sad on his face, something at odds with the strength that was usually there. "You're here by yourself?"

"Is that so surprising?"

"Yeah. I thought Deenie Crocker was your cook."

"She is, but there ain't much cookin' needed for just me. Same with cleaning. A man doesn't have to be helpless."

Cutter went back to his sandwich. His father had been helpless. So were most of the men he'd known, at least when it came to home chores like cooking and cleaning. There were certain things men didn't do, certain things they had women for. He didn't understand why Eugene St. George's wife wasn't doing those things for him, or why, if she had to stay in Boston, Eugene didn't have someone else here in her place. Cutter would have thought it a matter of pride that a wealthy man like Eugene not have to take care of himself.

But the kitchen was neat and clean. It was nice, with its big round table to one side and the comfortable chairs with arms and the large windows that looked out to the backyard. It was the kind of kitchen that the other families in Timiny Cove would have filled with people and kids.

"Do you get lonely?" he heard himself ask. He wasn't sure where the question came from, since *loneliness* wasn't a recognized part of his vocabulary. He looked Eugene in the eye.

Eugene turned away. "Sure. Lots." As he left the room, he called

over his shoulder, "Put that stuff back in the Frigidaire, and let's get moving."

Cutter did it, pausing only to take a long drink of milk straight from the quart bottle he found on the refrigerator shelf. By the time he returned to the front hall, Eugene was outside in the car. For a split second, Cutter hesitated. He wondered whether the next stop was the jail. He didn't want it to be. He *really* didn't want it to be. Being in Eugene's custody wasn't so bad because Eugene seemed to know what he was doing. It was like he was Cutter's protector, and if that meant driving through the rain in the big, warm car and getting enough food to keep his belly from growling, he didn't mind it. Life wasn't usually so good.

The next stop turned out to be Leroy Robichaud's store. Eugene pulled up to the curb; killed the engine, took out his wallet, and handed Cutter two large bills.

Cutter stared at the bills, then at Eugene. "What's this for?"

"Clothes. I want you to go in there and buy two pairs of jeans, two shirts, a jacket, and some boots."

"I can't buy that stuff."

"Well, I'm sure as hell not goin' to buy it for you. You're big enough to—"

"I can't afford to buy so many clothes at one time. I ain't got the money for that."

"I do. So go buy the clothes."

"But I can't pay you back!"

He thought he saw the ghost of a smile on Eugene's face. "Call it a gift. But get a move on. We haven't got all day."

That ghost of a smile bothered him. He didn't like being made fun of. "I ain't no charity case."

"You sure as hell are, since you haven't done much of a job looking out for yourself. But that's goin' to change. Now, get the clothes. And *underwear*, you need underwear."

"I know," Cutter snapped.

"I wasn't sure you did."

That irritated him all the more. "Maybe I'll just take the money and run."

"You won't do that."

"How do you know?"

"Because in the past hour you've had more 'n one chance to take something from me and run, but you haven't. You're not stupid. You smell a good thing when it's stuck in front of your nose. You're not ready to walk away from that yet, no matter what it turns out to be."

Cutter was furious at having been read so well. "Damn right I'm not," he vowed. "When I find a sucker, I take him but good." He slammed the car door, leaving Eugene's chuckle to die in the rain.

Needless to say, Leroy Robichaud was suspicious. "I heard what you tried at Judd's b'fore, Cutter Reid. If you think you're gonna do that in my store, you got another think comin'. I ain't leavin' this cash register till you're outta here."

Money had a way of making a man confident, and the bills Eugene had given Cutter felt warm and full in his hip pocket. So he didn't rise to Leroy's barb. Instead, he picked out the clothes he needed, then sauntered to the cash register and pulled the money from his pocket as though it were an everyday thing for it to be there.

"Where'd you get those bills, Cutter Reid?" When Cutter jerked his head toward the street, Leroy craned his neck to look out the window without leaving the till. "Eugene gave 'em to you? What's Eugene doin' givin' you money like this?"

Cutter didn't answer. Instead, he took a two-pack of Hostess cupcakes from the counter display, said, "Add these in," opened the pack, and devoured its contents.

Unable to deny that Eugene's car was parked out front with Eugene apparently alive and well inside, Leroy tallied up the bill and gave Cutter his change. "What I hear, you got a trip to Portland comin' up. Tryin' to look nice for the judge? Huh, Cutter Reid? Is Eugene gettin' you a lawyer, too?"

"That ain't your affair," Cutter said. Pocketing the change, he stalked out of the store carrying the things he'd bought.

Eugene scanned the packages. "Where's the food?"

"What food?"

"Didn't you get any food?"

"You didn't say nuthin' about food."

"For God's sake, boy, where's your brains? You got to eat, don't you, or do you just love havin' the walls of your stomach rub against each other?"

"If I'm goin' to jail, what do I got to buy my own food for?"

"If you were goin' to jail, what would you have to buy your own clothes for?" Eugene retorted and stuck out his hand. "Where's my change?"

Reluctantly Cutter dug it out of his pocket and handed it over, then watched Eugene leave the car and head into Leroy's. This time Cutter looked at the keys dangling from the ignition. He could drive; he'd lied to Eugene about that. He could get away if he wanted to.

Still, something held him back. Eugene had a plan, and it didn't sound like it involved going to jail. He wanted to know what that plan was. If it turned out to be worse than jail, he'd steal the car. Eugene had given him ample opportunity already; he was sure to do it again.

Dropping a sack of groceries into the backseat, Eugene slid behind the wheel and started driving again. He didn't stop until they'd reached the outskirts of town. Cutter recognized the low slope of Lampett Peak directly before them. Directly before that was a dirt pile that was muddy and deserted in the rain. Even with the windows up, the scent of wet earth seeped into the car.

"I was ten years old when my daddy found the first crystal," Eugene began, sitting back in his seat and stretching his long legs as best he could. "It wasn't here. It was over by Mount Blue. He thought it was the prettiest thing he'd ever seen, but he didn't know what to do with it. So he took it down to Boston and sold it for piddling little, and it never occurred to him to look for more. It occurred to me, though. I used to spend all my free time walkin' around, kickin' at the dirt, keepin' my eyes peeled for another one. I kept thinkin' that was an easy enough way to make money, and that we could sure use the money. We were poor as church mice."

Cutter couldn't imagine that. For as long as he could remember, Eugene had been rich. He didn't always act rich—he still hung around with his old friends—but he had the kind of confidence that came

from knowing he was set for life. Cutter couldn't picture him without that confidence.

"Year after year," Eugene went on, "I used to dream of finding more of that stuff. From the time I was little on up into my twenties, I was working at Grady's, doin' whatever needed to be done, but they were nearly as bad off as the rest of us. So they couldn't pay much, and my daddy was goin' blind, and my mama was takin' care of my older brother, who was sick, too. Things were looking pretty bad, but since everyone was kind of in the same boat, it didn't matter so much. We laughed about what we didn't have. There was a group of us used to sit around on the bench in the center of town and dream about makin' lots of money. I kept most of my own dreams to myself, because they seemed crazier than the rest.

"Then in the fall of '32, the rains came. It was the tail end of a hurricane, they said, and even though we didn't get the winds, we got three days of driving rain. The sun was out about a week before I had a chance to get back to Blue. The rain had carved a big gouge out of the side of the hill. And there they were."

"Just lying out there in the sun?" Cutter asked. He'd seen pictures in town of the Peary Necklace—everyone around was big on tourma-line since it supported the town—and was trying to imagine a hole with emerald-green stones sticking up for anyone to take.

"Not just lying there. Not like you think. Tourmaline comes bur-ied in pockets of pegmatite. Once in a while, natural erosion will be enough to expose a crystal, but usually you have to know what you're looking for in order to find it. That was where I had the advantage over most others in these parts. I knew what I was looking for. First thing I did was to stake my claim. Next thing I did was to learn more about the stone. I wanted to know how much there was around here and whether it was in demand. I wasn't about to let it go for next to nothin' the way my daddy did."

Cutter thought a bit facetiously of the big house in town and the one he figured to be just as big in Boston. He thought about the car and the fine leather wallet, the money Eugene had taken out of that wallet and the money that no doubt remained. "You sure didn't do that."

Eugene turned a sharp eye his way. "I worked hard for what I got. I took those stones out, as many as I could, and cleaned them up, then went looking around for the best buyers. And when I had all that arranged, I came right back up here and went looking for more."

"Why wasn't half the county lookin' along with you?" Cutter asked. He sure as hell would have been. If he'd been living at the time of the gold rush, he'd have been on his way to California as soon as word of the first lode came in.

"Because I had the sense that they didn't. I had the organization. I knew about tourmaline, knew how it was formed and where it was goin' to be found. By that time, I also had the chain set up to get the stones to market for top dollar. Tourmaline isn't as valuable as diamond. One stone won't make a fellow rich. The odd stone that's picked up may make someone a little money, but it's only on the larger scale of keeping a steady supply flowing into the market that the money comes. So I hired all my friends to work for me, and I guaranteed them the living they couldn't be guaranteed anywhere else."

"You were that sure you'd keep finding the stones?"

"No. But I figured that a week's wages was better than nothing, so I went week to week. And I'm still around." He straightened in his seat, overlapping his hands on the top of the wheel. "We're just about to open Lampett Peak. That dirt is from the start of the mine. We've got to dig a whole lot deeper if we want to come up with much. I'm looking for help." His hands slipped down. One closed around the keys, starting the engine again. The other steered the car around and back toward the main road.

Cutter watched him cautiously. He wondered if he'd been offered a job. He wasn't sure he'd take it if it was.

As though anticipating the argument, Eugene said, "Your daddy worked for me for a while, but that wasn't what killed him. What killed him was the booze. It rotted his mind so he couldn't see straight or think straight. He started drinkin' long before he went to work for me, long before he married your mama, long before they had you." He paused, then said almost casually, "I didn't see any bottles lying around your place. Were they stashed under all the mess?"

"You think I have to drink because my daddy did?"

"I don't know. Do you?"

"If I don't have money for food, how would I get money for booze?"

"People who want it find it." Eugene darted him a look. "Don't you want to tell me what a big man you are and how well you hold your liquor?"

Cutter turned his face to the window. "What's the point?" he muttered. "You've seen me with my pants down."

"You got some problem in that department, too?"

"I got no problem!"

"Lots of women?"

Cutter snorted. "Sure."

"Clean yourself up a little, and you will. You're not a bad-looking guy. Eat some, and you'll fill out. Put on a little weight. Give your body a chance to grow into itself."

Cutter snorted again. He was getting uncomfortable with talk about his body. Coming from Eugene, it had a ring of truth. "Look, are you goin' to drive me over to the jail, or aren't you?"

"Haven't you figured that one out yet, boy?"

"You're not?"

Eugene didn't answer. Without another word, he drove back to Cutter's place. Only when he'd stopped the car did he speak again. "Do you want a job?"

"I don't know."

"'I don't know' ain't gonna get you anywhere in this life. You want to go places besides courthouses and prisons?"

"I suppose."

"Then you want a job. Be at Lampett's Peak tomorrow morning at seven. We start early. Eat well before you come or you'll be hungry long before lunch. And clean up that pigsty in there. It's a disgrace."

Cutter wanted to argue. There were a number of pithy things on the tip of his tongue, the most immediate being, "Up yours," but he didn't say it. What he said was, "How are you going to swing it with Verne?"

"Verne isn't the problem. He's happy to have you off his hands.

The problem is Judd. I'll have to give him a good talking to. But so help me, boy, if you ever go back to that station for anything but to buy gas with your own money, you won't be working for me anymore. My men don't steal. They got a problem and need money, they come to me." He barely paused for breath. "Do you know how to cook?"

"I can make do."

"There's a bundle of wood in the trunk. See that you get the stove going. There's also a jug of gasoline back there for your cycle. You'll need it to get to the Peak."

Cutter was confused. "Why are you doing this?"

Eugene gave him a droll look. "Because I'm a sucker. Isn't that what you said?"

"You didn't get to where you are by being a sucker," Cutter conceded. He felt he owed it to Eugene, after all he was doing. "So why are you takin' the risk?"

"Maybe 'cause I want to. Maybe 'cause I think you'd'a had a better start if I'd been able to help your daddy. Maybe 'cause I liked the guy, and he ain't here to set you straight."

Things were getting too sentimental for Cutter. "You know what this town thinks of me. Anything goes wrong at that mine, I'm goin' to be the one blamed, and then they'll blame you for takin' me on."

"That'll be my worry. You just see that you're not responsible for anything going wrong at the mine, and you'll do fine."

"You're sure of that?"

"I'm sure. No one will accuse you of something you didn't do, not at my mine. I place value on honesty. And loyalty. I'm loyal to my men and they're loyal to me."

"I don't know nuthin' about loyalty."

"Then it's about time you learned. Unless you don't think you can. Is that it, boy? Are you worried you can't hack it?"

"I can hack it."

"Then get the hell out of my car and start putting your house in order. You got a lot to do before morning."

Chapter 7

◈◈◈

When Cutter first went on the payroll at St. George Mining, he worked hard out of sheer defiance. No one, not Eugene St. George or anyone else, was going to tell him he couldn't hack it. They thought he was good for nothing. It became his mission in life to prove them wrong. The more suspicious the looks people shot him or the more derogatory the mumblings, the harder he worked. After a week, then a month, the looks grew less suspicious and the mumblings died down. There wasn't exactly a warming to him, but in fairness, Cutter couldn't fully blame the miners for that. He kept to himself. Years of living alone emotionally and physically hadn't prepared him for the camaraderie that the others shared. Cutter put in his time, as much as the mine foreman would allow, and went home at the end of the day to his shack in the woods and his books.

Although he never quite lost that element of defiance, in time he became interested in what he did. It wasn't the everyday work that intrigued him; there was nothing fascinating about hacking away at walls of earth or chipping around stone. But when a new pocket was found, or a special crystal, the hacking and chipping were forgotten.

Cutter had Eugene to thank for that. From the start—though subtly, so that the other miners wouldn't take offense—Eugene taught him more than the simple mechanics of mining. At the end of a day, when most of the others had left, he took him aside to show him the stones they had unearthed that day. He explained how the crystals evolved

over millions of years from liquid caught in pockets in the center of lithium-rich pegmatites. He showed him stones of different colors and explained what caused the milky steaks in some, like the cat's eye tourmaline, and the two-colored effect of others, like the watermelon tourmaline. He gave him books on the geologic history of the earth, with those parts that had to do with tourmaline underlined.

In large part, Cutter's interest evolved because Eugene treated him as an intelligent adult. He had faith in Cutter before Cutter had it in himself. He seemed to enjoy the time they spent together, and little by little Cutter relaxed and began to enjoy it too. Eugene was the first person he'd ever been able to trust, and not once was the trust betrayed. Days could go by without their seeing each other, yet Cutter always had the feeling that Eugene was looking out for him. In return, Cutter gave his work his all. He was as determined and dedicated as any employee St. George Mining had ever had.

Away from the mine, his metamorphosis was slower. Cutter's bad-boy image lingered, and he did nothing to discourage it. Mindful of Eugene's warning, he gave up anything that could be considered criminal. But he was a dark and somber presence on Main Street. He answered deprecatory comments with lewd hand gestures, and drove his cycle through town as though the devil were in pursuit. For years, the townsfolk had thought the worst of him. He saw no reason to change their opinion. Not the most forgiving sort, he saw no need to start treating them like friends. He didn't owe them a thing.

Eugene was the one he owed. Well beyond anything to do with the mine, Eugene gave him more than his parents ever had. Within days of his starting work, Eugene had the electricity turned on at his place, had the roof fixed where it leaked, had the plumbing updated. He had food delivered. He bought Cutter an ax to chop wood. Even before his first paycheck came, Cutter was living more comfortably than he ever had, and when that first paycheck did come, Eugene put it into the bank in an account in Cutter's name. It was a full three months before Cutter had access to the account, but not once in the course of that time was he wanting for life's necessities.

For the very first time, Cutter had a taste of security. He had

clothes to fit his still-growing frame, food to fill the endless pit of his stomach, money to earn him interest at the bank. He put on some weight, stood taller and straighter, and spoke with less of the backwoods twang he had often deliberately deployed. The pride he took in being self-sufficient was profound.

Eugene was his role model, an example of a man who'd made it in life through common sense and determination. Cutter gave him the loyalty he asked, and then some. He found that it wasn't so awful to visit the laundromat once a week, that food lasted longer if it was wrapped and refrigerated, that the lights stayed on as long as he paid his bill.

Eugene was right about women, too. The taller and broader he got, the darker the beard that he shaved, and the more often he washed, the more they looked at him. He let them look. He wasn't in a rush to tangle with any and disturb the privacy of his life. Then came the day when, at the librarian's request, he helped carry some books to her small house behind Main Street, and found himself backed against her parlor wall while her hands slipped over his body. She was a pretty woman in her late twenties, and she knew what she was doing. Her mouth was warm and wet by his ear, her fingers warm and seeking inside his shirt. They dealt easily with the snap of his jeans and his zipper, and were inside his pants, taking hold of his erection without any hesitation at all.

Over the next hour, she did for him things he'd only dreamed of, and in the subsequent days and weeks she taught him all she knew. It was an ideal relationship. She was as private a person as he was, had no wish for ties, was perfectly happy to service him in exchange for those few moments of hard, fierce loving that her agile body and knowing tongue inevitably brought to him. He knew that she took others to her bed, but that only made him feel more the man than the boy he really was.

He didn't tell anyone about Lenore. He figured the town knew, but he didn't care. What happened between them was his business. She was like the money in his pocket, tucked away where no one could see but where he could feel it and know the pleasure of its presence.

She was one of the many secrets he had. Another was that he wished Eugene were his father. Another was that he was grateful he wasn't, since that would have made him a brother to John St. George, and if there was a single ogre at the mine, it was John.

Word was that John had an office in Boston and hated coming to Timiny Cove, and Cutter believed it. The man was stiff-backed and somber-faced. His concern was with tourmaline as a commodity rather than a gem, and he viewed the men the same way. Whereas Eugene was demanding when something displeased him, John was caustic whether he was displeased or not. He never had a good word for the miners and found fault where neither the foreman nor Eugene did. When he was around, the atmosphere in the mine was more tense than usual.

Likewise, when John was around, Cutter saw less of Eugene than usual. John came north only when Eugene ordered him there, either when Eugene couldn't be there himself or when his little girl was visiting. But it made things hard for Cutter. John didn't like him. Whether it was his age, or the fact that he was a reliable worker, or the fact that Eugene liked him, Cutter didn't know, but John went out of his way to hassle him in front of the others. If ever Cutter's self-control was tested, it was at those times when he'd have liked nothing more than to haul back and smack John in the face. But Eugene would never have approved of that, so Cutter didn't risk it. Self-control, too, became a matter of pride.

Cutter was amazed that someone like John could be Eugene's son. On the other hand, Eugene's little girl, Pamela, was as friendly as her father and ten times cuter. Cutter had been charmed the very first time he'd seen her at the mine. He stopped work, helpless to do anything but watch while she greeted all the men she knew with hugs. When she reached him, Eugene introduced them. There wasn't any hug, of course, and she suddenly grew quiet, but the shy smile she gave him when Eugene nudged her had stolen his heart.

She was nine then and filled with boundless enthusiasm. Eventually Cutter found himself becoming as protective of her as the other men were. If Eugene was called off while she was at the site, she had

her choice of guardians, and in the same subtle way that Eugene gave Cutter attention, she sought him out. She would smile and laugh with the other workers while she made her way to where he was. Then she'd stand with her hands locked behind her, and in a soft, near-whisper ask how he'd been, whether she could see the crystals he'd found, and didn't he think they were beautiful. Always, before she left, she gave him the shy smile that lingered with him until he saw her again.

She was eleven when she first showed up at his place. It was a Saturday morning, and he was sound asleep when she called his name. "Cutter?" It was soft, almost scared. "Are you in there, Cutter?"

Though he'd held his job at the mine for nearly two years he didn't socialize with the locals. Guests to his home were as rare as ever. Therefore, it took him a minute before he realized that he hadn't dreamed the voice. When it came again with the same cautious inquiry, he tumbled out of bed, pulled on his jeans, and peered out the window. Seconds later he pulled open the door.

Pam was sitting high on the bare back of the horse that Cutter had seen grazing in the meadow a short distance from Eugene's big brick house. She looked so small atop the horse that he couldn't help but smile.

"What are you doing, Pamela St. George?"

"Visiting."

"I didn't know you were in Timiny Cove."

"We came last night. It's the Memorial Day weekend. There's no school on Monday, so John drove Marcy and me up."

"And you came all the way out here on that horse?"

"It was nice. Besides, he did all the work."

"Does your daddy know where you are?"

"He's off with John. Marcy's at the house, and she knows I've gone for a ride. I wanted to see where you live."

"It's nothing like your house."

"I think it's more exciting, living out in the woods like this. Can I come in?"

"Not on that horse, you can't."

"Help me down."

Dropping the reins, she held out her arms. He swung her down and tied the horse to the birch at the side of the house. By the time he turned, she was running up his front steps.

"Wow," she breathed, looking through the doorway. Her eyes grew wider. "This is super!" Flashing him a smile, she stepped inside.

That eleven-year-old's smile made him proud of what he'd done to the house. The table was clean, sanded and polished, with a stool on either side. The potbelly stove had been freed of its grime, the shelves around it repaired and made sturdy for the dishes stacked there. The walls, once covered with peeling paint, had been stripped and stained. He'd made a small bookshelf, on which rested not only books but a radio, and beneath the old loft that he'd slept in for so long, in the space where his parents' bed had stood before he'd used it for kindling, was a large four-poster that gave his eighteen-year-old body the room it needed.

"I've seen that before," Pam said, pointing to the bed. "It used to be in our attic. It belonged to Nana and Papa."

"Your grandparents?" Eugene hadn't told him that.

She nodded. "They died a long time ago. I never met them. I was wondering where the bed went. I'm glad Daddy gave it to you." She sent him that shy smile of hers. "This is really nice, Cutter. It's like a secret hideaway in the woods. If I had this, I'd spend all my time here. How can you stand going to work?"

"If I don't go to work, your daddy will fire me. What would I do then?"

"Go to work for someone else. But then I wouldn't see you, so don't get fired." She went back outside. "What's in the woods?"

"Trees."

"I know that, but are there any fields or hills?"

"There's a stream."

Her eyes lit up. "Will you show it to me?"

"If you wait here while I get dressed. You woke me up."

"I'm glad," she said without remorse. "No one should sleep away a day like this."

"Is that you talking, or your daddy?"

"He said it first, but he's right. Hurry, Cutter. I'm going to start off. Which way do I go?"

Cutter had visions of her getting lost. "You wait right there until I come back out, and if you don't, I won't take you anywhere." After watching her for a minute to make sure she didn't move, he went back inside for a shirt and sneakers. Then he took her into the woods in the direction of the stream.

It was a warm spring day. The sun dappled their path, playing through the maples and oaks that rose above them. Cutter went first, with Pam following, and rather than talk they let the knock of the woodpecker, the coo-hoo of the mockingbird, and the rustle of leaves in the gentle breeze say whatever needed to be said. When they reached the stream, Cutter hunkered down and, cupping his hands, sluiced the clear, cool water over his head. It was the second best thing to a shower for washing away the vestiges of the night.

Tossing back his head, he looked at Pam. She was squatting not far from him, trailing her fingers over the pebbles that glistened by the water's edge. "I like it here," she said.

So did he. It was peaceful. And quiet. Taking a deep breath, he straightened and went to lean against a nearby tree while she continued to run her fingers through the water. After a bit, she took a small pebble in her hand, stood and gently lobbed it toward the middle of the stream. It landed with a melodic *plop* that sent out an echoing circle. When the ripples were gone, she bent, picked up another pebble, and lobbed it after the first.

Over and over she did this, seeming fascinated with the way each circle spread and broke up. "Every one's different," she mused softly.

"That's because of the flow of the current. If it's a little faster or a little slower, a little to the left or the right, the ripples are different."

"Like snowflakes."

"Kind of."

"Gone so fast."

"Yes."

"But so pretty."

As Cutter watched her, listened to her, he marveled at her

appreciation. It was hard to believe that her family was wealthy. She probably had a room full of pretty things all her own in Boston, and in Timiny Cove, too. That she should be entranced by ripples in a stream—and by snowflakes and by unpolished tourmaline crystals—was a tribute both to her and to Eugene.

Straightening, she wiped her damp hands on the seat of her pants. "I have to go, Cutter."

He led the way back through the woods to where he'd tethered the horse. When she was up on its back again, she said shyly, "I liked that. Will you take me there again?"

He nodded. Taking the reins, he began to walk her down the rutted road.

"You don't have to lead me."

"Just to the main road."

"You don't have to, Cutter."

But he did. Pam was Eugene's daughter; she was special. If anything happened to her, he wouldn't be able to forgive himself. He felt responsible for her. It was a new feeling, and not bothersome at all.

She must have sensed it, because she came to visit often after that. She always came alone, never stayed long, never made a pest of herself. She actually seemed afraid of taking too much of his time, which was amusing since he had neither family nor friends whose company he would prefer. He wanted to tell her to stay as long as she wanted and come back as soon as she could. But he didn't. It didn't seem appropriate. She was a little girl, seven years younger than he. He didn't want people getting the wrong idea.

Their friendship was innocent. They didn't even talk much at first. They explored the woods, or listened to Cutter's radio, or simply sat on his front porch, and Cutter enjoyed it. A whirlwind of chatter with others, Pam was calm and undemanding with him. He liked to think that she liked him, that she liked his home, that she chose to be with him over all the other options she had. He knew she trusted him. He liked to think that she felt as good as he did after their visits.

Gradually they started to talk. It happened during the year Pam turned twelve, when, for several visits running, she wasn't as ebullient

as usual. Afraid that he'd done something wrong, that she was finding her visits with him a bore but didn't know how to end them, he asked her about it.

"It's nothing," she said quietly.

"You don't look happy."

"I am." She produced a smile, but it lacked brilliance.

"If you'd rather be back at the house with your father—"

"He's with John," she interrupted, the smile abruptly replaced by a frown. "When I left, they were arguing. They're always doing that, Cutter." She told him about it in a rush, then when she ran out of breath she grew quiet again.

He sensed that she felt disloyal talking about John, so he didn't push. But she was back the next day, telling him a little more. She seemed to need the outlet, and though he didn't have any answers for her, he got the feeling that she was pleased that he listened.

The proof of that came over the course of the next few months, when talking became a vital part of their relationship. At first it was just Pam, opening up about the situation at home. Cutter wasn't one to open up; he'd been keeping his thoughts to himself for as long as he could remember. But she began to ask about his life, pointed questions that were like a step-by-step guide to the art of confession. Coming from anyone else, those questions would have made him suspicious. Coming from Pam, they weren't offensive. Just as she trusted him, he'd come to trust her.

"I heard Leroy telling Rufus about something that happened at the mine yesterday. You were there, Cutter. They said that you were talking right up. Was it bad?"

Cutter shrugged. "It turned out okay."

"What happened?"

"Jethro fell. He's okay."

"But he wasn't at first. Rufus said he couldn't get up. Poor Jethro. He doesn't walk so well. Was it his legs again?"

"He has arthritis pretty bad. Once he's up and standing, he's okay. It's getting there that's the problem."

"So what happened yesterday?"

Cutter recalled the incident only too well. Tightly, he said, "Simon and John were walking by. Jethro was sitting down, taking a rest. Simon doesn't usually say anything when he does that, because he still does his work. But John was there, so Simon complained. Jethro hurried to stand up. He lost his footing and fell."

"You helped him up."

"Rufus said that?"

"And that you said something to Simon."

"Well, hell, it wasn't right," Cutter argued. "Old Jethro tries. He does the best he can. He's there at work every morning and stays till the end of the day, and he's good. I've never seen him crack a stone. Eugene knows he isn't feeling good. So does Simon. And they're usually pretty easy on him. So now, all of a sudden, Simon yells. And John picks up on it and says that he shouldn't be working there. Right in front of him. So I told Simon that Jethro knew more about mining tourmaline than anyone but Eugene, and that he was the one who told us all what to do when Simon was out on another coffee break." He snickered. "Simon didn't much like my saying that."

"But he'd never fire you."

"He might, but not for that. Because I was right. And he knew Eugene would agree with me. Jethro's been working for Eugene even longer than Simon has. So now his legs're bothering him. What's he supposed to do? He's not trained for anything else, and anyway, no one would hire him. He's too old. But he still has to eat."

Pam's eyes were large. "Did you say all that to Simon?"

"No way. He was looking annoyed enough from my comment about the coffee. And John was standing right there," having already made a comment about Cutter's minding his own business. "I wasn't pushing my luck."

"You don't like John?"

Of all the questions she'd asked, that was the hardest to answer. He wanted to say a resounding no, but he still had to keep in mind that John was Pam's brother. She didn't like him, herself; she'd made that clear, but he shouldn't be the one doing the bad-mouthing. If

she were his age or older, it might have been different. But she was just a kid.

So he shrugged and said, "John's okay."

"You like him?" she asked in disbelief, and the issue suddenly became one of Cutter's credibility.

"I didn't say that. I said he's okay. He's not around too much. And besides, it's not my job to like him or not like him. He's your brother. He's my boss's son. He is my boss in a way."

"But how can you like him?"

"I don't like him," he shot back defensively, which went to prove, he realized later, that he was putty in Pam's hands.

She breathed a sigh of relief and said, sounding far older than her years, "I'm glad to hear that. I was beginning to think I was the only one who hated him so much."

No, Cutter thought, she wasn't the only one. Most of the men at the mine disliked John, but it was worse for Cutter. John went out of his way to put him down. Cutter found that hard to take, even when he told himself that it was because John was jealous. John didn't have anywhere near as smooth a relationship with Eugene as Cutter did. Cutter figured that any son in a like position would be jealous. But that didn't give John the right to punish him, especially not in front of everyone at the mine. He had his pride, too.

That pride took some twists that Cutter didn't expect in the months that followed. The incident with Jethro Lamall was the first of several in which he found himself speaking up against something he considered unfair. Eugene was never the problem. Once in a while, Simon was, but it was usually at John's instigation.

John was the problem. Cutter was sure that if John were around more, most of the miners would quit. The fact that he wasn't there for more than a week out of every four was some consolation to the havoc his presence wreaked. He had specific opinions on running the mines. Although Eugene had been running things well for some thirty-odd years, John was convinced he knew better. Inevitably he either wanted to work the men harder or pay them on a scale based on output. Even the younger men, who had strength and stamina on

their side and could produce more than the older men, were against that. The older men were their fathers, their brothers, their friends.

Cutter wasn't anyone's brother or son. He had no family to support. He didn't have to worry that if he angered John, retribution might take the form of punishment to people he loved. He didn't have as much to lose as the others.

That was one of the reasons why he came to their defense. Another was the same defiance that had driven him so often in the past. He didn't like John. He didn't like being put down by John. Speaking up to him in front of the other miners brought a deep satisfaction, particularly when it had to do with justice, and especially when it had to do with something he was sure Eugene believed in, too. In an odd way, Cutter felt that he, more than Simon, was Eugene's on-site representative at the mine.

The other miners came to feel that way too; increasingly they looked to Cutter when something went wrong. While he had no desire to be a hero and continued to keep to himself once he left the mine at the end of the day, he wasn't adverse to championing the workers' causes. It gave him a good feeling. It gave him a sense of power.

John didn't like that much, which enhanced its appeal. Cutter began speaking up just to let John know that the other miners respected him. Simon respected him too—or respected the fact that the other miners looked to him for leadership—and occasionally left him in charge of things at the site. Since John was never around at those times, there was little joy in it for Cutter. He didn't aspire to be a foreman. He didn't like the idea of ordering the other men around. Whatever leadership potential he had he used in his silent battle with John. Power, in any other context, didn't excite him.

"Daddy and John were arguing again today," Pam told him one late-summer evening. Cutter had gone into town for a six-pack of beer and had found her sitting on the steps outside Leroy's store. Unable to resist, he sat down beside her. "It was about you this time."

"About me?" he said with a half-smile. She looked so serious, so grown-up, so adorable in a T-shirt and cut-off jeans, with her hair in a single long ponytail and her feet bare.

"Daddy was saying that you'll be in charge of the mine someday. John didn't think so."

"No, I doubt he would. But he doesn't have to worry. I don't want to be in charge of the mine."

Pam looked startled. "Why not? You'd be in charge of everyone. You'd get more money."

"And more headaches."

"Do you get headaches now?"

"No. But Simon does."

"That's because John makes him nervous."

"John makes me nervous."

"But you can fight him," she urged with a touch of excitement. "Simon can't. He's too old. He senses a shift in power."

Cutter was always amazed at Pam's instincts when it came to the business. Nudging her side, he asked, "How do you know that?"

"I can see it."

"Little girls aren't supposed to see things like that. They're supposed to be sweet and innocent."

"For God's sake, Cutter, I'm nearly thirteen."

He grinned. "Hard to believe. Or not hard at all. Depends on how you look at it." He held his head back and peered at her. "You're gettin' taller, all right."

"Don't talk down to me," she said more soberly.

"But you are getting taller."

"And older. And I see things. I do, Cutter. And you're trying to change the subject."

"What is the subject?"

"John. You could fight him, and Daddy would be on your side."

"But John is his son," Cutter said, all kidding forgotten. "It's not my place to come between them that way."

"Not even so you could get ahead at the mine?"

"I don't want to get ahead at the mine. There are lots of other guys who want Simon's job, and they've been working for Eugene a lot longer than me."

"But Daddy likes you."

Cutter knew that. Still, it didn't change certain things.

"If you don't want to be a foreman, what do you want to be?"

He rested his weight back on the heels of his hands and looked out across the street. "I don't know."

"Are you going to leave here and get a job in the city?"

"I don't know."

"Are you going to work in the mine all your life?"

"I don't know."

"But don't you dream things?"

"Not much," he said. He didn't dream of being rich or famous. He didn't dream of being a boss and ordering people around. His life now was so much better than it had been before that he was pretty satisfied. Sometimes he dreamed of little things—a little more money, a little bigger house, maybe a car, maybe even a car with a stereo. He figured he'd have those things one day.

"I think you ought to come to work in Boston. That's what Hillary's doing. She just got a job working for the paper. It's interesting, she says."

Cutter knew Hillary Cox, just as he knew almost everyone in Timiny Cove. She'd been gone awhile, but word had a way of filtering back. "Hillary's a writer. I'm not."

"You could be. You read all the time."

"Reading has nothing to do with writing."

"We read *Lord of the Flies* in English class, by the way. I don't think I liked it. It was pretty depressing."

"It was supposed to be. It was supposed to be an example of what might happen if there wasn't any order to things." With deliberate nonchalance he asked, "What did your teacher say about it?" He liked it when Pam told him things like that. It made him think. Sometimes he even went back and reread a particular book after they had talked.

"Kind of what you did," Pam said, "about order and rules and laws. She said the author was making a statement that there's evil deep down inside us, but I'd never have done what Jack and Roger did."

He nearly smiled at the appalled look on her face. But evil wasn't

a smiling matter. More than once he had wondered what he'd have done on that deserted island. "Are you sure? Not even if you were in the situation they were? Not even if you were lost and frightened and started imagining all sorts of things?"

She shook her head. "I wouldn't have. I couldn't have."

Cutter wasn't so sure he could say the same. He'd have done almost anything to feel safer when he was younger. "Maybe that's because you're a girl," he said a little distractedly.

"No." She was about to elaborate when John drove up in his Thunderbird. Pam's features immediately darkened. "What does he want?"

Cutter grew alert. He allowed himself to admire the car, a shiny blue convertible with the top up. As soon as John climbed out, though, looking perfect in cuffed khaki pants and a shirt with a little alligator on the front, his admiration died.

"I'm going inside," Pam murmured. Very slowly she rose from the step where she'd been seated. She looked at John for an impertinent minute, then, with incredible dignity, Cutter thought, turned and walked into Leroy's store.

"Did I disturb something?" John asked in a voice that was nearly as cold as his eyes.

Cutter was determined to be just as cool. "Why would you think that?"

"Because you two were sitting pretty close. What are you doing with my sister, Cutter?"

"Talking. Right here on Main Street where everyone can see."

"You see her more than that. I know she goes to your place sometimes. Is that by invitation?"

Cutter didn't bother to answer.

"If you're hoping to use her to get something from my father, it won't work."

"I don't need anything from your father."

"You need a job."

"I already have one."

"At our discretion."

"I do my work, and I do it well," he challenged, beginning to burn

inside. "Fire me for no reason, and you'll have half of the others walking out on you."

"I'll have good reason if I find you diddling with my sister."

The burning increased. "Why would I want to diddle with your sister when I have a damn sexy woman doin' all the diddlin' I want?"

"She's not bad, Lenore isn't," John mused smugly.

Cutter couldn't help himself. "She doesn't think quite so highly of you."

John's smugness vanished. "Stay away from my sister, Cutter. You are aware that she's a minor, aren't you?"

"Minor? She's a *little girl*."

"No girl's too little to fool around with, but if I were you, I'd watch it. You touch a hair on her head, and you'll have me and half the lawmen in the state to answer to."

Struggling to contain his anger, Cutter rose. He was nearly John's height and every bit as strong, and while he didn't have money and polish on his side, he had pride. "Pam is my friend, just like she's a friend to everyone else in this town. And she's Eugene's daughter. I'd lay down my life to keep her safe." But he couldn't leave it at that. The demon inside wouldn't let him. "The way I see it, she has more to fear from you than from me."

"What's that supposed to mean?"

"You're the one with the brains. You figure it out." He started off, but John caught his arm.

"You're asking for trouble."

Cutter gave the hand on his arm a long stare before raising his eyes to John's. "I'm not askin' for a thing 'cept that you leave me alone." He shook his arm hard. John's hand fell away.

"Stay away from Pam," he growled.

Not trusting that he wouldn't tell John to go to hell, Cutter strode off to where he'd left his motorcycle, climbed on, revved the engine—never more appreciating the power of the mama he'd bought the year before than at that moment—and, without a look back, left a strip of rubber and a trail of dust behind him.

He rode hard, barreling out of town well past his place. He pushed

the cycle to its limits, roaring past the occasional car as though it were crawling, taking curves at a precarious tilt. Only after he came within inches of hitting a cottontail rabbit that was hopping across the street in ignorant bliss did he careen to a stop.

Parked on the side of the quiet highway, he took a deep breath, closed his eyes, and let his fury settle. John was a bastard in every sense but the literal. He'd known that, but it didn't help much in soothing the insult he felt.

He didn't like John's suggestion that he was fooling around with Pam, that he'd ever harm her. Mostly, he didn't like the suggestion that he stay away from her, because, unless John was going around town telling everyone the same thing, it implied he wasn't as good as the others. But Pam didn't seek out the others the way she did him. She didn't tell them the things she told him. If John knew half of those things he'd be furious.

That thought and the knowledge that John could threaten all he wanted and it wouldn't matter made Cutter smile. If Pam wanted to come out to his place, she would. If she wanted to visit him at the mine, she'd do that, too. And if he saw her on Leroy's steps, he was going to sit right down beside her.

He'd be damned if John would tell him what to do, especially when it came to Pam, and if John didn't like it, that was his problem. He didn't scare Cutter. After living on danger's edge for so many of his early years, Cutter welcomed the challenge. Baiting him would be fun.

So, in hindsight, the confrontation on Leroy's steps wasn't so bad. Cutter's only regret as he turned the cycle in an arc and headed for home was that he'd been distracted from buying the six-pack he'd originally wanted.

Chapter 8

◆◆◆

WHILE CUTTER HEADED HOME, John drove Pam back to the big brick house. "Get your things together," he instructed, feeling little affection and even less patience as he walked through the large front hall. "I want to be on the road to Boston in an hour."

Pam followed him into the living room. "To Boston? But I thought we were staying all week."

He heard her disappointment and wasn't touched by it in the least. He didn't care how she felt, especially after the snotty way she'd walked away from him with Cutter sitting right there watching.

"We've changed plans," he said curtly. He reached for the tallest of the three sterling decanters that stood on the bar. "I want to be at the office in the morning."

Pam came up from behind. Although she was growing taller, she still had the sweet look of childhood that never failed to annoy him. Sweet she might look, but she was not. She was too smart for her britches. "I thought Daddy wanted you here."

"Simon will cover while he's gone."

"But there's nothing to do in Boston."

He took a healthy swallow of scotch. "Maybe not for you. I have more than enough to keep me busy."

"Okay. You go back. Marcy and I will stay here."

"Uh-uh. You have to be back by the weekend. I'm not making the trip again."

"Then Marcy will drive me home."

"Marcy doesn't have a car."

"We'll borrow one."

"No way, princess." Highball glass in hand, he headed for the stairs. "Be ready in an hour. And tell Marcy to be ready."

"John . . ." Pam's plaintive voice followed him up the stairs. Neither missing a step nor looking back, he went down the hall to his room and began to pack. He had the few things he'd brought from Boston stowed neatly and was packing his shaving kit when Eugene appeared at his door.

"Pam says you're leaving?"

John shot him a sharp glance. "I should have known she'd run straight to you."

"She didn't. I saw Marcy downstairs. I'm off to New York tomorrow, John. I was counting on you to keep an eye on things here."

He was using his tempered voice, the one that he used more often now, the one John found patronizing. He preferred the big booming sound that had shaken him so as a child. He wasn't a child anymore, and he didn't shake. Moreover, he could give back what he got. He enjoyed a good shouting match with his father.

"Simon can do it. You trained him. He knows what you want."

"I want you."

"I have things to do at the office."

"I want you here. You're my son. I want you here when I'm not."

John's patience waned. It didn't matter that Eugene was getting older and more gray, or that there were a few times when he actually looked lonely. He represented all that John despised, and John was helpless to hide that contempt.

"You don't need someone here. You don't need to be here yourself, but it's the one place you can be yourself. You don't fit in the city. Timiny Cove is where you feel comfortable, so you hang around here and tell yourself that they need you. Well, they don't. The mines practically run themselves. If you want to waste your time up here, fine, but I don't." He tossed back the rest of his drink, then took mellow pleasure from his father's reddening face.

"This is your living, these mines. You seem to keep forgetting that. Without them, you'd be back in the city in some small office kissing some big shot's ass. That what you want?"

"It's a moot point, since we do have the mines."

"I have the mines. They're not yours yet."

"But they will be, because I'm the only one, next to you, who knows enough about the business to run it. You've done well in that sense. Even when I was fighting, you got me up here and involved. I have to hand that to you."

But Eugene shook his head. "I don't take credit for no failure."

John bristled. "You're calling me a failure?"

"I'm saying that I failed with you. Maybe I got you to know the business. Maybe I even got you to be important to the business. But I could never wring any feeling from you. You're cold as a fish, John. Ever since your mama died—"

"Don't bring her into this!" It was the one thing he couldn't take. Eugene had abused her. Even thirteen years after her death, it hurt John to hear her name on his tongue.

Eugene ignored him. "Ever since your mama died, you've been hard as a rock. You may know this business better'n anyone but me, but you sure don't have the love for it that I hoped you might."

John was incredulous. "Love? What's to love? A business is a business. We've got open pits and mountains and mines and dirt. We've got gemstones. We've got receipts from the sales of those gemstones. If there's anything to love, it's the bottom line—which would be a hell of a lot more impressive if you would let me broaden the company a little. But you're so goddamned narrow-minded—"

"Whoa," Eugene warned, his face heating.

"What? I shouldn't say that? But it's the truth, only you're still living like a hick so you don't know it."

"Watch it, boy."

But John wasn't intimidated by his father's flashing eyes. "It's been a long time since I was a boy. If I were to get full control of this company tomorrow, I could turn it into something big within a year."

"You'd ruin it."

"I'd build it. It's static now, standing still, just like everything and everyone in this godforsaken town." He couldn't resist elaborating on that, because he knew it would irk Eugene. "No one does anything here. Small brains, small thoughts. If not for St. George Mining, these people would be living like they did thirty years ago. They don't know what ambition is. Well, I do. I'd make something of the company that no one else around here could dream of."

Sniffing in a breath, Eugene drew himself up straight. "You may just live to eat those words, boy. Mind you, when it happens I won't be around to gloat, but you can bet your boots I'll be up there, leaning against those pearly gates, watching to see which one of you does what."

John felt his stomach tighten. "Which one of us?" He had assumed Eugene would leave something to the others, but he was thinking in terms of money or a trust. "You're going to let Pam have a say in running the company? Or Patricia? Neither of them knows anything about this business."

"Cutter does."

John didn't breathe for a minute. He was sure he'd heard wrong. "Cutter?" When Eugene nodded, he said, "Cutter *Reid?*"

"Ain't no other Cutter around."

John was incredulous. "Cutter Reid has nothing to do with this."

"Someday he will. I'm leaving him Little Lincoln."

"You're . . . leaving him . . . Little Lincoln." It was a statement, disbelieving, but a statement nonetheless.

"That's right."

"*Cutter Reid?*"

"That's right."

Talk of Little Lincoln, the mountain that John had been lobbying to open for years, was bad. Talk of Cutter Reid, who was a constant thorn in John's side, was even worse. But it was the smugness in Eugene's voice that broke John's composure.

"Have you gone mad?" he roared in an uncanny and unwitting imitation of his father. "You can't do that! Little Lincoln may contain some of the richest pockets of tourmaline we've found yet. You can't

leave that mountain to Cutter Reid! He's not in the family—he's not your flesh and blood—and he doesn't know a thing about management. *Cutter Reid?* You're out of your mind!"

"I don't think so. Neither did Joe Grogan."

"Then that old lawyer is as crazy as you!" He turned away, sure that what he was hearing was a joke, but in the next breath he turned back, less sure. "You're kidding, aren't you?"

Eugene shook his head.

"Cutter Reid is a no-good troublemaker!"

"He's a good worker."

"He's lazy! If he had his way, he'd have the men taking breaks every hour!"

"The others respect him. He's a leader."

"He's an instigator."

"He believes in human dignity."

"Is that why he lives in that filthy shack in the woods? Is that why he bombs around town on that motorcycle, making enough noise to wake the dead? Is that why for years he stole whatever money he could find?" When Eugene was unmoved, he threw in his ace. "Is that why he hangs around Pamela? I just came from town, and there he was, snuggling up to her outside Leroy's store. I'm telling you, he's sick. She's just a girl, not thirteen to his twenty. It's obscene!"

Eugene was perfectly calm. "I trust him."

"To fool around with your daughter?"

Eugene snorted. "He's not doing that. He likes Pam. Everyone likes Pam. She's friendly and agreeable. She's also one of the few people who knows Cutter for who he is, rather than where he came from. He'll go places one day, John, and I intend to give him a boost."

"But *why?*" John cried. "Why Cutter Reid? You've always had a thing for him, right from the day you hired him. Is he your little project? Your cause? Is that what this is all about? You took a kid who was headed for jail, put him to work and turned him around, so you have a personal investment in him now? Is it an ego thing for you? But you won't be around when he inherits Little Lincoln. Why in the hell would you waste a prime piece of mining property like that?"

"It won't be a waste."

"He won't know what to do with it."

"He'll know," Eugene said, and gave John a curious look. "But what I don't understand is why it's botherin' you so much, the thought that I'm giving him some land. You're goin' to have the business, and the good Lord knows how much other property the business owns. We've got mountains all over the county. Little Lincoln isn't much more than a hill, when you come right down to it."

"But it's rich."

"And it'll be years before he can get at it, for pity's sake. We have a contract with families who live there sayin' that no mining will be done till they leave. That may not be for another twenty or thirty years."

John had spent his share of time in the past thinking of ways to circumvent that contract. "I'd offer them money to move them sooner. Cutter wouldn't do that. He wouldn't have the money to do it."

"Which is probably why I'm willing that land to him," Eugene said. "I've already offered those folks money, and they don't want it. They want to stay where they are. You'd pressure them, but I won't have it." He shook his head conclusively. "No, Cutter was born and raised here. He feels for the people more than you ever could."

" 'Feeling for the people' isn't what keeps a business running."

"It's what's kept it running so far."

"And not terribly efficiently, if you ask me."

Eugene drew himself up to his full height, which, to John's frustration, hadn't shrunk at all with age. "I ain't askin' you." He started for the door.

But John wasn't through talking. He had to get Eugene to change his mind—and his will. "All right." He followed his father into the hall. "You have a personal interest in Cutter. If you want to help him, leave him some money. The guy lives like a pauper."

Eugene paused at the top of the stairs. "If he lives that way, it's because he banks most all of his paycheck, just as I taught him to. He's got money. He wants to spend it, he can."

"Okay." John could deal with that argument, too. "So he's being

prudent, just like you taught him. Leave him a little more money, and he won't feel that he has to be so prudent."

Halfway down the stairs, Eugene said, "He's happy with his life. He wants to splurge, he can."

John grasped the railing with both hands. "But he's going to need more money anyway. Pretty soon he'll meet someone and want to get married, then he'll have kids coming right and left. He'll need funds, but it'll be years before he sees a dime from Little Lincoln, and then only if he puts money into it."

Eugene's smile, as he looked up from the bottom of the stairs, was a knife twisting in John's gut. "You've got his life planned out for him, eh, John? You've always been orderly, ever since you were a boy lining your toys up in your room. But Cutter's life ain't your toys. You ain't got much of a say in it."

He took a breath and went on. "To be perfectly honest, I don't know what Cutter's got planned. Don't think he does. Don't think he wants to plan much ahead right now. And that's why Little Lincoln is the perfect thing for him. By the time it's ready to be mined, he'll know what he wants." He arched a brow and said pleasantly, "Tell you what. You keep *your* money in the bank, and by that time you might have enough to buy him out. Course, Little Lincoln won't come cheap. And by that time, at the rate you're goin', Cutter will hate your guts enough to take you for a real ride." He walked to the front door and left.

Pride was only one of the feelings that prevented John from going after him. The other was a raw anger that kept him immobilized, standing where he was gripping the second-floor railing, for a time. It was only when his fingers began to ache that he realized what he was doing. Returning to his room, he finished packing with a vengeance.

"Pam!" he bellowed, trotting down the stairs with his bag. "Get down here, Pam!" Had he not been her only source of transportation home, he'd have left without her. Having to suffer her company was bad enough under normal circumstances. Given his present mood, it was going to be unbearable. "We're leaving, Pam," he shouted. "Get her out here, Marcy! I'm getting the car!" He stormed out of the house.

It was another fifteen minutes before they got on the road. The

sudden departure plans had caught Marcy baking a chocolate cake. She had to clean up the kitchen before she could pack, then had to dash to take food to her mother, who was laid up with a broken rib.

"Did he hit her again?" John asked in disgust when, breathless, she finally climbed into the backseat of the car.

"She's okay," Marcy said and tucked herself into a corner.

Pam turned around in the front seat. "Is someone with her?"

"Lizzie."

"Where's Jarvis?"

"He ran off. He'll be back in a week or two. Always is."

"It's her own damn fault," John snapped. "He was beating her before they got married, still she went ahead with it. It was a stupid thing to do."

Pam turned on him. "She had her reasons for marrying him."

"Sure. She wanted someone to warm her bed, so she picked the first man who came along."

"Maybe she was lonely. Maybe she was scared. Marcy was just a baby. Honestly, John, can't you imagine what she was feeling?"

"Frankly, no. It was a stupid thing to do. So now she's living with the decision."

"She doesn't deserve what he does to her."

"Then she should kick him out."

"She does, and he keeps coming back."

"Then she should go to court."

"She doesn't have the money to do that."

"So she sits there and takes it. She's as stupid now as she was back then. Some people just don't learn."

Pam made a face. "You're a pill, John."

"The feeling's mutual," John said and stepped on the gas.

He made record time back to Boston. While the speed took the edge off the worst of his anger, enough remained to keep him geared up. He kept thinking of Cutter, then of Eugene. Then he thought about Patricia, and kept thinking about her, so that by the time he parked the car in the courtyard of the townhouse on Beacon Hill, he was sexually excited.

Pam and Marcy took off as quickly as they could, which was just fine with John. Dropping his bag by the back door, he took the stairs two at a time. Patricia was in the parlor, sitting at the roll-top desk, writing out invitations for a party she planned to give. Having already paused to greet Pam, she raised her eyes when John appeared at the door.

Tossing his head toward the upper floor, he turned and took those stairs two at a time also. He went straight to Patricia's bedroom—Patricia and Eugene's—and began to strip. By the time Patricia slipped through the door, he was naked and fully aroused. She barely had time for a whimsical smile before he pulled her to him and began to shove her clothes aside.

"John?" she asked.

He knew that she was puzzled; he was usually more urbane in his approach to her. He also knew, as he tugged one piece of clothing after another from her body, that she was a little frightened, and that suited him well. He was the one in charge. Eugene could do whatever the hell he wanted with his will; he could be smug and cocky, make fun of John, put him down without a care. But the final laugh was on Eugene, because here in his bedroom, on his bed, between his sheets, his wife was putting out for John.

Over the next few months, John sought out Patricia more and more. She became a vindictive compulsion for him, the only source of satisfaction he had in his war with his father. Eugene wouldn't change his will; John argued and argued, tried reason again and again, but the more he went at it, the more it seemed Eugene dug in his heels. Likewise, Eugene dug in his heels when it came to the business. He wouldn't hear of branching off into activities other than mining, and when John even mentioned the possibility of taking the company public, Eugene left the room.

So John left, too, and took out his frustration in Eugene's bedroom, on Eugene's wife.

Sometimes she protested. On the day he returned from Maine with Pam and Marcy, when he took her without even a moment of foreplay, she complained that he wasn't considerate.

"I'll stop," he said tightly, holding himself up on his fists while he was buried deep inside her. "I'll stop if you want. I'll get out of this room and never come back. I'll even move out of the house and take a place of my own. That's long overdue."

But she quickly relented, as he'd known she would. Just as she'd become an obsession for him, he was her addiction. With Eugene rarely there, John gave her peace of mind. She depended on him. He was her ally, the one who was going to convince Eugene to take the steps necessary to provide her with the security she needed.

John didn't always agree with her on what those steps should be. She remained fixated on real estate. She saw men in Boston making millions buying property and then renovating or tearing down and building from scratch. Restoration of the waterfront was just beginning. She was sure that St. George Mining could thrive in property development.

John had other ideas. Those men making millions in real estate were, in his opinion, relative upstarts. Some were from out of town. Others were local lawyers and politicians who had spotted a good thing and were capitalizing on it. None had real class, and he had no intention of aligning himself with people like that.

What he had in mind was something more sophisticated. He spent enough of his time with the upper crust to know the kinds of things that impressed them. Old wealth impressed them, but he didn't have that. Excessive wealth impressed them, but he didn't have that either. What he had was access to some of the finest tourmaline in the world, and while it wasn't worshipped as diamonds, rubies, and sapphires were, he had become deeply enough involved in the gem trade to know that jewelers were beginning to branch out. Tourmaline was a rising commodity. He could deal with it and other gemstones as well.

He wanted to build something exclusive and elegant, an establishment that would be to jewelry what Dior was to clothing, Gucci to leather, Chanel to perfume. Patricia thought he was dreaming far too narrow a dream, but he knew that given the choice between one

of their plans or nothing, she would opt for his against Eugene's insistence on the status quo.

In the meantime, she grew more and more dependent on him, and he encouraged it. When they were in bed, she clung. He wouldn't have stood it from another woman. God only knew Hillary didn't.

In the end, Patricia's dependence brought things to a head in a way he would never have dreamed. She wanted him, and with his anger toward Eugene at a high during those few months following the altercation over Cutter, he wanted her right back. So they were careless. Rather than waiting until Eugene was out of town, John came home from work early one day, pointed Patricia toward the bedroom, and made love to her long and hard.

Eugene found them there. Whether it was coincidence or whether he'd begun to suspect something, John never knew. Apparently, he had finished a meeting, learned that John had left for the day, and followed him home.

The look on his face when he opened the door and discovered what was taking place wasn't quite what John would have expected. There was neither humiliation nor defeat. He stared at the two in the bed, John lounging with measured nonchalance while Patricia jumped up and frantically began adjusting the clothes she'd never completely removed, and his features twisted into open disgust. "How long has this been going on?"

"It's not what you think," Patricia cried as she pushed her skirt down from her waist and turned her back to return her breasts to her bra. "It's not at all what you think."

But he was looking at John. "How long?"

John shrugged. His heart was pounding far louder than it had earlier, at the moment of climax. "A while."

"You scum."

Fumbling now with the buttons of her blouse, Patricia tried again. "Gene, I can explain. I know this must look fishy—"

"If I'm scum," John said, "what does that make you?"

"Nothing. No relation. I've had it. You're out."

"Don't *say* that, Gene! John is crucial to the company. He wasn't feeling well, that's all, and—"

"I don't want to hear it," Eugene said.

He didn't look at her once, but kept his eyes on John, who was beginning to worry. In all those times that he'd imagined the pleasure of telling his father that he was screwing his wife, it had never occurred to him that he'd end up on the street. But that was just what Eugene was saying.

"I want you out. Out of this house, out of my life. Today."

"Gene, no—"

"I don't think so," John said, ignoring her to answer his father. He drew himself slowly up on the bed. "I'm the one who's been holding things together both at the office and here, while you've been playing pool and poker with the guys up in Timiny Cove. You owe me."

"Seems to me," Eugene said with the briefest of glances at Patricia, "you've been paid."

"Not enough."

"John, explain it to him," Patricia pleaded.

But John wasn't listening to her. What was happening, what had happened, was between him and his father more than it had ever related to her. Wrapping the sheet around his waist, he rose from the bed. "I want more. If you want me out of this house, I'll go. I'll even resign from the company. But it'll cost you."

"You get nothing," Eugene barked.

"It'll cost you a lot. I want money."

"You get shit."

"If I leave, I'll take most of the management with me. I haven't been twiddling my thumbs all these years. You may have bent over backward to treat the miners like gold, but I'm the one who took the time to see that the movers and shakers around the office were greased. They'll come with me. One word and you'll lose them. There's your chain"—he snapped his fingers—"broken in a minute. It'll take you a while to get it fixed."

"By God, you're arrogant as ever. Well, it won't work this time," Eugene informed him, flushed with rage. "If anyone wants to leave, I'll

give him a push out the door. I place loyalty above lots of other things. If their loyalty's to you, you can have them." His jaw grew even tighter. "I'm going out now. By the time I get back, I want you gone."

"Gene, you can't—" Patricia began, running after him.

"It's done!"

John didn't move, couldn't move, but listened while Patricia tried to stop Eugene. She followed him down the stairs, her voice growing frantic in a way that mirrored the feeling in John's stomach. He heard the slamming of doors—once, twice, again—interspersed with Patricia's pleas and Eugene's terse replies. Still John didn't move, not even when there was a final loud slam and then total silence. For an interminable time he stood there in his father's bedroom wearing nothing but a sheet, fighting the panic that brought a cold sweat to his lip.

There was a feeling of déjà vu in it—the panic, the fear, the sense of having the floor knocked out from under his feet. He'd felt that way when his mother died, and he hadn't intended ever to feel it again. But there it was. His future hung in a limbo that was the antithesis of the satisfaction he'd expected.

Stunned, he let the sheet slip to the floor and reached for his clothes. He was pulling on his pants when he heard the first of the sirens. Life in the city was filled with sirens, and since he was embroiled in an emergency of his own, he ignored them.

With his shirt buttoned, though hanging loose, he scooped his tie and jacket from the floor, drove a hand through his hair, and went to his own room long enough to drop his things. He needed a drink. He couldn't think straight. He had to decide whether to stay or go, what to say or do, how to handle Eugene. It wasn't possible that his father had meant all he'd said. He was angry and upset. A man didn't just write off his son—his vice president—that way.

Mired in confusion, he was halfway down the stairs before he felt the draft from the door. Marcy had opened it and was leaning out, looking down Mt. Vernon in the direction of Charles. The sirens were louder than ever.

John wasn't sure what drew him to the door, whether it was a pre-

monition, a need for diversion, or simple curiosity. But he found himself looking over Marcy's shoulder at a jumble of blinking red lights.

"Fire?" he asked.

Marcy shook her head. It was a minute before she said, "The lights are in the middle of the street. Looks more like an accident."

John felt odd. "Where's Patricia?"

In the pause that followed he was convinced that Marcy knew precisely what had been going on behind her mistress's closed doors so many afternoons and evenings. But he was past the point of caring. "Is she in the living room?"

Eyes on the blinking lights, Marcy shook her head.

"The kitchen?"

"Isn't she with your father?"

"I don't know. Is she?"

"I heard them talkin', then they were gone. Maybe they're down there stuck in that mess."

John's heart was pounding again, not so loudly, but heavily. "Where's Pam?"

"At her friend Cindy's. She'll be home b'fore long."

He turned back into the house and called, "Patricia?" When there was no answer, he went to the foot of the stairs. He was sure he'd have known if she'd gone back up after Eugene had left, but he had to check. "*Patricia?*" The only answer was another siren.

Swearing softly, he grabbed his coat from the closet and threw it on as he trotted down the stone steps outside.

The closer John got to the lights, the faster he walked. There was something too familiar about the blue of the car that was crushed between the Mack truck that had rammed it and the unyielding brick wall of the corner drugstore.

"Jesus," he breathed as he wove through the emergency vehicles. "Jesus."

"Hey, fella," the police officer called, "better stay back."

"I know them," he managed to say. Breathing hard, he watched as the truck was hauled back from the wall.

"You know who they are?" the policeman asked, but John couldn't take his eyes from the mess that had once been his father's car.

"What happened?" he whispered.

"Looks like they came barreling down Mt. Vernon and either skidded into the intersection or ran a red. Who are they?"

"John!" came a breathless cry from a short distance away. He looked over to see Pam running up, her eyes wide and curious. "Cindy's parents dropped me two blocks down so they could turn off before they hit this. What happened?" She leaned sideways, then stood on her tiptoes in an attempt to see past the police cars and ambulances.

Swallowing hard, John put an arm around her shoulder. It was the first time he had ever touched her in what could have been called a protective way. Turning her away, he began to lead her quickly up the hill.

"Hey, bud," the policeman called, "we need an ID."

John ignored him. He held Pam's shoulder, squeezing tightly each time she tried to look back. He wasn't sure why he was protecting her; she had to know sooner or later. But later seemed better, when things were cleaned up and he knew who was hurt and how badly.

She tried to look back again, but he forced her forward. He didn't have to look back to see the crush of that car against the wall; it was a vivid picture etched in his mind. If he could save Pam that, it would go a long way toward easing his guilt.

"What happened there?" she asked, suddenly more frightened than curious.

"An accident. You don't want to see. I'll take you up to the house, then go back. I'll tell you about it later."

Pam didn't argue, but she must have known that his behavior was strange. Once more she tried to look back over her shoulder. When he wouldn't allow it, she asked, "Is my mother home?"

"I don't think so."

"Is Daddy?"

"No."

In a tone that was as unsteady as any he'd ever heard from her, she asked, "Do you know where they are?"

"I'm not sure. I'll find out." He quickened his step and hers along with it. Marcy was still at the door, too far away to see the car or its color or, mercifully, its contents. "Take her inside," he ordered, then jogged back down the street.

He arrived in time to see Patricia's broken body being put into an ambulance for a short, high-speed ride to the hospital. It was a while before Eugene was freed from the wreck. He too was put into an ambulance, but the ride was less rushed. He had died the instant the car hit the wall.

Chapter 9

New York, May 1990

Hillary glanced at Pam, who walked at a smart pace beside her along Fifth Avenue. Her hair was tucked up under a floppy hat, she wore a nondescript jersey and jumper, tights and ballet flats, and she carried a canvas bag with I LOVE NY stamped on its front. The effect was supposed to be tacky, but Hillary thought she looked adorable. Large dark glasses shielded her eyes, not so much from the glare of the sun as from recognition. She needed anonymity. They were on a spy mission, one of Pam's infamous incognito adventures into the world of New York jewelers. It was the first they had taken since Brendan fell ill, and though Pam was hesitant about leaving him, she needed the day away.

Hillary had often accompanied her on these jaunts in the past, simply because Pam was her friend and she enjoyed being with her. This time her motive was more pointed.

They had just left David Webb's showroom on Fifty-seventh Street and were headed for Tiffany's. Quite conveniently, Pam liked to talk while she was looking at what the competition had produced. She wanted to appear nonchalant, even a little disinterested. As fate would have it, coming in from the airport on this day she had passed the scene of an automobile accident, and while the particulars were different from the accident twenty-one years before, the blinking lights

had stirred memories. They had talked of these memories through lunch at the Polo Lounge at the Westbury and now continued talking as they walked.

"I knew John had the germs of compassion in him," Hillary commented after Pam had relived the details of those terrible days.

Pam shot her a dry look from behind the dark glasses. "No doubt they've all atrophied by now. But he was decent back then. I have to admit it. For about three days—between the time of the accident and the funeral—he was decent. He played the grieving son and the concerned brother. No doubt it was all for show."

"Give credit where credit is due."

"Okay. Three days. I'll give him three days."

"Generous," Hillary remarked, but her thoughts were on something Pam had said in the course of another talk they'd had, two weeks before when Hillary had flown to Boston. "Speaking of generosity, what happened to Cutter's bequest? He's never said a word to me about it, and the more I think of it, the more odd that seems. When he first came to New York he had his life savings in a bank note in his pocket. He had no intention of ever returning to Timiny Cove."

Pam didn't answer. Hillary suspected that she was thinking back to the circumstances preceding Cutter's arrival in New York. She was sure the memory brought pain.

But Hillary wanted to know about the bequest. "If he had owned Little Lincoln, he wouldn't have been so down about things. That would have given him confidence—not to mention money. Little Lincoln was developed within a year after Eugene's death." She had learned that while moseying around in Timiny Cove the week before.

"He never got Little Lincoln."

"Why not?"

They stopped at a light, pressed close together in the crowd waiting for it to change. Hillary felt Pam's shrug.

"Why not?" she repeated.

"Your guess is as good as mine."

"What's your guess?"

The light changed. They moved on. "John changed the will."

"He couldn't do that. A will is a legal document."

"More than one legal document has been tampered with."

"He wouldn't do that."

The look that came from beneath the floppy hat and dark glasses was facetious this time.

"He wouldn't, Pam. That's illegal. John wouldn't have risked his career that way, much less his reputation. Changing a will is premeditated. It's a blatant violation of the law. Are you sure, Pam?"

"I was there when the will was read," Pam insisted.

"And there was no mention of Cutter?"

"No."

"Or of Little Lincoln?"

"No."

Still Hillary resisted. She didn't want to think of John as a felon. "Maybe that part of the will was handled privately. Maybe Eugene had instructed that the bequest should be between the lawyer and Cutter. Maybe he got Little Lincoln and turned right around and sold it." The eventual development had been done by St. George Mining. "John must have bought him out."

"Sorry, Hillary."

"Are you sure?"

"Cutter didn't get anything. I know."

"Maybe there wasn't a bequest to begin with."

"I heard them talking. Clear as day that time in Maine, I heard it. Daddy was firm. It wasn't something they were discussing for discussion's sake. It was a fait accompli, and nothing happened after that that would have changed Daddy's mind. He and Cutter were on the best of terms right to the end."

They walked on in silence for several minutes before Hillary murmured, "The bastard."

"Uh-huh."

Several days later, Hillary went to see Arlan McGregor. He was her editor, the man she had worked with on two previous books, and a

friend. Looking up to find her at the door of his office, he flipped the glasses from his nose, sat back in his chair, folded his hands over a middle that had grown some of late, and grinned.

"Glad to see me?" she asked with a grin of her own. She had forgotten how much Arlan liked her, but the reminder was spreading from his grin to his eyes. No look could have been more welcome.

"Damn glad. I was beginning to think you'd dropped off the face of the earth. Or moved from New York. I've missed you something fierce."

"Uh-huh."

"I have. But a guy can only deal with unrequited love for so long." He gave her an appreciative once-over. "You're looking good, Hillie."

If there was one thing John had taught her, it was to project herself as she wanted to be perceived. She was wearing a chic, man-tailored suit that was all business. She wanted to look competent, confident, and in control.

"Thanks, friend," she said, then paused. Something was different. Something smelled different. Then it hit her. "No smoke?"

"Gave it up."

"Good for you, Arlan! I'm proud of you!"

"I miss it like hell."

"You'll get over that. You're looking good." In a more professional tone, she asked, "How've you been?"

He shrugged. "Pretty good." He glanced at the manuscript he had been reading. "Busy." After a few seconds he rocked forward and put his elbows hard on the desk. "Bored. I've been doing all kinds of fascinating stuff—a biography of the guy who invented sneaker deodorants, a collection of short stories written by gays about their mothers, a how-to book on keeping raccoons away from bird feeders, and self-help books on everything from peace of mind to gas pains. We're talking dry, here. Real dry." He widened his eyes. "I need something good, Hillie. My mind is shriveling. I need something with meat, something I can sink my teeth into. When are you going to give it to me?"

Smugly, she patted the briefcase that hung from her shoulder.

His eyes widened even more. "Are you serious?"

"Very."

"You've done something more than those crap magazine pieces?"

She didn't take offense. He was too good a friend, and besides, the excitement in his voice was what she had come for. "Those crap magazine pieces have been my bread and butter for the past few years, since nothing I've written for you has set the world on fire yet. But this could do it." She took a breath. "I only have the first few chapters, and they're in pretty raw form, but they're yours to see."

Arlan snatched up his pencil and jabbed it toward the chair. "And close the door. No one hears this but me."

Hillary closed the door and, in a cloud of composure, took a seat. "In March, there was a *20/20* piece on John St. George. Did you catch it?"

Arlan shook his head.

"It was interesting," she told him. "Highly favorable. Glowing, actually. It portrayed John as a pillar of the community, a philanthropist, an entrepreneurial genius."

Arlan rolled the pencil back and forth. "From what I hear, the genius part might fit. His stores are hot. How many are there now?"

"Five. The newest are in L.A. and London."

"Some pretty heavy names buy his stuff."

"Heavy names have heavy money, and what better way to spend it than on jewels? They're the ultimate luxury. Not that John buys jewels with the money he makes. He buys plaques on the sides of buildings, recognition for his name, and goodwill. He buys favors."

"Sounds political. Next thing you know, he'll be running for office."

Hillary went very still. "Not if I have any say in it. I know him, Arlan. I know the man; I know his family. I know his fears and his obsessions, and I know of things he's done over the years that would put that *20/20* piece to shame. There's a whole other side to John that no one knows, a whole other story. You want a hot book, that's it. And I can write it."

Arlan sat just as still as she for a minute. Then, in a flurry of movement, he opened a drawer, took a handful of something, and palmed

it into his mouth. "Sunflower seeds," he mumbled, brushing several from his shirt. As an afterthought, he raised his brows and lifted the bag from the drawer.

She shook her head.

He helped himself to a few more, then closed the drawer. "You've been personally involved with the man."

"Some of the best things are done by writers who are personally involved. The bestseller lists are loaded with books by a son or a daughter or a spouse, ex-spouse, or mistress."

"That makes for pretty strong biases."

"And pretty strong reading. For years you've been telling me that my work lacks fire. This won't. Believe me."

Arlan hesitated. He was rolling the pencil again. "I believe you. But this smells commercial. Your other work has been intellectual."

She tossed a glance at the ceiling. "So you say."

"The critics said it too."

"And what good did it do me? How many copies did we sell?"

"It takes time to build a reputation. Those books were a beginning. They were intellectually exciting."

"This one will be, too." She leaned forward, bracing her elbows on the arms of the chair. "Don't you see? That's my skill—to pull deeper meaning out of something seemingly shallow. That was what my biography of Dorothea DeBlois was all about. Her name meant nothing. She was a newspaper colunmist whose work had been buried. But she wrote things before 1910 that are right on the mark today. And there were good reasons why she saw things the way she did, reasons that had to do with the times and her family and where she lived. That was what I was able to bring out in the book. That was where the excitement came from."

Recomposing herself, she looked Arlan in the eye. "I can make the same kind of excitement with this one. The book will sell because of who it's about. The *20/20* segment is proof of that. John is a marketable commodity now, only I have a unique angle. I can offer insight into the man and his mind. I can analyze him in ways that no

therapist could because John would never open up to a therapist. But he's opened to me. I'm the one to do it, Arlan."

He was interested. She could see it in his eyes. Still he held back. "How long have you known John St. George?"

"The first time I set eyes on him, I was twelve. The first time I talked with him, I was fifteen. I was seventeen when we became friends. I'm forty-four now. You figure it out."

Arlan arched a brow. "Friends all that time?"

"Enemies on occasion. All friends are."

"And lovers?"

"I didn't say we were lovers."

"But you were. Did you have a falling out?"

"Why do you ask that?"

"Because writing a book like the one you're talking about won't please him. He may hate you."

"Making *The New York Times* list will be ample compensation for that."

"There are no guarantees. If you write the book and it doesn't make the lists, you'll still have made an enemy. What then?"

"Life goes on." The words came blithely. Lord knew she'd said them enough times in the last few days.

"Without John?"

"My God, Arlan, you have a one-track mind. Yes, life goes on without John! He isn't the be-all and end-all of my world! Why are you making such an issue of this?"

"Because I don't understand your relationship with him. It's another piece of the puzzle you are, and, dammit, you are a puzzle. Your life before New York is a big blank to me. Each time I ask, you evade."

"My life *is* New York."

"Baloney. You didn't just grow like Topsy in a corner of Central Park. You spent six years in Boston before you came here, and eighteen before that in Tammany Hall—"

"Timiny Cove," she corrected, smiling in spite of herself. "Why do you always do that?"

"Because the place has no meaning to me. You won't say a thing about it. There are times when I wonder whether it isn't fictitious."

"It isn't."

"Then it must be some kind of evil little town that you had to flee on threat of death."

"Not quite." Her smile went flat. "But we all move on. You did it when you left Poughkeepsie. Do I ask you what it was like as a little boy growing up there?"

"You already know it was boring as sin." He tapped a pen against his chin. "And anyway, maybe you're not into understanding my mind the way I'm into understanding yours. I adore you."

Hillary sighed and looked at the ceiling.

"I do," he insisted. "If I didn't have a perfectly good wife at home—"

"How is she, by the way?"

He settled back in his seat. "Pissed off that I won't take her to Puerto Vallarta next month, but otherwise fine."

"Why won't you take her to Puerto Vallarta?"

"Because every time I set foot in Mexico, I get sick. I told her to find a place in Florida, maybe one of the Keys. But she wants Puerto Vallarta. What's so special about Puerto Vallarta?"

"The person you're there with," Hillary replied, then paused, stricken. She'd spent her fortieth birthday in Puerto Vallarta with John. It was one of the few times they'd traveled together. John rarely took vacations. He was a workaholic in the truest sense of the word. His initial motivation had been building the business, but it had been a long time since the business had demanded the hours he still put in. To him, work was both an excuse and an escape. It was one way to keep people at a comfortable distance. For all his success, he had never come to feel totally accepted by, and therefore at ease with, society's crème de la crème.

Of course, that hadn't come out on *20/20*.

Spurred by that thought, Hillary took a breath. "I have to write this book, Arlan. It's something in me that's aching to be done."

"All of a sudden?"

"No. I've thought of doing it before." More than once over the years, as she'd watched John transform St. George Mining from a small-scale gem enterprise into the sophisticated parent of *Facets*, she had thought to document the change. Corporate reports told only half the story. "But I was never quite sure before now that John was a big enough somebody to make the book a success. And I want a success. I *need* one. I'm forty-four and growing older every day. I've had two books published, neither with much hoopla, and dozens of magazine articles that may or may not have been read. I've reached a plateau. My career is stagnating. If I don't hit it big soon, I'll run out of time. Or strength. Or sanity." She scowled. "Dammit, I want my turn on Donahue. I want to be written up in *People*. I want to go to parties and have people know what I do for a living. I want to be someone."

"Like John St. George?"

His words stopped her cold. "Yes, like John St. George." She didn't hide her pique. "I can't take away from what he's achieved. No one can do that. John took over St. George Mining after his father died and built it into something his father hadn't begun to dream of. Professionally, the man deserves kudos. As a person, he stinks."

She went to look out the window. The view was concrete and bleak. "John St. George is a totally self-centered man. At an early age he decided what he wanted in life and set out to get it. The real shrewdness hasn't been so much in how he built *Facets* as in how he used people along the way. No one steps in his path and stays there for long. He sweeps them away—threatens them, bribes them, manipulates them so cleverly that some don't even know it's happened. He may have done enough work to earn his place in the limelight, but there are a hell of a lot of people who should be right up there with him."

"Like who?"

"Like Pam. His sister, stepsister, actually."

"The jewelry designer?"

Hillary sent a wry grin toward Arlan's reflection in the dirty glass. The fact that he knew who Pam was made her point about the family's prominence. "That's right. Her work is what makes *Facets* so special. And successful. But John pretends not to see that. He concentrates on

the ledger's bottom line. God forbid he should acknowledge that Pam contributes something crucial to that bottom line." She turned. "And then there's Patricia, John's stepmother. I won't begin to tell you what he did to her. Suffice it to say that she lives in a private institution on the outskirts of Boston. And Cutter, who should have been Pam's husband—what John has done to Cutter is unconscionable."

Those three were the most obvious examples. Angry and tense at the thought, she said, "The hell of it is that he got away with it. He hasn't been called to account for half of what he's done in his life, and he blithely goes on as though he hasn't a thing to regret. We're talking warped values here. The man doesn't have a conscience."

"So what do you see in him?"

She should have known Arlan would ask. But how could she answer? How did one explain a case of idol worship that had turned into an obsession? She had been aware of John's faults for years, but they hadn't diminished her attraction to him. Even now, after he'd dumped her so cruelly, she wasn't sure that if she were face to face with him she'd be able to spit in his eye.

"You've been friends a long time," Arlan prodded. "What's the basis for the friendship?"

"Time, history, mutual appreciation of slow dancing—I don't know, Arlan." She wished he wouldn't push. The issue was too sensitive. "You reach a point where the relationship is a basis in itself. Maybe it's habit."

"Or compulsion."

"Maybe." She faced him head-on. "But if that's so, it'll make for damn good reading. Now, are you interested in this book, or aren't you, because if you're not, I'm taking it elsewhere." She felt in control again and filled with resolve. There was solace in knowing that John's betrayal was being put to good use. "I don't want to have to go elsewhere. We work well together, you and I. We both know this is your kind of story. It involves a smooth, good-looking, wealthy guy." She arched a luring brow. "Wouldn't you love to see him smeared?"

She'd pressed the right button. Arlan McGregor was a pleasant-looking man, only minimally stocky, with wonderful long dark hair

that showed no sign of thinning. There was something of the teddy bear about him, which was one of the reasons why Hillary liked him. Even without the girth, he had a cuddly quality, and though she'd never actually cuddled against him, she'd taken full advantage of his kindness. She respected his editorial expertise; she understood his need to ask pointed questions; but through it all he was gentle, which meant a lot more to her than dashing good looks.

He was not suave. He'd been known to mistakenly introduce a to-be-wooed reviewer as an art assistant, and at more than one publicity event he'd dripped cocktail sauce on his shirt.

Nor was he wealthy. He had risen from Poughkeepsie's working class, gone through college on scholarship, and held numerous jobs working with words before settling down in his present office. At forty-six, he was a senior editor with some status, and though he complained at times, he liked his job. But it would never make him rich.

That didn't mean he couldn't poke fun at those who were, or feel a certain satisfaction when one of the high and mighty took a fall. John St. George was one of the high and mighty. The look on Arlan's face told Hillary that if she could make John stumble, Arlan would be the first to tout her book.

Motioning toward her briefcase, he held out his hand.

One week later, she was back in his office, wearing the same calm look, though she felt anything but calm. The first part of her book lay on the desk. Arlan was leaning back, his hands linked over his stomach, fingers clenched more tightly than they should have been. She wasn't sure if that was because he didn't like what she'd done and didn't want to tell her, or because he wanted a cigarette.

"Well?" she asked when she could bear the suspense no longer.

"You didn't tell me St. George was engaged."

That wasn't what she had expected to hear. She had to work harder at looking calm. "Is that supposed to be relevant?"

"Could be," he said and smirked. "Do we bill the author as the woman scorned?"

The operative phrase was "bill the author." Her eyes lit up. "You liked it?"

"I liked it. You knew I would," he chided. "But you didn't answer my question. *Are* you the woman scorned?"

"Of course not. John and I never had any kind of formal arrangement. We're just old friends who go back a long way." Pleased with that explanation and the cool way she'd offered it, she asked, "Why? Would it matter if that weren't so?"

Arlan picked up a paper clip and began tapping. "I like this book. I want it done. But if your motivation for writing it isn't entirely professional—"

"I've been thinking of writing it for years. I told you that. If anything, it was the *20/20* piece that got me going. And the going's good, Arlan. This story flows." Her excitement grew as she spoke. "I've spent most of my adult life as a writer, and I've done my share of struggling with words and phrases. This book is different. It's the one I was born to write." She barely paused. "Couldn't you tell?"

He tossed the paper clip aside and squirmed in his seat. "I could tell."

She frowned. "So why are you fidgeting?"

"I'm fidgeting because I'm dying."

She tried to be sympathetic. "Still want one?"

The look in his eyes said he'd kill for a puff just then. "Your manuscript took my mind off it for a while."

She grinned. "I knew you'd like it. I could feel it. The words came so easily. Something connected."

Arlan nodded sagely. His fingers were steepled now, flexing like crab's legs. "That's because you're intimately involved with the situation and the characters. It's like they're your family." He paused. "But they're not. You have family of your own. So why is it," he slapped a hand to the papers, "that you come across in this manuscript as an orphan?"

"Because I'm not a major player in the story."

"But I want to know where you fit in. You refused to give us any kind of detailed bio to use for your other books."

"I gave you a bio. You got all the pertinent information—where I was born, where I went to school, what publications I have to my credit. That's all that matters."

Arlan shook his head. He reached for the sunflower seeds. "I want to know more. It's part of this story. You grew up in Tammany Hall—"

"Timiny Cove, Timiny Cove."

"You lived there, you knew all the people there, but you're not like them, and you never were."

"That's not my fault."

"But you lived there."

"My family lived there."

He popped some seeds into his mouth. "Go on."

"Really, Arlan. This isn't necessary."

"You want a contract?"

She knew that he was teasing, but it was a low blow. Rising slowly from the chair, she said, "I make my own way in life. I may not be as famous as I want, but what I've done, I've done on my own. Not once have I tried to pull strings."

"Too bad. Your dad has nice strings."

She stared at him in silence for a minute. "You knew?"

"Sit down."

She sat down but remained ready to bolt if the conversation took a turn she didn't like.

Arlan seemed to know that he'd found her Achilles' heel, because his voice immediately gentled. "Somewhere along the way, I read that Oliver Cox was living in a small town in Maine called Timiny Cove. The name stuck with me because it reminded me of—"

"—Tammany Hall."

"Then you came along and inadvertently mentioned you were from the place. I began to wonder. Same name, same town. A phone call was all it took."

"To my father?"

"To the postmaster—uh, mistress. What a lovely lady she was. No questions asked, she said you were Oliver Cox's daughter."

Hillary was too busy adding things up to be annoyed. "Then you've known for a while."

He nodded. "I figured you had your reasons for wanting anonymity."

"I certainly did!" she cried, sitting back in the chair with her faith in Arlan restored. "My father was a brilliant poet who'd won nearly every award in his field. My older sister graduated from high school when she was fourteen, went off to M.I.T., and to this day is doing advanced work in nuclear physics for the government. They were both odd, but my mother was the real eccentric of the bunch—which she'd have to be, to be able to live with the other two.

"Then I came along." She sucked in a breath. "Let me tell you, I was a disappointment. I wasn't a poet and I didn't multiply four-digit numbers in my head when I was six. When I was three, I did all the normal things that three-year-olds do. When I was four, I did all the normal things that four-year-olds do. Not that the townspeople believed that. They figured I had to be weird, too, so they didn't accept me any more than they did my parents and sister."

"Your father was known to be a recluse."

"He was. Not a social being at all. His mind was so complex that there was an odd simplicity about him. He could be lovable when he tried, but as the years went on, he tried less and less."

"Why Timiny Cove?"

She had never known the answer to that. "It was out of the mainstream, I suppose. Any rural town would have suited his purpose. He wanted the quiet to work."

"So the neighbors left you alone."

"Totally. They never claimed us as their own. They just stood back and stared. Well, I didn't like being stared at because I was his daughter or her sister, and I didn't like being a disappointment because I couldn't keep up with them. So I made up my mind that as soon as I was old enough, I'd leave and make a name for myself."

"Oliver Cox hasn't produced anything for a while."

"No. He's aged." But the earlier days were never far from Hillary's

mind. "Do you know what it's like growing up with brilliant people? I mean, really brilliant people?"

Arlan scratched his head. "Can't say I do."

She ignored his comical expression. "It's awful. They don't communicate. My father used to sit staring off into space. I could say something, and he wouldn't hear. Then he'd pick up a pencil and scrawl something on the back of an envelope or a bookmark or a matchbook, and it would be incredibly beautiful, only when I tried to tell him that, he was already off in some other mind-place."

"His work is highly acclaimed."

"As rightly it should be."

"Then you're not ashamed of him."

"I was never ashamed. I was just tired of being rated on a scale that was way off the boards to begin with. I didn't want to be thought brilliant when I wasn't. I didn't want to be thought eccentric when I wasn't."

"Apparently John St. George didn't think those things."

At the mention of John's name, she took a deep breath. She remembered those early days with John as though they had just been. A sense of visceral excitement rushed back. "No, John didn't think those things. I met him at a time when I was feeling pretty low. I didn't fit with my family, and I didn't fit with the locals. I was biding my time, waiting to escape to college. John was the link that I needed. He was from the outside world. He was as much of a misfit in Timiny Cove as I was." She smiled. "And you know something? He didn't care. He didn't care what the miners or their families thought of him, because he had this other life. And what a life." She sighed. "I used to ask him about it. I wanted to know everything. I could have listened to him for hours on end." More quietly, she said, "I idolized John. When we became lovers, I was on cloud nine. He was a cut above anyone I'd ever known."

"But he was playing with you."

"Maybe."

"You knew that he had other women. Didn't it bother you?"

"I didn't know it back then. I was seventeen and naïve."

"You didn't even see him that often. If what you wrote was the truth, he used to come and go from Timiny Cove at will. Did he call you when he was away?"

"No."

"Write?"

"No." She rushed on, "But I understood. Really. I adored him, but my dreams weren't centered around him." At his skeptical look, she insisted, "They weren't. I knew by then that I wanted to be a writer. I used to dream of that."

"When you were done dreaming of John. What was it you saw in him, Hillie? Was it the polish? The glamour? Given all you know now, it sounds like the guy's an ogre. What did you see in him?"

She thought about that for a while. What did she see in him? She saw the fire. He had it. He was his father's son in that sense. Fine, custom-tailored clothes were only a veneer. When the clothes came off, he could be earthy as sin. He tried to temper the passion, but the more he did, the more it built and the more powerful it was when released. Those were the times she liked best, the times when he was an absolute wonder in bed.

She wasn't about to tell Arlan that, though, so she simply said, "He was alone and different, just like me. That was what probably brought us together in the beginning. Then, when I got to know him, I was taken by his charm. Yes, charm," she insisted when he looked doubtful. "John was a charmer when he wanted to be. And he was bright in a normal way. I enjoyed being with him."

That was simplifying the issue, she knew, but using the past tense was getting to her. Glancing at her watch, she said, "I have to run," and stood.

"Hillie, about this book—"

"I'm going to keep writing."

"Have you talked with him lately?"

"No. I've had a couple of messages on the machine from him, but I didn't see much point in returning the calls." In fact, John hadn't asked her to return them, which was typical. He called the shots. If he phoned her and she was out, he figured that was her loss.

"What's happening with the engagement?" Arlan asked. "Have they set a date?"

Heading for the door, she tossed back a nonchalant, "No date yet, but the engagement's still on as far as anyone knows."

"Think you'll be invited to the wedding?"

"God, I hope not." Just thinking of it was painful. She would have to arrange a conflicting engagement. Perhaps she'd be out of town on business. She would be out looking for evidence that John had tampered with his father's will. She liked the idea of that.

"Stick it to him, Hillie!" Arlan called as she passed into the hall.

She didn't acknowledge the comment, but a small smile played on her lips during the elevator ride to the lobby. Once outside, though, her smile faded. She could do it, she realized. If she found evidence of a bequest to Cutter, she could really stick it to John. After all he'd done to her, that would be satisfying.

Chapter 10

❖ ❖ ❖

Boston, 1969

WHEN JOHN FIRST TOLD PAM that her father was dead, she refused
to believe him. She had been waiting, frightened, for hours and now
stood in the front hall regarding him mutinously. "You're lying. He
can't be dead."

"The medical examiner certified it."

"He wouldn't die."

"He didn't have any say in it. None of us do when it comes to
that."

"But he wouldn't have driven through a light. He was a good
driver."

"We don't know whether he drove through or lost control, but he
was at that intersection at the wrong time."

Pam struggled to make sense of what John was doing. "You're say-
ing that because you hate him."

"I'm saying it because that's what the witnesses said. The truck
had the green."

"It couldn't have!" she cried, but the most convincing argument
was right before her. John was acting strangely, more subdued than
usual. He was looking strange, too, tired and pale. And he was putting
up with her protests without yelling at her, without telling her what a

spoiled little pest she was. That was the strangest thing of all. For once in her life, she wished he were behaving like a rat.

Now he pushed his hand through hair that looked like it had been ruffled a lot. "Pam, he's dead. He's gone. There was nothing they could do to save him."

She shook her head and began to back away. "Where's my mother? She was with him. I know she was."

"She's at the hospital. She's been badly hurt, but she'll live."

"I want to see her."

"Tomorrow. They just brought her out of surgery. She won't be back in her room till morning."

Pam didn't ask what was wrong with her. She didn't want to think anything was, didn't want to know. "Can I see her then?"

He nodded, and he was true to his word. Not that it did much good. At the hospital the next morning, Patricia couldn't talk with her. She couldn't say that everything was going to be all right. She couldn't tell her that John was wrong, that Eugene was up in Maine and would be back in a few days. She was too doped up with painkillers and sedatives. So Pam returned home with little reassurance to cling to.

Then the phone calls started coming, and the visitors, and the evidence seemed to mount in John's favor. Various people from the office dropped by, as did some of those in Patricia's circle. There were calls from Timiny Cove, even calls from the mothers of Pam's friends. John handled the calls and the visits with a somberness that Pam found hateful. But he wasn't the only somber one in the house. Late that afternoon, when she went into the kitchen and found Marcy in tears, she knew that Eugene truly was gone.

The funeral was held on a Monday, an affair that John kept deliberately small, as he explained to Pam, because of Patricia's precarious condition. Pam suspected that he was only using that as an excuse. She suspected that he didn't want a crowd because it would be too much of a tribute to the man he hated.

He couldn't control the crowds at the burial in Timiny Cove, though. The entire town plus carloads of people from surrounding areas and as far as the state capital came to pay tribute to Eugene.

These were the people who might have been a comfort to Pam, but John hustled her off in a black limousine immediately after the graveside service and had her back in Boston that night.

She was too unsettled to cry or to protest. Her mind told her that Eugene was dead, but her heart kept waiting for him to call or walk in the door or laugh his wonderfully robust laugh. Second to that, she waited for Patricia to call her from the hospital and say that she was feeling better and would be home soon.

But Eugene didn't laugh, and Patricia didn't call. She remained in a somnolent state that wasn't quite a coma but what the doctors called a severe depression. Pam visited every day, but not once did Patricia acknowledge her presence.

So she asked endless questions of John, but with the funeral over, he was deeply involved in the business. "Picking up the pieces" was the expression he used, and Pam took it for the insult it was. She also knew it wasn't true. The business was solid. John was just going ahead with all the things Eugene had resisted. He had little time for Pam.

The doctors were the ones who answered her questions. From them she learned that her mother had suffered a spinal injury and had no feeling from the waist down. "She's paralyzed?"

"That's right." It was a female doctor who told her, sitting with her in the easy chairs at the end of the corridor.

"For how long?"

"We don't know yet."

"But you will soon?" Pam asked, not caring that she sounded frightened. Of all the doctors, she liked this one the best. She was young and softspoken, more approachable than some of the men, and she was very gentle with Patricia.

"Once the swelling goes down and the injury itself heals, we'll be better able to evaluate your mother's condition."

"Will she be able to walk when all that happens?"

"We don't know."

"She will. She has to. When she feels better, will she start talking, too?"

"Probably." The doctor paused, tilted her head, and asked, "Has she said anything to you yet?"

"No. She isn't sleeping. She just stares at the wall."

"She's upset."

"At me?"

"No. At herself, maybe."

"But why? She didn't cause the accident."

"Sometimes when people suffer traumas like your mother has, they don't think as clearly as you or I."

"Will that change, too?"

"We hope so."

"When?"

The doctor shrugged, smiled sadly, shook her head. "We just don't know, Pam."

Pam hated answers like that. So had Eugene. "There has to be something we can do to help her."

"There is. You can visit her like you have been and talk to her. Tell her about what you've been doing in school. Tell her that you miss her and want her home. Ask if you can bring her anything. She'll hear you, even if she doesn't answer."

Trusting that to be the case, Pam did talk. She told Patricia what she'd done that day and what she was planning to do the following one. She told her that she missed her and wanted her to come home. She told her about all the things they could do together when Patricia was feeling better.

Unfortunately, she couldn't tell her the things she really wanted to, for fear they'd only upset her more. She couldn't tell her about the funeral and how many people had come out in Timiny Cove. She couldn't tell her how much she missed Eugene. She couldn't tell her that she was afraid that her whole life was changing, that she'd never get to Maine again, that she'd never have the fun she used to have. She couldn't tell her how awful the house was, how quiet and grim, or how John seemed to go out of his way to annoy her during the rare times he was at home. He didn't talk with her, he talked *to* her.

He wasn't interested in what she was thinking or doing. He had no patience with her fears.

But day after day Pam went to the hospital, a comfortable walk from the house, and day after day she talked until she ran out of things to say. Then she sat in a chair by her mother's bed, doing homework sometimes, or watching television, wishing sometimes that she could curl up next to Patricia on that hard white bed and cry the way she ached to do. Most often, she simply watched Patricia, waiting for a sign that she knew she was there.

It came after a month. Patricia looked at her, gave her a small, sad smile, and Pam felt happier than she had in days and days. But the news that came at about the same time wasn't good. The spinal damage was permanent. Patricia would never walk again.

Whether because of that news or because of the depression she'd been in since the accident, Patricia didn't show any significant improvement after that. Pam was sure she'd given up, and nothing she said by way of encouragement had any effect. From time to time Patricia looked at her, offered a fleeting smile, but otherwise she remained in the silent shell into which she'd withdrawn following the accident.

After two months, the doctors recommended that she be moved. "Why can't she come home?" Pam asked John, when he told her their decision. They were eating dinner, just the two of them in the large dining room where John always insisted on taking his meals. He thought it was elegant. Pam thought it was empty.

"Because she isn't well."

"She's not on any machines," Pam argued. She felt she'd seen enough in the past few months to deserve a more substantial answer. "Some patients are hooked up to so many that you can hardly see them through the wires. Not Mom. There are no machines, and she isn't in a body cast or anything. She doesn't even take much medicine."

"Still, she's not well."

"Then let her come home and we'll get a nurse for her here."

"She needs more than just a nurse."

"Then we'll hire whoever she does need."

"Pam," he put down his fork to stare at her as though she were a half-wit, "this house isn't designed for a paraplegic."

Pam resented his tone. She resented the way he talked down to her—and she resented the way he could eat as though everything were normal, when there'd just been another turn for the worse in a tragedy that seemed to go on and on. "Don't call her that."

"It's what she is. Isn't it time you were honest with yourself? Your mother is paralyzed."

"I know that," Pam said, sounding as calm and grown up as she could. She was going to have to be both if she hoped to fight John. "She won't ever walk. But that doesn't mean she can't learn to use a wheelchair. The doctors said it. So did the physical therapist. And just because she can't walk doesn't mean she can't come home. We're not poor. We can afford to do what has to be done here so she can get around in a wheelchair. I was sitting right there when the physical therapist told her about it."

"And what did Patricia say?"

Pam remembered that well. She had been so sure her mother would show some sort of excitement. "She was pretty tired. They'd been working with her legs for a while."

"Did she say anything?"

After a minute, Pam quietly conceded. "No."

John began to eat again. "Um-hmm."

"But she'd be better at home. I know she would, John. She should be here with us and her own things. We could turn the library into a bedroom so that she wouldn't have to do the stairs. Most of the doorways are already wide enough for a chair to pass through. So if we put up bars in the bathroom—"

"Things aren't that simple. There are other factors involved."

"What factors?"

"Emotional ones."

"Her depression? But there are ways to fight that, too. She's been seeing a psychiatrist at the hospital. She could see one here. If she sticks with it long enough—"

"Pam, she doesn't *want* to come home."

Pam refused to believe that. "Of course she does."

"Has she told you so?"

"No, but that doesn't mean anything. She doesn't say much at all."

"Doesn't that tell you something?" he asked archly.

Pam's stomach was twisting. She had to work harder to keep her thoughts straight. "It tells me that she's still upset about the accident, but we already know that. She's upset about Daddy and upset about herself, and she can't talk with me until she deals with those things." One of the nurses had suggested that to her, and it made sense. "So she's been seeing the psychiatrist at the hospital."

"And what do you think she tells him?"

"I don't know. I'm not there."

"She tells him," he said slowly and distinctly, "that she doesn't want to come home. Why can't you accept that?" He forked a large piece of tenderloin into his mouth.

"How can *you* accept it?" she cried, throwing good intent to the winds. "And how can you eat that way, John? It's disgusting. How can you eat at all? Aren't you the least bit upset?" Tossing her linen napkin onto the table, she stood. "You aren't. None of this bothers you. You got over Daddy's death the minute he was in the ground, and now you're in a rush to put my mother away somewhere."

"Sit down, Pam."

"I'm not hungry."

"You need to eat. If you don't stay healthy, you won't be able to visit your mother."

As a threat, it was empty. "I won't be able to visit her anyway. You're sending her to some place in Wellesley. I can't walk there."

"Marcy can drive you there."

"But not every day."

"Of course not every day. You shouldn't be visiting her every day anyway. It's not healthy."

"She's my mother!"

With that, John lost his patience. Planting his forearms on the table flanking his plate, he said, "Right now she doesn't want to be your mother. Don't you see that? She has serious physical and mental

problems, and if she's ever going to work them out, she needs time by herself. You've been there every day, and it's not helping. So give it a rest, for God's sake. Leave her alone."

Pam's stomach churned harder. John always did have a way of making her sick. Lowering her head, she made for the door.

"Where are you going?" he barked.

"Upstairs. I don't feel well."

"You don't feel well because your stomach's empty."

But she continued on, climbing the stairs to her room and curling up on her bed. She didn't throw up. Neither, though, was she hungry when Marcy came up with a tray.

"Come on, honey, you got to eat."

Pam stared straight ahead. "It won't get better. This is it. It's not going to change."

"Sure it is."

"No. They're both gone now."

"Nuh-uh. Your mama's right down the block, and when they move her she'll be just a short drive off."

"She's not interested, Marcy. She doesn't care about being a mother anymore."

"Sure she—"

"No. And it's not just because of the accident. She hasn't cared about it much for a long time. It didn't matter when I had Daddy, but now that he's gone it matters. She doesn't care. How can a mother do that?"

"She's sick, honey. She's not feelin'—"

"She doesn't even care about this house. She always loved this house. She loved it almost before she loved my father."

Marcy smoothed a lock of hair back from her face. "She's grieving, Pammy. She's grieving for your daddy, and that's a hard thing to do sometimes."

Pam turned her head on the pillow and looked up. "But what about me? I'm not dead, and I need her. I keep telling her that, but she won't listen. Doesn't she know I miss Daddy, too? Doesn't she know how lonely it is without either of them? The only one I have now is

John, and he's worse than ever. He likes it when I'm unhappy. I can't believe that they left me here alone with him."

"You're not alone. You have me. I won't ever leave you."

Pam took her hand and held tight. She wanted to believe that, but so much of what she'd always believed had been torn away from her that she wasn't sure what to trust. She knew that if Marcy had her way, she wouldn't ever leave. But people didn't always have their way. After all, Eugene hadn't intended to leave either.

She took Marcy's offer of comfort, though, because she had nowhere else to turn. Patricia was moved to the small private hospital in Wellesley the following week. Pam visited her once, but she was received with such disinterest that she didn't go again. It hurt too much.

In time, the hurt spawned anger. Pam was angry at Patricia for rejecting her, for refusing to get well, for lying around in a semicatatonic state in a hospital when she had a daughter who needed her. She was angry at Eugene, too. He had betrayed her by driving his car into the path of a truck, then he'd compounded the betrayal by abandoning her. She was angry at John for surviving the other two.

John was, in essence, her guardian, which put her very much at his mercy. He ran not only the business but the house. He was civil to her, but she needed warmth and laughter. She needed someone to talk with, someone to hug her when she was feeling down. Marcy helped, but she wasn't family.

John was family, and she was desperate. She felt alone and frightened. So, for a time, she tried reaching out to him. She convinced herself that if she showed a little warmth, he might, too. She was her most pleasant, waiting for him when he came home from work the way Patricia always had. She showed interest in what he'd done with his day. She talked softly. She avoided riling him.

It didn't work. He seemed to know what she was doing and found it amusing, but when the amusement waned, he turned his back as he always had. He never asked how she was feeling or what she had done with her day, and he certainly never suggested that they spend time together.

Burned once too often, Pam pulled back, but the hurt and the anger lingered. As an escape from those, she devoted herself to school. She went out for basketball to lengthen the day, and she did more with her friends. When she was invited out for a night or a weekend, she always accepted. Thirteen was a social age, and she was a social creature. Forcing other thoughts aside, she sat with her friends in their bedrooms and, for a little while at least, laughed about silly things, poked fun at teachers, plotted ear-piercing expeditions, and dreamed about dating the cutest boys in the upper school.

The laughter died as soon as she came home. The townhouse was too big, too quiet, too empty. Seeing John was torture. He went about his business and seemed to thrive, while she was filled with a pain that swelled, then receded, only to return until she felt she'd explode from it.

By early March she was longing for Maine. It represented all that was right in the world, and although she knew that it would be different without Eugene, she needed to be with the people and things that had meant so much to them both. She hadn't been there since the funeral. It was the longest stretch in her life that she'd been away. John went up during the week while she was in school. She had asked to go many times, but he always put her off.

"My vacation starts next Friday," she told him one morning at breakfast. His only response was to turn a page of the *Wall Street Journal.* "I thought maybe Marcy and I could go up to Maine." She waited through what seemed an interminable silence. "John?"

"Marcy was up there last month, and before that at Christmas." He continued to read the paper, clearly not considering the issue of Timiny Cove or Pam's vacation worthy of his immediate attention.

"Her mother's having trouble, so she had to go up. But you wouldn't let me go either time. I really want to go now, John."

"There's nothing to do up there."

"There's nothing to do down here. It's a two-week vacation. Most of my friends are going away with their families."

That did draw a rise from him. Lowering the paper, he said, "I can't take you away for two weeks."

"I'm not asking you to take me." That was the last thing she wanted. "I know you're busy. That's why I said I'd go with Marcy."

He stared at her for a minute before returning to the paper. "I'll think about it."

"I really want to go."

"I said I'll think about it."

"It'll be good for you, too. You won't have to worry that I'm hanging around here with nothing to do." As if he would. "I really want to go."

"Say it a few more times," he informed her, "and the answer will be no."

She didn't say it again, and in the days that followed, she hoped against hope that he'd say yes. He kept her in limbo until the Wednesday before her vacation was to begin, when she couldn't hold back any longer. "Have you decided?"

"About what?"

"Timiny Cove. My vacation."

"Oh." He was getting ready to go out, adjusting his bow tie in the gilt-edged mirror that stood in the front hall. He was in a good mood, looking forward to the evening. Pam had been hoping that might help. "I've decided," he said. "I think you should stay here. Hettie wants some time off, so I'll need Marcy around to cook."

Her heart sank. "Did Hettie say she had to go next week?"

"I said she could go next week."

"Then let me go to Maine the week after."

"She'll be gone for two weeks."

"She never takes two weeks."

"Well, she is this time, and don't look at me that way. Your interests aren't the only ones in this house. Hettie works hard—a lot harder than you do. She deserves the time. Do you honestly think that everyone's schedule should revolve around yours?"

"No, but Hettie is flexible. She doesn't have family. When she takes a vacation, she usually takes a long bus ride to somewhere she's never been. She wouldn't care when she did it."

"Well, I do," He reached for his topcoat. "And she's doing it next week." Opening the front door, he stepped out.

Pam caught it before it shut and called after him, "Can I take a bus?"

"No." He trotted down the steps.

"When will I get to Maine?"

"When I say so," he called and disappeared into a waiting taxi.

That March vacation was the most miserable of Pam's life. Her emotions were raw, made worse by memories of past March breaks. She tried to keep busy. She read a lot, doodled and sketched a lot, and several times she dragged Marcy to the movies with her. Once she went shopping with Hillary, who had been good enough to volunteer when Pam told John that last year's spring clothes didn't fit.

It rained on and off through most of the vacation, so Pam couldn't go out much. She did spend one day under an umbrella window-shopping on Newbury Street. But the best day was the one she spent at the museum. It was peaceful there. Thanks to Patricia's attempts to make her a perfectly cultured young lady, she knew enough about the masters to appreciate their work. For a time, they diverted her mind.

John was out often. Of the fourteen days Hettie was gone, he was home for dinner only five times. Knowing that he could as easily have eaten out those five nights and done without Marcy, Pam was livid. She avoided him when he was at home, fearing repercussions if she vented her anger on him. But the strain built up inside her. She was grateful when the vacation ended and she could immerse herself in school again. Being busy helped. But the pain was still there, deep down inside, and the longing for Timiny Cove went on.

Then John threw a party. It was his first as master of the town-house and was a coming-out party of sorts. At least, that was what Hillary told Pam in a moment of pique. "He's invited everyone who's anyone. It's his way of announcing that he's a big man now that he's the head of St. George Mining. He's out to impress. Even hired some-one to make all the arrangements. I told him I could do it, but he said I didn't know how. Is that fair, Pam? I have good taste, and I'm com-

petent. So I haven't had the experience planning parties. How will I ever get the experience if I don't try it now and again?"

Pam loved Hillary. She couldn't understand why she wanted to hang around John in the first place, but given that she did, Pam hurt for how he treated her. "You'd arrange a great party. I liked what you did on Valentine's Day." Hillary had invited John and a few friends from the *Globe* to dinner at her small Back Bay apartment. Since one of those friends had asked to bring his daughter, Hillary had insisted that Pam come, too. The apartment looked adorable, the food was delicious, and the fresh flowers that filled the place were arranged with an eye for art—not that John appreciated that, but Pam did and was lavish with praise.

What John had thought of the rest of the party, Pam didn't know. He never shared his feelings about Hillary with her, although she put in good words as often as possible. She liked it when Hillary was around and wouldn't have minded at all if John decided to marry her.

Marriage wasn't the issue then, however. The issue was the party he was throwing, for which he had assigned Hillary the role of passing through the crowd making sure that everyone had access to the bar, the wine tray, and the caterer's spread.

Pam was beginning to wonder what her own role would be. She didn't know if she was even invited. John hadn't said anything about buying a new dress, and she would need one, she knew.

A week before the party, he settled the matter in a way that instantly banished all thought of buying a new dress. "I want you and Marcy in Timiny Cove for the weekend. This place will be a madhouse before the party. You'll only be in the way."

The fact that he didn't want her at the party might have hurt if the alternative weren't so welcome. She counted the days until she could leave, spent every free minute thinking of what she was going to do first, and second, and then after that. She didn't share the extent of her excitement with John lest he realize how much it meant to her and cancel the trip out of pure malice. She tiptoed her way around him

through the course of that week, trying to be invisible, not giving him the slightest cause for anger.

Between the excitement and the fear, she barely made it through the week. She didn't sleep well, didn't do well in school. On Thursday night, when she felt certain he'd say something, he didn't. He wasn't home when she ran in from school on Friday afternoon, and within thirty minutes she and Marcy had the car packed and were off.

Not until they were out of the city and on the highway headed north did Pam feel safe. She relaxed back in her seat. The excitement was there. Increasingly, though, it wasn't the only feeling. She remembered the last time she'd been north, when they had buried Eugene. So much had happened since, and it all came back—the fear, the grieving, the anger, the worry, the loneliness. By the time she and Marcy arrived in Timiny Cove, she felt choked by it all.

Running into the house, which Deenie kept open and fresh, she dashed to her room and changed into jeans and the old shirt her father had given her to use as a paint smock years before. It wasn't as big on her as it once had been, but under its rainbow of spatters, it was loved. Back downstairs, she took a twill jacket of his from the closet. It smelled old and familiar.

"Pammy?" Marcy joined her in the hall.

"I have to go out."

"Deenie left dinner. I could heat it."

"A little later?" Pam asked. She swallowed against the hurt in her chest. "Maybe you should visit your mom."

"I'll wait here for you."

"Don't, Marcy. I need some time. Visit your mother. I'll feel better that way."

Marcy hesitated. "You sure?"

Pam could only nod. In the next instant, she was out the door and running down the street. It was suppertime in Timiny Cove. Those few people who were still in their yards or on their porches waved as she ran past, but she didn't stop. She ran to vent the anguish she felt inside, ran on and on, not caring that her hair came free of its ribbon or that the ribbon floated to the ground on a gust of evening air. She

didn't feel the coolness, didn't feel a thing but the need to keep running and running and running.

By the time she reached Cutter's she was out of breath but no more peaceful than she'd been before. Banging on the door, she yelled, "Cutter?" She waited, panting, never quite standing still, before banging again. "Cutter!"

When he didn't answer, she sat on his front step, pressed herself to the rail post, hugged her knees to her chest, and waited. She didn't consider the possibility that he might be off doing something private and adult on a Friday night, that he might not be back until late, that he might not be back until morning or even the one after that. She just pressed herself to the rail post, hugged her knees to her chest, and waited.

It wasn't long before she heard the roar of his cycle. She stood. He slowed the instant he saw her. Barely taking his eyes from her, he parked the cycle under a shelter by the house. Scooping up a brown paper sack, he came to where she stood. He didn't speak, simply looked, taking in each of her features one at a time, until his eyes met hers.

Pam felt the same choking sensation she'd experienced earlier, the crowd of emotions, so long stifled, now gathered and working their way into her chest and throat. She tried her best to produce a smile, but there was desperation in her high and broken voice. "Take a walk with me, Cutter?"

His fingers grazed her cheek. "You bet." Setting the paper sack on the porch by the door, he took her hand and led her around his cabin and into the woods.

She knew the way well; they'd walked it many times in the past. But she held tight to his hand and let him lead. Only when they reached the stream did she let go, moving to the water's edge, squatting. She felt Cutter's presence beside her. Something about his solidity and his warmth was so genuine, so strong, so like Eugene's that everything she'd tried so hard to keep inside for so very long filled up and overflowed. Tucking her face tight against her knees, she began to cry.

Cutter murmured something, but the sound was lost, just beyond the realm of her misery. Then he put his arms around her and, jacket and all, drew her close to give her the comfort she'd been wanting and needing. He didn't speak, didn't tell her that she shouldn't cry. He hugged her more tightly when the sobs came faster, stroked her hair when they eased, pressed her face to his chest when low, mournful moans came in their stead.

In time, her hands relaxed their grip on his shirt. She sniffled but didn't pull away. With her cheek flush to his chest, she whispered, "I miss him, Cutter. I miss him so much."

He scooped a swirl of hair from her cheek and tucked it behind her ear. "I know. I do, too."

She'd guessed that, which was probably why she had needed so badly to see him. "In Boston, there's just this awful emptiness when I think of him." She took a hiccuping breath. "I thought it would be better here, but when we were driving up today, I kept remembering all the times I knew he'd be waiting for me. Then we drove through the center of town, and everywhere I looked he was there. Only he wasn't. The house was just the same, but so different, and I thought I'd die if I didn't find you. I ran through town like I was crazy. That's what people must have thought."

"Nah. They'd never think that. They love you."

"They loved Daddy."

"They miss him, too."

Her thoughts flew back to the day of the funeral, when so many of those people had come out to say goodbye. Remembering their faces, remembering the huge coffin and the way it had disappeared into the ground, she started crying again. "I'm sorry," she whispered between sobs.

"Don't be." He sounded as distressed as she felt. "You need this. So do I. It helps me with all I'm feeling myself."

"You hurt, too?"

"I loved your daddy," he said, and there was a sudden fierceness in his voice. "He did more for me than any other person on this earth

ever did. I loved him like I'd'a loved my own daddy if he'd been worth a dime—" His voice broke.

Pam held tighter to him until she felt she was in control, but even then she didn't pull back. Cutter's heartbeat was the most reassuring thing she'd heard in four months.

After a time, he asked about Patricia, and she told him. She also told him about John and how he was in charge of everything, and about Hillary and how good she'd been, and about school and her friends and Marcy. When she asked, Cutter told her about things on the mountain and how they'd tightened under John's command. He told her about her old friends, who was doing what and how.

By that time they were facing each other in the dark, no longer touching but closer than ever. "What are we going to do, Cutter?" she whispered.

"We'll go on. That's what he'd have wanted. We'll go on and do the best we can."

"But it's so hard sometimes. Sometimes I just want to yell and scream, I get so angry. It isn't fair, all that's happened. It isn't fair that Daddy died, or that my mother's in a hospital, or that I'm stuck with John. Life shouldn't be like that."

"But it is, and it's the strong ones who survive. You're a strong one, Pam. You'll do fine."

"But it hurts so."

"I know." He pulled her close for a final minute, before standing and drawing her up. "I'd better give you a ride home."

"We're here for the weekend. Can I see you again?"

"You bet."

They'd gone about halfway back to the cabin when she said, "Daddy loved you, too. He really did."

"I don't know about that."

"He did. He wanted to leave you something in his will. Did you know?"

After a pause, Cutter said, "He mentioned it once. Little Lincoln."

"I don't know what happened." She remembered the argument her father and John had about it. "I heard him tell John and he was so

definite. He wouldn't change his mind. Not about that. I think he wished you were his son, not John—and John knows it." She looked up at him. Lit by the moon, his face was all hard, bold angles that should have looked harsh to her, but didn't, couldn't. Cutter was special. "He would be mad as anything if he knew I ran out here first thing."

"Well, you're not gonna tell him," Cutter vowed, looking defiant, "and I sure ain't, so unless he's got spies up here, he won't know. Right?"

For the first time in what seemed an eternity, Pam smiled.

She did more smiling that weekend. She saw all of her friends, and while there was always an awareness that someone was missing, being with them was healing.

Being with Cutter was the best part. His life was so different from hers, but somehow he understood what she was feeling and thinking. When she was with the others, she felt well tended and guarded as those people who loved Eugene would guard his daughter, but still there was an element of loneliness. When she was with Cutter, she didn't feel alone.

For that reason, she squeezed every possible trip to Timiny Cove out of John. It turned out to be easier than she had thought it would be and had nothing to do with either kindness or compassion on John's part. On the weekend of that first party in April, he discovered that he liked having the townhouse to himself, which he told her bluntly. She didn't care. Going to Maine meant the world to her. She was happier there than she could ever have been with John on Beacon Hill.

Cutter was her dearest friend. Sometimes they talked at his cabin or walked through the woods to the stream. Sometimes they went to the mountain he was working so that he could show her through the mines that had been opened since she'd been there last. Sometimes he watched while she doodled with a stick in the dirt or with a pencil on the back of his pay envelope. He kept all her sketches posted on the wall by his bookshelf and was particularly enthralled by those she made of tourmaline in each stage of discovery.

"I'd wear this one in a ring," she told him once, and when he asked what the ring would look like, she drew that, too, then took delight in his appreciation.

She knew of his reputation for toughness, but she saw none of it. She saw his eyes harden when he was angry, saw him grow guarded when he was in town, but in the next breath he'd look at her and everything in him would become gentle. That made her feel special. She liked the exhilaration she felt when she was with him. Like Eugene, he was spontaneous, not programmed. He liked to talk about books he read, or about what Washington was doing to help out the local dairy farmers. He hadn't ever traveled, hadn't ever gone to the theater or the ballet or the opera, didn't own a suit, wasn't thinking of leaving Timiny Cove or moving up in the world. Still he was the most interesting person she knew.

John found out that she saw him, of course. She wasn't sure how, but when he confronted her, she lied. She said that she'd bumped into him by accident, and that it wasn't her fault he happened to be walking along the sidewalk at the same time she was.

John warned her that it wasn't to happen again. She nodded and said that it wouldn't. And her smile was that much wider the next time she arrived in Timiny Cove and went straight to Cutter's cabin in the woods.

Chapter 11

◆◆◆

JOHN'S SPY WAS A MAN NAMED Sylvester Crosey, known to the townsfolk of Timiny Cove for his cat grin and his slyness. He had worked for Eugene until the day he was found doctoring his time charts, when, for the sake of the morale of the others, Eugene let him go. John rehired him in a supervisory position in one of the less productive mines and paid him a salary that far exceeded his position. Once Sylvester grew accustomed to a lifestyle he did not want to forfeit, John added the responsibilities that he'd hired him for in the first place. Spying became paramount among them. Not only did John want a bead on what was happening at the mines, but he wanted to keep a pulse on the town without having to spend anything but token amounts of time there.

Sylvester was the one who told him that Pam was spending time with Cutter.

John had mixed feelings about that. On one hand, it infuriated him that Cutter—and Pam—would blatantly disregard the warnings he'd given. On the other hand, the friendship had possibilities. The longer it went on and the stronger it got, the greater a bargaining tool it became. If Pam did something John didn't like, or if he wanted something from her that she was reluctant to give, he could threaten to keep her away from Maine. Likewise, the knowledge that he could slap a child-molestation charge on Cutter at any time gave him pleasure.

He didn't dwell on it, though, because within six months of Eugene's death, the bulk of his mental energy was channeled into the business. As Eugene's will had been written—with Cutter Reid no longer a part of it—John received a share of the business equal to Patricia's and Pam's. Small pieces of the pie had been left to Eugene's lawyer, his long-time accountant, and certain select friends in Timiny Cove, but the three family shares determined the power structure. Following Eugene's instructions, Pam's shares were put into trust until she turned twenty-five or married, with Patricia and John sharing discretion over her interest in the company until then. But Patricia wasn't in any condition to exercise discretion over her own interests, let alone Pam's, as John easily convinced the court. With the passing of documents granting him guardianship, he had full and unconditional control. The business was his to do with as he wished.

It was a heady feeling. Whether walking through the offices in Boston or the mines in Maine, he felt the power of such control. People regarded him differently. They went out of their way to please him. He didn't delude himself into thinking that they liked him any better; they knew he planned changes and were seeing to their own best interests. But whatever the cause of their deference, he liked it. Being the boss was a fine thing.

Being in control of his own destiny was even better. The dreams he had had when he was younger were reemerging and seeming more attainable by the day. The party he gave at the townhouse was a success, as were others that followed. In turn, he was asked out often. People were taking greater notice of him.

That wasn't to say he was where he wanted to be. He wasn't known much beyond Boston, and he certainly wasn't nearly as wealthy as he wished to be. While he made the occasional A-list for parties, he wanted to make it consistently, and not only in Boston, but in New York, Washington, Palm Beach, wherever he chose to go.

He could see such success happening. If he played his cards right, he could have it all. It also meant closely following a carefully devised plan. He made several immediate changes at St. George Mining. First, he moved the headquarters to a new and prestigious address in

Boston's financial district. Second, in a reorganization of his staff, he promoted the most intelligent and enterprising, demoted those who were mere technicians but necessary to the functioning of the office, fired others who were either old, boring, or still mourning Eugene. Third, he hired people chosen for their creativity, daring, and connections to fill newly created posts, most notably in public relations and marketing.

Once his staff was operating satisfactorily, he formally changed the name of the business to the St. George Company and went about taking it public. It was a complicated process, involving lawyers, bankers, brokers, and large amounts of paperwork and legal maneuvering, but he'd analyzed the market well. Precious and semiprecious stones, of which tourmaline was one, were considered a solid investment. By the end of the first day of trading, he, Patricia, and Pam were each millionaires many times over.

With the proceeds from sales of common stock, plus the capital that the business already had at its disposal, he was finally able to begin work on what he felt was the company's future. He rented a prime piece of storefront property on Newbury Street near the Ritz, and remodeled the inside according to the advice of one of the city's most savvy interior designers. He studied the work of dozens of jewelry designers in Boston, New York, and Los Angeles. Hiring the youngest and most talented of the lot, he set up a studio over the store itself and provided them with the tourmaline and other gems and metals they'd need to design the kinds of pieces he had in mind. Well before the first of those pieces were ready for sale, he hired an advertising agency to launch a campaign designed to appeal to customers with class.

Facets opened in May 1971, nearly eighteen months after Eugene's death, with the kind of gala champagne reception that would have driven the elder St. George to the street in a sweat. John, on the other hand, was calm, cool, and in his glory. The guest list included the best and the brightest of Boston, from society's cream to business leaders, members of the diplomatic corps, luminaries in the professions, and philanthropists. The bubbly flowed freely but was consumed with the

kind of temperance to be expected of people who were self-assured and successful.

They loved the store. John spent the evening accepting praise and congratulations. His designers, attired in tuxedos and gowns, spent the evening fielding inquiries as to whether they could make a piece of jewelry like a particular one on display but with a sapphire here, a bit more gold there, a pair of diamond trilliums somewhere else. His salespeople, chosen for their good looks and poise and well tutored in every aspect of the merchandise, spent the evening wandering through the crowd smiling, answering questions, inviting people back for a more personal look at a quieter time.

Everything clicked. The store was elegant, the jewelry exquisite, the mood exclusive, all of which appealed to people who were used to the same but usually had to leave Boston to find them. John was applauded for that by more than one grateful patron. By the time the evening was over, he was sure the venture would succeed.

Sales were good in the weeks that followed. He made sure that his designers' work was traditional enough to appeal to Boston's upper crust, but he allowed them enough freedom to create pieces for the more eccentric of the chic as well. Differences between styles were subtle in some cases, more distinct in others, but nothing was radical and nothing was cheap. *Facets* prided itself on the quality of its product, its setting, its service, and its personnel. People were willing to pay well for the privilege of bringing home a purple velvet box with the tiny gold marquise, *Facets'* insignia, embedded in the upper right-hand corner.

That insignia, the product of extensive consultation with art and advertising experts, had cost a bundle. So had renovation of the store. And while John had relatively easy access to tourmaline, the cost of buying the other gemstones for his designers was high, as was his operating overhead. He was shaken by the amount of money he had spent. More quickly than he'd have imagined, the funds gathered from taking the company public were depleted, and while that increased the pressure on him to see that *Facets* was a success, it didn't affect his personal spending. He was the figurehead, as he saw it, the

personification of *Facets*' clientele, and in that sense he had an image to uphold. That image involved a five-star lifestyle that mandated wearing the finest clothes, driving the newest cars, eating at the trendiest restaurants, and being seen at the poshest parties.

The bills came in, and the pressure mounted, although no one would have guessed it from the calm and confident way John carried himself. It wasn't part of his persona to look worried. Not once in any social conversation did he give the slightest suggestion that *Facets* was treading on shaky ground. That wasn't anyone's business but his own. Still, the pressure was there, making him tense deep down inside.

It was only natural that he should want a woman to divert his anxiety. Although his sexual appetite had been on hold in the months following the accident, it had returned in bits and pieces, and was back with a vengeance now.

Patricia was lost to him. She refused to see him—not that he wanted to see her either. She was a blemish on his record, a miscalculation on his part. Every time he saw how shattered she was, he remembered the cause. The accident wasn't his fault, of course. He hadn't been driving the car. Like the affair, the accident was Eugene's fault. Eugene had driven them to sleep together.

Now there were other women, strangers to him, whom he bedded. Having one woman, one night, added to the mystique of John St. George. It also kept him safe. He didn't want any woman getting close enough to interfere with his plans for the future. He didn't want any woman getting under his skin, discovering his needs, finding that he wasn't made of steel after all.

Hillary already knew that, which was one of the reasons he kept returning to her. She was privy to his past and wasn't part of the crowd he was trying to impress. She wasn't part of any crowd at all. Although she had plenty of friends, they were from diverse groups. She was an individual in that sense, which definitely fit into his plan.

"I like you, Hillary," he told her one night. They were lying among the twisted sheets of her bed, their lovemaking so recent that their bodies were still damp with sweat.

She lay on her stomach with her head turned away, but she faced him at his comment. "Thank you, John. It's nice of you to say that."

"Are you being sarcastic?" Usually he could tell, but her voice was faintly muffled by the pillow.

"No. I'm serious. It *is* nice of you to say it. You don't usually say things like that."

He took a long drag of his cigarette and let the smoke linger in his lungs before sending it out in a leisurely stream. "Does it bother you?"

"When you say it? Of course not."

"When I don't say it. Does it bother you that I'm not a big one for sweet words?"

"No. It bothers me when you don't call me for weeks and weeks, then expect me to think that you haven't been with other women in between. I'm not stupid. I know the score, and it's fine, John. Really it is. You have a right to do what you want. I have my own life, too. I'm not climbing the walls waiting around for you."

He didn't like the sound of that. "You see other men?"

"All the time."

"I mean socially. Sexually. Are you sleeping with other men?"

She lifted one bare shoulder in a negligent shrug. "I have."

He breathed in another lungful of smoke, exhaled it. "Are you now?"

"I'm with you now."

"How many? When you're not with me, how many are you with?"

"At a time? Only one."

"You know what I mean, Hillary. How many other men are there?"

Again she shrugged. "Two, maybe three in the last year."

He was annoyed to feel so bothered. "Are they as good as I am?"

She turned her head away again, but not fast enough to keep him from seeing the small, smug twitch of her lips. Snuffing out his cigarette in the ashtray on the night stand, he kicked aside the tangled

sheet and came over on top of her. Grabbing her wrists from under her breasts, he pinned them high to the sides.

"Are they?"

"You're crushing me, John."

"I'm not crushing you. You're used to my weight. Are you used to the other guys' weights, too? Do they do it to you like I do?"

"I don't know what you mean," she said primly.

"No?" Releasing one of her hands, he slid his own beneath her. It cupped her breast, rolled over her nipple, slid down her belly and between her legs. "Do they light a fire down here?" he murmured in her ear. His voice was deeper. He felt himself growing hard against her bottom.

"A fire? They'd have to do that, now wouldn't they, if they wanted me wet."

His stroking fingers told him that she was plenty wet for him then, but she always was. "Do you come?"

She was a minute in answering. Her voice was a little higher. "I try."

He increased his penetration. "Once? Twice? More?" He bit on her earlobe, then sucked it hard into his mouth.

"John," she whispered, "what are you doing?"

"I want to know what it's like with them. Do you cry out the way you do with me? Do you ask them to do it harder?" Spreading his hand over her belly, he drew her to her knees.

"John, no," she began, but his fingers continued to stroke her and her next breath was a helpless moan.

"Do you let them do this?" He touched her where he knew she was ultrasensitive and, at the same time, probed for entry.

"John, don't—"

But he was rock hard, needing to take her this way. "No, you don't let them," he whispered hoarsely, nudging deeper and deeper inside her. "You don't, because this is our way."

"You're hurting me," she whimpered.

"Only because you're fighting it. Don't resist. Take it easy." He withdrew, then pushed back into her. The pleasure was so intense

that his voice was little more than a growl. "That's it. That's it." He felt her hand covering his between her legs, pressing, rubbing, all of which excited him more, but when she began to move against him, drawing him in deeper, holding him there, he lost all thought of caution. With her cries of pleasure ringing in the air, he thrust into her again and again, harder and harder, until he felt sure he'd split her apart. His climax was long and hot. She was trembling when he finally pulled out.

"Help me," she whispered, turning under him and reaching for his head. He lowered it, took her mouth in a savage kiss, then moved down her body. With the same savageness, his mouth brought her to one climax, then another. By that time he was rock hard again, so he entered her that way and brought her to yet a third. Their bodies were hot, slick, and spent by the time they finally sank back against the pillows.

Closing his eyes, John let his pulse calm while he listened to the way Hillary panted, mixing sighs with low moans of pleasure. He loved the sound. It was one of the ways she was different. She wasn't ashamed of taking her pleasure. She didn't try to hide it. She let him do what he wanted, and she enjoyed it. Not all women did.

"So," he said. "I ask you again. Are they as good as I am?"

It was a minute more before she caught her breath enough to answer. Looking up at him, her dark hair a riot of tangles exotically framing her face, she whispered, "No one is as good as you are, John. You can bet that if I ever find one who is, I won't be waiting around for you anymore."

He saw the same twitch at the corner of her mouth. "Bitch."

"You're full of compliments today. So what brought on the first? What prompted you to tell me you like me?"

The comment had come in the aftermath of passion, when his defenses were down. She'd been an outlet for the tension that had built inside him for a long time, and he had felt relieved.

Hoisting himself up against the headboard, he reached for another cigarette. "I just realized that I did, so I thought I'd say it." He flicked the silver lighter that she kept around for his use, and talked

with the cigarette in his mouth. "You're easy to be with. You don't make demands. I like that." He drew deeply on the cigarette, only then taking it in his hand.

"Go on."

He was feeling mellow enough to indulge her for once. "You don't cling. You don't curl up on top of me after we've made love, like you're afraid I'll run off somewhere if you don't."

She gave a throaty laugh. "If you wanted to run off, I wouldn't be able to stop you. Besides, I'm hot and sweaty. The last thing I want is to curl up on top of you." She ran a hand under her breasts to catch the dampness there. "Go on. Tell me what else you like."

"You're independent. You have your own life. You work."

"For what that's worth. It doesn't seem to be getting me far."

He didn't expect that it would. Newspaper journalists were a dime a dozen. The ones who made it big were aggressive to the point of ruthlessness. They had guts and grit. Hillary might be independent, but she wasn't sharp-edged. Not that he minded. He didn't want her name in lights. He wanted her to stay the nobody she was. She wasn't any threat that way.

Knowing that she wouldn't understand his line of thinking, he said, to mollify her, "You haven't been at it long."

"Three years. I think I've been stereotyped. The assignments they give me are fluff pieces. I need a change."

"To a different department?"

"To a different paper."

"You're at the best Boston has."

"New York's got a lot more."

"New York?" He grunted. "Don't start in on that again." Annoyed, he took another drag on his cigarette.

"It's just a thought."

But he worried that it was more than that. "Not a terribly good one. Living in New York is different from living here, Hillary. For every dollar more you earn, you'll need two to maintain the same standard of living."

"I don't care how I live. It's the professional opportunity that I want. I want to be somewhere I'll be noticed."

"You think you'll be noticed in New York? Think again. New York is big business. Hundreds of people wanting to be noticed step off planes there every day. You'll be the smallest fish in the biggest pond in the world."

"But I'm a good writer. All I need is a chance to show the world that."

"So they all say."

She propped herself on an elbow to face him. "Do you have a problem with my trying to make a name for myself?"

"Of course not. But if you go to New York, you'll be setting yourself up for a fall. I know New York, Hillary. New York won't take kindly to girls from Timiny Cove."

Her mouth grew tight. "I'm from Boston now, and in case you hadn't noticed, I'm a woman."

"I'm the one who made you a woman. How could I not notice? And I just told you I like you. So why do you want to change things?"

"Because I want to be someone. You should be able to understand that. You've spent years working for a name and an image. Is it so wrong for me to want the same thing?"

Dropping his cigarette in the ashtray, he drew her to his side. "I want you to stay the way you are. I like you this way. Why do you think I keep coming back?"

"Because the others won't put up with you the way I will."

"The others would love to put up with me if I'd let them, but I won't. I've never had a relationship with another woman like the one I have with you."

"Not even with Patricia?"

He went very still. Of course, she'd known. She had been around the house a lot during that time, and she wasn't blind or dumb. But she hadn't mentioned it before. If she was hoping to one-up him, though, she was in for a let-down. He had no intention either of denying what he'd had with Patricia or of apologizing for it.

"Not even with Patricia." Setting her aside, he climbed from the

bed and went to the window. He drew the sheer drape back only enough to give him a look at the alley. It was a bleak view, oddly compatible with what he felt inside when he let memory take him back. "Patricia was weak. She had to be protected from every little fear. She wanted to know all about the business, but she couldn't take half of it."

"Do you discuss the business with other women?"

Letting the drape fall back into place, he turned. "No. It has nothing to do with them."

"It has nothing to do with me, either."

She was propped against the headboard the way he'd been moments before, looking lazy and replete. The fact that she wasn't rushing out of bed was another of the things he liked about her. She didn't jump up to smooth her hair or repair her makeup or take a shower. She was perfectly content to linger with the sight and scent of their sex-play on and around her.

Looking at her, the pique he felt at the thought of Patricia began to ease. "I tell you about the business because I trust you. I trust that you won't take what I say and turn it against me."

"I wouldn't do that!"

"That's what I just said." He came back to the bed and reached for another cigarette, but she snatched the pack from the nightstand.

"You're smoking too much."

"It relaxes me."

"Why are you so tense?"

Staring her down, he held out a hand. When she put the pack of cigarettes in it, he shook one out, lit it, then sank onto the edge of the bed with his back to her. "I'm human. I have pressures like everyone else. Right now, they're pretty heavy."

"Is there a problem with *Facets*?"

"Nothing that time won't fix."

"What do you mean?"

He was a minute in answering, reluctant to air his worry but, finally, wanting her encouragement. "We spent a lot of money getting started. It'll be a while before we show the kind of profit I want."

"You knew that would happen."

"Anticipating it is different from living through it. I've done a lot with the business since I took over, but it's not easy. There's always a risk that something unexpected will happen. I'm the guy in charge. It's my future that's on the line if something goes wrong."

Her voice was closer, bolstering him in the irrationally effective way that neither his banker nor his lawyer nor his accountant, for all their facts and know-how, could do. "It's a super idea, *Facets* is, and it'll be a huge success. You've done it right, John. You don't need to worry."

"Maybe not," he said. He felt her hand on his shoulder, working tension from the muscles there. He couldn't have taken it from another woman, but Hillary had just the right touch.

"You'll see," she went on in that same gently enthusiastic voice, "the profits will come rolling in pretty soon, and then you'll be thinking of opening another store. Is New York next on the list?"

He'd been so embroiled in establishing the flagship Boston store that it had been months since he'd thought ahead. But New York was the one. "If all goes well."

"So. You set up your New York store, and I'll get a job with one of the papers there, and we'll see each other the way we always have."

Grabbing her hand, he hauled her around his body and onto his lap. "Dammit, you had that whole conversation planned."

"I did not!"

"Then why did it wind up so conveniently in your favor?"

"Because it makes sense. Doesn't it?"

He didn't answer. The feel of her naked hip against his naked groin was arousing, as was the warmth of her body, the softness of her skin, the musky scent surrounding them both. So he kissed her hard by way of punishment for her good sense, then kissed her hard again by way of recognition of her sexiness, then kissed her hard a third time by way of expressing the unbridled desire that her sexiness sparked. His last thought before he tumbled her to the floor was that he would enslave her to keep her in Boston until he was good and ready to let her go to New York.

*　　*　　*

Four months later, when plans for the New York store were still in the dream department, she went. John supposed that he might have been more attentive during those four months, but a string of social engagements had kept him busy. He hadn't had time for her. Weeks had gone by when he had been so engrossed in all *Facets* was becoming that he didn't think of her. Then, typically, when the pressure built inside him, when he found he needed someone to talk to, when he found himself hungering for the fire that only she had, he called.

She didn't complain. She didn't nag or whine or ask why he hadn't called sooner. She gave him her all for the weekend that he spent at her apartment. Three weeks later, she moved to New York.

He knew that it was revenge, and it infuriated him. Pam had been the one—what pleasure she'd gotten from that—to hand him the new address. Hillary hadn't even had the guts to tell him herself.

So he fought fire with fire. He didn't call, didn't try to see her, although he was often in New York buying gems. Two months went by, then a third and a fourth. He tried to fill the gap with other women, but no one excited him for longer than an evening. There were none of the prolonged orgies he and Hillary had, none of the wild, impulsive couplings where he could really let himself go and pour everything he had into uninhibited sex. That wasn't part of the image. Nor was talking over his worries. He missed Hillary for that, too. When she had lived in Boston, she was his for the taking. When the mood hit, he could be at her apartment within the hour. He couldn't do that now. Seeing her required forethought, which was an annoying imposition.

After stewing about that imposition for a good long time, he finally capitulated and called her, which annoyed him all the more—which in turn meant that when they saw each other for the first time in New York, he had a plethora of anger and frustration to slake on her. It made for hot, hard, heavy sex.

Hillary didn't complain. She was as hungry as John was, which told him that she hadn't yet met anyone to take his place. Buoyed by that thought and by the fact that she had received him with open arms despite the long silence, he returned to Boston feeling smugly content.

She had been right after all, he realized. It didn't matter where she was. They could still see each other.

In some respects, having her tucked away in New York was very convenient. It meant that he could move freely through the Boston social scene without worry that he'd be associated with her. No matter how sophisticated she became, she was still from Timiny Cove. She wasn't part of the *Facets* lure. She didn't have the sparkling clear shine that his future did.

She did take the edge off his hunger, though. Because she satisfied his wildest sexual needs, he was in greater control with other women. He could play the consummate lover, be gentle and considerate, put his partner's satisfaction before his own. He could foster the gentlemanly image without worrying that the more earthy of his desires would be exposed.

Unfortunately, sex wasn't as exciting that way, so he found himself cutting back. There were still a few women—he had no intention of anyone thinking him queer, and his appetite was in no way diminished—but his playmates were chosen more for their social importance than for any physical satisfaction they might bring.

The tactic paid off. He came to be regarded as a slightly aloof, vaguely mysterious, but highly appealing and eligible bachelor. He rather liked the image. It had the scent of the upper crust—clean, controlled, dignified, genteel. It went a long way toward countering the image of the miner from Timiny Cove.

It also held an element of truth. Aside from those bawdy weekends in New York with Hillary, he *was* clean, controlled, dignified, and genteel. As for aloofness, he chose to call it individuality. He wasn't a groupie. He mingled with society's cream, but only on a pick-and-choose basis. He wasn't afraid to go his own way or to let people know that he did. It added to his mystery.

It also compensated for the fact that, despite his connections and the inroads he'd made, he remained apart from the Beautiful People. He went to their homes, entertained them at his own, but still he wasn't fully accepted. No matter how elegant an appearance he made,

how intelligently he spoke, how impeccably he behaved, he was still, somehow, an outsider.

He told himself that he was different, special, superior. But none of those arguments held much weight on the occasional nights when he was home alone and feeling restless. Occasionally he would hustle up a squash partner for a last-minute game or call a woman for a late dinner. Often, though, he stayed home, prowling the library, thinking about *Facets*, plotting the next step in his ascension to prominence.

But his restlessness remained. He didn't understand it. At thirty-two, he had the world at his fingertips. He was already a man of substance and was becoming more so by the day. He'd become a patron for the Institute of Contemporary Art, had had his name listed at benefits for the Cancer Society, the Opera Company, and the Lahey Clinic in that year alone. *Facets* was doing well, as was the St. George Company. The media were familiar with his name and face. What more could he ask?

He wasn't sure. And the restlessness persisted. That was when he went looking for Pam.

Chapter 12

PULLING THE CAR INTO THE courtyard, Pam cut the lights and the engine, pocketed the keys, grabbed her books, and slid out. She'd been up late three nights running and was tired, still her step was quick and light as she trotted up the back stairs. Thanks to four cups of coffee, the adrenaline would keep flowing for another few hours, which was all she figured she would need. She had to read through one last chapter and her notes, then pack. She'd crash over the weekend.

Breezing through the front hall, she checked the table beneath the mirror for messages. Finding none, she swung around toward the stairs without breaking stride, only to bump into John.

She gasped. "Sorry. I didn't see you there."

"You're late."

She didn't have to check her watch. She'd had an eye on the Cougar's dashboard all the way home. "It's eleven. That's when I told Marcy I'd be back. Didn't she give you the message?"

"I didn't ask for the message. Eleven's late for a school night. Where have you been?"

He didn't sound angry, exactly, still Pam was cautious. She had found that that was the best way to handle him. Arguing did nothing but raise the level of tension between them, which made living in the same house unbearable. "I was at Ginny Taylor's. We were studying. The American history midterm is tomorrow."

She held her breath while he considered that.

Sounding benign, he asked, "You've been studying all this time?"

"Uh-huh. I went to Ginny's straight from school. Mr. Harris piled extra reading on top of everything else, so like there are gobs of names and dates to memorize." She slipped past him and started up the stairs. "I have to finish."

She went straight to her room. Quietly closing the door behind her, she leaned against it for a minute, then quickly crossed to the bed, dropped her books and jacket, and picked up the phone.

"It's me," she said softly when Ginny answered. "Did he call?"

"Not yet. What's his problem, Pam? He said ten-thirty. He promised ten-thirty."

Pam slid down to the floor, back braced against the bed. She kept her voice low. "He must not be home yet."

"They were having dinner at seven-thirty. He thought for sure they'd be done by ten. Ten-thirty was playing it safe."

"He has a big family. Maybe it took a while to serve them all. Maybe they got a bad waitress."

"I don't know. Oh, Pam, I don't need this. Not tonight. Not with this test in the morning."

"You'll ace the test. And we'll get off like we planned. And they'll both be there, Robbie *and* Bill."

"Robbie will. He's wild about you. I'm not so sure about Bill and me."

"He'll be there," Pam insisted gently, then looked up when a movement caught her eye. John was opening the door, pushing it back all the way, slowly scanning the room before dropping his gaze to her.

"Maybe something happened to his car," Ginny went on. "I mean, like it's been making strange noises all week. What if he can't get it started?"

John just stood there, saying nothing, giving Pam no hint of what he'd heard and what he hadn't. She had been speaking softly enough that he shouldn't have caught the bit about Robbie and Bill unless he'd had his ear to the door. She wouldn't have put that past him.

Speaking in the same soft voice that implied she had nothing to hide, she asked Ginny, "Did you finish the chapter?"

"What chapter?"

"I've got to do it now. So we're on for seven?"

"Uh-oh, someone's there. Is it John?"

"Be ready, please? I'll be dead if I don't get to the library before assembly."

"What if Bill doesn't call?"

"Relax. You'll do fine."

"Pam, what if—"

"Gotta run," she said smoothly and hung up the phone. Seconds later, she was on the bed, reaching for her books. "Was there something you wanted?" she asked John.

He leaned against the doorjamb, arms crossed on his chest. "What was that about?"

"I was reminding Ginny to be ready in the morning. She has a way of forgetting that I'm picking her up, not the bus. If she wants to keep them waiting, fine. But, like, I've got lots to do."

He seemed to consider that while he looked around the room. "She must like being driven."

"Uh-huh."

"I'm surprised her parents haven't given her a car."

"So am I. She's envious of me."

"Do you like the car?"

Pam freely admitted it. "I *love* the car." She'd had it for only four months, but it had changed her life. It had given her the kind of freedom for which she had waited for years. She'd been independent and self-sufficient for a while; without a mother in the picture, she did her own shopping, took herself to the beauty salon, the dentist, the doctor. Having wheels made it all much easier.

When he asked, "Where are you off to this time?" her heart beat a little faster. She followed his gaze to the canvas duffel on the floor. Marcy, bless her heart, had neatly folded and packed the things Pam had piled on top.

"We're going to Ginny's place on the Vineyard. Just for the weekend. We'll be back Sunday night."

"Will Ginny's parents be there?"

"Uh-huh."

"The whole time?"

"Uh-huh."

"Like Allison's parents were in Vail the whole time?"

She'd known that was coming. He wasn't about to let her forget it. But if he used it to spoil the weekend she and Ginny had planned, she'd be furious. "Allison's parents were supposed to be there. They flew out with us, then Allison's grandmother took sick, so they had to fly back early. But we weren't alone. Allison's brother was there. He's a freshman at Duke."

"Why doesn't that make me feel better?"

"Because you're a naturally suspicious person. Nothing happened, John. I'm telling you. We went skiing, we went to dinner, we went to bed. Nothing happened. We were fine. Ginny's parents called every day. They were comfortable. So were we."

"I'm sure you were," he said. "You've been comfortable a lot, lately. It's a pretty nice life—ski trips to Colorado, weekend trips to New York and Martha's Vineyard, a car for your birthday—"

"Did you have any less when you were my age?"

"I wasn't flunking out of school."

So that was it. "I'm not flunking."

"I wouldn't call C's and D's a stellar report."

"There was only one D, and that was in math because I happen to have the worst teacher in the school. I'm getting a B-minus this term. And there were only two C's. And you didn't mention the A's and B's."

"In art and literature enrichment. Both electives."

"Both interesting, not boring like the rest."

"Boring or not, if you want to get into a decent college, you'll have to get your marks up."

"I'll get them up."

In point of fact, Pam didn't care what college she went to, as long as it was beyond commuting distance from Boston. That would mean she had only two more years of living at home, which was a wonderful thought. She was tired of tiptoeing around John, tired of being grilled

about what she'd been doing and whom she was with. Things were okay when he was busy and out of the house. When he was home and had time on his hands, his favorite activity was bugging her, which was just what he proceeded to do.

"It might help if you cleaned this place." His lip curled as he eyed the desk. "What is all that crap?"

"Note cards and research stuff for a term paper I'm doing." When he arched a brow at another pile, she said, "Drawings. I have to do zillions to get the one I want."

"Doesn't Marcy clean?"

"She does everything but the desk. I won't let her touch that. I know where everything is."

"But you can't possibly work there."

She patted the bed. "I work here. It's more comfortable."

"You talk on the phone there." His expression was growing darker. She could see that he was getting caught up in his cause. "You've already blown it for Penn. Even as an alum, I couldn't pull enough weight to get you in with C's and D's."

"B's and C's," she corrected quietly, knowing she wouldn't go to Penn even if John paid her. It was his school. And it was in the wrong direction. She didn't want to go south of Boston. She was thinking of going north, to Bates or Bowdoin.

"You may not think it matters where you go, Pam, but it does. The contacts you make in college are important."

"I know."

"Do you? Go to a lousy school, and you'll meet lousy guys. Bring a lousy guy home, and there's no way I'll approve of the marriage."

"Marriage?" She held up a hand. "Whoa. I'm sixteen years old. I'm not thinking of marriage."

"Isn't that what you and your friends spend hours talking about?"

"No!"

"Girls always talk about boys," his eyes fell to her breasts, which pushed gently against her sweater, "and since you're finally looking more like a girl than a boy—"

"John—"

"You are."

"I know that." But she could still remember the agony of being the flattest of her friends, year after year. She couldn't begin to tally the sleep she'd lost worrying that she was never going to develop or get her period. After suffering in silence for months, too worried to mention her fears to Marcy or Hillary lest they confirm that she had a problem, she finally took herself to a gynecologist whom one of her friends had seen. The examination was uncomfortable and embarrassing, but the doctor found nothing wrong that time wouldn't fix. Pam had been fifteen then. Sure enough within three months she started to fill out.

"You're looking pretty, Pam," John went on. "Don't tell me the boys don't notice."

She shrugged.

"And don't tell me you don't notice them back. You're out with boys as often as you're with girls."

"We're all friends. We have been for years." She waited, wondering if she'd been set up. If he had overheard her talking about Robbie and Bill and suspected that Ginny had invited the two to spend the weekend in the boat house, she'd be in big trouble. Robbie and Bill weren't schoolmates of theirs. They were freshmen at Boston University. Pam wasn't in love with Robbie, but he was fun.

But John made no mention of specifics. "I know how things work with groups like that. You pair up, then break off and pair up with someone else, and through the whole thing the girls are sitting in class doodling 'Mrs. So-and-so' on their books. High school is just practice. The serious manhunting takes place in college."

"Times have changed," Pam informed him, straightening her spine. "Women aren't going to college to get married. They're training for careers. Look at Hillary. Like, she's a perfect example."

"What's with this *like*, for God's sake?" John barked. "If it's supposed to be cool, it's wasted on me. As far as I'm concerned, it's nothing but poor English."

Pam was more interested in making her point than in arguing idiomatic usage. "Isn't she a perfect example?"

"Hillary is an exception."

"Maybe among the women you know."

"And the ones you know are different?" He straightened, preparing for battle. "Come off it, Pam. Your friends come from families that are loaded. Do you honestly think they're planning to work their way through life? You can bet their fathers have said the same thing to them—more than once—that I just said to you."

But Pam doubted that Eugene would have said it. He wasn't like that. Lord, she missed him. She missed his robust laugh, missed the way she could tell him anything, missed the way he used to hug her for no reason at all except that he loved her.

She missed Patricia, too, but that grief wasn't as simple. It was mixed with loneliness, wishful thinking, and guilt. Patricia was still hospitalized. Her psychiatrist, Robert Grossman, whom Pam had begun calling for updates on her mother's condition, had suggested that Pam visit each month. If she missed a month or two, though, it never seemed to matter. Patricia was pleasant; she responded to things Pam said with simple replies, but she never asked questions, never expressed interest or concern. She never called Pam on the phone, never remembered a birthday, never took the initiative in any aspect of their relationship.

By keeping busy with her friends, Pam was able to forget how much that bothered her.

"Besides," John went on, "if you're planning on a career, the college you go to is even more important."

"Not if I'm going into the family business."

"Yes, if you're going into the family business. I can't put you into a top slot if you've barely squeaked by at a second-rate school." He seemed egged on by his sense of superiority. "You want people to respect you? You want them to think you've got something up here?" He tapped his head. "You need the credentials for that."

"I already know more about the mining end of the business than most of the men in your front office."

"Mining is only a small part of the business. *Facets* is where we're going."

"I'll find my place." She had been watching things closely and

knew that taking over the presidency was a pipe dream. John was firmly entrenched in that spot, and he was a powerful force. But there would be another spot, one where she could build her own power. She intended to show him up. Somehow, sometime, somewhere, she would.

"Not if you don't settle down and study."

"How can I settle down and study if you don't leave me alone?" Having reached the limit of how much of John she could take at one time, she lost her cool. "I told you that I have a big midterm tomorrow. You told me that I should get better grades. How can I do that if you don't let me study?"

"How do I know that the minute I walk out of this room you won't pick up the phone?"

"Because I have to study! *Go*, John."

He stared at her for a long minute, during which she aged a dozen. She was sure he was going to tell her she couldn't go for the weekend—which wouldn't stop her, she'd find another way to get to Martha's Vineyard, but it would complicate things.

"I'll go," he said finally in the slow and deliberate tone that augured a threat. "But I'm telling you, be careful, Pam. I've been generous with you. I've given you a liberal expense account—"

"I haven't gone over—"

"—which gives you expensive clothes, expensive skis, dinners, and movies and shows with your friends. I send you to New York every few months. I let you travel to this summer place and that winter place. I gave you your own phone. I've given you a car and unlimited gas. And I've looked the other way each time you've gone to Maine."

Her heart skittered to an abrupt stop-start. "It's important that I go to Maine," she said quietly. "It's important that the men at the mines see one of us. You hate going. I don't."

"But you're still seeing Cutter Reid."

She felt another sharp skitter. "He works at the mine, so I see him."

"You see him other times, and I've told you not to."

"Timiny Cove's a small place. I can't help but see him."

"You go looking for him. Why do you bother?"

Someone was snitching. She wanted to know who, but she didn't get so muddled in the question as to fall into his trap and admit to seeing Cutter. "The miners are important. They're human beings who put in good, long days for us. They're the backbone of this company."

"Not anymore. Tourmaline is the most reasonably priced of the gems we work with. If we closed the mines, we could buy it at the exchange like we buy the rest."

No matter how quickly Pam wanted John out of her room, how reluctant she was to prolong the conversation, she couldn't let his statement stand. "You're assuming the business could survive on *Facets* alone. But even I know that we gross eight million a year from the mines, apart from the stones our designers use. That's a nice cushion. Without it, our stockholders might get nervous."

He was quiet for a minute. Although nothing showed on his face, Pam fancied he was stunned that she could speak so knowledgeably about the business. Rather than bask in her moment of strength, though, she too remained silent. One of the things she'd learned in dealing with John was that gloating only brought retribution, and retribution hurt. She didn't want to be hurt. Nor did she want Cutter hurt.

She had two more years before she reached majority. Two more years.

Ten more hours before she took the American History exam.

Fourteen more hours before she left Boston for the Vineyard.

And, God willing, no more than five minutes before John left her the hell alone.

"I think," he said at last, "that the mines are the least of your worries. Get those grades up, or you won't be going to Maine or anywhere else for a while. Do I make myself clear?"

He was more than annoyed. His eyes sparkled with resentment despite his otherwise iron control. She'd bested him, and he knew it. It was all she could do not to grin.

"Yes, John," she said docilely.

Her grades remained mediocre. When a note of concern came from her math teacher, John relieved her of her car keys and forbade

her to go out that weekend. She simply waited until he'd left, then walked down to Charles Street and was picked up by friends. When he decided, two weekends later, that he didn't like the term paper she'd written for English, he took the cars keys again, along with the ticket she had for a Saturday night concert in Cambridge. She wasn't fazed. She hopped on the T and went to a party at Boston University with Robbie.

John was not thrilled with her final report card in June. "This is pathetic," he said, tossing the incriminating sheet of paper onto the library desk.

Pam had been preparing herself for his anger since she'd learned of the grades several days before. "It was a hard course load. I shouldn't have taken biology. It took so much of my time that it messed me up for everything else."

"What messed you up had nothing to do with school. It has to do with that bunch you hang out with. You're always out. Are the others doing as poorly as you are?"

"My grades aren't that bad. Really. You knew I was having trouble in math, but that won't be a problem next year because I'll be taking geometry, which is a lot easier than algebra."

"You got a C-minus in history."

"That's because the entire grade depends on three tests, and I don't do well on Mr. Harris's tests. I listen to what he says and try to psych him out, but I guess wrong every time."

John wasn't buying the argument. "If you studied everything he assigned, you'd be ready for the test regardless of what he asked."

"I do study everything."

"Don't you want to do well?"

"Yes."

"So why aren't you? If you set your mind to something, you can do it. It's not so long since I went through school that I don't remember what it's like. If you work hard, you do well."

He didn't blink. Nor did he seem to be breathing, which was something that always amazed Pam. It was as though he was in such

total control of his body that every function was pared down to its most spare and efficient. He was a cold-driving machine.

"The problem," he went on in distaste, "is that the only thing you're working hard on is your social life. I think you ought to take biology over at summer school."

Pam's stomach knotted. "I can't go to summer school, John. I'm signed up to go out West. The trip starts in two weeks."

"They'll fill in with someone else."

"But I've been looking forward to this trip! I've been counting the days till I leave!"

"If you'd spent less time counting and more time studying, you'd have been better off."

"Please, John." She'd go mad if she had to hang around Boston all summer, which was her only other choice, since John had told her she couldn't spend twelve weeks in Maine. "I'll do anything. I'll work with a tutor when I get back from the trip, I'll go for extra help next fall, I'll come home every afternoon after school to study. I'll do better, I promise. I mean, like, junior year is the one that really counts, anyway, and if I do okay on my SATs, the colleges won't hold one mark against me."

"One mark?"

She wasn't about to bicker. "A few."

"I'll have to think about it."

"Please?" she begged, not caring that she did. She was tired of butting heads with him, tired of losing and being punished and slipping out on the sly. She welcomed the promise of seven weeks away from home.

"I said I'll think about it." He handed her the report card. "Take it. It embarrasses me."

She took the report card and left, knowing from experience that further argument would not help her cause. John was behaving true to form. He would keep her dangling while he made up his mind in his own sweet time, and only when he knew she was suffering.

Indeed, she was suffering. She was furious at him and at herself. With the school year over, her friends had dispersed, so she had no

ready diversions. She tried to be available and acquiescent whenever John was at home, but he gave no clue as to which way he was leaning. He was perfectly content to let her swing.

Needing a respite—and unable to help herself, although she doubted it would help her cause—she took off early one afternoon and drove to Timiny Cove. She went to the mountain first to say hello to Simon and the men. When she was certain Cutter had seen her, she left for the stream in the woods.

He joined her there soon after the workday ended. At the sight of his tall frame emerging from the trees, she felt the familiar brightening inside. Grinning, she rose from the rock on which she'd been sitting and ran to meet him.

He swept her up and swung her around. When her feet touched ground again, he held her back. "Jeez, do you look grown-up. I wasn't sure who it was when I first saw you. This is a change from jeans."

She was wearing a short white skirt, a lavender jersey, and flats, which was what she'd put on that morning when she hadn't expected to go farther than Beacon Hill. The impulse to leave Boston had been so sudden that she hadn't thought to change. Given the admiration in Cutter's eyes, she was glad she hadn't.

He twined a long strand of her hair around his finger and gave a light tug. "You're looking pretty, Pam."

John had said the same words to her not so long ago, and in the echo of the words he had looked at her breasts. She suddenly wondered if Cutter had noticed she was getting bigger there. Maybe he'd even felt her breasts when he hugged her.

Her cheeks grew warm. "Thank you." Her eyes couldn't quite hold his. They angled off, then returned. "You're looking pretty good yourself." It occurred to her that what with his height and his laborer's build and his long, light brown hair that never seemed dirty but was always mussed, he was more handsome than anyone she knew at home. "How've you been?"

"Not bad. Arguin' with Simon. Stickin' up for a thirty-minute lunch hour. Steerin' clear of John. How 'bout you?"

"Pretty much the same as you. Not bad."

But he was studying her closely. "You look tired," he decided, and she knew then why she'd felt such a dire need to see him. He cared in a way that no one else did. He was a haven she could run to when she was lonely and discouraged. He knew her, understood her. He gave her his full attention.

In no time they were sitting side by side on the rocks and she was spilling the whole story about her grades and John and the trip that was up in the air. She also told him that John knew they were seeing each other.

"He must have someone up here, Cutter. You joked about it once, but I think it's true. He knows I spend more time with you than I do with the others."

Cutter's features had hardened the way they always did when John's name came up. "Is he taking it out on you?"

"Not yet. But he's holding it over my head."

"Typical."

"Who do you think is watching us?"

He stared at a spot across the stream for so long that Pam looked that way, wondering if someone was there. The trees were in full bloom, fresh and lush in a June sort of way, so that though sundown was a ways off yet, the shadows were deep. She couldn't see a thing.

"I'm not sure," he said at last and looked back at her. "You came anyway."

"Of course."

He gave her the smallest smile, a tiny twitch of the lips that told of his pleasure. "Does he know you're here now?"

"He'll know when he gets home from work and finds my note. I was going to tell him I'd gone to a friend's house, but I figured someone would see me up here anyway. If John catches me in a lie at this point, I can forget that trip."

"When's the trip?"

"Next Thursday."

"And you really want to go?"

"I really want to spend the summer up here, but John won't hear of that." Tucking her hands between her knees, she gritted her teeth

and threw back her head. "I'm so tired of this, Cutter. He's impossible. He decides what's important, forgets about what isn't, and takes everything that is as seriously as if it's the end of the world. He's such a prig!"

Cutter flattened a hand on the rock behind her hips. "I won't argue with you there." He looked down at her more gently. "How long can you stay here?"

"Not long. I said I'd be back later tonight."

"You can't just turn around and drive another three hours alone."

"Want to come along for the ride?" she teased, then her grin vanished, her eyes grew wide, and she grabbed his arm. "Do, Cutter. Come back with me. You could stay across the Common at the Parker House. I'd love to show you the city. You've never been there, and I know everything there is to see. It's five days before I'm going away—if John lets me go; and if he doesn't, that gives us even more time. It would be such fun. I mean, like there's nothing else I'd want to do more than that. I wouldn't even mind not going on the trip if you came to Boston."

She felt the flex of a steely muscle in his arm even before she heard the hardness in his voice. "Wouldn't John just love that."

"John wouldn't know!" She hurried on, "Don't you see, Boston's so much bigger than Timiny Cove that he wouldn't ever know you were there. We'd be lost in the crowd. It happens all the time. He doesn't know half of what I do, and since he wouldn't be expecting—"

"Not a good idea, Pam."

She dropped her hand from his arm. "Why not?"

"First, because I have a job to do."

"Take time off."

"Second, because you'd be in big trouble if he found out."

"He won't find out," she said, but nervously. Cutter's voice was growing harsh.

"Third, because it's bad enough that I have to be under the guy's thumb at work, but I'll be damned if I'm goin' down to Boston just to be looking over my shoulder to see if he's there!" After a minute of silence, he muttered, "Besides, I've been to Boston before."

Pam knew Cutter didn't like John, but she hadn't known the force of his dislike until then. Nor had she known that he'd been to Boston. But before she could ask him about it, a sound in the woods caught her ear. At nearly the same time, Cutter put a cautionary hand on her thigh. Silent and still, they listened. Together, they looked in the direction of the sound.

"What is it?" she whispered.

He leaned closer. She felt the reassuring brush of his arm across her back. "I'm not sure."

"Footsteps?"

"Sounds it."

"Human?"

"Uh-huh."

Their whispers were exchanged over the space of an inch.

"Do you think it's John's spy?"

"No."

"Too obvious?"

"Too small."

"Who is it?"

When Cutter was slow in answering, she looked up at him. His eyes were trained on the woods, looking sharp in a way that was in keeping with the heavy shadow of his beard. So was the firm set of his jaw and the squaring of his chin. She wondered if that squaring was from tension or if it was always there. Funny, she hadn't noticed. She'd always looked at the whole, she guessed.

Then his lips moved. "Bumble," he whispered, and the tension left his features as quickly as it had come.

"What?"

"It's Bumble."

It was a minute before the word registered, a minute more before she realized what he was talking about. Dragging her eyes from his face, she looked off in the direction of the rustling in the woods in time to recognize the small creature who emerged from the trees.

Of the people in Timiny Cove, Pam liked most, disliked a few, and was frightened of one. That one was Bumble. She was a wizened

old lady who dressed in layers of dark clothes even on the hottest of summer days. Pam had always fancied that the clothes were the only things covering her bones, that if she'd ever had any flesh it had disappeared at some point during the course of the 110 years that she'd lived. The age, of course, was based on town gossip and was clearly an exaggeration, still Bumble was eerie. She lived in something that was half underground and not unlike a packrat's midden—but that was town gossip too, since few had ever actually seen where she lived. She appeared to be entirely self-sufficient. She spent her days wandering through the woods gathering plants and herbs, and while she had never harmed anyone or anything, she was given wide berth. No one knew her real name. She was called Bumble after the sound she made when she talked.

Pam leaned closer to Cutter and whispered, "What's she doing here?"

"Looking for mushrooms probably," he whispered back.

"Why here?"

"Because the mushrooms are good here."

"But these aren't her woods. They're yours."

He whispered a chuckle. "Not quite."

"You know what I mean. Cutter, she's coming straight toward us."

"It's okay. She won't hurt you."

"Are you sure?"

"Trust me."

She did, of course. She trusted him with her life. Tucked up against him, she wasn't half as frightened as she'd have been if she were alone.

The old woman didn't stop shuffling until she stood directly before them. Her watery eyes focused on Cutter. Pam felt him nod a greeting. Then Bumble looked at her, and Pam felt skewered. She managed a small smile. "Hello."

Those watery eyes stared at her for what seemed an eternity to Pam. Then a wizened hand came from the pocket of something that looked like a worn gunnysack, which was layered over a faded smock, which was layered over a frayed dress—all three in varying shades of

dun. The hand disappeared into another sack, this one of canvas. It was burgundy and looked far newer than the rest of her.

When the hand came out, it was clutching a sprig of flowers, which she promptly extended to Pam. "Wi'zalis," the little voice buzzed.

"Wild azaleas," Cutter interpreted softly. He gave Pam a gentle nudge at a spot on her back that Bumble couldn't see.

Pam took the flowers. She'd seen wild azaleas in the woods before, but never ones as delicately pink. When Bumble gestured toward her nose, Pam smelled them. Their scent was nearly as delicate as their color.

"Thank you," she said. "They're lovely."

Even before she had the last word out, the old woman turned and resumed her shuffling trek through the woods. Holding the flowers to her nose, Pam watched the wrinkled figure until it blended into the forest and was gone.

"Weird," she whispered then. She rested comfortably against Cutter for another minute before lowering the flowers and looking up at him. What hit her, though, wasn't the intent look on his face but his scent. It was familiar in the way of something long taken for granted, new in the way of an awakening. He didn't smell of aftershave like John, or of leather jacket like Robbie. He smelled of earth and of sweat, of man.

Feeling a fluttering in the pit of her stomach, she drew away from him and stood. Holding the flowers to her nose again, she said, "I should go."

Cutter rose. "Can I take you to supper?"

She couldn't think of anything nicer, but she felt strangely awkward. "We can make something at your place." They'd done that many times, then had eaten out on the porch. It was fun and familiar.

But Cutter shook his head. "I'd like to take you out. I haven't ever done that. You're looking so pretty and grown-up. Let me."

Her heart melted.

"There's a steak place over in Norway," he went on. "We could celebrate your finishing school for the year."

"You don't have to—"

"It may be the last time I'll see you for a while."

Abruptly, she felt close to tears. Just then she would gladly have given up her trip for the few weekends she might have in Timiny Cove. She had passed seven weeks before without seeing Cutter, but never being quite so far away. Only now did she realize the comfort she drew from knowing he was just three hours away.

"Okay," she said softly.

So they went back to his place while he showered and changed, then he took her out to dinner. She had eaten at fancier restaurants and had better food, but she'd never treasured a dinner the way she did this one. The memory of it stayed with her through the long drive back to Boston later that night, and the tense days that followed.

Chapter 13

❖❖❖

JOHN ALLOWED HER TO GO ON the trip. She wondered if he did it because somehow he knew she was having second thoughts herself, but any reservations were gone by the time she was to leave. Hanging around the house for the first time in months, she found herself thinking about the past and the future, brooding about things she couldn't change. She was on edge even when John wasn't at home. She knew that if she spent the summer at home, regardless of how many weekends she spent in Timiny Cove, she would be a basket case come fall.

The trip was fun. Pam easily made friends, saw Yellowstone, the Grand Canyon, San Francisco, Beverly Hills, and Las Vegas. She would have kept going when the seven weeks were finished if it weren't for missing Cutter. And, of course, there was school.

Despite her good intentions, the fall semester didn't get off to quite the start for which she hoped. John was right, she knew. If she paid attention in class, did all the assignments, stayed home and studied more, she would do better. But it was hard to pay attention in class when her mind kept wandering. The same went for homework. There was always something better to do in the afternoons than to study, and as for the evenings, if she could linger at a friend's house so that she didn't have to return to the townhouse and John, she was happier.

She was his whipping boy, the one he lashed out at when any little thing in his own life wasn't quite right. He found fault with what

she was doing, how she was doing it, where she was going, and with whom she was going. He never yelled—he was always in control—but his words were sharp, quite effective in telling her how irresponsible he thought she was. In moments of pique she wondered what she'd done to deserve his torment, but when those moments settled and she thought clearly again, she knew. She was Eugene's daughter. John took one look at her and was defensive. By the same token, he had come to represent everything negative in her life.

Come late October, when her midterm grades came in, he imposed a weekday curfew. When three nights running she dashed in late filled with excuses, he took the car away for a week, but that didn't slow her down. She simply arranged for transportation with her friends. On various occasions he threatened to cut off her allowance, to disconnect her phone, to sell her car—but none of that would have crippled her. John was the materialistic one, far more so than she. There were things that meant more to her than a telephone or a car.

It took him a while, but he finally came to that realization. So when her term grades arrived at the end of December showing no sign of improvement, when she came in at two in the morning from a party he'd told her not to attend, when she ran off the next day on a ski trip to Vermont without asking permission, he lowered the boom.

"Enough," he declared from the door of her room the evening after she returned. "From now on, I want you home for dinner and the evening on weeknights. You can do what you want when you're here. If you don't want to eat, you don't have to eat. If you don't want to study, you don't have to study. And you can do what you want on the weekends—come and go as you please, go to Maine, whatever."

Pam held more tightly to the book she was reading. It was *Love Story*. She had started it while she'd been away, when the others had driven off to another party and she hadn't felt like going. She was thoroughly caught up in the pathos, or had been until John had intruded. Now, listening to him, she waited for the other shoe to fall. Nothing he had said so far was particularly new or upsetting, but she had an uneasy feeling that something was coming.

"I don't like feeling foolish when I tell you to do something, and

you don't," he went on in such a reasonable tone that her unease grew. "I've had it with laying down laws you ignore. I can't watch you every hour of the day. It's time you show some responsibility. You'll be seventeen in a few months."

She waited. He was making her nervous by deliberately drawing out his ultimatum.

"All I ask," he said finally, "is that you make honor roll at school."

"All," she echoed.

"It's not so much. You're not dumb. Just unmotivated."

She thought about that for a minute before saying slowly, "If the problem is motivation, what's to make the difference?"

"Responsibility. I'm wiping my hands of it. It's all in your lap. It's your responsibility to make the honor roll."

"And if I don't?" She held her breath.

"If you don't, I'll do two things. First, I'll fire Marcy. Then I'll sell the house in Timiny Cove."

Pam sat forward so suddenly that the book tumbled to the carpet, but she didn't notice. "You wouldn't."

"I would." His dark eyes gleamed. "Make honor roll, or Marcy will be out of a job. She can look for another, but she'll have trouble matching the pay I give her. Besides, she'll have a hard time of it with no letter of recommendation."

"You *wouldn't*."

"I would."

"But I love Marcy!"

"I know. Did you know she's been helping her mother out with what I give her? If I let her go, it's done. Do you want the responsibility of that on your shoulders?"

Pam didn't, not in a million years. The look of horror on her face must have encouraged him, because he went on more smugly. "As far as the house in Timiny Cove goes, it's superfluous anyway. I make day trips mostly. The house has outlived its usefulness."

"But *I* use it!" Pam cried. She was trembling inside and with good cause; the scaffolding around the frail fabric of her life had been shaken. "I love that house. Daddy loved that house."

"Daddy's dead," he mocked coldly.

"But it's all I have of him!"

"Fine. Make honor roll, and I'll keep it."

"John," she pleaded.

"Make honor roll, Pam. It's all in your hands." Before she could do more than cry his name again, he left the room.

Her first impulse was to run after him and tell him exactly what she thought of him, but then she thought of Marcy and quickly reconsidered. Her second impulse was to grab her coat and keys and go out, but it was Thursday night, and although she was still on vacation, it was a weeknight. Her third impulse was to call Hillary—but Hillary was in New York, and besides, John wouldn't listen to her when it came to something like this. He felt that he'd found the way to make Pam toe his mark, and maybe he had.

Her fourth impulse was to call Cutter. But Cutter didn't have a phone. So she had to settle for leaving first thing Saturday morning for Maine. It was noontime before she arrived and three in the afternoon before Cutter pulled up in the small pickup he'd bought the year before. She had been pacing the inside of his cabin for three hours and was in a mood to beat all moods when he arrived.

"You need a phone, Cutter!" she cried the minute he opened the door. She knew she looked a little wild, but that was just how she felt. "I've been needing to talk with you since Thursday night, and I couldn't! Can't you get one? You've made so many other improvements around here, and a phone doesn't cost that much. I'll pay for it if you want. I have to talk with you sometimes!"

Cutter was standing in the open doorway, caught short by her outcry. Closing the door behind him, he crossed to where she stood, but when he tried to touch her she batted his hand away.

"I'm serious, Cutter. I was stuck in that house and couldn't go anywhere because of John's threats, and the one thing that might have helped was talking with you. But I couldn't." Again he reached for her; again she stepped away. "I thought of sending a message through Simon, but if I'd done that, he'd have called John in a minute. Same with Leroy or any of the others. They're all afraid of him."

Cutter came toward her once again, but this time she wheeled around and went to the window. It was too clean, clearly depicting the winter woods dappled with patches of snow. What wasn't cold and white was dismally gray, perfectly matching her mood. "A telephone isn't such a big deal," she cried, hugging herself against the chill. "I mean, I couldn't call you. I couldn't call Hillary. I could call my friends as much as I wanted, except they don't understand what I'm feeling. They aren't the ones living with a sadistic monster. They aren't walking a tightrope. They may have fights with their parents, but at least they have parents!" She whirled to face him. "More than anyone else, you would have understood, but I couldn't talk with you!"

When he next started toward her, she made for the kitchen, but he'd had enough of her evasion. A long arm reached out and snagged her. She tugged, but he tugged right back, bringing her fully against him. She tried to twist away, but he wouldn't allow it.

"Cutter!"

"Easy, babe."

"I wanted to talk with you!" she protested, but her words were muffled in the sheepskin lining of his jacket, and her will to fight was dying fast.

"I'm here now," he said in a low, soothing voice. "Calm down. You're all tight and shaking. Relax, Pam."

She felt his hands on her back, coaxing the tremors from her, while his cheek rubbed the top of her head. Slipping her arms inside his jacket, she took a deep breath and let herself be sedated by his strength and his scent.

"Oh, Cutter," she murmured.

His lips brushed her forehead. "Better?"

"Mmmm." She listened to the steady beat of his heart. "Pretty stupid of me, huh, to start in on you like that when you were the one I came to see?"

"Y'could say that."

"I thought the weekend would never come. I've never been so impatient to get here in my life."

"John didn't give you trouble about coming?"

"Oh, no. I now have carte blanche as far as that goes now."

He looked down at her. "He'll let you come up here whenever you want?"

"On weekends." Reluctantly she dropped her hands from his waist. This time when she left him, she sank into the easy chair opposite the foot of the bed. From there, hands folded like the demure young lady she hadn't been acting, she explained John's terms. As she talked, the brief peace she'd found in Cutter's arms dissipated. By the time she was finished, her hands were fluttering in the air to emphasize her protest. "Have you ever heard anything so cruel? Marcy's job is dependent on my grades! I mean, it boggles my mind! And the house here—he'd actually sell it to spite me!"

Having removed his jacket, Cutter was sitting on the foot of the bed, his legs spread wide, elbows on his thighs. "Sounds like he'd have sold it awhile back if it hadn't been for you."

"No. If he'd wanted to sell it before, he would have."

"Then he wouldn't have had it to use as a lever. Don't you see, Pam? That's what he does. He finds what it is that means most to people, then threatens to take it away if they don't comply with his demands."

"But what's so critical about my getting good grades?"

Cutter clasped his hands between his knees. "You're smart. You could be doing better than you are."

"But what does it matter? I did well on my SATs. I'll get into a decent school. Why is it so all-fired important that I make honor roll?" Her eyes were glued to his face. She couldn't figure out his expression. "Why, Cutter?"

"Because you can do it."

"But I don't want to. I don't care about grades. They just don't matter to me. I don't like my classes, and I don't see the point in killing myself for the sake of a mark."

"You wouldn't have to kill yourself and you know it. All you'd have to do is to pay attention in class. You're quick, Pam. And you do like your classes—at least some of them. You like French, and you really like English. You don't want to admit it, because you think that

would be capitulating to John, but I don't see why you're sabotaging yourself because of him. You could graduate at the top of your class if you wanted to."

She learned forward in disbelief. "What are you saying?"

His voice was gruff. "I think I said it pretty clearly."

"You want me to study? You want me to do well in school? You want me to join that . . . that rat race worrying about grade-point average and class rank? Cutter," she protested heatedly, "what's with you?" When he didn't answer, she said, "You didn't think school was so terrific when you were going through it. You skipped it whenever you could and dropped out the day you turned sixteen. You didn't care about grades or class rank or college. It was fine for you to do what you wanted. Why is it so awful for me to want to do the same thing?"

He had straightened and was looking appalled. "Is that what you've been doing—following my example?"

"Not directly, but what was okay for you should be okay for me."

"Well, it isn't!" he declared. Rising from the bed, he stalked halfway across the room before turning back to glare at her. "I skipped school because I thought I was stupid, and I didn't like feeling stupid. I decided I didn't need that any more than I needed parents. I could make it on my own." He took a tight breath. "The truth is that I was scared shitless of life, and angry at the world and everyone in it for making me scared. Do you know that I actually liked it when Verne locked me up for a night? I was in a warm, safe place and there was someone else near. I'd have bought prison for a lifetime sooner or later if it hadn't been for your daddy. He put me to work and made me feel less afraid and more sure of what I was doing, but by that time I was too old for school. I was a working man. The life I knew and trusted was goin' back and forth to the mountain each day."

"Is it so awful?" she asked. She hadn't thought Cutter was unhappy.

"It's not awful at all, which is why I keep doin' it. But I'm missing things, Pam. I'm not stupid like I thought. I like to read. I do it all the time." The only clutter in his cabin was the reading matter piled on his

shelves. "I'd have been embarrassed to say that a few years back, but not now. I can understand things to do with the company, or things to do with the economy or the government that the old coots sittin' over at the bench on the green can't understand. If I'd gone to school when I was supposed to, if I'd paid attention and tried once in a while, I'd'a made something of my life."

Pam was out of her chair like a shot. "You have made something. You're—"

"A miner," he cut in with a grunt of disgust. "I've been a miner for the last eight years and I'll be one for the next eight and the eight after that. I'm not going anywhere, Pam. If I'd been smarter when it mattered, I might'a gone to college. But it's too late for that, too. So I'm stuck in a rut."

She tried to take his hand, but he turned away. Grabbing a log, he hunkered down before the wood stove to push it inside. "I'm not moving, Pam, but you are. You've got a future ahead of you. You can do well in school and go on to college, then you can work in the company way up there at the top of the ladder. I'll never be able to do that. Don't you see? I'm down here at the bottom. I'll always be down here at the bottom. I ain't got nuthin' to boost me up."

Pam ached for him. Squatting before the stove with his head down, he looked defeated. "That's not true. You have a record for eight years of good, hard work. You could be a supervisor—"

"Not under John. Maybe if Eugene were alive, but there's no way John would move me up."

"I could ask," she offered, and would have done it in a minute if the look he shot her hadn't been so quelling. Her asking John for a promotion on Cutter's behalf would be asking for trouble for them both, and anyway, Cutter had too much pride to let her do it.

"I thought you didn't want to be a supervisor. That's what you told me once."

"It was a long time ago. Things have changed."

"What things?" she asked more quietly. When he didn't answer, she grabbed a handful of his hair. It fell thick on his neck and was perfect for tugging. "Tell me, Cutter. What things?"

He twisted on the balls of his feet to face her directly then, and she almost wished she hadn't pushed. His look was so intense that her insides quivered.

"If I was a somebody—"

"You *are* a somebody—"

"If I was a somebody—" He cut himself off this time.

"What?" she prodded.

He stared at her for another agonizing minute before giving a short shake of his head. Hands on his thighs, he pushed himself up. "Nothing."

"What were you going to say?"

He went to the refrigerator. "And anyway, being a supervisor at the mine isn't what I'm talking about." He popped open a beer and took a swallow. Reaching in again before the door swung shut, he tossed her a can of Coke. "I'm talking about moving up and out. Getting a fancy apartment or buying a house. Wearing a shirt and tie. Driving a sports car. Traveling."

"You can do all that."

"How? I'm not trained for a damned thing besides mining, and even if I was, I don't have any degree. Pick up the papers any day and see who the big men in business are. Most of them went to college and graduate school. I didn't finish high school."

"So go back and finish. You could do it. You could go to college—"

"Not now."

"Why?"

"I'm too old."

"You're barely twenty-four! Loads of people are still in school at that age."

"Not high school."

"You could do it if you wanted." Coke can in hand, she went to the refrigerator and nudged him aside. "No one's stopping you."

"But I have a job here. What are you doing, Pam?"

"Getting a beer."

"I keep the Coke for you."

"So keep it for another time. I want a beer." Fully aware that he was watching, she popped the tab and took a swallow.

Cutter leaned back against the sink. "You do that pretty smoothly. Go to lots of beer parties?"

"Some."

"It's fun, huh? Kind of defiant? Makes you feel big?"

"You should know. You've been drinking beer for years."

"And I'll be drinking it long after you've outgrown it and moved on to wine. That's what I'm trying to say, Pam. What I'm doing now, I'll be doing for the rest of my life, but you—you have the whole world open in front of you. You're still growing. There'll come a time, not too far off, when you won't want to be up here. You'll have a full life in the city—"

"Never a full life there. Part of me was meant to be here."

"But your future is there. You'll be part of the business someday. You won't have time to go for walks in the woods—"

"With you, always."

He shook his head. "You're growing up. Your life is just starting. You're going to go back to Boston and get those good grades—not because of John's threats but because you want to. You'll go to college, then go into the business, and somewhere along the way you'll meet someone just as smart and successful as you are. You'll get married and have kids, and once in a while you'll bring them up here and show them to me, only I'll be exactly the same then as I am now."

That wasn't at all how Pam imagined it. "You're wrong. I may go to college, and I'll surely go into the business, but I'm not getting married so quickly." She tipped up her chin. "I'm waiting for you."

"Waiting for what?"

"You to get married."

"I won't ever."

"Then I won't either."

"That's the craziest thing I ever heard."

"No more crazy than your not getting married or not going back to school or not getting a better job if that's what you want. Not that

you need a better job. The one you have now is just fine. It's honest and it's important."

"You say that because you're young and idealistic."

"For God's sake, Cutter, you're only seven years older than I."

"Seven years and a lifetime."

She rolled her eyes. "Please."

He regarded her for a long time. "You don't get it, do you?"

"Get what?"

"What I'm trying to say."

"You're saying that I'm going places and you're not, but you're wrong."

Coming away from the sink, he took her chin in his hand. His voice vibrated with feeling. "I'm saying that if things were different, if I hadn't thrown it all away because I was young and dumb and scared, I'd have a chance with you now. You're the only girl I've ever met who I'd think of marrying, but I'm all wrong for you."

Pam's heart had started to pound against her ribs. "No—"

"You're poised and polished. You've got money. You've got class and breeding." His thumb brushed her mouth. She felt its touch deep inside her. "Me, I've got nothing but this house, a pickup, and a job. Sure, I've got a little money in the bank, but not so much that it would make a difference. We're from opposite sides of the track."

"There's no track here," she argued, nearly breathless because he was so close to her. "That's what Daddy proved. He had money, but he was always one of the miners, and he was happiest that way. I'm the same. I'm happiest when I'm up here."

Cutter seemed distracted following the movement of his thumb on her mouth. "You won't be. Not forever." He took a shaky breath. "There are times when I wish—"

She was barely breathing now. "Wish what?"

His thumb skimmed the new glow on her cheek.

"What, Cutter?"

"There are times—" he faltered, brought his thumb all the way around her cheek to her jaw, then went on in a smoky tone, "times when I wish I could take you away someplace where it wouldn't

matter who you were or who I was—" His voice broke off, but his eyes stayed on her mouth.

Pam had kissed and been kissed before. But she'd never felt the sudden need for both that she felt then.

Cutter stepped back.

Grabbing his hand before it reached his side, she carried it to her mouth and held tight. Her eyes were wide and pleading.

But he shook his head.

"Why not?" she whispered.

"I won't start something I can't finish."

"You can finish it."

He squeezed his eyes shut. "No."

"You can, Cutter. I want you to."

"You don't know what you want."

"I want you to kiss me."

His eyes came open, dark and dangerous. "I want to do more than that."

"You *can*."

Suddenly his hands were against her scalp, immobilizing her head while his heat immobilized her body. "Listen to me, Pam. We're not playing games here. Making love is serious business."

"I know. Lots of my friends have—"

"Have you?"

"With the guys at home? No way!"

"So you're a virgin."

"I want to do it with you."

"No."

"Why not?"

"No!"

"It's okay, really it is."

"*No!*" He took a breath. "No. And if you can't accept that, we won't be able to see each other. Is that what you want?"

She felt teary. "You know it isn't."

"Then I don't want to hear any more about it. We've discussed it. We've decided. It's done." He looked at her for a minute longer, then,

swearing softly, hugged her hard. "You're enough to drive a sane man mad, Pam."

She didn't answer. She was too busy breathing him and feeling him, storing up memories for the time when she was back home.

Those memories came in handy in the weeks that followed. Seeing no way out of her predicament, Pam spent more time at home than ever before. Her room became her haven. She talked on the phone some with her friends, but the frivolity of it was gone. She slept some, daydreamed some, brooded some. Mostly she studied. John had put the weight of responsibility on her shoulders, and she felt it keenly.

She didn't see him much at first. True to his word, he seemed to have stopped playing watchdog. He had told her the rules and was doing whatever it was he did with his time while she abided by them. If anyone was her guard, it was school. Her midterm report would be telling.

Her grades rose dramatically. Pam was relieved to know she could do it, and in that sense the pressure eased. It didn't go away, though. John wasn't satisfied simply to know that she could do well; he wanted her to do it on a regular basis. He made it clear what would happen if she didn't.

He also made it clear that he was pleased with her progress. She suspected it was his own cleverness that pleased him most—he had effectively, and painlessly on his part, brought her to heel—but the fact that he was less odious than usual was some solace. He took her to dinner at the Ritz when she received those first improved grades, even invited her to several business functions. He took to stopping by her room when he came home from work, then again before he went to bed, and while she told herself that he was just checking up on her, there seemed more to it. He was actually being pleasant.

"How's it going with Mrs. Ditmar?" he asked one night. Mrs. Ditmar was the American-literature teacher with whom Pam had locked horns at the start of the year.

Pam was propped against the headboard of her bed. A pencil was in her hand, a notebook on her lap, a textbook beside her. Wary as

ever at John's appearance, she held the pencil more tightly. "Not bad. She's mellowed, I think. Or maybe I'm just getting used to her style."

"That was a nice paper you wrote for her last week."

"You read it?"

He nodded. "You left it on top of your books in the kitchen. I always liked Steinbeck. *The Grapes of Wrath* was long—all my friends complained—but it was my favorite."

"I liked it, too."

"That came through in the paper. You write well, Pam. Clear and concise. You organize your thoughts nicely."

She nodded her thanks and looked down at her notebook. She felt awkward, not quite sure if he was being patronizing and in any case not knowing what to say or do.

"I got a call from Jennifer's mother before." As Pam looked up at him, he went on, "She wondered if we'd reached a decision on spring break. You didn't tell me they invited you to their villa on Nevis."

"I didn't tell you because I don't want to go. Jennifer started mentioning it last fall, and she won't let it rest. I've given her every excuse in the book."

"So I gathered. Her mother said that if I was worried, she'd see that you put in some time every day studying so you'll make the honor roll." He arched a brow. "That's going a little too far, don't you think?"

"I guess, but I didn't know what else to say."

"Why don't you want to go?"

She began to doodle on her notebook. "Jennifer's been getting on my nerves lately. She's so silly sometimes and we're not that close anymore. It'd be pretty hypocritical of me to use her to get to the Caribbean, when I wouldn't even want to go on a weekend trip to New York with her."

"How about a weekend trip to New York with me? I thought I'd go down to see Hillary. We could do some shopping, maybe take in a show. What do you think?"

Pam didn't know what to think. He'd never offered to take her away before. She searched his face for some sign of teasing or sarcasm

or even treachery, but he looked perfectly sincere. "Uh, won't I be in the way? I mean, you'll want to spend time with Hillary."

"I could take a suite at the Pierre. If you want, we could even go down to Palm Beach from there. I can always drum up some business while you lie in the sun."

She wavered. The last person she had imagined vacationing with was John. But she loved New York. And she loved Hillary. And she loved the idea of working up a tan. She had hoped to spend part of the vacation in Maine, but only part. Being with Cutter, while necessary to her survival, brought an odd kind of torment now. It might be nice to have a diversion from that.

"You have two weeks," John pointed out.

"I really should study," she pointed out right back.

"You're studying plenty here."

"But if I don't make honor roll—"

"Going away for spring break won't affect that. It's not like you'll be partying all night and waking up every morning hung over." He seemed to catch himself, and for the first time his expression darkened. "Unless you think you'll be bored."

"Of course not. John, I don't live to party, and I've never once been hung over."

The darkness eased. With its passing, she almost imagined he had been hurt to think she might not want to go. Given that they hadn't been a family for years, it was a fanciful thought.

"I'd like to go to New York," she surprised herself by saying. "And Palm Beach. I've never been there. It would be fun."

A good deal of Pam's fun lay in anticipating the trip. In a school as private and elite as hers was, everyone went away for spring break. Most went with their families, and Pam had always envied them. This time, she was looking forward to a family trip of her own. "My brother and I are going to New York, then on to Palm Beach," she told whoever wanted to know. It didn't matter that her brother had been her enemy for most of her life; there was something right about being with family.

She almost imagined that John felt the same way. In the weeks preceding the trip, he was uncharacteristically affable. He asked questions about school, not in the grilling way she hated but as though he were truly interested. He engaged her in discussions about the business. He complimented her on the way she looked. He even came home with a pair of gold bangles that he had had one of *Facets'* designers make especially for her.

"It's weird," she told Marcy the day before she and John were to leave. "All this just because I started studying?"

Marcy carefully wiped the corners of the window she was cleaning. After a thoughtful silence she said, "He's proud of you."

"He's never been proud of me before."

"But he puts store in school marks. They mean something to him. The pictures you draw don't."

Pam knew that, which was why she didn't show him the things she showed Cutter. "Still, he's been so polite. He actually held my coat for me when we were going out last week. There has to be a reason."

Marcy considered that while she cleaned another pane. "He's getting older. Maybe he's tired of the fighting."

"Maybe."

"And you're getting older. Maybe he sees that."

No doubt he saw the physical growth. But he hadn't relented on his threat, which Pam thought he'd surely do if he trusted her as an adult. Of course, Marcy knew nothing about that threat, and Pam had no intention of telling her.

"Maybe." She took a deep breath. "He's probably thinking that when I turn eighteen I'll be able to control my own stock in the company. I'll be attending shareholders' meetings. I could make things tough for him. Maybe he's scared." It was a lovely thought, to have a little power for a change.

Moving to another pane, Marcy wet it with her sponge. "Don't jinx it, Pammy. The peace is good."

Pam agreed, which was why she stopped asking questions and left with John the next morning for New York. Even more so than she had expected, he did things first class. The suite at the Pierre was large and

sumptuous, the restaurants they ate at were lavish in food and decor, their theater seats were front and center. Although Hillary spent the weekend with them, John never left Pam alone, and while one part of Pam felt guilty about that, the other enjoyed the attention.

Monday morning, Pam and John flew south. Again their accommodations were without fault, and although John did leave Pam by the pool while he saw to business, she was happy enough there not to mind. The sun was bright, the water warm, the lifeguard friendly. She was feeling grown-up and attractive when John took her out to dinner, particularly when he kept her wineglass filled. He smiled at her with what she could have sworn was true affection, brushed a long wisp of hair from her bare shoulder, even put an arm around her as they left. She felt sheltered and cared for, warm and content, when, muzzied by the wine, she fell asleep on top of the covers.

She didn't know what time it was when she woke up. The room was dark, and she was on her stomach, but John's voice came to her quickly. It was low and gentle. "You're still dressed, honey. That's no way to sleep." She felt her zipper open, felt the air whisper over her back.

"I can do it," she murmured, but she was too groggy to move.

"I've got it."

He slipped the dress down past her hips, rolled her over, and took it off. When he started on her stockings, she made a slurred protest. "John, really—"

"Let me. It's my fault. I should have known you weren't used to drinking."

Exhausted, she lay back and let herself be taken care of. It had been a long time since anyone had catered to her quite so intimately. The luxury of it sent her off into a dreamy state. She imagined that Cutter was with her, that he was the one rolling down her stockings, unhooking her garter belt, removing her bra, then her panties. She imagined that his hands were the ones touching her body lightly and sweetly, making her moan.

When she opened her eyes, though, Cutter wasn't the one looming

over her. "John?" She fought for clarity. It was dark, hard to see. "John? Oh, my God!" She tried to scramble away, but he held her to him.

"No, no," he whispered. "Don't be frightened. You liked what I was doing."

She twisted away. "You shouldn't—we shouldn't—" He followed the twist and took her breast in his hand. "Don't, John!"

"It'll be good." His mouth was against her throat. "I'll make it good."

"No!" She writhed against the arm that restrained her, bucked against the one that slid down her body. "God, John, *don't do that!*"

"If you fight, it'll hurt."

Fully awake and aware that she was a poor match for his strength, Pam clawed at the hand that had slipped between her legs. "God no, God no, God no," she whispered. She twisted and turned, tried to get a foothold on the bed and push herself away, but he was half on top of her, his semiclad body large and hard as a rock. "You're my *brother*. You can't do this, John! Don't, oh, please *don't!*"

"Lie still, Pam," he warned.

But she had no cause to listen. There was nothing he could threaten her with that would be worse than rape. That realization brought her a burst of strength. "Get your hands off me!" she screamed. When he covered her mouth, she bit his hand, then took advantage of his surprise by bringing her knee up against him. Her aim was off; the angle wasn't right and she didn't have enough room to put force into the blow, but she startled him enough to buy a minute. That was all she needed. Scrambling out from under him, she scurried to the edge of the bed, fell to her knees on the floor, then staggered to her feet. A split second later, she was in the bathroom with the door locked.

It seemed an agonized forever before she caught her breath. Then, wrapping her hands over her head, she slid down the length of the door, huddled in a ball, and began to cry. Nausea, revulsion, fear, horror—she suffered them all. Soft, tortured sobs shook her. At some point, feeling chilled to the bone, she swaddled herself in a bath sheet, but that did little to help. She had no idea what to do.

"Pam?" His voice came to her after a time, low and somber.

She didn't answer.

"You can't stay in there all night, Pam."

For lack of a viable alternative, that was just what she planned to do.

"You'll have to come out sometime."

The thought of looking him in the eye after what he'd seen and done sent a new wave of nausea through her.

"I'll call the concierge if I have to." He knocked hard on the door. "Are you all right?"

"I feel sick."

"That's the wine. Open the door. I'll give you an ice cube to suck."

"It's not the wine," she murmured, but for a minute she wasn't sure. What had happened was horrendous enough to have been unreal. She would have given anything to believe she'd been hallucinating.

The hallucination, though, was all that had come before—the attentiveness, the compliments, the seemingly genuine interest—and in that, John had been at his cruelest. He had led her to think that they might be a family, when all along he had other things in mind.

He was sick. She had to get away from him. But sitting in a locked bathroom wasn't going to do it.

Leaning heavily against the sink, she rinsed her face with cold water. Then she tied the hotel's thick terrycloth robe around her, picked up the shoeshine machine, and opened the bathroom door.

John was sprawled in the bedroom chair looking dark and disheveled. His head was low, but he was staring at her. Holding the makeshift weapon at the ready, she flipped on the nearest light.

"I want to go home."

"We have reservations to stay for two more days."

She gave a rigid shake of her head. "Tomorrow. I want to be on the first flight out."

"It's not necessary."

"I think it is."

"I won't touch you."

"I can't trust you."

His eyes drilled her. "It was the wine, Pam. We both had too much."

"I had too much. You planned it that way."

"No. I was enjoying myself. I had more than I should have, and then when I saw you lying like that on the bed—"

"Don't," she interrupted, cringing. "Don't say it. It's sick."

At the last word, his jaw clenched. "There could be an argument made," he said slowly, "as to which one of us is sick. You've been leading me on ever since I mentioned this trip. You've been playing up to me—"

"I have not!"

"—looking sweet and sexy. You may be seventeen, but you acted like twenty-five tonight. The way you were writhing when I was trying to get you ready for bed was indecent. Is there a problem that I don't know about, Pam?"

She was aghast. "I don't have any problem. You're the one—"

"Your mother was like that. She came on to me too."

"You lie!" Pam cried.

"No. She was a hungry bitch."

"Don't *say* that."

"Ask her, if you don't believe me."

Pam's stomach was churning, pushing her anger up and out. "I can't ask her and you know it! She's too fragile. And anyway, it's not true. It's one more thing your sick mind has dreamed up." Her voice shook. "You're the one with the problem, John. You've always had a problem, but this time you've gone too far. I'm not forgetting what happened tonight. What you tried was disgusting. It was immoral and illegal. It was *sick*. As soon as I get back to Boston, I'm going to report you—"

"To who?" he asked, but he didn't look particularly upset, which made her madder.

"To the police. To Bob Grossman. To my guidance counselor."

"I don't think so."

"Why not?" she asked indignantly.

"Because given your age and the mental instability on your

mother's side, they'll never believe you. They'll think you're a hysterical young girl, lashing out at the brother who is trying to keep you on track. They'll think you need psychiatric help. You'll be taken for a fool."

Pam swallowed hard and shook her head. "They'll listen to me."

"But you haven't got any proof, Pam. There are no bruises on your body. And you're still a virgin."

"How do *you* know that?"

"Precisely." He gave a silky smile. "I don't know for sure, but a doctor will. If you've given it away, we'll know that it wasn't to me. But I'll want to know who you did give it to, so I'll go to your school. I'll question your friends and their parents. I'll make a lot of noise about my 'wronged' sister. Mmmm, I'll relish playing the role of the injured brother. It would add a nice twist to the image."

"You're sick," Pam whispered, but despair was creeping up on her fast. She was a virgin, of course, so John's threat was empty. By virtue of the same fact, though, no one would believe what he'd tried to do. He was right: she didn't have any proof. And much as she wanted to think differently, his credibility was greater than hers. People would believe what he said.

She was back to square one, without any idea of what to do. The problem was temporarily alleviated when all that had been churning in her stomach came up. She ran to the bathroom in time to be violently sick and stayed there until John appeared at the door.

"Go to bed, Pam," he said in a coldly familiar voice. "And don't worry. I won't touch you. You're pretty unappealing this way."

By the time she mustered the strength to turn her head, he had disappeared into his own room and shut the door.

Chapter 14

❖❖❖

PAM BARELY SLEPT THAT NIGHT. Although she bolted her door, she didn't trust that John wouldn't find a way in. And even apart from that fear was the memory of what he'd done. No sooner did she doze off than the image of his hand on her flesh jolted her awake. She was alternately nauseated, shaky, and tearful. By the time she boarded the plane for Boston the next morning, she felt as though she'd been through the wringer. Back in the townhouse, she was pale and wan and had little to say about the trip.

After watching her silently suffer through a kitchen dinner she barely touched, Marcy finally spoke up. "What happened down there?"

Pam's eyes shot to hers. "Down where?"

"In Palm Beach."

Pam shrugged and looked away. "It was a disappointing trip. That's all."

But Marcy's voice held quiet conviction. "It was more than that." She was still for a long minute. "He touched you."

Pam didn't take the time to wonder how she knew. Her head came up again along with a quick denial. "He didn't do anything."

"But he tried." Marcy was still for another long minute, then her voice rose in remorse. "I should'a known. I should'a warned you."

"He didn't do anything."

"B'cause you fought him off."

Pam shrank into herself.

For one who rarely did anything with great speed, Marcy was surprisingly fast into the chair beside her. "Talk about it, Pammy. You can't keep it inside."

"It's ugly."

"The good Lord knows I've seen ugly before. Jarvis taught me all I had to know about that."

Pam's eyes widened. "He hit you, but he didn't—"

"He tried. More'n once. That was another reason your daddy wanted me out of there."

"Oh, Marcy," Pam whispered, feeling sick, "I didn't know."

"There was no need for you to know then. But you know now, so you know I know what you're feeling." She took her hand. "Tell me."

Needing to confide in someone, Pam did. At the end, she said pleadingly, "Did I ask for it? I went out of my way to be nice because it felt so good to be a family. He was pleased, so I was pleased. Did I go too far? Did I lead him on?"

"No."

"I didn't mean to."

"You didn't lead him on!"

"He's my brother. I'd never do something like that with my own brother. I've never done it with anyone." But she wanted to. She wanted to do it with Cutter, and each time she was with him she felt the pull more. Now she couldn't even tell him about John. He'd be livid. "What am I going to do, Marcy? I can't sleep. I can't eat. I feel sick."

Marcy stroked her hand. "When is he coming back?"

"I don't know. We didn't talk this morning. He just handed me my ticket and looked at me like I was dirt."

"He's trying to make you feel to blame for what happened, but you're not, Pammy. He is. There's something wrong with that man."

His words kept crowding her mind. "He said I was like my mother. He said she came on to him, too. Did you ever see her do that?"

"I never saw anything," Marcy said immediately.

"When I threatened to tell what he did, he said no one would believe me, and he's right. I don't have any proof. But I can't stay here

anymore, Marcy. I can't live in the same house with him." She had
been agonizing over the problem for hours. "I'd move up to Timiny
Cove and live there, but he'd never allow it."

"You should be here with your friends at school."

Pam wanted that. She had two more months to go in her junior
year, then her whole senior year. It wasn't the time to transfer. "I'll
have to board. The dean will let me do it if there's space." When Marcy
looked stricken, she hurried on. "I don't want to. I'll miss you. If there
were any other solution, I'd take it, but there isn't one. John would
never let me live in an apartment. I can't just move in with a friend and
her family without explanations, and I can't make the explanations."

"The school will ask."

"I'll say I want to try out dorm living before I go to college."

"Will John fight you?"

Pam had asked herself that more than once, and each time she felt
stymied. "I can't prove what he did. He didn't get far enough—"

"Thank the good Lord."

"And it only happened once. If I make noise about it, he can say
I'm mentally unbalanced." She raised her chin a notch. "But if I make
noise, he'll feel it. People will wonder. It'll embarrass all of us, but if
John gives me trouble, so help me, I'll do it. He makes a big thing of
his image. If he wants to protect it, he'll let me move into the dorm."

John returned two days later. By then, Pam had spoken with the
school, found a place in the dorm, and made arrangements to move in
at the end of spring break, given John's approval. He gave it, but not
without a parting shot. "The same rules apply," he sneered. "Honor
roll, or else."

For a brief minute, Pam considered countering with a threat of her
own. She ached to call his bluff. But she couldn't. Marcy's well-being
was at stake, as was the house in Timiny Cove. Tarnishing John's im-
age was nothing compared to the loss of either of those.

The days that followed were long and tense. John seemed to take
pleasure being around her, eyeing her in his scornful way, knowing
that his presence was a threat. She couldn't move into the dorm until

the Sunday night before classes resumed. Meanwhile, she was stuck at home.

She spent a good deal of time trying to persuade Marcy to look for another job. "Daddy hired you for me as much as for the house. If I won't be here, what's the point of your staying? You could be doing the same work for someone far more reasonable than John."

"He pays me well, Pam. I couldn't match that somewhere else."

"Would it be so terrible to take less money?"

"I need it."

"For your mother?"

Marcy nodded. "Things are real bad between her and Jarvis. I give her everything I can."

Judging from what she saw, Pam believed that. Marcy lived simply. She bought few clothes, cut her own hair, and most often spent her days off babysitting for the three-year-old son of the housekeeper who worked around the corner. "I could help."

Marcy shook her head. "You don't have extra money."

"I do too. I don't need all I have."

"I won't take your money!"

"Then let me make some calls. Someone must need help—either my friends' parents or one of my mother's old friends. Maybe the pay wouldn't be so bad."

"But the freedom wouldn't be the same. I get up to Timiny Cove one or two times a month to tend to the house. John pays me, but I get to go home, too, and he lets me use the car. He even helps out with the medical bills at my ma's. I can't afford to quit, Pammy."

That was pretty much what John had told Pam, and it angered her. Cutter was right: John bought people; he gave them what they badly needed, then held the threat of withdrawal over their heads. She wanted only the best for Marcy, but the day when she could guarantee it herself was a long way off.

Everything good seemed a long way off. Pam brooded on that during the nighttime hours when she lay awake with her eyes on the bedroom door. She felt constrained and defenseless. If she were older,

she'd be safe. She'd have money to use at her own discretion. She'd come and go at will. She'd be free of John.

If she were older, she'd have Cutter. She would be in a position to offer him a place in the company, and he'd do well. He was too smart not to. He could wear a tie and jacket as well as the next man.

She thought about that a lot. She pictured him dressed up, driving a sports car, pouring scotch into a glass in the waterfront apartment he might have if he was working in Boston. She pictured him approaching her, looking urbane and sexy—but the image was superimposed by one of him in his cabin in Timiny Cove, wearing nothing but jeans, his hair rumpled, his jaw shadowed. Urbanity couldn't improve on his sex appeal, she decided. Thoughts of him just as she'd always known him made her feel restless and achy inside.

Still, she resisted going to Maine. Being with Cutter, wanting him badly but knowing that he wouldn't even kiss her, was agony. So she stayed home during that first weekend after her return from Palm Beach, and kept busy getting ready to move into the dorm. By the second weekend, though, she had done everything there was to do, and she was on edge. She was tense from the minute John walked in the door to the minute he left, and she hadn't once slept the night through.

So, early Saturday morning she left for Timiny Cove. Cutter was out when she reached his place. She pictured him buying food or browsing for books or getting a haircut. In a way, she was glad to be alone. She was dead tired.

Climbing into his bed, she pulled the sheets and blankets up to her neck and, wrapped in his scent, was asleep in minutes.

For a time, her sleep was deep and dreamless. Then, as had happened every night since Palm Beach, the nightmare of John's assault brought her awake with a cry. It was a minute before she realized that she wasn't in Boston, another before she realized that the man whose arms flanked her shaking body wasn't John.

"Cutter," she whispered. Sitting up, she threw her arms around his neck and held on tight. "God, I was dreaming awful things."

He hugged her close, ran a soothing hand over her back. Slowly

she stopped trembling, but still she clung to him. For the first time in days, she felt secure.

"It's been so long," he said, voicing her thoughts in a low, gritty tone. His arms tightened around her.

"Three weeks."

"I missed you."

"Me too."

His mouth brushed her forehead, nudging her face away from his neck. "You were sleeping soundly. You look tired."

She nodded and closed her eyes against his chin. Seconds later, she nestled closer. If she'd been able to dig her way inside him and curl up there, she would have.

"Pam? Are you okay?"

"Just hold me, Cutter. It feels so good when you do."

She wasn't sure if he heard the desperation in her whisper. She hadn't deliberately put it there, but after the way John had touched her, Cutter's embrace was healing. She needed that badly.

When he hugged her more tightly, she sighed in relief. For the longest time they sat there holding each other. It was all Pam wanted, a balm that was penetrating and pure. Then, slowly, she began to notice things like the fullness of his chest, and his warmth, and she wanted more. When he nudged her face again, she turned it up.

His mouth brushed her forehead, her eyes, her cheeks. She turned the tiniest bit to catch his kiss, but it was an elusive whisper. She looked up to find his eyes soft but troubled.

"I shouldn't do this," he said.

"I love you."

"You're too young."

"I've loved you forever."

"Not this . . . way." In the next breath, he lowered his head and kissed her.

Pam melted. Her eyes closed, her lips softened. She was his to mold, which he did with leisure from first one angle, then another. Finally drawing back, he put a finger to her lips and said in a thick voice, "I'm in trouble, I think."

"Do it more," she whispered and ran her hands through his hair.

"Pam—"

"More." She pulled his head down. Everything inside her cried with the wanting. She loved him too much to let him go so soon. And she could tell he wanted her.

His kiss was harder, and she loved it. He taught her to move her lips the way he liked, taught her to open them wider, taught her to give him her tongue. She was trembling when he finally raised his head.

"I've never done that before," she said in a broken whisper.

"Never?"

"Never. Was it good?"

He rolled his eyes and laughed. "Was it ever." The laugh ended with a sharp gasp when she reached up and touched the tip of her tongue to the corner of his mouth.

In the next instant she was on her back on the bed, with Cutter on top of her. His hands were in her hair, holding her still, while his mouth took hers in a kiss that was raw with need.

Pam had never tasted a man's hunger that way. If the force of it was frightening, the excitement of it was beyond belief. It made her ache the same way her daydreams had. Without conscious thought, she arched her body against his.

He swore and slipped to the side.

"What's wrong. Cutter? What did I do wrong?"

"Nothing. Oh, baby . . ." His face was against the pillow, shoulders hunched and rigid. He moved his hips against the bedcovers. His voice was muffled. "You did everything so right that if I'm not inside you soon, I might just embarrass us both."

His words stole her breath. Her eyes were large when he raised his head.

"Do you know how much I want you?" he asked in a tormented whisper. His face was flushed, his eyes hot, his features tight.

The thought made her soar. Looking at him then, she knew she was the luckiest woman on earth. She touched his cheek, the bridge of his nose, his eyebrow. Catching her hand, he brought it to his mouth

and pressed it there hard for a heated minute. Then he carried it over his chest, past his waist to the distended front of his jeans.

Pam remembered the way John had felt there when he'd flattened her against the bed. He'd been hard and ugly, threatening a violation. But there was nothing threatening about Cutter. Nor anything ugly. He was very, very hard. But she loved him. She wanted to touch him.

Opening her hand, she explored his shape. He allowed it for no more than a minute before he forced her hand away. When she protested, he silenced her with a kiss that distracted her, and by the time he let her up for air, he was stroking the side of her breast. Her flesh grew warm with pleasure. She made a small sound, then waited, breathing raggedly, wanting more but unable to ask for it.

Something of her desire must have reached him, because before he'd even fully cupped her he began to unbutton her blouse. She felt the air on her skin, then the strength of his large hand. Again, helplessly, she thought of John.

When she closed her fingers on Cutter's wrist, he looked into her eyes. "Too much?"

She felt she could drown in his gaze. Not John, but Cutter. Not dirty, but right. "Too little," she whispered. Struggling to a sitting position, she pushed her blouse from her shoulders and unhooked her bra. There she faltered. "I've never done this before."

Cutter drew the thin straps from her shoulders and set the bra aside. Then he looked at her as though he never wanted to look away, as though her breasts were the most beautiful things he'd ever seen.

The soiling that Pam had felt at John's hand was washed away by Cutter's gaze. When he touched her she gasped, smiled self-consciously, then bit her lip when she felt the urge to cry out. While he kneaded her breasts, he sucked her lip away from her teeth.

"Say what you feel," he ordered against her mouth.

"I'm burning. Burning."

"Here?" He brushed her nipples with his fingertips.

She did cry out then. But he was still waiting for an answer when she finally caught her breath. "Inside," she cried, not caring how desperate she sounded. The sensations were too new, too strong. She

didn't know how to handle them. "I'm burning inside. I *need* you, Cutter."

When he slipped a hand between her legs, she closed her thighs on it and moaned. What she felt was so excruciatingly beautiful that she didn't know whether to laugh or cry. She had always imagined it would be like fire in heaven with Cutter, but she hadn't dared think her imaginings would come true.

Suddenly, when the reality of it was so close, she was terrified. "You're not going to say no now, are you?" she asked in a high-pitched voice. "I'll die if you do." Hands shaking, she unsnapped her jeans and dragged down the zipper.

He caught her hand. "What are you doing?"

"What 1 should have done when I first got here."

She rolled away. He lunged for her, but she was off the bed, pushing down her jeans and panties before he could reach her.

"Pam—" He snagged her around the waist and tumbled her back to the bed, with her jeans still hanging on one leg.

She wore a defiant look and little else. "If you don't like what you see, you can send me home. I may be only seventeen, but I'm a woman. I can be woman enough for you if you give me a chance. Teach me, and I'll make you burn, too."

"You already do that," he growled. With his body angled across hers to hold her still, he freed her leg of the last of her clothes. Then he took a long look at her.

Whether from pride or arousal or even shyness, she didn't know, but she felt herself swell inside. "Help me," she whispered, all defiance gone. "I don't know what . . . It's hurting."

Fully clothed, he came over her. "Be sure, babe," he warned, sounding hoarse. "Past this, and I won't be able to stop. I've dreamed about doing it once too often."

"Do it."

"I'll hurt you."

"Never."

"Physically. You'll tear."

Her voice had a frantic pitch. "I don't care. Hurry. Hurry, Cutter."
She was pushing futilely at the waistband of his jeans.

He tore off his shirt, then his pants. In the broad light of day,
he was more beautiful than she'd ever imagined, all long limbs, lean
muscles, and sandy hair.

The touch of his bare skin against hers was like fire. She gasped.
Then gasped again when he touched her. Before she knew what was
happening, her body erupted into spasms of incredible pleasure. She
threw back her head, eyes closed, panting for breath as the pleasure
went on and on. She was still in its grip when she felt a searing pain.
Her eyes flew to Cutter's face, and although the pain lingered, the
sense of fullness that came with it told her what had happened.

"I'm there, Pam. Inside you. You're mine now. Mine."

"I've always been yours," she whispered on a thread of breath and
smiled. "I love you."

"I know. Me too. Does it hurt?"

"I feel so full."

He gave a broken laugh. "You are."

"Here, too," she said, pointing to her head.

"Jesus."

"What?"

"I'm gonna come." He scrunched up his face, went tight all over,
then pulled out of her just as his large body began to pulse.

"Cutter?"

It was a while before he could answer, and then it was a grunt
from between her breasts.

"Why did you leave me?"

After another while, he raised his head. His hair was damp, flat-
tened in spikes against his forehead. "I couldn't put a rubber on. Not
the first time."

"I feel empty now."

A crooked smile tugged at his mouth. "Not sore?"

"Empty. I want you back." What she'd felt had been too beautiful
to be so short. It was everything her life had been missing. She needed
him more.

"In a minute," he said and began to kiss her gently. In time the kisses grew hungry again, and she strained closer. He touched her breasts, her belly, between her legs, and with each pass of his hand she loved him more, until she felt she'd burst from it.

He left her for only a minute before entering her again, and this time there was no pulling out. The pleasure built until explosion was the only possible route back to earth.

Pam spent the weekend in Cutter's bed. He made love to her over and over again, forcefully sometimes, tenderly at other times. Having set aside his qualms, he seemed bound to prove how much he loved her, and she didn't complain. She surprised herself with her own hunger, which was barely sated when Sunday afternoon arrived. By that time she had told him that she was moving into the dorm, although she hadn't said why. She didn't want him to get angry at John, when it would only be self-destructive. More than that, she didn't want the smallest reminder of John when she was with Cutter. Their time together was too precious.

In the weeks that followed, they saw each other several times a month, either in Cutter's cabin or in one nameless motel or another on the outskirts of Boston. Knowing he was waiting for her, Pam didn't mind the restrictions of dorm life. She had no interest in dating the boys at school and was content to spend her time studying. When she checked out of the dorm for weekends, she gave the name of a friend. John didn't ask questions.

Things were more tricky over the summer, when John insisted she work in the Boston office. She had to lie directly to him. She might have felt guilty had he not been making her miserable. In his dark, silent way, he taunted her. When she was at home, he made his presence felt. Although he didn't try to touch her again, the threat was always there. That was justification enough for her lies, she reasoned.

If her life had been dichotomous when she was a child, it was even more so now. During the week, she was a dutiful office gofer. She kept to herself when John was at home and slept only in bits and snatches, always with a plumber's wrench close at hand. On the

weekends when she was with Cutter, she was in another world. They did whatever took their fancy as long as it didn't involve the risk of discovery. That meant staying near the cabin when Pam was in Maine and steering clear of Beacon Hill when Cutter was in Boston. Pam didn't mind. As long as she was with Cutter, she was happy. She loved him more each time she saw him and was sure he felt the same.

So she easily lied when John pointedly asked, "Have you seen Cutter Reid?"

"No."

"Simon saw your car taking his turn last weekend."

"Simon's lying."

"I don't want you seeing him."

She schooled herself to indifference. "Why would I want to see him?"

"Because I don't want you to," John answered with a menacing look. "Stay away from him. I'm warning you. Stay away from him."

The warning fell on deaf ears. Much as Pam loved Marcy, much as she loved the house in Maine, Pam loved Cutter more. Being with him was as vital to her as breathing.

Summer ended and she went back to school. Aside from being able to sleep at night, little changed. She studied as hard as she could and lived for the weekends with Cutter.

Then, on the day after Thanksgiving, Tommy Willow, Marcy's seventeen-year-old half-brother, bludgeoned his father to death with the handle of a rusty water pump. It was a crime of passion, but a willful one, prompted by one too many instances of violence on Jarvis's part—and it gave Pam an excuse to go north.

A week later, Marcy came to see her at the dorm, looking as though she'd been through hell. "He knows," she whispered as soon as the door to Pam's room was closed.

Pam had assumed that Marcy's anguish had to do with Tom's predicament. "Who knows?"

"John. He knows you been seeing Cutter." She covered her face and started to cry. "He asked me straight out, and I told him, Pammy. Didn't know what else to do. He said that if I didn't tell the truth, he

wouldn't help Tom. He's payin' for the lawyer. We could never do it ourselves, and without it Tom goes to prison. He's a good boy, but he's never had much of a chance, and if he's sent away, it would kill Ma. So when John asked, I told him that you been seeing Cutter." She wept softly. "I'm sorry, I'm sorry."

For a quick minute, Pam felt betrayed. Then she thought about Marcy's situation and her own, and the choices she might have made if the tables were turned, and she couldn't remain angry. Upset, yes, and frightened—very frightened. She put her arm around Marcy as much to steady herself as to offer comfort.

"How much does he know?"

Marcy sniffled. "Just that you see Cutter in Maine. I told him I don't know what you do when you're at school." She raised fearful eyes. "He'll do something. He's an evil man."

Pam knew that all too well. Sinking down on the bed, she gave Marcy a pleading look. "I can't stop seeing Cutter. He's my life." Then the unfairness of it all hit her again—her father's senseless death, her mother's hospitalization, John's tyranny. With a hard swallow, she squared her jaw. "I'm nearly eighteen. I can do what I want, and I want to be with Cutter. If John has trouble with that, that's his problem."

John kept her on pins and needles for two days before showing up at the dorm. In a private corner of the living room there, he confronted her.

"I told you not to see him, but you did it." He kept his voice low, but it was no less deadly than his look. He wore an impeccably tailored business suit that added to his aloof demeanor. "I warned you, Pam. I even asked you if you'd seen him, and you lied. That wasn't very nice."

She thought of lying again, but it was too late for that. "I love him."

His lips curled. "You don't know the meaning of the word."

"I *love* Cutter."

"Then unlove him, because it's over."

She shook her head. "I'm seeing him."

"Over my dead body."

"What is it you hate so about him? He's good, and he's kind. He works hard. He keeps up the morale of the others. Is it because of that that you hate him? Or are you still sore because Daddy liked him?"

"The man is a waste."

"Daddy didn't think so. He wanted to leave him Little Lincoln."

She scored with that one, if the muscle that twitched in John's jaw meant anything. "What are you talking about?"

"I heard the two of you talking once. Arguing. Daddy wanted Cutter to have Little Lincoln. Why didn't he get it?"

"The old man must have changed his mind," John said. He didn't blink, but came close before catching himself. "He must have realized what a mistake it would have been. Cutter Reid is trash. He's nothing, he's going nowhere, and I'll be damned if he'll have you."

Pam was infuriated by the insults. "He already has," she informed John, uncaring when his eyes grew darker and more vicious.

He was very quiet for a minute. "Is that true?"

"Yes."

"I'll get him on rape."

"It wasn't rape."

"You're a minor. I'll get him on a corruption charge."

"I begged him for it."

"The court won't give a damn. You're a minor. He violated you."

"What he did was beautiful. What you did was the violation."

John went rigid. Pam had never seen him quite so angry. "Don't you ever," he muttered, "ever say that again."

But she was fighting for her life. "I'll say that and more if you bring Cutter to court. I'll embarrass you, John. It'll all come out."

He gave her a look of pure hatred, and for a minute she wondered if he'd lose control. In the next minute, though, he straightened his shoulders and started for the door.

She had fought fire with fire. Suddenly she wondered if she'd played her cards wrong. Nothing was settled. She went after him. "Where are you going?"

"Someplace where I don't have to look at you. You disgust me."

"That's nothing new—"

He whirled on her so quickly that she fell back a step. "What's new is that I've sold the house."

She sucked in a breath. "You didn't."

"As soon as I heard you were seeing him."

"To who? Who did you sell it to?" She'd just buy it back.

"It's none of your affair. Nothing about Timiny Cove is your affair anymore."

"It is!" she cried, her heart hammering wildly. "I loved that house! It was mine!"

"At my discretion. But you blew it. I gave you fair warning, and you blew it."

Her eyes brimmed with tears. "You hated it. You wanted to sell it all along. You waited until you knew it would hurt the most, then you used me as an excuse. You're a sadist, John."

"Sadist or not, I'm your legal guardian."

"Not for much longer," she argued, and the meaning of that hit her. "I'm nearly eighteen. That's why you did it, isn't it? Once I'm of age, I can fight you."

"You can try, but you won't get very far. I run things around here. What I say is law." He raised a finger in front of her nose. "And I say that you'll keep your goddamned mouth shut and behave. You won't call Cutter Reid. You won't see Cutter Reid. Because selling the house is for starters. If I catch you anywhere near Timiny Cove or Cutter Reid, I'll can him from the mine."

Pam swallowed the thick knot in her throat. "You wouldn't do that. He's a leader there. He sticks up for the others. They respect him. Fire him, and you'll have a rebellion on your hands."

"Not," he said, punctuating his words with jabs to her chest, "if I fire every goddamned miner he's ever championed right along with him." His hand formed a fist and fell to his side. "And I'll do it, Pam. Times are hard. The old guys are dead weight. For every one of them, there's another able-bodied man dying to work. Don't think I don't control the hiring and firing. And don't think you can sneak off and

see Cutter Reid without my knowing, because I'll be watching. I'll have people listening in to his phone calls—"

"That's illegal."

"Keep your mouth shut!" he roared, then quickly lowered his voice. "Judge Nowell, in Bangor, is a friend. He'll make it legal with few questions asked. And it's perfectly legal to hire a private investigator. You'll have someone on your tail every time you leave this dorm."

"You're bluffing."

"Try me."

She didn't know if she dared, which made the agony that much worse. "Don't do this," she cried softly.

"Don't see Cutter."

Desperate, she clutched at his arm. "But I love him."

He shook her off. "Then you're a fool. He's only after the name, don't you see? He tried to get what he could from the old man, but he came up short, so now he's shooting for you."

"That's not true," she said without any doubt. "He loves me."

"He loves who and what you are."

"He loves *me*."

"You're his ticket out, Pam, only you're too stupid to see it." He was in control again, speaking with the voice of authority. "I know how guys like that work. They latch on to a good thing, get what they can, then move on to greener pastures."

"But he hasn't gotten a thing from me."

With a sneer, John looked her up and down. "That wasn't what you said a minute ago."

She didn't have to remember Palm Beach to feel dirty again. His look was lewd enough to do it. She wrapped her arms around herself to ward off the feeling. "I've never given him money or tried to get a promotion for him. I haven't given him a thing. So why's he hanging around?"

"Because this is all part of the plan. First he seduces you, then he makes you dependent on him physically, then he starts hitting you up for favors."

"Is that how you work?" she blurted.

He slapped her hard across the face.

Her hand flew to the spot, but she was more aware of the tears in her eyes. They were a sign of weakness, which was the last thing she wanted to show John. So she said, "Did I hit it right?"

"You have a fresh mouth. I should have done that years ago."

"If you had, I'd have reported you for child abuse."

"For a slap across the face? I think not."

"But you've got it in you for more," she lashed back, "and we both know it. You have a mean streak. Deep down, under that expensive suit of yours, you're no better than a street fighter."

Before she could move from his reach, he closed a large hand around a fistful of her sweatshirt and hauled her close.

"And you," he said in a fury of clenched teeth, "are a bitch. I don't want to hear what you have to say. I don't want to see you. Just stay here and study. Stay away from Maine. And stay away from Cutter Reid. If you don't, you'll have yourself to blame for what happens. Do I make myself clear?"

"Let go of me."

He hoisted her higher. "Do I make myself clear?"

"I hate you."

"The feeling's mutual. Now, are we in agreement about the other? Do you understand what I expect of you?"

"I understand that as soon as I'm legally of age, I can tell you to fuck off."

His nostrils flared at her choice of words, but that was the only satisfaction she got. "Wrong, sweetheart." He twisted his hand to lift her even higher, while he put his mouth by her cheek and spoke with lethal quiet. "What I'm saying has nothing to do with age. It has to do with power. I have it, you don't. I control the trust fund, I control the stock. You won't have a voting seat on the board until you're twenty-five, and by that time I'll have the board stacked my way. So the best you can do when you turn eighteen is run away, and I won't be able to bring you back." He took a deep breath, seeming to inhale her essence before spitting it out in a contemptuous snarl. "If you want

to run away, be my guest. I don't want you." Releasing her forcefully, he turned on his heel and left.

Pam went to see her mother the next day. She sat quietly with her, not saying much, staring blindly out at the gray December landscape. After a time, she took her hand. It was pale and delicate, not quite limp, not quite directed, an apt representation of Patricia herself. The longer Pam looked at it, the more carefully she traced the fragile web-work of veins, the more devastated she felt. She was thirteen again, lost and alone and frightened because everything that had been good in her life was being taken away. And suddenly it didn't matter that she was nearly eighteen or that Patricia was to be protected. Unable to hold it in any longer, Pam bent over that hand and began to cry.

"I don't know—what to do—things are so wrong—I need help—Mommy."

She wept softly, losing track of time in her grief. Somewhere in its midst, she felt Patricia's fingers close around hers, and she held on for dear life.

Chapter 15

◈ ◈ ◈

CUTTER PUT HIS BACK TO THE phone booth door and lowered his head over the receiver. "Pamela St. George, please."

"Just a minute." The voice was that of another of the students in Pam's dorm and was accommodating enough. Whether the girl could produce Pam was another story. He had already tried twice without luck and was uneasy. They hadn't talked in five days, which wasn't unusual, but he had expected her in Timiny Cove that morning, and she hadn't shown. He had checked the big brick house and found it locked tight. He wasn't waiting to get back to his place to try her again at the dorm.

"I'm sorry," the voice came back, "but she isn't here."

"Do you know where she is?"

"No."

"Do you know when she'll be back?"

"Has she signed out?"

"I don't know."

"Can you check?" he asked impatiently, then sighed. "I was supposed to meet her this morning. I'm worried."

"She was here a little while ago. I saw her myself, and she looked fine. Do you want to leave a message?"

The words echoed in his brain. She wasn't sick. Or in a car crash. He'd already left two cryptic messages that only Pam would understand. "No," he murmured and hung up the phone.

Leaving the booth, he slid into his truck and sat for a long time staring out the windshield. He was scared to death. He loved Pam so much that she was his first thought in the morning and his last thought at night. She was with him wherever he went, was everything poetic in a life that was otherwise ordinary.

He didn't know what in the hell was wrong. It wasn't like Pam not to call if she couldn't come. Or not to answer his calls.

Starting the pickup, he backed away from the phone booth and headed out of town toward the highway. Minutes later he was pushing the speed limit, heading south, toward Boston.

He'd find her. If he had to wait all night and all of Sunday outside her dorm, he'd find her. He had to know what was wrong. She meant far too much to him not to worry, and it was even worse since they'd made love. Her body was perfect. It was fresh and clean, and it responded to his body as if it had been created especially for him. When he was hugged tightly inside her, he felt securely loved.

It was an illusion, of course. Pam did love him, but there was nothing secure about it in the sense of longevity. She argued that they had a future, but he didn't believe it. He was a townie, she was a city girl. He was born to dirt, she was born to money. He knew he'd have to give her up one day, but he just wasn't ready for it yet. He hadn't had her long enough. He wanted more time.

In the fall she'd go off to college, and her world would open up. He could follow her, could leave the mine and take a job where she was, but that would only be worse because then she'd see him out of the context of Timiny Cove. In comparison to the college guys, he would seem a dud.

Flashing lights suddenly filled his rearview mirror. He didn't have to look at his gauge to know he'd been speeding. Muttering a choice epithet, he slowed down and moved out of the fast lane. When the cruiser sped past him after another target, he stayed where he was. Someone had given him a reprieve.

He prayed for another one when he reached Boston, but it wasn't to be. Pam wasn't at her dorm. She had signed out to a friend's house, which meant she could be anywhere. Leaving another cryptic

message, he checked in to a nearby motel. Pam never showed. He stayed there, watching the phone, until midday Sunday, then staked out a position within viewing distance of the brick-flanked drive to her school. It was cold and dark at 6:00 P.M. when the Cougar finally turned in. He quickly followed, pulled into the parking space beside hers, and caught her as she got out of her car.

She screamed with fright, then with anguish. "Cutter! Oh God." She covered her face with shaky hands, but rather than falling into his arms as he thought she would, she shrank back against her car. "Go away, Cutter! Go quickly!"

He didn't like the sound of that at all. "What's wrong?"

"Leave! *Please*, leave!" She parted her hands and shot a frantic look around. "If we're seen together, there'll be awful trouble." She grabbed hold of his heavy jacket. Not even the darkness could hide the fear in her eyes. "Go now, before someone sees!"

He'd never seen her this way, and it was making him more nervous by the minute. "Not until I find out what's wrong. You were supposed to drive up yesterday morning."

"I couldn't. He said he'd have me watched."

Cutter felt a ripple of cold fear. "John?"

"He knows about us. Everything. And he'll do awful things if he catches us together." She glanced worriedly over her shoulder.

Cutter pulled her down against the baseboard of his pickup. "What things?"

"Fire you."

"I'll quit first."

"No." She held tight to his jacket. "He'll fire the others—Jethro, the MacMorgans, Hugo Wall, all the men you fought for—and he said he's already sold the house."

"I haven't heard about that, and I would've. Word spreads fast."

"Maybe it's too soon."

"Maybe he's lying."

"You didn't see his face, Cutter! It was awful! The man is mad! He'll do everything he says!"

Cutter refused to believe it, but Pam clearly did. Tugging her

shaking body to his, he held her tightly for a minute. Then he gave her a kiss that was rough, telling her of the hell he'd been through for the last two days. When he raised his head, he was angry. "John is full of crap."

"No. He'll do it. All of it."

"He isn't God."

"Close to it."

"He can't control us."

"But he does!"

"We'll escape him."

"He has everything covered, Cutter. I've thought and thought and I can't find a way out."

"We'll run away."

"He'll be right after us."

"We'll get married."

"I'm too young. He'll take you to court."

"No court will listen if you say you love me."

"His court will. He knows the judges."

"So we'll wait three months. You'll be old enough then."

"That won't do any good," she cried. "He'll ruin you!"

"There's not much left to ruin if I lose you."

With an anguished sound, she pressed her face to his chest, then looked up and reached for his mouth. He tasted the desperation in her kiss—or in his, he didn't know which, and it didn't matter. What mattered was that they were together then and there.

All but bodily lifting her, he opened the door of the pickup, slid her in, and followed. Pressing her flat on the bench seat, he kissed her and touched her until the December air turned hot and heavy between them. Then, disturbed by what she had said and needing a reaffirmation of her love, he began pulling at her jeans.

"God, no, Cutter!" she cried.

"I need you." He caught her mouth again and ate hungrily from it until his need surpassed that. Rising to his knees, he used both hands on her pants.

"Not here!" she whispered, frantic. "We can't!"

He tugged the denim over her hips. "We can, dammit. We can do what we want."

"If someone comes—"

"No one will." He unzipped his fly and released himself, then came down to her. "It's dark. No one will see." He entered her in a single strong stroke, then thrust again and again, grasping her bottom and lifting her to deepen the penetration until she cried out at the pleasure he gave her.

She came, clutching his shirt, murmuring, "I love you I love you," and he climaxed seconds later. But he stayed hard, because having her once was never enough. Her breathing had barely slowed before he was moving again. He pushed deeper, harder, and again she rose to meet him. The sound that tore from his throat when he climaxed this time came from deep in his soul. It echoed in the cab of the pickup long after their passion was spent and their clothing repaired.

The chilly air seeped over them quickly. "What are we going to do?" Pam asked. Her cheek was against his chest. She was as curled around him as a human being could be on the front seat of a small truck, and he held her tightly.

"I can't give you up yet."

"He'll do something awful."

"Then we'll fight him."

"How?"

"I don't know, but there has to be a way."

"Maybe when I'm eighteen."

"I'm supposed to stay away from you till then?"

"If he catches us, there'll be hell to pay."

"I don't care. I'll face him. Maybe it's time."

"But it's not just us," she insisted; and, much as he didn't want to, he had to listen. "There are others involved. Innocent people. He'll hurt them, too."

"Maybe he's bluffing."

"What if he isn't?"

"He can only hurt people so much before the hurt boomerangs."

"And in the meantime?"

Cutter thought about the meantime, and there was nothing comforting about it. He could quit the mine and leave Timiny Cove, but it was his home, the only place he knew. If he belonged anywhere, it was there, where he finally was respected to some extent. And the respect was two-sided. While it wasn't exactly affection he felt for the people, he recognized their struggles and felt loyalty to them. They depended on him in subtle ways. While he wouldn't go so far as to call them friends, he couldn't desert them.

Nor could he desert Pam. She depended on him too. Even if he hadn't loved her so much, he would have wanted to be there to protect her as Eugene would have done.

A spark of light came from his left. Pam whispered a frightened, "Oh God," while he peered through the fogged-up windows. "It's the security patrol." She pushed away from him. "I have to leave. If the guard finds me here with you—"

"Too late." Cutter caught her hand. He rolled down his window as the guard approached. "Evening, sir." He glanced at the wrist where a watch would have been if he owned one. "We still have some time, don't we?"

The guard aimed his flashlight into the truck. Pam held up a hand against its brightness, but she took Cutter's lead and calmly leaned over his thigh toward the window. "We won't be long. Another five minutes? It's freezing out here."

The guard, who looked far too old and wrinkled to protect active young women, gave a grunt. "I was thinking that myself when I stopped. But I never seen the truck here before, and it's my job to check."

"That's good," Cutter said. "I'm glad to know someone's looking out for her when I'm not."

Touching the flashlight to his forehead in a salute, the guard returned to his car and slowly drove off.

"He saw the truck," Pam gasped as soon as the window was up again. "He'll remember it now. Oh, God, I knew this would happen."

Cutter linked his fingers through hers. "Nothing happened," he said as smoothly as he could, although his heart was pounding. "As

far as he's concerned, we're both happy and healthy. The old geezer's probably already forgotten he saw us."

"If he'd come five minutes earlier, do you know what he would have seen?"

Cutter grinned.

"You laugh!" she cried. "If we'd been caught like that, John would have strung you up by your heels."

"It's okay, honey. We weren't caught." But his grin was gone. Everything that had come before was crowding in on him. He started the engine.

"What are we going to do?" she asked again as he drove the short distance to her dorm.

He was asking himself the same question. The answer eluded him, but he knew one thing. "I won't give you up, Pam. Not on John's say-so. If you were to find someone else and tell me you didn't love me anymore, that would be different."

"I'll always love you."

"Someday you might not."

"No. Always."

His need to hear the words was enough to stop him from arguing more. "Then we'll find a way to see each other now." He drew her close for a kiss. "You're my life," he whispered. She ran her fingers over his forehead, across his cheek to his mouth, following with her eyes in a way that made him uneasy. "Don't memorize things, Pam. We'll be together next weekend." Still she looked at him as though her heart were going to break. "Pam?"

"Gotta run." The words were no more than a broken breath, but they hung in the air for a long minute. Then she came up the few inches to his mouth. Her lips were soft and hungry, desperate in the way they clung to his. In seconds, his own desperation had him taking ravenous control of the kiss, but his tongue had barely filled her mouth when she tore herself away. Seconds later, she was out of the truck and running toward the dorm.

He started after her, then caught himself and straightened behind the wheel. She was upset, it was late, and the eyes of whoever cared

to watch were on them. If he followed her, it would draw unwanted attention. He'd call her later to make sure she was okay. Maybe by that time he would come up with a brainstorm.

The brainstorm didn't come during the ride home. Snow did. It fell gently, reflecting in his headlights to make the night look unnaturally bright. But the brightness didn't spread to his insides. He was feeling cold and bleak when he pulled up to his home and cut the engine. Head down, he trudged to the door, only to stop short when he felt a prickling at the back of his neck.

His footprints weren't the only ones in the snow.

His head came up, eyes focusing on the shadowed figure that stood by his door. Before he could identify it, a second, larger figure materialized from the side and rammed a fist into his stomach. The force of it sent him reeling. He had barely hit the snow when he was hauled back up by a third man. Another blow caught him in the ribs. He staggered in pain and tried to deflect the next shot, but it hit him in the gut. When his arms automatically went to his stomach, he took a wallop in the jaw that sent him backward.

The pain was explosive. Time and again he staggered to his feet, only to be slammed to one side or another. He tried to fight back, but with each attempt the pummeling came harder. He couldn't catch his breath. He couldn't straighten. In sheer self-defense, he curled on his side with his arms covering his head, only to be kicked everywhere else.

At a low sound that he couldn't make out through the pain, the beating stopped. He gulped for air, unable to open one of his eyes, unable to turn over. That was done for him by the same booted foot that had inflicted such damage seconds before. The sharp movement made him cry out in agony. A lingering shred of sense urged him to catch sight of his assailants, but he was too dizzy to see much. He panicked when his jacket and then his shirt were crudely torn from him. Bare-chested in the December snow and hurting all over, he was dragged halfway up the steps.

"I'll take that belt now," came the voice behind him. "And hold him down."

Dredging for remnants of strength, Cutter wrenched free and stumbled down the steps, only to be caught and hauled back. This time two pairs of boots pinned his shoulders and upper arms to the snow-covered edge of the porch. He tried to get a foothold at the bottom of the steps, but between his bruised body and the slippery snow, his efforts were futile. He was aware of movement by the man on his right, the giant whose fists had wreaked such havoc, but all he could see was a hulking black shadow.

For a long, terrible moment, time stood still. Cutter tried to wake himself from the nightmare but couldn't. Deep inside, mixed with all the pain, was a stomach-churning fear as he waited in the quiet, snowy night for a punishment he didn't deserve.

The belt hit him then, and pain exploded across his back. He panted against it, broke out in a sweat, and barely had a chance to brace himself when it came again. The pain was excruciating, totally engulfing, simultaneously mind-blowing and numbing. Through a fog of screams inside his head, he heard the voice by his ear.

"In case you're wondering," it seethed, "this belt is covered with metal studs raised in rows of fives. It's going to leave some very interesting marks on your back. I wanted to tell you that now, because you might pass out before I'm done, and since there won't be any evidence of this visit left behind, I didn't want you wondering."

"You're mad," Cutter managed to whisper, although even that small effort cost him.

"And you're through," returned the voice, with less control now. "Out. As of this weekend, you've resigned your job at the mine. You won't tell anyone why, and you won't make any accusations. Your phone's already been disconnected. You'll take whatever piddling money you have and pack up and leave Timiny Cove, and if you know what's good for you, you'll never come back."

"Go to hell," Cutter wheezed.

In the little time it took for the belt to be swung again, the five rows of metal studs raked another gully through his back. He made a guttural sound and convulsed against his bonds, but they gave no quarter. The belt found him again and again, driving him hard against

the iced edge of the steps. Each crack was preceded by a grunt that, in Cutter's near delirium, sounded obscenely sexual.

His back felt like it was on fire. He was shaking all over. He fought for consciousness, which came and went along with flashes of searing pain, stark terror, and nausea. Finally, wanting nothing more than escape, he let the darkness take him.

But escape wasn't to be so easy. A handful of snow in his face brought him back to nearly unspeakable pain. Through it came John's voice, filled with the anger that, once unleashed, could not be restrained.

"That's for screwing my sister, you goddamned son of a bitch." He pulled Cutter up by the hair. Through the haze of one slitted eye, Cutter saw the blade of a knife. "And this is what I'll use if you touch her again. I'll make it so you don't ever touch another woman."

"Should'a done it this time, boss," said one of the men.

"No way," John replied through clenched teeth. He pulled Cutter's head back in a way that would have hurt if Cutter hadn't been so far beyond pain. "If I did it now, he wouldn't want her. But he's gonna want her. He's gonna be rock hard with it night after night, and he won't have her, because he knows I'll do what I say." He tightened his hand in Cutter's hair. "You diddle with the St. George family again, and I'll close the mine, I'll cancel out Pam's inheritance, and I'll cut off your balls. Got that, bastard?"

He gave Cutter's head a shove. The last thing Cutter heard before he passed out was so sick that only the words registered. Their meaning was left for another time.

He awoke to pervasive pain and tried to steel himself against another round of flogging. When it didn't come, he lay very still. His mind went dark again; he pulled himself back. Not moving a muscle, he listened for human sounds, but nothing disturbed the whisper of the snow falling around him.

Again he drifted. His body, drenched with snow, sweat, and blood, was so riddled with pain that he couldn't get his bearings. Reality held no meaning.

In time he felt the cold. He felt the racking shivers that compounded the pain. He felt a deep, dark loneliness. Then fury. Then, out of anger, he regained his will to survive.

Summoning fragments of strength, he struggled to his knees and painstakingly made his way up the steps. He collapsed at the top, but the memory of what had happened there goaded him on. Fighting nausea with jaw-clenching determination, he crawled to the door. He fell against it. When it opened, he fell inside.

Consciousness came and went. He managed to get the door closed behind him before he faded, then regained consciousness long enough to crawl to the bed before losing it again. He didn't give a thought to the wood stove, or heat, or the blood that covered his back. All he wanted was to bury himself under the down comforter and rest.

He was lying on the floor on his stomach, trying to find the strength to hoist himself onto the mattress, when something touched his shoulder.

Thinking that John had stayed after all, he whipped out an arm in rage and tried to roll away, but the movement cost him dearly. He gave an anguished cry, then broke into a spasm of coughing, and the agony of that was pure hell. He was beginning to think that death wouldn't be so bad when he realized that the murmur above him was coming from Bumble.

He let down his guard and went as limp as his cold, cramped body would allow. Bumble was there. When he'd been alone and hungry as a little boy, she had come by sometimes with food. She would know what to do.

The hours that followed were harrowing. The pain was relentless, worse at times when Bumble bathed him, turned him, and put salves on his mangled skin. He floated in and out of consciousness, breathing shallowly, swallowing moans that kept coming and coming, but he let her do as she wished. He had neither pride nor modesty. The full force of his energy at any given moment was focused on surviving until the next.

Survive he did, through that endless night, and then for two days

during which he was alternately feverish and chilled. By the third day, the fever had broken, and he slept. By the fourth, he was pushing himself to get out of bed. By the fifth, he was beginning to understand what had happened and what it meant to his life.

One thing was clear. He was leaving Timiny Cove. Pam had been right: John was vicious enough to carry out every one of his threats. Lying in bed all those hours, helpless and hurting, he had come to the realization that there were two things he wanted above all others in life.

One was Pam.

The other was John.

He intended to get both.

Chapter 16

◆◆◆

New York, early June 1990

HILLARY STARED AT CUTTER. "I don't believe you."

He shrugged, raised his champagne glass to his mouth, and sipped the sparkly as his eyes skimmed the crowd.

Her eyes didn't leave his face. She was trying to find some sign that he was putting her on. "John wouldn't do that."

Cutter remained silent. After a minute he gave another elegant shrug.

"Say something, Cutter. Tell me that of course he'd do it, because he's a monster at heart."

He looked at her with what she thought was a flicker of pity. In an instant it was gone, replaced by the hardness that attested to the truth of his words. "It's not my place to tell you what to think, Hillary. You asked why I deserted Pam while I claimed to love her so much, and I answered."

"You never mentioned it before."

"You never asked before."

"But it was such a significant thing. If what you say is true, he left you for dead."

"I didn't die."

"You could have. You could have bled to death, or frozen to death."

"I didn't."

"Because Bumble was there."

He nodded his head subtly. "And because I made up my mind not to die." He extended his hand to the man who approached. "Steve." He introduced Hillary, then gave the connection: "Steve and I lost money together in a fiasco in Kansas City last year."

If true, Hillary decided, it had to have been a rare experience for Cutter. Barring those few months when he had first come to New York, Cutter had managed to make money hand over fist. Looking at him now, at the way he held himself with his shoulders back and his head at a confident angle, at the comfortable way he wore his tuxedo and handled both the slim, fluted glass and his erstwhile partner, it was hard to believe that he had dropped out of school at sixteen and spent eight years in the mines in Maine.

". . . read everything he's written," Cutter was saying as she tuned back into the conversation. That she believed. He was as voracious a reader as ever. She might be the writer, but he was the one who had received the engraved invitation to the reception they were attending. It was in honor of the newest Fletcher Grady thriller, which, rumor had it, was about to debut at the top spot on the *Publishers Weekly* best-seller list. Not that Cutter had been invited simply because he read Fletcher's books. The two were good friends.

Hillary marveled at Cutter. He wasn't showy or gregarious. But something about his silent way spoke of competence and dignity, plus an independence that intrigued people. As a kid, he had had a renegade streak. Now, softened, it worked in his favor. He was nearly as charismatic as John.

"The figures are impressive," his friend was saying.

"It's a solid company. Efficiently organized and well run. A good investment, Steve."

"Ten grand worth?"

"More."

Steve's eyes widened, and Hillary was about to ask what the investment was, thinking that maybe she'd chip in a little herself if the company in question was so solid, when Cutter caught her eye.

"Sorry. Didn't mean to talk business. It just creeps up sometimes." To Steve he said, "Talk with you next week?"

The man nodded, smiled at Hillary, and moved on.

"His business is . . . ?" she asked.

"Commercial appliances. He supplies some of the largest hotel chains."

"How did you meet him?"

"I was on a shoot in Palm Springs seven or eight years back. He'd just outfitted a new resort there. We played golf together. Still do, sometimes."

She gave him a wry smile. "Golf. Who'd'a guessed?"

He gave another of his negligent shrugs.

This time the gesture drew her eyes to his shoulder and she was reminded of the punishment he had suffered. Her smile faded fast. "John *beat* you?"

Cutter was silent for so long that she wondered if he was retracting his story. Her hopes had barely risen, though, when he said with quiet purpose, "Had me beaten, then tore my back raw with a belt he borrowed from his biker friend."

"John doesn't have biker friends."

"Change 'friend' to 'lackey.' I'm sure he was hired, then paid well to forget what he'd done and seen. And to dispose of the belt."

Still Hillary resisted. "Timiny Cove is a small place. Someone would have known."

"In the middle of winter? The snow fell for three days. It was a while after that before anyone moved far, and anyway, the gem pits were closed for the winter. We were just sifting, sorting, and matching. Work was sporadic."

"But no one called?" It seemed bizarre. "No one came looking for you?"

"The phone line had been cut. By the time anyone came looking—if anyone did, which I doubt, since I didn't have that kind of relationship with the guys—I was gone."

"Two weeks after the beating," she said skeptically.

"That's right."

"And you showed up at my door looking hale and hardy."

"Did I?"

Thinking back, she recalled that he had looked unsettled. At the time, she assumed he was overwhelmed by New York City. "You were standing straight."

"I was stiff. My ribs were still hurting, and my back was scabbed over."

Feeling vaguely ill, she tipped the glass to her lips with far less finesse than Cutter affected. "You stayed at my place for a week," she said. "If you'd been suffering, I would have known it."

"How?"

"You'd have moved funny."

"I didn't move much. I slept."

He was right, she realized, but still she insisted, "I'd have known it."

"Did I show you my back?"

"No."

"Did I ever walk around without a shirt?"

"No." She grew quiet. "I thought you were modest." Something struck her then. "If your back was all mangled and scarred, how could you do the work you did?"

"I had the face they wanted. The look." He came close enough for their sides to meet, and his voice softened. "Touch my back."

She eyed him questioningly.

"Go on," he coaxed. "Run your palm over it." He waited until she raised her hand. "No, not over the jacket. Slip it inside. That's it. Now move your hand. More. What do you feel?"

She swallowed. "Texture." And she knew it wasn't his shirt, since that was of finely pressed silk. The flesh beneath the silk felt rutted, the way the ground used to be in Timiny Cove at the end of mud season.

Unable to deny the evidence, she gripped his cummerbund buckle and whispered in horror, "Why didn't you tell me?"

"What was the point? You had a thing for John. What he did to my back was between him and me."

"But you came to my place. *Knowing* I had a thing for John, you came to my place. If it wasn't for vengeance, what was it for?"

"I needed a place to stay," Cutter said simply. "I wanted money and I wanted power. New York had more of both than any other city, and you were the only person I knew in New York. So I went to your place. I figured we had a hometown in common. It never occurred to me to take vengeance on John through you."

But he had in a way, just then, by giving her proof of John's cruelty. She felt sick inside.

A week later she met with Arlan at the United Nations Plaza. She had hoped to be uplifted by the bright June sun and the delegates in their native garb, but there were few in sight.

Arlan, who had been drinking Coke from a super-size take-out cup, released the straw. "You're doing good, Hillie. You were right. You've got a story."

She said nothing.

He nudged her. "Aren't you pleased?"

"Very."

He stopped walking. "You don't sound it."

She ambled on another few steps before stopping at a large geometric sculpture with a concrete base. She lowered herself to the base. "I thought I had a story without all this."

"This makes it stronger." He propped a foot on the concrete. "How well did you know Cutter in Timiny Cove?"

"Not well. He was three years behind me in school—when he was there."

"Do you remember him as a troublemaker?"

"I remember that the town thought of him that way. I always felt bad for him. He was different. Like me."

"And John."

"Uh-huh."

"So out of the blue one day Cutter just showed up at your door. What excuse did he give for leaving Timiny Cove?"

"He said that he was tired of being a nobody, that he wanted to

make it big, and that he wouldn't be able to do either in Timiny Cove. I could identify with that."

"Did you know he wanted to get back at John?"

"Not at first. He talked about wanting to make something of himself so that he could have Pam. He wanted somehow to get into the upper echelons of St. George Mining, but I didn't realize he wanted it for revenge until we'd talked more. After a while, his anger came out. No wonder. There was so much of it."

Arlan had the straw in his mouth again. Without quite taking it out, he said, "I'm surprised he didn't go to the cops."

"Where?" She slanted him a droll look. "Timiny Cove? You think Verne would have done anything?"

"He could have gone to Portland. What John did was assault and battery."

"Of which Cutter had no proof."

"His back. His back."

"No proof that John did it. Besides, he wanted to put space between himself and Timiny Cove. He believed John's threats. He was sure that if he caused trouble, the men at the mine would suffer."

"Then he was being altruistic?"

"He was being selfish. He didn't want the responsibility."

"Would John have carried out his threats?"

She let her eyes travel up the East River to the spot where the tram carried people from Roosevelt Island to Manhattan. The aerial car was halfway across. She felt she was the one hanging in mid-air. "Maybe."

"You don't believe it?"

"I don't want to. But then, I didn't want to believe that he whipped Cutter, but it's true. Pam confirmed it, and she has seen Cutter's back. Even Bumble confirmed it."

Arlan looked surprised. "You talked with her?"

"Went up there last week, a day after the party."

"She must be ancient," he said in a hushed voice.

Remembering the bent and weathered woman, Hillary gave a small smile. "Not as old as people think. Maybe seventy-five."

"That's old enough," he drawled.

"But we thought she was double that twenty years ago!" He eyed her with the utmost admiration. "So you went to the pack rat's midden."

Hillary's smile tilted. Arlan was reacting just as the people of Timiny Cove would have done if they'd known she had visited Bumble.

"The pack rat's midden," she enlightened him, "is actually a small house on the far side of the woods from Cutter's place. I wouldn't exactly call it a dung heap. It is quite well equipped."

"You mean, she has Teflon-coated caldrons?"

"I mean, she has a modern stove and refrigerator, a microwave oven, a television with a small satellite dish, plus a VCR and an extensive collection of films. Seems she's a sucker for situation comedy. *Three's a Crowd*, *Who's the Boss*, *Cheers*—you name it, she has taped collections."

"Where did she get them?"

"Cutter. He's been sending her stuff for years."

"The microwave and the stove, too?"

Hillary nodded.

"In gratitude for nursing him?"

She nodded again and turned her face to the breeze. It lifted the hair off her neck, offering pleasant relief from the warmth of the sun and the tension of her thoughts.

"And you? Did you take Cutter in for old times' sake?"

"And for Pam's sake. I knew she liked him. I also—" She hesitated, feeling guilty.

"You also what?"

She sighed. "I had mixed enough feelings for John to take Cutter in out of defiance. I knew that John had given him trouble over the years. Somehow it seemed right that I give him his start in the big city. Not that I dreamed he'd actually make it. He seemed harmless. I knew that he had worked hard at the mine, but there was no correlation between mining and anything in New York. It never occurred to me that he would pose any kind of threat to John."

"Does he? Have I missed something here?"

Hillary wasn't sure. Since she'd seen Cutter the week before, there had been times when she wondered how on top of things she really

was. "He's become a somebody, all right. He knew the movers and shakers at that reception last week, and they knew him."

"Does that make him a threat to John?"

"Not per se." She was trying to figure out her unease. "But back then he had so much anger. He said there were two things pushing him when he left Timiny Cove—getting Pam, and getting back at John. He doesn't have either yet, but I can't believe he's given up. Especially now that I know . . . this."

She felt Arlan watching her closely. Seeking to escape his scrutiny, she rose and began walking again. It wasn't long before he was beside her.

"It bothers you, doesn't it?"

"Of course it bothers me. I hate violence."

"It's great for the book."

That was true. Whether it was great for her peace of mind was something else.

"Hillary?"

She continued walking.

"Talk to me, Hillary."

"About what?"

"About whether you're getting cold feet. You're not having second thoughts, are you?"

"No." But she knew she sounded hesitant. She also knew that if she didn't offer an explanation, he'd hound her forever. "I just didn't expect to start unearthing surprises. Like this business about the beating."

"And the will. Don't forget the bequest that was never bequeathed."

She couldn't. It ate at her.

"Pretty eye-opening," Arlan remarked, chewing on his straw. "The guy really is a bastard."

"He has his strong points."

"But they aren't what will make your story."

"I know," she said softly.

Arlan stepped directly in front of her, forcing her to a stop. "The

contract is in the works, Hillie. We've agreed on the terms. You're on the schedule for next July. Don't fink out on me now."

"I won't. I'm writing the story."

"Including the good parts?"

"Of course."

"Even though you love the guy?"

"I don't love him," she muttered and looked away. "He's getting married next month."

Arlan leaned close. "But he doesn't love her."

Her eyes flew to his. "Does it matter? Since when do people marry for love? Since when is love enough to sustain a relationship? Things don't work that way, Arlan. Love is a frivolous concept. It's something we entertain when we're too young to know better. It doesn't have much of a role in the real-life scheme of things."

"Would Cutter agree with that?"

"Probably."

"Has he stopped loving Pam?"

"No, but she's married to someone else, and he's alone."

"Has he given up on her? She was the other half of what he swore he'd get when he left Timiny Cove. Seventeen years have gone by since then. Has he conceded defeat?"

Of course not, Hillary thought, but she didn't say it. She couldn't believe that Cutter had conceded defeat where Pam was concerned—any more than she could believe that he was done with John. Maybe she didn't want to believe it. Maybe it was the old-fashioned part of her that wanted love to win out and justice to prevail.

And yet, Cutter had seemed satisfied. But was he so content because he anticipated greater satisfaction?

Cutter had had the look of a man expecting vindication.

Or had she been imagining it?

She'd have to ask Pam.

Chapter 17

◆◆◆

Boston, 1974

Pam hurriedly locked the bathroom cubicle and whirled to hang over the toilet. She had to throw up. She felt it coming. She wanted to, if that would settle her stomach. She had a class in thirty minutes, and she'd absolutely die if she made a fool of herself there.

But nothing happened.

Nothing had happened in ten days, which was how long she'd been waking up nauseated. Morning sickness. She guessed it was as emotional as physical. Being pregnant was both a miraculously wonderful and a positively terrifying prospect.

Suddenly giddy, she leaned against the cubicle door and grinned at the ceiling. In the next breath, her eyes filled with tears. Lowering her head, she buried her face in her hands.

It had happened in Cutter's truck on that cold night in December. Neither of them had been prepared. Neither had expected to make love, much less there. It had been spontaneous, uncontrollable, and more than a little desperate.

She hadn't seen him since.

Hit by the ache of that hollowness, she leaned over the toilet again. Her arms shook as they propped her up. Her skin felt clammy. Closing her eyes, she took an unsteady breath. She knew she had to get control

of herself. She would forget the class in twenty minutes; she had the rest of her life to manage.

Straightening, she brushed the tears from her eyes, left the cubicle, and went to the sink. The cold water felt good on her skin. Time and again she splashed her face, and would have gone on for a while had another student not come in. She mumbled a wet hello, buried her face in a towel, then, when it was marginally dry, left.

Mercifully, she had a single room, so she was spared having to make explanations when she took a cracker, propped herself up in bed, and began to munch on it. She'd feel better once she ate, she knew.

She didn't feel better when she thought of Cutter, though. She ached. Being without him for the last two months had been as bad as losing her parents. Neither loss made sense. In Cutter's case, the loss was even harder because he was out there, somewhere, and she didn't know where.

Unfortunately, it had taken her a while to realize that. She had assumed, back in December when the days went by without a call, that he was very wary. After all, she was the one who had pushed for caution. She was the one who'd been terrified that John might find them out. After a week, her frustration mounted. She thought for sure that Cutter would call her from a pay phone, where nothing could be traced. Several days later, she used one herself, but he didn't answer his phone. She kept trying. After three weeks, she began to feel frightened.

Marcy, who was in constant touch with her family, told her that Cutter had vanished.

"Vanished? He can't just have vanished," she argued.

But Marcy held firm. "He's off the payroll, out of the bank, gone."

"But *why?*"

Marcy looked helplessly blank.

"Someone has to know where he went. All the men he stood up for—"

"I had Lizzie ask. They don't know."

"Aren't they worried?" Pam certainly was, and angry. "Aren't they

wondering whether maybe he's in some kind of trouble and needs their help for a change? Aren't they asking questions?"

Marcy was slower, more reluctant in answering. "That's not how they are. They don't ask. They accept. They adjust. Cutter left. Life goes on."

Pam wasn't so sure of that in the weeks that followed. She was miserable. One minute, she was sure that Cutter had abandoned her, that he had decided that loving her was too hard, that he'd given up the fight. The next minute, she was sure that John was involved in his disappearance. She couldn't ask him; it would be revealing and dangerous. She couldn't talk with Simon Blaise or Verne Walker, or even the FBI, for the same reason. So she was as helpless as the miners. Only she felt ten times worse.

The first time she missed her period, she attributed it to worry. The second time, she knew the truth. She didn't have to go to a doctor for confirmation. The sun was rising inside her, a little bit of Cutter growing there, making her feel full, worthwhile, and redeemed.

And scared.

She was going to have the baby. There was no question about that. It didn't matter that the Supreme Court had made abortion legal and easily obtainable. She wanted the baby. She figured that it would come in September, which meant that she could graduate with her class in June without many people even knowing of the pregnancy.

But John would know. His eagle eyes would see it. He would be furious, particularly if he knew the baby was Cutter's. Maybe she wouldn't have to tell him. Maybe she could run off, take her own apartment, and have the baby alone. She would be eighteen, an adult. College could wait.

Then she realized that John would be furious regardless of what she did. Her stomach churned at the thought. But she was going to have the baby, and if it looked like Cutter, she'd be thrilled. John could threaten all he wanted. He could resort to blackmail. He could try to manipulate her as he had in the past, only this time it wouldn't work. There was a life growing inside her and it was as precious to her as her own.

She wondered if it was a boy or a girl.

She wondered if it was hard to take care of a baby.

She wondered if people would look at her like she was a slut.

She wondered if John would disown her, and if he did, what access she would have to the trust fund her father had left her.

She wondered what Patricia would say. And Marcy. And Hillary.

She wondered where Cutter was.

As the next two weeks passed, though, she wondered most if she could make it through the semester. The nausea was nearly constant, and no matter how much she slept, she was tired. She didn't dare let up on her schoolwork lest her grades slip. She didn't want anyone at school, even her friends, to guess she was pregnant, so she had to deny the symptoms. And although she feared that something was wrong, since she was so sick, she feared seeing a doctor more. She was still underage. A doctor would report back to John.

The matter was taken out of her hands during the first week in March, when, rising from her chair at the end of Art History, she passed out cold. When she came to, she was on the floor, looking up at a ring of concerned faces. She struggled up, and might have convinced those around her that she was fine, had the headmaster not been passing by. He insisted that she be taken to the infirmary. Worse, he called John, who deemed it important enough to pick her up and take her to his personal physician.

"You look like hell," he said on the way there, and she knew she did. She *felt* like hell. Pregnant women were supposed to be radiant, but the only thing she radiated was exhaustion. Something was wrong. She was nearly as frightened for the baby as she was about John finding out she was pregnant. One scenario after another raced through her mind. By the time they reached the doctor's office, she was a bundle of nerves.

The first thing the doctor did was give her a sedative. When it had taken effect enough to silence her protests, he gave her the kind of examination the doctor at school hadn't thought to give. When he was finished, he removed her feet from the stirrups, covered her shivering body with a blanket, and left the room.

She was lying with an arm thrown over her eyes when the door opened again, then closed, and she knew the moment of judgment had come. She wished she felt up to it, but the world seemed vaguely distant. Still, she tried to steel herself for a fight.

"You've really done it," John said in a low, controlled voice. "Three months along."

Instinct made her deny the charge, albeit weakly. "He didn't do any tests. He can't be sure."

"He doesn't have to do tests. Not this late. He saw."

She swallowed tightly. The nausea was there, but it, too, seemed distant.

"Is it his?" John asked.

She thought of denying it, but she didn't have the strength. Besides, one part of her was furious at Cutter for not being with her just then. "Yes."

"Didn't you use anything?"

"Once we didn't."

"That's all it takes."

She was aware of feeling lighter—perhaps from the sedative, perhaps from sheer relief that the secret was out and she was still alive. John didn't sound as angry as she had thought he would be.

"When was it?" he asked.

"December. Early December."

"Have you seen him since?"

She swallowed. "No."

"Are you sure?"

Annoyed that he was prodding right where she hurt, she took her arm from her eyes. "I can't *find* him. He's gone. He doesn't even know about the baby."

"That's good."

"It's not good. It's his baby, too. He should be here with me." Turning away from him, she tucked up her knees and pulled the blanket to her chin. She felt cold and alone. She should be used to feeling that way, she knew, but the thought didn't help. The trembling wasn't

from a surface chill. It came from deep inside and was the kind that a blanket couldn't stop.

"I'll help you."

Tears came to her eyes. "I want Cutter."

"He's run off. Gave Simon a day's notice and left. No one knows where he is. Maybe he knew you were in trouble."

"He couldn't have."

"He has no sense of responsibility."

"He just doesn't know I'm pregnant, and I can't find him."

"What would he do if he knew? Race back here?"

"Yes."

"That's the last thing he'd do. He doesn't have money, and he doesn't have a job."

"Maybe he does. Somewhere else."

"Doing what? Flipping burgers? Working on an assembly line? Face it, Pam, he's a loser. You have the rest of your life before you. You're better off without him. He would only drag you down."

"But I want him."

John was silent for a minute. "You're tired and confused. You've been through a lot." He sighed. "Why didn't you tell me about this? Did you plan to go through it all alone?"

She peered at him over her shoulder. He looked sympathetic. Then again, she wasn't sure she trusted her eyesight. The sedative was probably clouding her vision. She was probably seeing what she wanted to see. "I couldn't tell you. You'd have hit the roof."

"Did I?"

She hesitated. "No."

"I can be reasonable."

"You aren't usually, when it comes to me."

"Because I insisted you get your grades up? But you've done it. Doesn't that make you feel good?"

She stared at him. His voice was gentle. She recalled another time when it had been that way. He had nearly raped her then. But he couldn't have rape on his mind now. Not in a doctor's office. Not with her pregnant and sick.

He guided damp strands of hair away from her temple and said quietly, "Come on. Get up and get dressed. You need rest."

"Is the baby all right?"

"You're weak. Haven't you been eating?"

"I'm nauseated most of the time."

He went to the door. "We can do something about that. I'll be waiting out here."

She watched the door close, then pushed herself up. The sedative slowed her, weighing down her limbs. Or perhaps it was due to fatigue. Or to confusion. John hadn't reacted at all as she'd expected. She didn't know what to think. He was being uncharacteristically nice. Remembering Palm Beach, she didn't want to trust him. But she needed someone to lean on. The thought of going through pregnancy and delivery all by herself was more than a little daunting. She wanted Cutter, but, damn him, Cutter wasn't there. If John was willing to accept the baby, she couldn't turn her back on his help. After silently carrying her burden for nearly three months, she was relieved to share it.

Back in the car, he was solicitous. Was she too warm? Too cold? Did she want to lower the back of her seat? Exhausted, she did that, then closed her eyes and dozed. When she came to, she was disoriented.

"Where are we?"

"Route Six."

She raised her seat, but even looking out the window she couldn't make sense of it. "This is the road to the Cape."

"That's right."

"What are we doing here?"

"There's a private hospital in Chatham. It's a restful place."

She sat straighter. "I thought you were taking me back to school."

"Pam, you passed out there. You're exhausted. That's the last place I'd take you."

"I have exams coming up. I have to study."

"You have to regain some strength."

"Then home. Take me home."

"This will be better. You'll have plenty of care."

"I don't need plenty of care. I want to go home."

"Relax. Everything's going to be fine. You'll spend a few days here. Come Monday, you'll be back at school. You'll have plenty of time to study then."

"I don't like this."

"It's the sensible thing. You're in lousy shape. Let me take care of you for a change, okay?"

Hit by a wave of nausea, she didn't argue further. But she was distinctly uneasy. Something didn't feel right, and it had nothing to do with her stomach.

John pulled up at a large Victorian house surrounded by low trees and shrubs, and guided Pam inside. They were expected. She was immediately ushered to a pretty room where a soft-spoken nurse helped her undress and get into bed, then returned a short time later to give her an injection.

"Just something to take the edge off and help you sleep," she explained. She looked so straightforward and kind that Pam trusted her. Within minutes, she was asleep.

When she woke up, the room was dim, lit only by a small lamp on the nightstand. She looked around. Her head was heavy, her eyelids even more so. She dozed off again, then came around to the awareness of movement by her side. It was the same smiling nurse.

"How do you feel?"

"Sleepy."

"That's to be expected."

"I've been so tired." She moved her lips very little, but even that was an effort.

"From the pregnancy. You'll be getting over that now."

"Past the first three months?"

The nurse gave her an odd look and made an adjustment that drew Pam's attention to the pole by the side of the bed, then the tube that led to her hand.

"What's that?" she asked, feeling as slurred as she sounded.

"Glucose."

"Am I that sick?"

"You're not sick at all, just a bit weak. After a procedure like this, we like to make sure you have enough fluids in your system."

Pam struggled to focus. "Procedure?"

Again the nurse looked at her oddly. "D and C."

Something ached in Pam's chest. "D and C?" she echoed in little more than a whisper.

The nurse squeezed her hand and said kindly, "It's a nicer word than the other, don't you think?"

"What other?" Pam whispered, but she knew. She knew. The pieces were fitting—John's calmness, his solicitousness. "What other?" she asked more loudly.

It was a minute before the word came. "Abortion."

"Oh God!" Pam cried. She put a hand on her stomach. "I had an abortion?"

"You had a D and C."

"God!" Her heart had begun to pound, and her eyes filled up. She looked around frantically, as though there might be someone or something there to tell her it wasn't so, but with even that small movement she felt the telltale pad between her legs. Her eyes flew to the nurse's. "I'm not pregnant anymore?"

"No."

"My baby's *gone*?"

"It wasn't viable. That was the whole point of doing it so soon."

Tears trickled down her cheeks. "The point of doing it so soon was to have it done before I knew what was happening." She brought her hands—IV needle and all—to her mouth and stifled an anguished scream. Enough of it escaped to frighten the nurse, who ran to the door for help. Within minutes, a doctor was there, with John in tow.

Fragments of the nurse's murmured words reached Pam from the door: ". . . woke up . . . didn't know . . . procedure . . ."

The doctor sent her out and came toward Pam, whose eyes were large and wet. "Is it true?" she asked in a shaky voice.

"That the baby's gone? Yes."

Pam gasped. "I wanted that baby."

"You came here for a D and C."

"I didn't know it." She avoided looking at John. He was reprehensible and repulsive. "I want my baby. I want it back."

The doctor put a pacifying hand on her arm. "What you're feeling is perfectly normal. You've been through a trauma. Something like this is hard enough for a woman in her twenties, but for a seventeen-year-old, it's worse."

"I want my baby."

"There's bound to be a sense of loss. But you made the right decision. You're very young to be having a baby—"

"I could have done it. I wanted it. I loved it."

"And now you feel guilt. That's natural, too. You're tired. Feeling drained. Is your stomach bothering you?"

The cramps she felt were nothing compared to the pain in her heart. "I want my baby!"

"Enough, Pam," John said, coming forward. "It's over. Done. The baby is gone. You can't bring it back."

"She needs time—" the doctor began in an undertone, only to be interrupted.

"She needs to be told the facts." John's eyes bore down on Pam with the anger that must have been festering inside him all along. "The baby's gone, and it's no loss. The pregnancy was a mistake from the start. You said it yourself; it wasn't planned."

"It was *my* baby, and Cutter's. You had no right—"

"*You* had no right—" John boomed, only to interrupt himself this time. To the doctor he said, "I'd like a few minutes alone with her."

"She shouldn't be upset."

"Give her a sedative."

"It's on the way. Still—"

"I don't want another sedative," Pam sobbed. "I want my baby!"

The doctor looked over his shoulder at the returning nurse. "Ah, there it is."

Pam rolled to the far side of the bed, only to be caught by John. "Get your hands off me!" she yelled.

"You'll hurt yourself. You're not well."

"I'm perfectly well. I'm pregnant." She made a choked sound. "Or

was until you stopped it. I don't want that," she told the doctor, who held a syringe in his hand. She struggled against John's hold, but the needle found its mark. "You *bastard!*" she screamed between sobs.

"That's right," John goaded. "Call me names as much as you want if it gives you satisfaction."

"Bastard! Dirty, filthy bastard! You won't let anyone else have what you can't, and you can't have kids because no woman wants you near enough—"

John took her chin in his hand and squeezed hard, effectively stemming her flow of words. He looked at the doctor. "Leave us?"

"She'll be asleep soon," he warned.

"Then I'll just say a few things before she is. I want her in a better frame of mind by the time she wakes up."

"I don't think—"

"Don't," John ordered. The single word was enough to send the doctor from the room. John's glare sent the nurse along in his wake. By the time he looked back at Pam, her lids were heavy.

"I want you to listen and listen good," he said.

The pressure on her mouth was painful. She closed her eyes, but tears continued to seep from their corners; it seemed the only way she could express her defiance and blot him out.

But he wouldn't have it. "Look at me, dammit," he growled and gave her chin a painful shake. When her eyes flew open, he said, "You had no business seeing Cutter Reid in the first place. I told you not to. I warned you that he was nothing but shit, but you thought you knew best, so you saw him. You let him touch you. You spread those lily-white legs and he screwed you." His teeth were gritted at the last. "And where did it leave you? In a big fat mess! How were you going to take care of a baby? Hmmm?"

Pam couldn't answer. He was hurting her jaw, preventing her from speaking. Her only sounds came from the back of her throat, against her will, from the crying she couldn't control.

"You're seventeen. Not even out of high school. Did you want to be a dropout like him?"

Pam grabbed his wrist and pulled with every bit of her dwindling

strength. "You're hurting me," she whimpered, and he eased the pressure on her jaw.

"I'm doing what's best for you," was his answer. "Someone has to, since you can't do it for yourself. You got yourself knocked up. I solved the problem."

Her tears came faster. "It wasn't a problem."

"An unwed, pregnant teenager isn't a problem?"

"I wanted the baby!" she sobbed.

"You have no idea what having a baby entails. You don't know the work involved or the dedication or the expense," he stuck a finger in her face, "and don't say I don't know, because I have friends who have kids. And don't," the finger jabbed her chest, "say I can't get a woman, because if I wanted, I could have five women happily pregnant in a matter of months. I choose not to have a child. I don't have the time or the interest."

"I do. I wanted one."

"You wanted his, because you knew it would drive me wild." His face came lower. "Well, you can't have it. It's gone. Flushed down some toilet, or whatever it is they do with unwanted refuse around here."

She cried out at the cruelty of his words. Tears streamed from her eyes. She felt close to drowning and far too weak to save herself or even to try.

"You'll thank me someday. When you're old enough to realize what a favor I've done you, you'll get down on your knees and thank me."

"*Never.*"

"When you're married to someone well known and successful, when you have a brick house bigger and nicer than the one in Timiny Cove, when you have a ski place and a Mercedes and three adorable kids who take gymnastics and soccer, you'll thank me."

The tears kept coming, despite the medication she'd been given, but her voice was losing strength. "I wanted Cutter's baby."

His eyes flashed. He took her shoulders and shook her. "Not another word. Not one."

"You can't stop me."

"I can come close. Haven't you learned that yet? Don't you know

that I control things around here? I'm the one who determines what happens. Not you."

"But why?" she cried. She fought the heaviness of her eyes and the lethargy that slowed her weeping and threatened to drag her down. "Why does it matter what I do if I mind my own business? I'm not hurting you."

"But you are," he said and squared his shoulders. "What you do is a direct reflection on me. Why do you think I've ruled with such a firm hand all this time? If it didn't matter, I'd have thrown you out on your own a long time ago." He paused. "That might have been fun to watch. The little girl all by herself. Justice, after the way they always fawned over you."

He leaned toward her, propped his fists on the bed, and stared at her. "I've worked hard to make a name for myself. I've walked softly when I wanted to yell. I've kissed ass when I wanted to spit. The St. George name is finally getting to be known and respected, and it had nothing to do with the old man and everything to do with me. You're a St. George. You do something stupid like getting pregnant by a miner and it's a mark against me. I'm the one they'll laugh at, and I've worked too hard for that. I want the recognition due me, and I'll be damned if I'll let you put the slightest blemish on it."

"I'm almost eighteen," Pam whispered weakly.

"Almost of age," he conceded. "But if you choose to make a fool of yourself, you'll do it without a cent from me. I don't give a damn whether you're twenty-five or married, I'll fight you every way I can. You lucked out this time. I've cleaned up this little mess without anyone the wiser. But in the future, when you make a spectacle of yourself, things won't be so neat. The only way I'll be able to stay clean will be to publicly denounce you. And I'll do it. Act up, and I'll do it. Loudly and clearly. Understood?"

His face swam before her eyes, partly from the tears that clung to her lashes, partly from the medication she'd been given. In a last, token show of defiance, she turned away and denied him an answer.

Chapter 18

❖❖❖

PAM DREW THE BRUSH GENTLY through Patricia's long hair. She had just trimmed the ends, as she'd promised during her last visit, and she imagined that the brush moved more freely. Certainly the neat line it produced was more pleasing than the splits and straggles. Then again, much of Pam's pleasure was in the doing. She enjoyed visiting her mother, more so in the last few months than before. Being with Patricia was calming. The whole hospital setting was calming. She was beginning to understand how a person could retreat there and want to stay. It was a world unto itself, a haven when reality became too hostile.

Gripping the wheelchair handle, she leaned sideways to look assessingly at Patricia's face. "Bangs. You need bangs."

Patricia blushed and murmured a soft, "At my age?"

"You're only thirty-seven. It'll look great." She touched her own. "Just a few. We'll be twins."

They could well have been, Pam knew. Their features were alike, and Patricia's skin was still smooth and dewy. If there was any sign of her age, or of the mental anguish she'd suffered since the accident five years before, it was in the color of her hair. Once blond, it was now pure silver. Pam thought it was beautiful. But then, she'd always thought her mother beautiful, even during those awful times when Patricia had been in her own isolated world.

"No bangs?" she asked with a gentle smile. When Patricia mouthed

an echo of the words, she said, "A French braid, then. Okay?" They'd done French braids before.

Patricia nodded.

Moving behind her again, Pam continued to use the brush for a little while before dividing the hair into thirds. She took her time. There was no rush here, no clocks posted on the grounds of the hospital. Instead, there were trees, tall pines and maples, lower-growing dogwoods and junipers separating one house from the next. There were eight houses in all, of differing sizes, for patients with differing needs. When Patricia had first come, she'd been in one of the larger houses that offered more intensive care. Now she lived in a small one for long-term patients with a degree of self-sufficiency. On warm days like this, she was free to enjoy the outdoors.

"Is school finished?" Patricia asked.

"Almost." Pam worked the silver plaits over and under one another. "Exams are next week."

After several minutes Patricia asked, "Are they hard?"

"Sometimes. But they don't matter much for seniors. Unless we botch them. But I won't." Not that she'd ace them, either. She would make just enough of an effort to pass. She didn't care about doing more. "Is the sun too strong? Want to move into the shade?"

"This is fine," Patricia said quietly.

Having reached the end of the braid, Pam needed something to hold it in. So she took a slim green ribbon from her own braid and tied it on. Standing back to admire her handiwork, she decided that it looked better on Patricia than it had on her. The contrast was there, green on silver. Green on brown was bland. But that was how Pam's life was. That was how she wanted it. She didn't have the emotional strength for more.

"Hey, you two!" came a voice from across the lawn. Pam looked up, saw Bob Grossman approaching, and smiled. He was a nice-looking man, lean, partially balding, but his manner was his strong suit. He was kind, gentle, surprisingly normal for a psychiatrist. "Hard to say which is the mother and which the daughter. You're looking

more grown-up every day, Pam, while you"—he put an easy hand on Patricia's arm—"go the other way. Pretty braid."

Patricia's cheeks warmed. "Thank you."

"No thanks necessary. You brighten my day." To Pam he said, "How's it going?"

She shrugged. "Okay."

Taking her hand, he pulled her down to the grass in front of Patricia's wheelchair. "Just okay?"

Pam folded her legs. "Just okay."

"It's the end of your senior year. You should be having the time of your life, partying up the kazoo. No?"

Pam managed a small smile and rolled her eyes. "No."

"Why not?"

She shrugged. "I just want out. It's all pretty boring."

"Ahhh," Bob drawled to Patricia, "the world-weary woman. We should only be back in her shoes."

"I wouldn't wish that on either of you," Pam said with more force than she'd intended. She sighed. Resting her elbows on her thighs, she combed her fingers through the grass in the circle between her legs. There was an apology in the eyes she raised to Bob's. "Sorry. I shouldn't have said that."

"You felt it," Bob said quietly. "I'm glad you said it. We all go through rough periods. Sometimes it helps to talk."

Pam darted a quick look at her mother.

Bob leaned closer to Patricia so that his shoulder touched her knee. "You're afraid of upsetting your mother. But she's come a long way. Maybe it's time we see what she can take." He sought confirmation from Patricia, but she was looking at Pam.

After a very long moment and in a very soft voice, Patricia said, "Yes."

It wasn't exactly an inquiry into Pam's feelings, but it did imply an interest, which was so much more than what used to be. Pam's throat knotted up; she swallowed the tightness away and forced a self-conscious smile. "It's no big thing, really. I'm just feeling down. School is unequivocally uninspiring."

"Big words," Bob mused. "Sounds like you've outgrown it."

"Oh yes," Pam said. She felt years older than her friends. The frivolity of graduation didn't interest her in the least.

"When's the big day?" he asked.

"The fourth of June."

"Do you have anything special planned?"

Pam shrugged and pulled at the grass. "I've been invited to dinner with some of the other families after the ceremony, but—" She scrunched up her nose.

"Don't want to?"

"Nah."

Patricia's voice was low. "John should do something."

"Spare me that," Pam said, but the attempted joke fell flat when tears came to her eyes. Blinking them away, she looked at her mother. "I wish you could come."

Patricia pursed her lips and gave a short shake of her head.

"Then I'll come out here afterward with a picnic lunch." With a glance, she extended the invitation to Bob. She'd rather be with him than with John any day. "The three of us can celebrate."

Again Patricia gave that quick shake of her head.

Pam didn't push. She knew that Patricia still had problems. Bob explained that they had to do with security and real life, and while Pam didn't see how a picnic lunch on the hospital grounds posed a threat, apparently Patricia did. And that was what mattered.

"Have you heard more from Swarthmore?" Bob asked.

Pam nodded. "They sent me health forms and questionnaires to fill out about what kind of roommate I wanted. I'd rather have a single room, but freshmen don't often get that."

"A double would be healthier."

"I figured you'd say that."

Bob grinned. "Typical shrink talk?"

"Yeah."

"It's true, though. Freshman year can be daunting. A bond formed early on with a roommate can go a long way toward easing anxiety."

Pam shrugged.

"Such enthusiasm," he chided. When she said nothing to that, he asked, "Are you looking forward to it?"

"Yes and no."

"Nervous about leaving home?"

His question hit a nerve. Levelly she met his gaze. "I left home a long time ago. There's nothing for me there."

"You and John?"

"Nothing. Worse than nothing. If I were the violent type, I'd have stabbed him in his sleep long ago."

"You don't really mean that."

"I do. Do you know what college means to me? It means going far enough from Boston so that he can't watch me every minute."

Bob glanced at Patricia, who was staring blandly across the lawn. Returning to Pam, he said, "You're very angry."

Pam was grateful for the reminder of her mother's fragility. Bob was a natural, the kind of man who invoked confidence and encouraged confession. She had poured her heart out to him more than once in the past few months, but never in front of Patricia. It was one thing to share gentle thoughts and mild frustrations, another to share all-out anger. Patricia wasn't ready for that.

As fate would have it, the physical therapist came across the lawn at that moment. Pam gave Patricia a hug, then stood with her arms hugging her middle while the therapist wheeled her off.

"You really are angry," Bob said, regarding her closely.

"Yes."

"It's right there, just below the surface. Doesn't take much to bring it up."

"No."

"Is it still the abortion?" He was one of the few people she'd told.

"That does it pretty quick."

"Are you okay?"

"Physically. Other than constantly feeling empty."

"But the guilt is still there."

"I keep thinking I should have known what John was up to. I should have fought harder. I let my baby down. And Cutter."

"Sounds like Cutter let you down. Any word from him yet?"

She shook her head.

"Still miss him?"

"Oh yeah," she whispered. "And now I'm leaving school. Leaving the city. Leaving the *country*. He won't be able to reach me."

"Where there's a will, there's a way."

His quiet words gave her pause. She studied her thumbnail. "Maybe I'd be better not knowing that. Then I could imagine that he isn't calling because he doesn't know where to call."

"You're too strong a person to delude yourself that way."

"I don't feel strong."

"But you are, Pam. Put that strength to work for you."

"How?"

"I can't tell you that. You're the only one who knows what you want in life. Or maybe you don't yet. Maybe it's too soon. Maybe that's what going to college is about." He paused. "Is the trip still set for this summer?"

"Uh-huh. Four of us hitting ten countries in nine weeks. I'm not sure Europe is ready—at least, not for the three of them. Me, I'll be Milquetoast."

"Heart's not in it?"

"No."

"It could be fun."

She sighed. "Well, it's the thing to do after graduation, and I committed myself to these friends over a year ago, so I couldn't very well back out. I suppose it's a good enough way to spend the summer. There's not much I'd rather do."

"Do you know how many people, grown-ups, would give their right arms to be in your shoes?"

She caught his grin, still she was duly chided. Sheepishly she said, "I know."

"You'll have a good time."

"Maybe."

"You'll learn a lot."

"Maybe."

"The art. The art. Think of the art."

"Believe me," she drawled, "that's the only thing that's keeping me going."

The art was wonderful. Pam and her friends started in London, hitting the National Gallery, the British Museum, the Victoria and Albert Museum, and the Tate Gallery, not to mention Big Ben, the Tower of London, and Westminster Abbey. From London they flew to Rome, where they caught the Sistine Chapel, the Galleria Borghese, and ruin upon ruin. They went by train to Florence, where Pam instructed the others on the magnificence of Michelangelo's *David*, as well as the treasures of the Pitti Palace and the Uffizi Gallery. By the time they reached Milan, her three friends were beginning to rebel. They met a group of local students and chose partying over spending hours before *The Last Supper*, as Pam wanted to do. She went along, but was miserable. By the time they had worked their way through the French countryside into Paris, she was spending part of each day off on her own, seeing what she wanted to see, then turning in early, while the others availed themselves of the local nightlife.

Then, on a small side street on the Left Bank, after she had thoroughly exhausted her enthusiasm at the Louvre, L'Orangerie, and the Jeu de Paume, the Musée Picasso, and the National Museum of Modern Art, Pam's fancy was caught. She was wandering by herself, having long since left her friends to check out Le Printemps and its kind, when she chanced across the small shop of a jewelry designer. She was first caught by samples of the woman's work—bracelets and rings of gold and silver with stones worked intricately into the designs—on display in the window. The pieces inside were even more impressive, far bolder and more innovative than anything Pam had seen produced by the designers at *Facets*. The artist, Monique Geffe, worked at the back of the shop. She was a quiet woman, in her thirties, Pam guessed, and she was amenable to letting Pam watch while she worked.

Watch, Pam did, through the rest of that afternoon and most

of the next day. She was fascinated by the way Monique worked from a drawing, the way she pounded the metal, cut it, molded it, shaped it, the way she mounted a stone, then remounted it when it wasn't quite right. Pam asked questions. She also drew simple sketches, often replicas of ones she had in her portfolio at home. She was totally drawn into the process of forging something beautiful out of rough goods, and what Monique made was beautiful indeed. At the end of the second day, she begged Monique to let her stay for the summer.

"Kind of an apprenticeship," she said in a voice that was soft but urgent. "No pay. I don't want any pay. I just want to learn to do what you do. I want to watch."

Monique spoke only broken English, yet Pam managed to make her point. "And your frienz?" she asked, rolling the *r*. "Zey say you do ziss?"

"My friends have each other. They can go on without me. They'll know how to contact me if anyone from home tries to reach me."

For a split second she allowed herself to dream that Cutter would call, that he would fly over, that they would hole up in a small Parisian pensione, madly in love with each other and with life.

When the second ended, she thought of John. He wouldn't try to reach her unless something happened to her mother, and she could forestall that by letting Bob Grossman know where she was. She'd tell Patricia, anyway. She was writing her long letters from each of the cities she visited. Whether they were read or not, it felt good to pretend that there was someone at home who cared.

Monique let her stay. Pam wanted to think it was because she saw promise in her sketches, but she suspected it had more to do with the respect Pam showed her. Not all Americans did. Pam was astonished by the derogatory comments made within easy hearing range of Monique. On more than one such occasion, Pam surprised the offender with a comeback in English, until Monique assured her that it was a waste of time and energy. Time and energy, she claimed, should be channeled solely into the craft.

Following that credo, Pam spent July and August by Monique's

side. She concentrated intensely and learned everything she could. Living in a small room not far from the shop, she worked six days a week. On the seventh, she either wandered through Paris on her own or went on outings with Monique and her husband. He spoke even less English than Monique. But Pam knew French. By the end of the summer she was fluent in it. By the end of the summer she was also turning out surprising professional pieces of jewelry.

Pam wanted to stay on. She had been happier working with Monique than she'd been in what seemed a very long time. In light, hopeful moments, she imagined becoming Monique's official assistant. She didn't need a salary. She would happily live on the commissions her work brought in. But Monique insisted she return to the States.

"Why do I need a liberal arts education," she asked in French, "if this is what I want to do?"

"You need more formal training. I can't give you that. You want to develop your own style. Some of it is there, in your sketches, but it is rough."

"It may be rough, but it's more than I'll get at Swarthmore."

Monique was shaking her head and a hand along with it. "No, no, no. Not Swarthmore. I've been talking with Phillipe. He knows people who studied in America. They say that Swarthmore is a fine school and has a good art program. But there is a better one." She took a piece of paper from her pocket, unfolded it, and put it flat on the table before Pam.

Pam looked at the name written on it. "I don't believe it," she murmured in English. Returning to French, she said, "But this is in Boston. I want to *leave* Boston."

"Have you heard of this school?"

"Of course. I've taken courses at the Museum of Fine Arts. Some of the teachers were students at the Museum School. I've seen shows by others."

"They were good, no?"

"They were good, yes. But I don't want to be in Boston. I don't want to be anywhere near John."

"You'd be near your mother."

Monique knew about that, too. One day Pam had received a letter from Bob telling her that Patricia not only read her letters but held them in her hand for days afterward. Monique had seen Pam's tears.

"Yes," Pam conceded. "I'd be near her. I'd like that."

"And you'll get your own apartment, something near the museum, maybe with other students, and you won't have to see John any more than you would have if you went to Swarthmore."

"But I wanted a change of scenery."

"Is Boston so small? Wouldn't you be living and studying in an area that's different from what you're used to?"

Pam supposed she would. Monique was being sensible.

"It's the best place for you, Pamela. Phillipe says so, and he's seen your work. So do I. If you want to come back here next summer, I would be very happy, but by then you may have moved beyond me."

"I doubt that."

"No. You have talent and enthusiasm. You love working with the materials. I can see it in the way you handle them. You love them and respect them. You have a vision for presenting them that few artists have. You need to work at enhancing that vision. Once you've done that, your pieces will be superb." When an innate modesty made Pam protest, Monique waved off the protest. "This is where your future lies, Pamela. You can establish a name for yourself. You can be very successful. If you want."

Si tu veux. The words echoed in Pam's mind during the flight across the Atlantic, and by the time she'd landed at JFK and transferred to a flight to Boston, she knew that she wanted to be successful more than anything in the world. By making a name for herself, she could be independent of John. She could take her legacy when she turned twenty-five and tell him to drop dead. If she was successful enough, she could even open her own shop and rival *Facets. That* would be satisfying.

Letting her imagination run wild, she envisioned the atelier she might have on Newbury Street, perhaps not as close to the Ritz as *Facets* was, but at a lower number, where the newer and more daring

artists worked. She would fit in well, and once she'd established a client base of her own, she could move higher, closer.

She could rival John on the social scene. That would make him croak. She could lure clients from *Facets*, and she'd do it without a second thought. Best of all, Cutter could visit her in her chic little shop, and John wouldn't be able to do a thing about it.

That would be the most satisfying of all.

Chapter 19

❖❖❖

STARING AT THE BANK STATEMENT he'd just received, Cutter indulged in a few fantasies of his own. It was a new experience, but then, having a six-figure balance in his personal account was a new experience. Barely nine months out of Timiny Cove, he had a steady income and a promising future. Hard to believe, given the way he'd arrived in New York.

He was cold, tired, and slightly overwhelmed when he'd rung Hillary's bell that night. The trip from the airport had been a mess of bus changes and subway connections. Even at night, the city was ten times louder, more crowded, and faster paced than Boston. But New York was the place to be if a man wanted to make it, and Cutter did. He didn't know how, but being in the right place was the first step.

In hindsight, he realized that showing up at Hillary's had been an act of daring. She had been close to John in Timiny Cove. Cutter had no idea whether she still was. But he had to take the chance that she'd let him in. He didn't know where else to turn.

Besides, she and Pam were friends, and he needed to be in touch with someone who was in touch with Pam.

Not only did Hillary let him in, she gave him a bed and food. She seemed pleased that he was there, even when he told her that he and John were archenemies.

"Then it's a good thing he isn't here," she said smugly.

"Is there a chance he'll come?"

"Not much. He was here last week. Twice in a month and I might think he was serious. He wouldn't let that happen."

So Cutter stayed. There was a certain gratification in encroaching on John's turf. He knew that Hillary felt it too. It created a subtle bond between them.

He slept for most of the first few days. His back hurt, and he hadn't fully regained his strength. He didn't tell Hillary about the beating; the trouncing he'd taken embarrassed him. He couldn't hide his over-all anger, though, since it was largely what kept him going. It also kept her aware that she was cavorting with the enemy. He wanted her to remember that.

Still she took him under her wing. She took him to the bank to deposit his savings, took him to Bloomingdale's to buy job-hunting clothes, took him to an employment agency run by a friend to look for a job. There was nothing, of course—at least nothing that he wanted to take. He didn't want to be a janitor or a short-order cook or a salesman.

"I think you should consider the chauffeur job," Hillary told him as they walked back to her place.

"And wear a uniform and a cap?"

"Head too big for it?"

"Yeah. It is. I've got pride."

"You also have no skill, no training, no job. If you took this one, you'd be working for the president of a large brokerage firm. You'd be listening to high-power conversations involving some of the most suc-cessful businessmen around. You'd be in a position to make contacts. The exposure would be incredible."

"I'd be a chauffeur."

"Play your cards right, and you'd be someone's discovery. You're a bright guy. Ask the right questions of the right people, and you could find yourself in a super entry-level job that you wouldn't have been able to get without that personal contact."

But Cutter doubted that things happened that way in real life. Besides, New York traffic unsettled him. He figured he could afford to

wait around, looking, for a week or two before taking something just for the sake of the money.

The waiting depressed him. He slept late every day, then just hung around Hillary's, hoping the phone would ring. When the silence had him climbing the walls, he went out for long walks. He immersed himself in the crowds. He timed his stride to match the business-like gait of those around him. He did his best to be part of the city's hustle.

Deep down inside, though, he felt like an impostor. He wasn't thinking New York thoughts as he walked those streets. He was think-ing Boston thoughts. Pam thoughts.

He wondered how she was, what she was doing, if she was think-ing of him.

He stared at every phone booth he passed, then walked on by. Hearing her voice would hurt too much. He would want to see her. But he couldn't. It was too dangerous. As soon as he knew who he was and where he was going, he would call. As soon as he had some hope of battling John and winning, he would be back in her life. She was his. If she loved him as much as she said, she'd wait.

The problem was that he didn't know how long the wait would be. He wanted her next week, next month. But that was asking for a miracle. He was at rock bottom—no job, no prospects, no training. He had so far to go to gain a foothold on John.

His mood darkened progressively as the days passed. Hillary tried to cheer him with one success story or another, but he wasn't inter-ested in anyone else's luck. She tried to lure him to parties, but one raucous, strobe-lit encounter was enough to show him how alien he was. Then, on a dark and rainy night, out of sheer desperation, he was sure, she dragged him to a lower Manhattan bar. He went along with the sole intention of getting drunk. Barely two beers into the process, he saw something that annoyed him.

"What's their problem," he growled under his breath.

"Whose problem?"

"Those two guys at that back table. They're staring. Do I look funny or something?"

Hillary was on her second scotch and feeling mellow. She tossed an easy glance over her shoulder toward the men in question. "You're imagining it. They're not staring."

His eyes didn't leave the men. "They're staring. Like I've got horns."

"If they're staring, it's because you're a gorgeous hunk. You really are, Cutter." She grinned and raised her glass to her lips. "Maybe you turn them on." She took a drink.

"Shit, here they come. I'm leaving." He started to get up, but Hillary's hand was suddenly like lead on his arm.

"Sit. We were here first. I refuse to be chased away by two ignominious creeps. If they cause trouble, I'll hail the bartender. He'll toss them out." She grinned. "Create a little excitement. Might do us good."

The men reached their table. One was taller, darker, leaner than the other. Both wore business suits with the jackets off, sleeves rolled up, ties loosened. They looked clean-cut, if hassled, and they continued to stare at Cutter.

"I wonder," said the shorter of the two, "if we could talk with you for a minute."

"What about?" Cutter snapped.

"Who you are," the taller said, "where you're from, what you do."

Only two people had ever expressed as much interest in Cutter in as short a time—Eugene and Pam. Neither of the men struck Cutter as having the heart Eugene had, and neither of them in any way, shape, or form resembled Pam.

"That's none of your goddamned business," he answered. The men exchanged quick grins. Cutter didn't like the looks of it.

"If you guys are queer, get the hell away from me and stay away."

The taller man reached into his pocket and handed Cutter a business card. The name on it was Douglas Verrana, and it claimed that he was the vice president of a firm whose name meant nothing to Cutter.

He turned the card forward and back. "Nice feel."

Hillary took it from his hand. Her response was more respectful.

"I'm not familiar with your name, Mr. Verrana, but I am with Wald, Newcomb." To Cutter, she said, "It's one of the leading advertising firms in the city." She extended her hand to the man. "I'm Hillary Cox, and my friend is Cutter Reid. What can we do for you?"

"Your friend," Verrana said. "Is he new around here?"

"Relatively."

"Where is he from?"

"Maine."

"Hillary . . ." Cutter warned, but she silenced him with a hand on his arm.

"What line of work is he in?"

Hillary hedged. "Why do you ask?"

The second man answered. "My name's Pete Shorb. I work with Doug. We're looking for a model. Your friend has the face we want."

The face in question donned a look of distaste. "Model?"

"For an ad campaign we're doing."

"An ad campaign for what?" Hillary asked.

Cutter couldn't believe it. She actually sounded interested. "Hillary—"

She tightened her hand on his arm. "What are you advertising, Mr. Shorb?"

"A collection of clothes by Girard Jondier. He works out of Paris. His line has a loyal following on the Continent, but he's only now thinking of going for the American market." He regarded Cutter assessingly. "The idea is to get one man with the right look—the right American look for the clothes—and make that face instantly identifiable with the line. You look different. Independent. Like a rebel." He lowered his gaze to Cutter's shoulders and chest. The table cut off the rest. "How tall are you?"

Hillary spoke up before Cutter could tell him to get lost.

"What are his clothes like—this Girard Jondier?"

"Elegant. Expensive."

Verrana elaborated. "He got his start in informal wear, but he's recently branched into sportswear. He's introducing both lines in this country. We're talking high fashion. The man who wears Jondier's

suits is affluent and self-assured. He's a leader. His clothes make a statement, but it's a subtle, classy one."

Cutter liked the sound of that hypothetical man. He was everything he wanted to be but had virtually no chance of in the immediate future unless something drastic happened. Being discovered in a bar and turned into a model, though, went beyond the drastic to the absurd.

"How tall are you?" Shorb repeated.

The thought of being a pretty-boy model was ridiculous to Cutter. But Hillary was listening as though there might be something to it. He figured he could go along and listen, too, at least until he heard the bottom line. Somewhere along the way he'd read that models made big money. He could use big money.

"Six-two," he said.

"Weight?"

"One-eighty."

"All in the shoulders," Hillary put in. "He's narrow from the waist down."

"What does he do for a living?"

"I'm a miner," Cutter declared.

That seemed to please the men immensely. Again they grinned at each other. "Are you just visiting here?" Shorb asked.

"Maybe. Maybe not."

"Depending on whether you can find a job," Verrana guessed. "You won't find much here by way of mining. And I can guarantee that nothing you find will come close to matching the kind of money you can make if you work with us."

"What kind of money is that?"

"Fifty thousand a year."

Cutter was thinking that fifty thousand was more than four times what he'd been getting and had to be too good to be true, when Hillary burst out with an indignant, "Are you kidding? If you want Cutter Reid's face, you'll have to pay a lot more for it. And then there's the rest of his body to consider. He's worth a lot more than fifty thousand a year."

"I'm not adverse to negotiation," Verrana replied, but to Cutter.

Cutter said nothing. It occurred to him that Hillary had been taken as the more sophisticated of the two and therefore the more shrewd. Indeed she was. But he was a quick study. A minute before, he'd have taken the fifty thousand and run without any idea that there was more in the pot. Now he knew better.

"We're getting ahead of ourselves," Verrana went on. "Before we can talk money, we have to know how you photograph. Have you got a portfolio—no, of course you haven't. Sorry. We're used to working with professionals."

Cutter heard the put-down and knew it was deliberate. The message was that as a novice in the profession, he shouldn't expect the fee of an experienced model. What Verrana didn't know was that he didn't give a damn about modeling. The money was the only reason he'd do it. If he was going to demean himself by being photographed in designer clothes, he was damned well going to be paid as much as possible for it. If that turned out to be fifty thousand, fine. All the better if it turned out to be more.

Shorb was jotting something on the back of his business card. "Can you be at this address at ten o'clock tomorrow morning?" He handed the card to Cutter.

"What for?" Cutter asked, handing it on to Hillary as if she were his business manager. He liked that idea. John would have a fit if he knew.

"Photos."

"Who'll be doing them?" Hillary asked.

"Brian Webster."

The name meant nothing to Cutter, but he could feel the excitement radiating from Hillary's hand. "Brian Webster usually works on location. Are you sure he's in the country?"

"He's here."

"And he'll have time for us on the spur of the moment?"

"We've paid him a hefty retainer to do this ad campaign," Verrana said. "He'd better."

Shorb was looking at Cutter. "Will you be there?"

After a long minute, Cutter nodded slowly.

Shorb beamed at Verrana. "See the defiance? It's what we need."

Verrana wanted to know how they could reach Cutter if there was any change of plan. Hillary promptly produced a business card of her own, which he pocketed. "You won't regret this," Verrana told Cutter.

Cutter didn't say a thing as he watched the two leave the bar. The minute they were out the door, he sent Hillary a hard look, then drained his beer in a single chug.

"Sure beats playing chauffeur," she said.

Cutter agreed, but it took him a while. He didn't enjoy the photo session the next morning. Too many people were there—the photographer and his assistants, a clothes person, a hair person, a makeup person, Verrana and Shorb and half a dozen of their associates—all looking at him. For the private person he was, it was unnerving. Moreover, he didn't like having to wear strange clothes or have his hair fiddled with or his nose powdered. He felt like a fool on parade.

But he did like the photographer. He was a straight sort of guy who talked quietly as he worked. He sensed Cutter's awkwardness and dealt with it in subtle ways that made an uncomfortable situation bearable.

So that was one good point. The other was the sum of money Cutter was offered to spend a year working exclusively as the man in the Girard Jondier suit. John Torvall, an agent whom Hillary contacted when it became clear how excited Verrana and Shorb were with the preliminary prints, negotiated a contract that made it well worth Cutter's while to put up with embarrassment and discomfort.

So there he sat, studying his bank statement, indulging in dreams. He already had his own apartment, taken immediately after he signed the contract, and although it was small, it had everything he needed. It wasn't far from Hillary's, but even if it had been, he'd have seen her often. He liked her. He was grateful to her. And she was still his link to Pam.

He knew that Pam had graduated from high school, that she had spent the summer in Europe, and that she was studying at the Museum School in Boston. Classes would have started the week before.

He thought of calling; she was rooming with two other art students, Hillary said, and he was sure she had the number. But he didn't call for the same reason as he didn't fly up to Boston to visit. He didn't trust what John would do if he found out.

Occasionally he wondered whether things might be different now that Pam was eighteen and he was gainfully employed in New York. All he had to do at those times was finger the raised ridges on his back, and he knew he couldn't take the chance. Not with a man as prone to violence as John. In the nightmares he still had about the beating, two things always stood out: the first were the sounds John had made with each blow, the grunting that had been almost sexual, and, in that, obscene; the second were the last words John had said, muttered in his ear in a venomous voice.

If I can't have her, you sure as hell can't either.

The words haunted him. He tried to think back, to remember anything Pam might have said or done to hint that John had molested her, but there was nothing. It was a good thing. If John ever abused her sexually, he would strangle the man. Literally. Even if he ended up in prison.

There were, though, other ways to handle him, and those were the ones Cutter most fantasized about when he considered the money collecting in his bank account. He let his mind wander two years, three years, four and five down the road. If during each of those years his income remained steady, and if he lived simply and banked every spare cent, he would have a substantial amount of money amassed. If he invested that money, the amount would grow even more substantial. The greater it was, the more power he would have, and the more power he had, the better a position he would be in to get back at John. He didn't know exactly what he wanted to do. He had wild visions of riding in on a black charger and stealing the St. George Company, but things didn't happen that way, he knew.

Still, Cutter would do something. John was going to live to regret what he'd done.

* * *

While Cutter's dreams were broad and sweeping, Hillary was at-tuned to the smaller satisfactions of life. "I'm going to show John the ad," she announced. It was late September. Cutter's face was in every classy magazine on the stands.

"Don't."

"Why not?"

"He'll wonder how you knew to look."

"No, he won't. I read fashion magazines all the time."

"Don't, anyway."

"But I'd think you'd want him to know."

They were eating breakfast, danish and coffee to go, on a bench on the east side of Central Park. Cutter set his coffee on a worn wood plank. "It's enough that I know for now. There's satisfaction in that. Don't worry. People talk. He'll find out. Maybe he'll choke on his cav-iar in the middle of some important party."

"Shhhh."

Cutter gave her a dry look. "He'd wish the same on me."

Hillary didn't argue. "What about Pam? I talk to her every few weeks. I see her when I'm in Boston."

He already knew that. Like a starving man begging for crumbs, he grilled Hillary on every detail of those visits.

"She asks, Cutter. She asks if I've heard anything about you. I feel lousy not telling, and it's not even so much because we're friends. She thinks about you a lot. She worries. It's only a matter of time before she sees those pictures. She'll be hurt."

"She won't recognize me. I look completely different."

"It would take a lot more than shorter hair and fancy clothes to disguise you from Pam. She'll know it's you the instant she sees one of those ads. Let me tell her. Prepare her. Better still, you tell her. Give her a call."

"I can't."

"Why not?"

"John forbid me to do it."

"Screw John."

"That's your job."

"Oh, Cutter."

"I can't call her, Hillary. Not yet. There are too many people John can hurt if he wants to get back at me, and I'd be helpless to stop it."

"Don't you miss her?"

"I miss her so much I hurt, and it's not for sex."

"So *see* her."

"I will."

"When?"

"Soon."

And soon it was. Barely a week later, when he had a rare free day and was feeling rash, he flew to Boston and staked out the path in the Fens between the museum and Pam's apartment. Late in the afternoon, she walked by with a friend. Cutter's chest tightened. He was leaning against a tree, separated from her by shrubs, people, and several hundred feet, but he took in every detail of her appearance.

She looked beautiful. Young, but grown-up. Artsy. She was wearing loose pants, a voluminous blouse, and a long vest, and she carried a canvas satchel over her shoulder. Her hair was in a thick braid that fell from the nape of her neck to the middle of her back, secured so that the breeze couldn't ruffle it, as it did her bangs. Large gold hoops swung from her ears.

Once she looked up and around. His heart started to hammer—he was sure she sensed his presence. Then she looked back at her friend and laughed at something the other had said. A minute later, the two went into their apartment building.

If she'd been alone, Cutter might have followed. But seeing her with someone, seeing her smile, seeing how comfortable she looked in her new life, he couldn't do it. He couldn't take the chance. They had no future yet. One day, dammit. One day. . . .

So he returned to New York. Fall became winter, and by the time spring arrived, Cutter had seen more of the country than he'd ever thought to see. He was photographed wearing Girard Jondier suits in San Francisco, sweaters and slacks in Aspen, cruise wear in Key West. If the fall line was well received, the spring line was even more so.

Girard Jondier was pleased with Cutter. In turn, Cutter was pleased with his new contract.

There were still times when he wondered if he was crazy to be doing this. Real men didn't model. But he wanted to be rich enough to ruin John, and given that he wasn't trained for much, modeling seemed the fastest way to wealth. He abided the graceful male hands that smoothed suit jackets across his shoulders, the hovering of makeup artists and hair stylists, the glare of lights. He even abided the innuendos about his sexuality. All that was less humiliating than what he'd suffered at John's hands, and this time around he was being handsomely compensated for the indignity.

His private life was quiet, modest, and brief. Big bucks brought big demands, he learned. There were different clothes to model each season, different ads to shoot, then reshoot if the prints weren't just right, different stores to visit as Jondier's representative. At times he felt he'd made a bargain with the devil. But the devil wasn't Jondier, it was John, and regardless of how tired Cutter was at times, he was determined to triumph.

His face became known in high-fashion circles, more so with each season. He was invited to parties, where he became known—but only to a small extent. He remained a private person, carefully picking his points of exposure. He didn't make friends idly and had no use for large groups or shallow ones. He chose friends for their intelligence, their success, and their sense of discretion. They were, by and large, businesspeople. They became his teachers.

Through them, he connected with a financial adviser, a stockbroker, and an investment banker. By the time he'd been in New York for four years, the portfolio of which he was most proud wasn't the one filled with glossies that his agent kept on hand. It was the one that listed his financial assets.

Throughout those four years he ached for Pam. He had seen her many times—glimpses similar to the one on the Fens that day, only at places like Symphony Hall or Locke-Ober's or even, when he had been daring enough to hang out on Newbury Street, around *Facets*. There was a *Facets* New York now, too, opened two years before, and

she had come down for the festivities. He had seen her. He had seen
John. Neither of them had seen him, and as far as he could tell, neither
had been interested in seeing the other. Hillary confirmed that they
barely talked. Cutter wanted to know more.

Mostly, though, he wanted to hold Pam. The need was so great
that there were times in the night when he was bent up in pain. He
found satisfaction in other women, but it was brief, strictly physical,
and offset by the agony of opening his eyes and seeing a face that
wasn't Pam's.

That was why, shortly before she graduated and left her apartment
on the Fens, he drove up to Boston and, cloaked by the night, broke
into her room.

Chapter 20

❖ ❖ ❖

Pam hadn't slept heavily in years. Her mind was too active to be turned off for more than three or four hours at a stretch. It woke her at least once each night with thoughts of a lecture she'd heard or a paper she was writing or a piece of jewelry she was making. Once in a while it woke her with thoughts of John or Patricia. Regularly it woke her with thoughts of Cutter.

It did so this night, and, as always, she imagined he was with her. She turned over, curled into a ball, and gave the kind of sigh that was part pleasure, part pain. Then she heard a soft sound on the far side of the room, and the peace of her half-dream state vanished. Completely awake, she jolted to a sitting position and was about to cry out when a figure emerged from the darkness and clamped a hand over her mouth.

"Shhhh. It's me."

The room was dim and his voice a whisper, but something about the scent of his skin and the feel of his lips against her forehead painted a picture in Pam's mind. When his hand left her mouth, she whispered, "Cutter?"

"Yes."

She was sure she was dreaming. She hadn't seen him in four and a half years. But her hands were touching solid arms, a strong jaw, a warm neck. And there was the scent. And his lips. "Cutter?"

He looked down at her and whispered, "I couldn't stay away any longer. I had to see you."

Her pulse raced. "Oh, my God." She wrapped her arms around his neck. "I don't believe it." The words were no sooner out than she held him back. She touched his face with a trembling hand, each feature in turn. "What—oh, my—how did you—what time—"

"Shhh." He kissed her cheek, the bridge of her nose, her other cheek. "I climbed the fire escape."

"How did you know where I live?"

"The same way you know where I live."

Hillary. "But you've never come before."

"Not inside."

"You've been outside?"

"Um-hmm."

She made a small sound. "How did you know which room was mine?"

"I waited till it got dark, then watched."

"You didn't."

"I did."

"Oh, Cutter!" She hugged him again, and this time when she held him back, her mouth found his. If she'd had any lingering doubts, they vanished. No one kissed like Cutter did. No one devoured and adored at the same time. No one else could arouse her with a breath. She gave herself up to it, floated, rose, until sheer excitement had her gasping for air. "Oh, Cutter," she whispered, "I can't believe you're here."

"I am."

"After all this time."

"Four years."

"More."

"Four and a half."

"An eternity. I've missed you so." She went into his arms again, and this time warm tears flowed against his neck.

He hugged her tightly. "Ahhhh, babe."

She was in heaven. "For the longest time I didn't know where you

were, and when Hillary told me, I was angry that you hadn't written or called."

"I couldn't."

"She said you were afraid."

"I still am."

"But you have a name now." She caught her breath at the reminder and, incredibly, felt a twinge of shyness when she drew back and looked up. "You've done so much. I see those magazine ads and pinch myself. I show them to my friends and tell them that I knew you before you were famous. You travel all the time. You meet lots of people. It must be an exciting life."

"It's a means to an end."

"But it's so glamorous." She tried to make out more of him in the dark, without success. She would have turned on a light, but she feared she might find him a stranger. So she left the light off and ran her fingers through his hair. It was as thick and vibrant as ever and had the feel of casual disarray. The disarray was far more sculpted, though, than it had been in Timiny Cove. "You've changed," she whispered timidly.

"No."

"You must have. You've come so far."

"I'm still me."

"Do you love me?"

"I'll love you till the day I die."

"Oh, *Cutter.*"

He kissed her once, then again, longer. He buried his face in the crook of her neck, wound his hand around her braid, and held her close. Catching her lips a third time, he bore her back on the bed. "Love you till the day I die," he said hoarsely, "and want you till I can't get it up. I need you, babe."

She needed him, too, needed his hands on her breasts and her belly, and he gave her that. He touched her, stroked her, and when she began to burn, he took off her nightshirt and stroked her even higher. She was nearly in flames when he finally undressed, and there, with nothing between them but air, and then not even that, they were as

they'd always been, so in love with each other that the rest of the world fell away.

She wasn't sure she wanted to return. Long after the quivering stopped and her heartbeat leveled, she clung to Cutter, and he held her tenderly. After a time he stretched out beside her, propped himself on an elbow, and ran the backs of his fingers over the moist skin from her throat to her navel.

"You're more beautiful than ever," he whispered. "More mature."

"I'm the same."

"Ready to graduate."

"Still the same." She touched his jaw. "I've missed you so much. I dreamed of seeing you. There were times when I thought I had, when I'd be in a crowd somewhere and think you were there, but I could never find you. After Hillary told me where you lived, I dreamed of parking on your doorstep. I dreamed of picking up the phone and calling. I almost did, lots of times. But I was so scared. There was John. And you."

"Me?"

Her throat tightened. "I wasn't sure you still loved me."

He cupped her face with a firm hand. "I told you I'd love you forever. I always said that, and it's true."

"But you didn't call. You didn't come. I didn't hear from you after that night . . . after . . . that night."

He stroked her hair and held her closer.

"I'm sorry," she whispered. If she'd been stronger, if she'd paid more attention, if she'd expected the worst of John instead of deluding herself that he cared, the baby would be alive. "I'm so sorry."

He raised her face with his hands. "Not your fault. John's fault."

Her heart skipped a beat. "You knew?" When she had finally spilled it to Hillary, she had sworn her to secrecy. She blamed herself for the abortion. She didn't think she could bear it if Cutter blamed her, too.

But Cutter had mistaken her apology. "You told me about his threats. You were terrified that last time, and you had a right to be. He's a vicious man. But he'll get his, Pam."

Relieved, she felt a burst of strength. "I showed him your ads. It was worth going near him to see the astonishment on his face."

"Astonishment?"

"Then anger. He got quiet and tight, and for a minute I thought maybe he'd take it out on me. But I didn't care. I was so proud of those ads. I'm so proud of you. You've done so much."

"I've been lucky."

"You've been smart. You saw an opportunity and took advantage of it." Her hands made an admiring circle of his chest before meeting near his navel. "What's it like being a model?"

"Tedious. What's it like being an artist?"

"I don't know. I'm not a real one yet."

"You had an exhibit at *Facets* last winter."

"It wasn't much. Just a few pieces."

"They were beautiful."

"You saw them?"

He nodded. "Put on a duster and a Stetson and a pair of sunglasses. Didn't look a bit like myself."

"You saw my work but you didn't see me?"

The smugness disappeared from his voice. "I wanted to, Pam. I wanted to see you so much I could taste it. Then I thought of John, and I thought of how well things were going for you, and I couldn't risk ruining that."

"What's changed from then to now?"

"You. You're getting ready to graduate. It's a whole chunk of your life I've missed. I had to see you before you moved on."

"Oh, Cutter," she sighed. She kissed his throat and the underside of his jaw before letting her mouth rest on the pulse point at his neck. She had always loved that spot. It was a bellwether of his state, slow and steady when he slept, strong and steady when he woke, less steady but stronger than ever when he wanted her.

He wanted her now.

"Look at me," he whispered.

She did. His eyes were dark and hot in the night. He lifted her thigh over his, slid his hand to cover her bottom, and drew her

forward. His entry was smooth; she was moist and ready for that, but the sense of utter fullness stunned her. She closed her eyes to savor the pleasure.

"Look at me," he repeated.

When she did, he began to move, and the pleasure of that was so intense she thought she'd die of it. Over and over she breathed his name. She held tight to his arm, which held her tight to him. Then, sure she was dreaming since nothing had ever felt so good as his slow, deep stroking, she dropped her hand to his belly, then lower to clutch at the course hair that hit hers at each thrust. She breathed his name louder this time, a cry when her climax began. Her arms went around his neck. She held on for dear life while it shook her. By the time awareness returned, Cutter was at the end of his own release. She watched him as he fell back to the bed, panting, eyes closed, skin glossy with sweat.

When the panting eased, she put her thumb to the corner of his mouth. "I love you so much."

He snagged her neck with an elbow and pulled until she lay half over him. "Didn't use anything, Pam."

It was a minute before she realized what he meant. "It's okay."

He opened an eye. "You take something?"

She nodded.

He opened both eyes. "Do you date much? Hillary would never tell me."

"She couldn't. I never told her. But there's no one special, Cutter. The guys I know are just friends."

"Students?"

"At Tufts, mostly. I take my academic courses there. Sometimes there's a party or a lecture, and it's nice to be with someone."

"You're on the Pill."

The accusation was mild, but it was there. She put her forearms on his chest and swallowed before she spoke. "I never heard from you. I wasn't sure if I ever would. Once I learned what you were doing, I thought for sure you'd forget me. You were with so many people. So many women."

"I wasn't."

"Well, I thought you were. I thought you had a really busy and exciting life of your own and didn't need me anymore. There were times when I felt so empty inside, and I thought that maybe if I was with someone it would help, only it didn't." She paused. "I'm sorry," she whispered, wondering how often she'd have to say those words. She felt guilty about so many things.

Cutter held her head to his chest. His voice was gruff. "Don't keep saying that. I can't blame you for what you did. I may be jealous, but I don't have the right."

"Have there been many women?"

"No."

"One, two?" She raised her head. "Would I know them?"

He studied her face and smiled gently. "No. And I won't tell you their names. It's irrelevant."

"Are they my age?" When he didn't answer, she asked, "Are they models?"

"Pam."

"They must be beautiful."

"You're beautiful."

"Are they good?"

He flipped over and pinned her to the bed. "I'm not telling you a damn thing," he growled playfully. "It doesn't matter who they are, how old, how pretty, how good. I had to drive for five hours, sit outside in my car for another two until the cops staking out the Stop sign left, climb a fire escape, jimmy open a window, and then sit with my hands between my legs until I couldn't take it anymore and woke you up. If I'd wanted any of them, would I have done all that?"

Of course he wouldn't have, she realized, and that made her feel a little better. "The guys I was with were awful. I couldn't respond, not the way I do to you. One of them asked if I was frigid. The other kept apologizing because he couldn't make me come. No man does it for me like you, Cutter."

"No?"

She shook her head.

He watched her, half-smiling, then trailed a look down her body. "You're so beautiful." He scooped her close. "Holding you is like holding heaven." He rolled to the side and framed her face with a hand. "You're so good. Sensitive and kind. I've never been able to understand how you could be related to John."

"I've dreamed that I wasn't. It was wonderful."

"Do you see him much?"

"As little as possible."

"I was surprised you went to school here. I thought you'd want to go away."

"I did. Until I met Monique." She told him about that summer and how it had changed her direction. "I've been back to Paris every summer since. Monique is wonderful. She was the one who pushed me into having the show at *Facets*. If it had been up to me, I'd have stayed as far from John as possible. But she said I was a fool, that I had a contact most artisans would die for, that there was no reason why I shouldn't use *Facets* to launch my career. And I realized she was right. It was only fair that I should get something out of the grief John has caused. Besides, part of *Facets* is mine. It may not be a big part, and I may not have any say for another three years, but I am a St. George. Daddy would have wanted me to have the show there."

"I'm surprised John let you."

"He wasn't wild about the idea until I told him I'd go elsewhere."

"Did you? Good girl!"

"He's a bastard, Cutter. They hate him at the mines. He treats them well, but there's always a price to be paid. He likes being able to pull strings and make people dance to his tune."

"Does he bother you here?"

"No. He calls once in a while just to remind me he's around. God forbid I should forget." But that was exactly what she wanted to do just then. Cutter was there. To spend her time with him talking about John seemed a sacrilege. "Tell me about your work, Cutter. Tell me how it happened."

He skated a hand down the slope of her hip. "Didn't Hillary tell you that?"

"I want to hear it from you."

With a bit more prodding, he told her about the two men in the bar, the initial shoot, the contract, the early assignments. She asked question after question, and when the answers he gave were too vague, she told him so. She felt she was emerging from a four-year vacuum. Nothing was too trivial, nothing too mundane. She wanted to know what was in his mind when he posed, how long the sessions went, whether he preferred studio layouts to location shoots. She wanted to know which ads of all the ones he'd done he liked the best and why. She wanted to know whether Girard Jondier wore his own clothes, what kind of camera Brian Webster used, whether Cutter's hair stylist was gay, and where Cutter spent Thanksgiving and Christmas. She made him describe his apartment. She asked whether people recognized him on the street. She wanted to know whether he still read a lot, and when he said yes, she wanted to know what.

She was surprised when he told her. "You used to like fiction."

"I still do. But I haven't had much time, lately, and nonfiction takes precedence."

"Why books on business?"

"Some of the people I'm with are heavyweights. It helps if I can understand what they're saying."

"Wow," she said with a smile. "If Daddy could only see you now."

"If he could only see you," Cutter echoed, then paused. "Do you think he'd have minded us, Pam?"

"Not for a minute."

"Me neither." He paused again. "Does your mother?"

That was harder for Pam to answer. "I don't think so. I've mentioned you a lot. I'm not sure she takes it in. Bob says she does."

"Bob?"

"Grossman. Her psychiatrist."

"The same one? He's been working with her all this time?"

"Uh-huh. I think he's sweet on her."

Cutter frowned. "Is that legal?"

"Perfectly. He's divorced."

"Is it ethical?"

"She's a paraplegic. What can happen?"

"Lots."

"Are you serious?"

"Dead serious. Brian has a friend who comes to watch him work sometimes. The guy was hit in 'Nam and can't walk. He always comes with one girlfriend or another. He has a really active sex life."

Pam tried to picture Patricia with Bob. "I don't know, Cutter. I can't see it with my mother. Even if she can feel things down there, she isn't the passionate type."

"How do you know?"

He had a point. "I don't."

"Would that guy who thought you were frigid believe you if he saw you now?"

She laughed and draped an arm on his shoulder. "Probably not." She kissed his chin. "Thank you."

"For what?"

"Giving me hope for my mother." But he was always good at things like that. "I worry about her. I wouldn't mind it at all if she and Bob had something going. She deserves a little happiness."

"So do you," Cutter said in a voice that was low and concerned. "Where to from here? What happens after graduation?"

"I'll be working."

"At *Facets*?"

"With the designers. I want my own line."

"Will John give it to you?"

"If he doesn't, I'll go elsewhere."

"Even if he starts making threats? That's his way, Pam. You know it as well as I do."

"But at some point, it won't work. I'm not a child anymore."

"Age has nothing to do with it. He's a madman."

"But it's not fair. It's not right." The old anger returned, the old

sense of injustice and helplessness. It was never far from the surface. "Nothing is right, where John is concerned."

"*Facets* is right," Cutter pointed out. "It's turning a handsome profit. The dividends paid to stockholders have increased steadily over the past few years."

"How do you know that?"

"I've seen the prospectus."

"Do you own any stock?"

"A little."

She grinned. "That's great! Buy more, Cutter. He'll *croak*." Then her grin faded and she wanted to cry. "Such small victories. I want a big one."

"Someday."

"When?"

"Someday."

She didn't like the sound of that. It was too vague, too far off. "What do we do in the meantime?"

He rolled onto his back and stared at the ceiling. "We grow. You make a name for yourself. I make money."

"I'd rather have you than a name for myself."

His voice was harder when he said, "You need a name. It'll give you power."

"And the money? Do you need it?"

"Yes."

"You never used to."

"It was a pipe dream then. Now it's real."

"It's just money. It buys things."

"It buys power."

She felt a chill. She'd grown up knowing people with money and power. Her impression had been that one corrupted the other. John was a perfect example. "Does it mean so much to you, having power?"

"Yes."

"It didn't used to. I can remember when you didn't want to be a supervisor at the mine. You didn't want the responsibility."

He turned his head on the pillow. His eyes were dark as the night and hard as his voice. "We're not talking being supervisor at the mine anymore. The stakes are higher. And they're within reach. I'm making good money. Good money is self-perpetuating. I'm starting to think that it'd be nice to have as much as I can get."

"You were never money-hungry."

"I am now."

She felt an ache inside. The Cutter she'd known had simple tastes and desires. Most of them had focused on her. "Is making money more important than our being together?"

Angry, he came up on an elbow. "We can't be together. He won't *let* us be together. It's not safe."

"What can he do? Couldn't you and I, between us, counter anything he tried?"

"Not yet."

"You'll let him go on directing our lives?"

"No. I'm directing my own life."

"How?"

"By becoming as successful as I can."

"But what about us?" she cried. When he didn't answer, she rolled to the opposite side of the bed and sat up. "You don't really care. You're caught up in your own life now. Your own power trip."

"Wait just a minute. What I do, I do for you as much as for me."

"I don't want the money."

"It's not just the money. It's the power. The money buys the power, and the power buys our freedom."

"When? Five years from now? Ten years from now?" She was groping through the tangled sheets for her nightshirt. "We'll be old then, Cutter." She pushed her arms into the sleeves and made for the door.

"Where are you going?"

"The bathroom." She opened the door and looked back to see him staring over his shoulder at her. The pale light from the hall cast eerie shadows on his face, his arms, his back. The shadows didn't distort his face, which she knew so well, and his arms were fine, as

leanly muscled as they had been during his mining days. But there was something strange about his back. Odd marks.

Frowning, she closed the door again. She leaned against it for a minute, her eyes glued to his back. Slowly, she returned to the bed. She reached for the lamp, hesitated, finally clicked it to its lowest setting. Then she sucked in a breath and held it there with the back of her hand.

Cutter's eyes held hers, angry and defiant for the space of an eternal minute before he kicked his foot free of the sheet and got off the bed. "Turn off the light," he growled and went to the window. He stood there with a hand high on the jamb and his weight on one hip. His shape was incredibly beautiful, broad shoulders tapering to a lean waist and hips, legs that were long and well formed. His skin was every bit as firm as it had been, and now faintly bronzed.

She used to be able to look at him for hours, feeling nothing but pleasure. Now, unable to take her eyes from the canvas of scars on his back, she was appalled.

"Turn off the light," he repeated.

She did, but it didn't obliterate what she'd seen. Crossing to where he stood, she stared at the scars, then reached out a trembling hand. Her fingertips lightly grazed one of the ridges.

He flinched. "Don't."

"What happened?"

He was silent, staring out at the building across the alley.

Again she tried to touch him. Again he flinched. "You were whipped."

"Not whipped. He didn't use a whip. That would have been too neat."

Her stomach churned and she started to tremble. "John did this?" She glanced up to see a movement of the muscle at Cutter's jaw. It was answer enough. Her hand went to her mouth again. For a second, she thought she might vomit. But the second passed, leaving her cold and sick. "When?" she whispered.

"That December. A couple of hours after the last time."

"Where?"

"My place."

"Just him?"

"There were two others."

"Oh God," she gasped. Eyes riveted to his back, she was imagining the absolute horror of what must have taken place. "How could he?" she whispered.

She reached to touch him again, but barely made contact when Cutter whirled around and caught her hand. "They beat the shit out of me first," he ground out. "John just watched that. He wouldn't have touched me himself. Wouldn't have dirtied his hands. But he must have gotten one hell of a kick out of the way I was ricocheting off rocks and trees. It was snowy that night. You think snow cushions? Think again. It was cold and ungiving, and then when I was bruised enough to be hurting something fierce, he started in with the belt."

"Belt?" Pam was breathing in shallow bursts. Her wrist ached, he held it so tightly, but she forgot it in a deeper anguish.

"One of his men was a biker. The belt was wide and had rows of metal studs."

She cried out in alarm and started to shake.

But Cutter wasn't done. His eyes were wide and angry, faraway, cruel. "They stripped me from the waist up. In the freezing cold. Not that I felt the cold for long. When that belt hit, it was like fire. It tore through my skin, raked right across it."

She stifled another cry.

"Know what blood looks like when it spatters on new-fallen snow?"

She swallowed an answer; none was called for.

"And he was enjoying it! The bastard was enjoying it. The other two held me down while he swung that belt. Again and again and again—" He stopped abruptly, blinked, seemed to refocus. His voice was less brutal, but no less determined. "So now you know why I want it so bad. I was totally helpless that night. Never again."

She stared up at him, breathing quickly, feeling everything he had that night, including the helplessness. "The police?" she whispered.

"I couldn't go to the police. I couldn't do a damn thing. He threatened *you*." He looked as though he was going to shake her to drive home his point. Instead he dropped her wrist and turned back to the window.

Pam had thought she knew what love was. She had thought it was thinking about a person, wanting to be with him, aching to make love with him. She had spent years loving Cutter that way. But she had a lot to learn. Love involved things like protectiveness and self-sacrifice. Cutter had felt those for her. She was humbled.

She touched his back, then pressed her palm flat when his muscles tightened. Her hand inched its way down one long welt, over a series of small surface knobs, across a jagged ripple. By the time she moved onto another, tears blurred her vision.

Coming forward, she flattened her cheek to his rough skin. Her arms stole around him, palms scaling his ribs until each covered a nipple. *"Cutter,"* she whispered. She kissed his marred skin, one knotted spot, then another, wishing her mouth could erase them, and if not her mouth, her tears. The scars remained, branded indelibly, still she continued to kiss him. Her mouth moved up one furrow to its end. She stood on tiptoe to kiss his neck and the smooth spot beneath his ear. She leaned sideways to kiss along his shoulder, then the silky patch of hair under his arm. Fingers splayed, her hands slid down his body until they closed around his growing erection.

"I love you," she whispered and moved against him, feeling her bare breasts on his scars, her belly on his buttocks. She stroked him, arched into him, spread her fingers and touched him everywhere. When he turned and braced his back against the wall, she worked her way down his body until she was on her knees, making love to him with her mouth. She had done it before because he'd wanted it. This time was for her. She heard his labored breath and increased the pressure of her lips. Her hands slid over his lower abdomen, along his inner thighs, between his legs. She stayed with him when his hips moved, and even when his fingers knotted in her hair, she refused to leave. Only when he'd climaxed did she release him. Sec-

onds later, she was on her back on the floor, and, he was still hard, thrusting inside her.

He wasn't gentle. His large body drove hers over and over into the oak planks, but she didn't complain. She loved him too much. She understood his need. When he came a second time, she wrapped her arms around him and held him close.

For a long time he lay on top of her. His weight was significant, but she didn't complain about that, either. After being without him for so long, she would have suffered almost anything to have him near.

At last he roused. He hoisted himself to his knees, hung his head for a minute, then lifted her in his arms and carried her to the bed. After settling her gently on the pillow, he came down on a knee beside her.

"Did I hurt you?" he asked quietly.

"No. No, Cutter. You're the one who's been hurt. I wish there were something—some way—"

"Just be here when I need you."

She'd known it was coming. After all he had said, she'd known he wouldn't stay. "Will you come often?"

He shook his head. "I won't risk that."

"But he can't hurt you that way again. You're too well known."

"He could hurt you to hurt me. I can't let that happen."

The dark didn't hide the sadness on his face. She touched it, tried to smooth it away, but it was in his eyes and soul-deep. "I'm hurt now without you. What more can he do?"

"He can cheat you out of your share of the company. He can refuse to show your work and bribe his rivals not to show it either. He can rape you, and then say you started it."

She caught her breath, wondering whether he knew how close it had come to that. She'd been sixteen then. She was twenty-two now, but she felt the same revulsion, the same fear.

"He could do something to hurt Patricia," Cutter went on. "Say ugly things, spread rumors. She's as vulnerable as a person can be. And Marcy—she's back in Maine now, and married to a guy at the

mine. John could mess them up. And what about Hillary? She's been a good friend. A *good* friend. Her career is finally getting off the ground. Can you protect her, if he decides to destroy her?"

Pam thought of all the times Hillary had been there to listen, give news of Cutter, offer support. Incredibly, given her on-again-off-again affair with John, Pam loved her like a sister. "No."

"Neither can I, but he might do just that if he's riled. I've learned my lesson. I don't put anything past him."

She could understand why. More so even than she, he knew firsthand John's capacity for brutality.

"So I'm being cautious. I'm building a name and a kitty. It's not that I want money for money's sake—or power—"

She stopped the words with her fingers. "I know. I was wrong."

"It's freedom for us." He took her fingers away and held them. "Do you know how often I've thought of killing him? I mean, actually committing murder? Catching him in an alley and beating him to death? Bludgeoning him with a baseball bat? Running him over with my car? I'm not proud of those thoughts, but they come, and I hate him more for making me think them." He eased his grip. "But I'm gonna do it right, Pam. I'm gonna fight John on his terms. I'm gonna fight him with money and power, because that's what I'm going to have. You can do it with the jewelry you make. Think about it."

She didn't want to. Not just then. She wanted to think about when she'd see Cutter again. "I'm going back to Paris for the summer. Meet me there."

He shook his head. "I'll be working the country pushing the fall lines. I won't be home for more than a weekend until October. That's one of the reasons I had to see you now."

"Then October." She came up and put both hands on his chest. His skin was warm, the hair there soft. "I don't know where I'll be living—I'm looking for an apartment in the Back Bay—but Hillary will know my address, and my phone will be listed."

"I don't know where or when it will be, Pam. But we're on the right track. I'm not blowing it now by being careless."

"We'll be careful." She clutched his shoulders, fearful that if she didn't make her case, another four years might go by before she saw him again. "Once I start at *Facets*, I'll have to visit the New York store sometimes. I'll make excuses to visit it. I'll stay at the Park Lane—no, the Hilton; that's busier, people get lost there. If you're in town, we could meet. John would never know."

Cutter gave her a sad look before drawing her close. He wrapped his arms around her, enclosing her in a cocoon of his warmth and his scent. He didn't speak. As the minutes passed, his arms tightened.

"Sleep with me?" she whispered. "Just for a little while?"

When the silence stretched on, she wondered if he'd heard. She was about to repeat the plea when he took her down to the sheets and tucked her snugly against him. Taking his hand, she brought it to her mouth. She kissed it, curled it around hers, held it there so she knew it was real.

In time she fell asleep. When she woke, as she had known he would be, Cutter was gone.

She cried. It was one way to fight the silence and fill the emptiness. When the tears were finished, she wrapped a love-scented sheet around her and went to the window. Dawn was just breaking, casting a pale glow on the building across the way. She opened the window higher. It was going to be another warm day. She wondered how many warm days would pass before she saw Cutter again.

The more she wondered, the more frustrated she grew. She was twenty-two, graduating from college within days. By fall she'd be a full-fledged member of the workforce, a functioning adult. It wasn't right that John should still be controlling her life.

Make a name for yourself, Cutter had said. *Fight him on his terms.*

He sounded so sure of himself, but that was easy for him to do. He didn't have to see John. His income wasn't dependent on him.

You can do it with the jewelry you make. Think about it.

She did. She thought about it often during those days before graduation, and by the time she stood up to receive her diploma, when the one person she wanted most to be there wasn't, because

there would be trouble if John found him around, she was angry enough to understand.

She needed power over John. That meant sinking her fingers into *Facets* and holding on. She could do it one of two ways—through her say as a shareholder, or through her own work. Since she wouldn't control her stock until she turned twenty-five, she was determined to become the jewelry designer of note at *Facets*. By making the store's name synonymous with her work, she would have the power she needed to fight John and win.

Chapter 21

Palm Beach, 1979

JOHN WORKED THE CROWD with his usual aplomb. He knew most of his guests, and those he didn't, he greeted with a smile, an outstretched hand, and a clever word. Small talk was his forte. It didn't demand much. While engaged in it, he could be thinking about more important issues, like whether the triple-tiered chandeliers were too sparkly, the caviar canapes too spare, the champagne too dry.

Turning from a guest to stop one of the tuxedoed waiters as he passed, he murmured so that only the young fellow heard, "Your friend on the other side of the room is flirting. Please tell him to do that on his own time. On my time, he'll pass the hors d'oeuvres."

"Yes, sir," the waiter said and moved off.

John rejoined the ongoing chitchat for several minutes before moving on to another group. People seemed impressed. That pleased him. He had wanted the opening of *Facets* Palm Beach to be an event, and it was. A fair number of the press were there, more than had attended the opening of *Facets* New York three years before, and that pleased him, too. The name was growing. The following was growing. Fashion reporters and society columnists called often, which was all well and good until they asked for Pam. John had mixed feelings about that. On one hand, their interest in her was good for business. On the other, it was interest diverted from him.

He had to admit that her work had flair. Her pieces were unique. They were large and simple, relying on an undulation of gold or a twist of silver to provide an exciting backdrop for one or more stones. She worked exclusively with tourmaline, claiming it was in her genes. He was a diamond man, himself, but he couldn't deny that her pieces sold well. For that reason, he gave her free rein with her designs.

On the matter of press interest, though, he wasn't as free—or he hadn't been in the past. His people had been able to soft-pedal the press response to her original show, saying that she was still a student and wouldn't be available for interviews. Now, he was losing his hold. The press could find her whenever they wanted, either at *Facets'* workshop on Newbury Street or at the one in New York.

Raising his champagne glass to his lips, he looked over its rim to the spot across the room where she stood. She looked beautiful. Her white silk dress was strapless. It fell to her ankles, showing just a hint of high-heeled silver sandals. Her hair was swept into a loose knot at the top of her head. Her makeup was as simple and tasteful as her attire.

He knew her strategy. She wanted nothing to detract from her jewelry, and nothing did. Around her neck she wore a wide silver collar embedded with pink and purple tourmalines of various sizes and shapes. Her earlobes displayed silver disks, each with a single off-center stone. Her bracelet echoed the collar, with a ripple worked through it for good measure.

As he watched, he saw a woman touch the collar in admiration. He saw Pam smile in response, then turn her smile on another person in the group. He saw her talk, saw her nod, saw her accept the two-cheeked kisses bestowed on her when that group yielded to another.

She knew how to handle herself. He wanted to think she'd learned it from him, but if that was the case, she'd learned it from afar. She avoided him whenever possible. If he was on one side of a room, she stayed on the other. Generally she excused herself from affairs that she knew he was attending. But she went to many

parties, and after each there were orders for replicas of the jewelry she'd worn.

Pamela St. George Originals, she called them. When she had first come up with the name, he had indulged her. He had doubted she had the experience or ability to produce a steady flow of designs. She was proving him wrong, though, and it was too late to change the name. People had latched on to it. They wanted "a Pamela St. George" or "a St. George Original." He supposed that mention of the family name did him good; but he could have done without the quips about "the other St. George—the pretty one."

Drawing himself straighter, he turned to welcome the junior senator from Florida. They talked for a bit. John had met the man at a reception in Washington several months before, and since plans for the Palm Beach store had been well under way at the time, they had much to discuss.

He wasn't the only senator John knew. With the steady expansion of his circle of contacts, he made frequent visits to Washington, which put him in the company of politicians on a regular basis. They fascinated him, or rather their game did. He was intrigued by the jockeying that went on when one wanted something from another. Political blackmail was subtle and called by any other name.

He played the game, but from a distance. He was content to contribute money to one candidate or another, even to contribute big money to some. But he wanted none of the impermanence of Washington, where a man's career was at the whim of voters or, worse, the media. He wanted his own fame to be solid and long-lasting. Given how far he'd come in his thirty-nine years, he had a good shot at it.

Only half-listening while the senator talked, he ran through a mental roster of his guests and considered how he ranked on the list. He wasn't as wealthy as some. He didn't have as many homes as others. And the St. George Company was a baby compared to some of the other corporations represented.

But what a baby. She was a gold mine, and he had made her so. His timing had been right, his shrewd management on the mark. Any

financial crises he'd endured after the opening of *Facets* Boston were history.

He couldn't help but be smug at the thought of his yacht moored in Newport Harbor and his Rolls-Royce parked on Beacon Hill. The townhouse, redecorated from top to bottom, had been the scene of many an elegant gathering of late. His parties were prized affairs, well attended and chic. He never had a shortage of guests.

But guests were guests, women were women, and superficiality was the name of that game. When he wanted to relax, Hillary was still the one he went to. She knew him. He didn't have to play the gentleman with her.

She wasn't here tonight, though, because he never invited her to the most important of his parties. It wasn't her place. Unlike Pam, she wasn't the glamorous type.

Excusing himself from the senator at a breaking point in the conversation, John wandered to a spot where he had a view of Pam again. She was talking to the applesauce heir. He wasn't a bad-looking guy, twenty-five or twenty-six, not a bad match for her. She claimed she wasn't getting married, claimed—right to his face no more than a month before, when he'd raised the issue—that if she couldn't marry Cutter Reid, she wouldn't marry at all.

He didn't like her boldness or the arrogance that came with professional recognition. Even more, he didn't like her mention of Cutter Reid. She only did it to bother him.

Cutter was one of his few mistakes. He hadn't dreamed that the guy could pull himself up by the shoestrings and make something of himself. Not that John considered modeling as something, but Cutter was making good money. He assumed Cutter would squander it. His kind didn't have brains to think ahead to the day when their skin would crease and their hair would turn gray.

Although Cutter Reid's days in the sun were numbered, it rankled John that he had enjoyed any such days at all.

The irony of it all rankled, too. Cutter would never have modeled if John had been freer with the belt and scarred his face. Nor would Cutter have ever modeled if John hadn't made him leave Timiny Cove.

He would still be there. Mining. Making eyes at Pam, who was so far above him. She was beautiful. Talented. Smart.

John reached for a cigarette, only to remember that he was no longer smoking. His doctor had advised him to stop, and that made sense. It would be tragic to build an incredible life and then die of cancer at fifty. He planned to live until eighty at least, enjoying respect, adulation, and great wealth.

Eighty years was a long time to live. A person could get lonely after a while. A person could get lonely, period, but life at the top was that way. Loneliness was the price paid for prominence. Even in this large, lavishly appointed room with four hundred people, he felt alone.

Pam should see that. She was his sister. She should know how he felt. She should help. She should be there for him.

But she was more interested in furthering her own name and career. If it hadn't been for him, she wouldn't be sashaying her way among the rich and famous. She wouldn't be an up-and-coming jewelry designer. She wouldn't have any career at all.

If it hadn't been for him, she would be an unwed mother trying to raise a child on her own. Maybe it was time he reminded her of that. She was a little too ungrateful and enamored of herself. She needed to be taken down a peg or two.

By the time the last of the guests had left and the caterers were stacking their silver trays, Pam was gone. John might have guessed it. She never made things easy. He called the hotel and learned that she had checked out before the party. One of his PR people reported having seen her change clothes in the ladies' room. Another reported having seen her leave the store and jump into a cab. A third called the airport and found that her name was on the passenger list for a flight that was now taxiing onto the runway.

He tried calling her in Boston later than night, but she didn't answer. He tried calling her at the company's suite in New York, although he knew she rarely stayed there. She preferred the Hilton. Or Hillary's. So he tried calling her there, but a groggy Hillary was the only one to answer.

He wondered if she was seeing Cutter Reid. The thought drove him wild. He simmered all night, took the first morning flight back to Boston, and went to her apartment and pounded on the door.

He never expected her to be there, but within a minute she opened the door. She was tying the sash of a long white robe. Her face was clear of makeup and flushed from sleep. Between that and the hair tumbling over her shoulders, she looked warm and womanly. John felt an instant physical response, which annoyed him all the more.

She was wary. "What is it, John?"

"No bright 'hello'? No 'how are you,' or 'didn't that go well yesterday'?"

"Sorry, but I OD'd on small talk."

She did look tired, which got all of his suspicions going again. "Where the hell have you been? I thought you would stick around after the party."

"What for? It was a success. We both knew it would be."

"There were people to thank. That's your responsibility, too. We're business partners, for Christ's sake."

She arched a slender brow. "Business partners? Are you kidding? I'm a company employee. Just one of the designers."

Since he wasn't about to acknowledge that her work was in any way superior, he focused on the family connection: "You're a St. George. You have a stake in the company."

"Only in theory. I don't get my say for another two years."

"Keep up the bitchiness and you won't get it at all."

"Bitchiness? For God's sake, John," she threw up a hand, "I'm stating facts. I don't control my share of the company. You do. I just work there."

"And when you're not working there, you're running around drumming up business for yourself and your designs. Think you're pretty hot, hmmm?"

"I don't need this." She started to close the door. He caught it with a foot and stepped inside before she could stop him, then kicked it shut.

Whirling around, she retreated into the apartment. He followed

and reached the kitchen in time to disconnect the call she was making, then snatched his finger away seconds before she would have crushed it slamming down the receiver.

"Who were you calling?"

"The police. I don't want you here, John."

He drew himself up. The taller he towered over her, the more dominant he felt. "Tough. I want to talk."

Incredibly, she held her ground. "Not now. Not here. This is my apartment. The lease is in my name. I pay for it with money I earn, and you're trespassing."

"I'm your brother."

"Half-brother. Get out."

He knew then that he had riled her. That was something—certainly better than the way she looked through him sometimes, refusing to admit he was there. Leaning back against the wall, he folded his arms on his chest. "I want to talk."

"About what?"

"You. What you're doing. Where you're going."

"You already know all you have to." She was standing by the counter, looking defiant but just that little bit nervous, which enhanced his sense of control.

"Not by a long shot. I want to know whether you like what you're doing."

"If I didn't like it, I wouldn't be able to do it so well."

"No modesty there."

"Why play games? We both know that my pieces are selling faster than every other designer's but one, and his figures are high because he has a contract with an Arab who has him making things for every woman in his entourage. My jewelry wouldn't sell if it weren't good, given the prices we charge."

"Do you think they're too high?"

"No way. We design for the wealthy, and the wealthy can pay."

"So what's your gripe?"

"I don't have one. You do. At least, I assume that's why you're here.

What's the matter?" She tipped her head. "Uptight because I'm doing well?"

He laughed. "You're doing well because I allow it."

"Try again."

"It's true. How do you think you got started? Do you think all those people came to see that first show because they heard your work was good? Good pieces of jewelry are a dime a dozen. Stunning jewelry is what's rare, and yours isn't stunning. Most of those people came as a favor to me. I made calls, told them about the show, asked them to drop by. I do things for other people; they do things for me."

"If they came by as a favor to you, they came back later because they liked my work. I'm not that naïve, John. People don't spend thousands for a ring or a necklace, then wear those pieces out in public and send their friends in for more if they don't like what they're getting."

"The Phelans? The Goodmans? The Andersons? They're all my friends."

"They were *Daddy*'s friends."

"The Phelans introduced you around Philly. The Goodmans did it in Scarsdale. The Andersons were your entree in Southampton. Those were my contacts."

"They were St. George contacts. I made the initial phone calls. I made the trip arrangements. If favors were paid, they were paid to Daddy. He was the one who began dealing with those people twenty-some years ago. They were St. George clients long before *Facets* was conceived. You call them your contacts. I call them my contacts. We can stand here arguing about it, or you can get out of here and give me some air."

"You have an answer for everything, don't you?" he asked, working harder to appear complacent. "I'd be careful if I were you, Pam. You forget that Pamela St. George Originals are part of *Facets*."

"Only if I want them to be."

He shook his head. "Whether you want it or not. Remember that standard contract you signed when you started working? It gave *Facets* the right to your name."

"It did not," she said, but she pulled her robe tighter.

He saw it as a nervous gesture and took heart. He also took a leisurely look at the curves she'd inadvertently emphasized. "Check it out. You'll see I'm right."

She wrapped her arms around her waist. "It gave *Facets* the right to any and all pieces I made while in the company's employ. I take my name, my skill, and my following with me when I leave."

He shook his head slowly. "I think not."

"I read it carefully, John, and I had a lawyer read it after me. If that contract gives *Facets* the right to my name, then it's been altered. Not that I'd put that past you. You did it before, with Little Lincoln and Cutter."

"Cutter." The name alone dented John's composure. "Don't bring him into this."

"Why not? You owe him. You stole Little Lincoln."

John wasn't about to confirm or deny the claim. "From what I understand, he doesn't need it. He's earning big money."

"Little Lincoln was his legacy from Daddy."

"Little Lincoln is barren. It isn't worth two cents."

"Then that's poetic justice, I'd say."

"And Cutter?" John shot back, determined to catch her in a trap of her own making. "What does he say?"

She stared at him without saying a word.

"You're seeing him behind my back," he accused, his anger rising. It was always that way when it came to Cutter Reid, right from the first, when Eugene had dragged him off the streets and shown him the kind of care and compassion that John had always wanted.

Pam's eyes were cold. "I see lots of people behind your back, because if you found out who they were, you'd try to control them, too. At some point it won't work, John. I'm getting older and smarter. If shrewdness was what I lacked, I have a fine teacher in you."

"I told you not to see him."

"Oh, yeah," she said with a sudden snap. "Way back in December that time, you told me that if I ever saw him again, you'd have him canned from the mine and run out of town." She stood straighter. "You made the threat, then without waiting to see what I'd do, you

carried it out." She started to tremble. "Only you weren't satisfied with firing him and making him leave. You beat him, too. You beat him, then went at him with a belt that left horrible, ugly gouges all over his back. You almost killed him, John."

The murderous look in her eyes might have unsettled him if he hadn't been so furious. "I should have. I should have known he'd come crying to you."

"He wasn't crying. Cutter doesn't cry. He survives. He did it when he was a kid. He did it when you left him for dead. And he'll do it again, if need be, because that's the way he is. He's far stronger, far more of a man, than you'll ever be."

Without thinking, John lunged. He had no idea what he intended. Red fury drove him on. A flash of silver stopped him before he reached her, though. It was a long, wide kitchen knife. A butcher's knife. And it was in her hand, pointed at him.

"Don't you touch me," she warned.

He straightened, but he didn't back off. She wouldn't use the knife. At least he didn't think so. "Relax, Pam."

"And don't tell me what to do."

"You're getting upset."

"As well I should! I saw his back! I saw what you did! It was horrible!"

"So it turned you off? That's good, at least."

"It didn't turn me off. I kissed every one of those scars, but they didn't go away. So I'll kiss every one of them the next time I see him, and each time after that. You're an animal, John."

He would have gone at her again if it hadn't been for the knife. But she was holding it like she meant business. "Put it down."

"No way."

"Put it down, Pam."

"When you leave."

"You don't . . . need . . . a knife."

"I'll be the judge of that. Give me the slightest excuse, and I'll scar you like you scarred Cutter." She upped the angle of the knife. "Only I'll go for the face."

He half-believed she'd do it. "Look who's the animal," he said, but he wasn't about to take chances. He didn't want to be cut. Whether she scarred him or not, there would be talk, possibly even a scandal, and he'd come too far to chance that. So he took a step back.

That didn't mean he accepted defeat. "You can't have him, y'know."

"Why not? What would be so terrible? I've been asking myself that for a good long while. Cutter is a 'someone' now. He has money. He has friends. What would be so terrible if he and I were together?"

"He's nothing but a miner."

"He's sophisticated, and he's successful."

"He'll be back at the bottom of the heap someday."

"He will not."

"He's a flash in the pan. He won't last."

"That's what you're praying. You were so jealous that Daddy took to him—"

"I wasn't jealous—"

"But that was years ago. You can't still be harboring a grudge."

"There's no grudge."

"There's pure hatred. It's irrational. Sick. You're a successful man, John. Why is Cutter such a threat to you?"

John had had as much as he could take. When it came to Cutter—maybe even when it came to Pam—his feelings were irrational. He didn't have to make excuses or discuss them with anyone.

"Cutter Reid," he stated with force, "will never be part of this family." He came forward again, angry enough to dare it. "And if you so much as scratch my skin with that knife, you'll regret it."

She sighed. "More threats? They're getting tiresome."

"Then I haven't used the right ones. Try this one on for size. You scratch me with that knife—you carry on with Cutter Reid so the press gets wind of it—so that anyone gets wind of it and it comes back to me—and I'll destroy your mother."

"That's a joke. She's been paralyzed from the waist down, confined in a mental hospital for ten years, and you're going to destroy her? What more could you do?"

"Plenty."

"Like what?"

"Like tell the world why she became catatonic after the accident."

"She was overcome with grief."

"She was overcome with guilt."

"Because she wasn't the one to die. Any woman who loved her husband the way my mother did my father would feel the same."

John shook his head. "There was more to her guilt than that. She was responsible for that accident."

Now he had her attention. "Are you saying that she was the one driving after all?"

"No. She was the one who upset Eugene so much that he drove through that light."

"They never knew whether he drove through the light or skidded."

"Either way, he was driving recklessly, and it was because of what she'd done."

"But she was in the car with him. If she'd done something so awful, he'd have taken off alone."

"She followed him into the car to calm him down."

Pam continued to hold the knife like a spike rising from her chest, but its tip wavered. "They had their fights, but it was never so bad that Daddy would have raced off into an accident."

"It was this time."

"Why? What had she done?"

"She slept with another man."

"You lie! She wouldn't have done that!"

"She did. He found them together."

"You *lie*."

He stared at her, waiting for her to make the connection. He knew she would. She wasn't dumb.

The tip of the knife came up at the very same time as a look of loathing so intense as to be palatable came to her eyes.

"Get out," she whispered.

Given the excuse, he straightened his shoulders and backed away

from the knife. He kept his voice low. "I'll spread the word, Pam, and I'll let it be known that she was the seducer. Then I'll tell her what I've done. Think she can bear up under that kind of shame?"

"Can *you*?"

"I have a solid image. I also have a PR department that can make me come out smelling like a rose. I'm not fragile. Your mother is."

"*Get out.*"

"I'm going," he said. She was upset. He had made his point. From the kitchen door, he turned and said, "So if you want what little is left of your mother's mental health salvaged, I'd watch it with Cutter. I'll go public, Pam. I'll destroy her and then get permanent control over her stock."

"Over my dead body."

"If it comes to that, fine. I don't have any more use for you than I do for her."

"Get out," she said again, coming slowly toward him this time. "And don't you ever set foot in this apartment again. Your presence soils it."

"I mean every word I say."

"Your word isn't worth a thing. I know better than to trust it."

"Stay away from Cutter, or I'll destroy Patricia."

"Destroy Patricia, and I'll marry Cutter so quick you won't know what hit you. Then we'll both fight you."

"Fat chance you'll have of winning."

"Try us."

"There won't be any need for that as long as we have an agreement."

"Get out."

He opened the door, then turned back to her and winked. "See you at work, hon." When she slammed the door in his face, he grinned.

Chapter 22

◈◈◈

New York, late June 1990

JOHN WASN'T GRINNING WHEN Hillary opened the door. Still she felt the same rise of excitement she always felt, a conditioned reflex deep inside, whenever she laid eyes on him. Three months had passed since his engagement announcement. She should still be angry. She was still angry. But the excitement was there, even when he strode in without a word of greeting and turned to glare at her.

"What in the hell are you up to?" He was wearing a dark summer suit and would have looked perfectly civilized had it not been for his eyes, which were dark and feral.

"Me?" Her heart was beating fast. That, too, always happened when he was close.

"You've been in Timiny Cove."

She struggled to think straight. He wanted an explanation. "I come from Timiny Cove. My dad still lives there. I go up to visit him sometimes. You know that."

"You've been visiting other people. You've been asking questions about me. What's up, Hillary?"

She didn't have to ask who had told on her. Half of the townsfolk were beneficiaries of John's charity. Over the years he had helped this one with housing, that one with medical bills, the other one with

education expenses. The repayment came in the form of loyalty—in this case, intelligence.

Given that he'd probably been in touch with more than one source, she saw no point in denying what he'd heard. "I've been thinking of doing a piece on you. My questions were by way of preliminary research."

"Make them final. Dump the project."

She felt a spark of annoyance. "Just like that?"

"Just like that."

"Any special reason?"

"I don't want you writing about me."

"Why not? You're important. There have been articles written in the past. There'll be more in the future. Why shouldn't mine be one of them?"

"Because I say no."

She stared at him. Not even the pleasure of seeing him again blunted her frustration. She couldn't believe that he had the gall to barge in and demand that she act simply on his wishes, particularly after the last few months.

"Don't do it, Hillary. You know things no one else knows. I won't be betrayed that way."

"*You* won't be betrayed?" she burst out. "What about *me*? After I've been here for you all these years, you turn around and make plans to marry someone else!"

"I never promised you a thing. I thought you understood that."

"Oh, I understood it. But I'm not made of steel. What you're doing hurts."

He said nothing for a minute. Then his eyes fell to her breasts. She felt their touch, saw the spark in their depths, and felt some satisfaction in knowing that she still turned him on.

He came toward her. "Is it revenge, then?" he asked in a soft voice.

She couldn't help but be caught up by his grace, the smooth way he walked, his sexy darkness. At fifty, he was as tall and good-looking as he'd been at thirty. She knew she ought to turn

and run, particularly given all she'd learned about him in the past weeks, but her heart was the only thing that moved. It beat faster than ever.

"I haven't yet decided what to write."

He slipped his fingers into her hair, then ran his thumb over her cheek with surprising gentleness. "Don't write anything."

"Do you have a better suggestion for how I should spend my time?"

"Definitely."

He brought her face up and kissed her with the kind of force that never failed to arouse her. It didn't fail then. She let herself luxuriate in his hunger for a minute before tearing away.

"I don't want this, John," she said in a breathy, singsong way.

"Bullshit."

When he reached for her again, she dodged his arms and ran down the two steps into the living room. There she sank into the corner of the sofa, looking as defiant as she could, and waited for him to make a move.

Slowly and deliberately, he squared his shoulders. "You're still in a snit about Janet."

"I sure am."

"There's no need. The engagement's off."

Her heart started speeding again. "Off?"

"Broken. Over."

"Why?"

"I decided I didn't want to marry her after all."

"Why?"

"I don't love her."

Hillary sniffed. "Love was never an issue."

"Then like."

"You liked her fine when you got engaged."

"I decided I didn't like the confinement."

After a minute's consideration, she understood. "Ahhh. You went to bed with someone. She found out and made a fuss."

"Something like that."

She searched his face for remorse or regret but found neither. "You bastard."

He actually looked wounded. "I thought you'd be pleased."

"Pleased that you see nothing wrong with cheating? Pleased that you sleep around with half of the women in the Western World?"

He came down the steps toward her. "One woman, Hillary, and only after you said you wouldn't sleep with me."

"And I meant it. Even I have to draw the line somewhere."

"There's no need anymore. The engagement is off."

"That's convenient." She tucked her legs up under her skirt and wrapped her arms around her knees. It wasn't the most sophisticated of poses, but she didn't care. She felt vulnerable and very much in need of protection from John. "You break up with Janet just in time to get it off with me. Will you go back to her when we're done?"

"That doesn't even merit an answer."

She laughed and shot a sad glance at the ceiling. "My God, you sound pious." Abruptly looking as grim as she felt, she met his gaze. "You don't understand, do you, John? You live by a different set of rules from the rest of us. You didn't see anything wrong with cheating on Janet, and you didn't understand when I refused to do it."

"I offered her a hell of a lot in return. I thought she knew the score."

"That's not the point! The point is that people don't like being used. It doesn't matter what you give them in return. At some point the abuse isn't worth it."

"Abuse?" His expression hardened. "Hold on a minute. I never abused Janet. I never so much as raised a finger to her."

"There are different kinds of abuse."

"So let's keep them straight. You say I used Janet. People use each other all the time. It's a mutual thing in an engagement or a marriage. Physical abuse is something else entirely. I didn't do a single thing in my relationship with Janet that could remotely be considered physically abusive."

"My, you're defensive," Hillary observed.

"What's that supposed to mean?"

She realized then how much she'd learned in the three months since she'd seen him last. "It means that you have it in you. You have a mean streak. Mean streaks turn violent. Maybe Janet saw that."

"I broke it off with Janet, not the other way around."

"Maybe she let you think that. Women aren't as dumb as you'd like to believe."

He watched her cautiously for a minute. "Are you trying to tell me something, Hillary?"

"Me? I'm just sitting here telling you why I won't have sex with you. I don't trust your motives."

"My motives are pure. I want you."

Her insides began to hum. She ignored it. "You want me to stop writing my story."

"That too," he had the grace to admit. "But mostly I want you."

"You want me, but you proposed to Janet. You want me, but you went to bed with someone else when Janet wouldn't put out. Was your need so great?"

"For you? Yes." He chewed on the inside of his mouth, looking younger, almost awkward. "Take a look, Hillary. You're the only one I want this way."

Her eyes dropped to his trousers. The smooth fabric did nothing to hide his arousal. The sight of it increased the humming inside her, making it harder to ignore. She pressed her thighs together and prayed for strength. She didn't want to give in.

Dropping her forehead to her knees, she murmured, "That doesn't change a thing."

"Doesn't it tell you something?"

"It tells me that you're a horny bastard, but I've known that all along."

"Horny, yes. Bastard? What have I ever done to you that's so awful?"

She looked up in astonishment. "Aside from the whole business with Janet? You pick me up, then drop me, pick me up again, drop me again. You come to me when you feel the urge and leave as soon as it's filled. We spend a long weekend making love, then days go by before

you think to give me a call. You keep me separate from the rest of your life, as if I'm not good enough, as if I might spoil something for you. I satisfy one need, and one need alone. You *use* me, John."

"If I use you, it's because you allow it."

Hillary was incensed. "So it's my fault? Just like it's Janet's fault the engagement ended because she didn't understand the rules?"

"You could say that."

"And Pam's fault that you forced her into an abortion she didn't want? And Patricia's fault that you seduced her behind Eugene's back? And Cutter's fault that you gypped him out of Little Lincoln—or that you had him beaten? I know about it, John. I know about all of it. So if you're thinking that I'm going to look up at you like you're some kind of idol, forget it. You've got feet of clay, just like the rest of us."

He said nothing. After staring at her for a time, he put his hands on his hips and looked at the ceiling. He raked his upper lip with his lower teeth. He hung his head. Then, when she was beginning to feel guilty for all she'd said, to wish that she could go over and wrap her arms around him, he met her gaze.

"Those are some pretty strong accusations."

She shrugged.

"Is that what you're planning to write about?"

"I don't know."

"I wouldn't, if I were you."

She held her breath, then said softly, "Don't, John."

"Don't what?"

"Lay down rules. Make threats."

"I'm simply giving advice."

"Advice that's in your own best interest. But what about mine?"

"It's yours that I'm thinking about," he said and came to her. Bending over, he propped a hand on either side of her hips and lowered his mouth to hers. But while she steeled herself against a kiss, what she got were a series of teasing touches that left her breathless and aching. Moaning softly, she turned her head away.

"You want me." He ran a hand up her leg. "Have you been heavy with it, too?"

"Shhhh."

His breath was warm against her cheek. "You always liked it when I said things like that. It heated you up." He tongued her earlobe. "Are you dripping for me, Hillary?"

She was sure she was. She was melting inside, despising herself for it, but needing him, just as he said. "Go away, John."

His hand was on the outside of her thigh, then sliding around. "Open your legs."

"No."

"Open them. Let me feel."

"No."

But he found his way there anyway, and his breath came sharply. "Oh, yeah. You want me."

"Doesn't mean a thing," she managed to gasp. She was losing her grip, hating it, loving it.

"Hillary?"

"Mmm?"

"Touch me."

"No."

His fingers paused in their deep stroking. "Do it."

Letting out a low whimper of frustration, she unwrapped her arms from her knees. As they spread apart, she felt his arousal through his trousers. But it wasn't enough. Touching him brought back images of what he was like bare, and she was suddenly desperate to feel him that way again.

Hating herself for what she was doing but half-wild with need, she pulled at his belt, unfastened his pants, and lowered the zipper. She slid her hands inside, under the band of his briefs, and with the very first touch she sucked in a breath.

"It's for you," he said in a voice that was low and gritty. "Doesn't get like this for anyone else."

She wanted to believe him, wanted so badly to believe him that when he began to unbutton her dress she didn't protest. She stroked him, then raised her hips at his urging. He had her panties off in a

second, and in the next had her against the sofa with her dress and her bra wide open, her knees bent and spread.

He dominated her world then, took control, blotted out everything else there might have been. If she'd ever wanted more in life, she couldn't remember. There was nothing but John—John needing her in ways no other man had, ways no other woman could possibly understand. In the afterglow, she truly believed she'd found her place.

Then, speaking quietly in her ear in a voice that was still faintly husky, he ruined it. "Proof is hard to come by, Hillary. Without it your claims are worthless."

They were sprawled on the sofa, a tangle of arms and legs and clothes that hadn't been fully removed. She lay still, trying to take in his words, but the deeper they sank in, the more they hurt.

He raised his head. "Are you listening? Write that story, and there'll be trouble."

For a minute she couldn't move. Then suddenly she felt she was suffocating. Scrambling out from under him, she withdrew to the far side of the room. She held her dress together with a shaky hand.

"Did that mean anything to you?" she asked.

He sat up. "It was damn good."

"Besides a lay. Did you feel anything here? Or here?" She touched first her head, then her heart.

"Ah, shit," he said and reached for his pants. "Are you going to start in on that? All these years, you were good. That was one of the reasons I kept coming back. You didn't pretend that there was more than there was. You didn't expect there to be." He stood and jerked up his fly. "Do you know how tired I get hearing women talk about love?"

"It scares you, doesn't it?"

He tugged his shirt into place. "It does not. I just find it a waste of energy."

But she had hit on something worth pursuing. "It scares you, scares you shitless. Love implies a commitment to another person— not a business, or a stone, or a marketing strategy, but a *person*. More than that, it involves expectations, and that's what you can't take. You don't want to be let down. Don't want to be hurt. So you keep people

at a distance. You order them around. You maintain full control, because then when you don't get what you want, you have someone to blame. You have someone to punish."

Draping his tie round his neck, he snatched up his jacket and started for the door. "You've been reading too much of the wrong stuff. Self-help books are a menace. You're getting analytical, and that's very boring." At the door, he turned and pointed a finger at her. "Don't write about me, Hillary. I'm warning you. Don't do it. Keep your nose in your own affairs, or you'll find yourself in over your head."

"Do you love him?" Pam asked.

Four days had passed since John stalked out of Hillary's apartment. Naturally, she hadn't heard from him. When Pam had come to town on business and called to meet for lunch, she had jumped at the chance. She needed to talk. Now, as they picked through their salades Niçoise at La Caravelle, she knew it was time.

"I suppose." She held her breath while the admission registered, then asked in an unsure tone, "Do you hate me for it?"

"No. I wish I could understand, though. How can you love a man who has treated you so horribly all these years?"

Hillary twisted her fork against a sliver of tuna. "I don't know. I just can't remember *not* loving him. From the first time I saw him, something was there." She looked up. "Wasn't it the same for you with Cutter? Right from the beginning, he was forbidden, still you felt something. Is there an explanation for that?"

"But Cutter is a giver. He's sensitive and gentle. He's as different from John—"

"I know." Hillary didn't want to go into that. "Don't ask me to tell you what I love about him. It's irrational. When we were young, I worshipped him. I saw his potential. I rooted for his success. I look at him now, and he has that success, but he's not happy. There's no personal peace. He won't let anyone get close enough to touch him where it really counts. I look at him, and I hurt. I wish he would let me help, but he won't. And I hate him for that."

She put a piece of lettuce in her mouth, simply to have something

to do. She chewed it, swallowed, ate another piece. "I'm filling the emptiness," she said with a wry half-smile. "This is why people gain weight. When there's a hole in their lives, they stuff something in. Food is the natural stuffer."

"So why do you look like you've lost five pounds?"

"I've been working too hard." She took a long drink of Perrier, then watched Pam sift through the remnants of her salad. "Speaking of which, aren't you going to ask?"

Pam pushed an olive through several revolutions before setting down her fork and sitting back in her chair. "I figured you'd tell me when you're ready." After a minute, she said with quiet resignation. "You're writing it, aren't you."

Hillary nodded. "It's mostly about John. But there's some about the rest of you, too." When Pam looked pained, she said, "You're my friend. My closest friend. You know I wouldn't do anything to harm you." Still Pam said nothing, so she added, "I thought it was a dynamite idea at first. I'm not so sure now."

"Why?"

"I wanted to tell the truth about John. Give the other side of the story. I thought I knew almost everything, but I was wrong. I've learned some things I wished I hadn't."

"Like the beating."

"And the will. For God's sake, I don't want to destroy John."

Again Pam was quiet. She frowned at her water glass, ran her thumb over its rim.

"Say something, Pam."

"Like what?"

"Like he deserves it."

"He does."

"Then you should want me to write this book."

Pam looked torn. Her response was a while in coming. "My goal isn't to hurt John so much as to be free of him. I want him out of my way. And he will be. But it has to be done right."

Once again, Hillary felt a premonition. "You have something in the works, you and Cutter. What is it?"

Pam eyed her sadly and shook her head.

"You can tell me. I won't say a word. Hell, John walked out on me. I won't hear from him again in months."

"I can't tell you, Hillary. I wish I could, but I can't."

"Because you don't trust me?"

"No. Because I love you. It's enough that you know something might happen. If I tell you anything more, I'll be putting an awesome weight on your shoulders. You love John; you hate John. The less you know, the less torn you'll be."

"You're taking over the company, aren't you?"

Pam didn't say a word.

"You've been courting the shareholders, and you're going to oust John as president."

Still Pam didn't speak.

"Is Patricia in on this?"

"You can ask all you want, but I'm not free to say. And anyway, I don't know much. I'm just an artist."

"Just an artist," Hillary echoed. "Hah. You're the backbone of the family."

Pam rolled her eyes. "I don't know about that. At this point I'm spread so thin I feel like I could break apart with the slightest provocation."

"Brendan?"

Pam shrugged, then let out a breath. "Not great. I shouldn't have come down today, but I've been putting off this trip for too long."

"Is there anything I can do?"

"Just be here if I need a friend. You always have been. I count on that."

"I'm here." Hillary paused. "Pam, about the book . . ."

"Do what you have to. I can't tell you to stop."

"Will you hate me?"

"I could never hate you. I'll worry, though."

"About what?"

"You. Writing about John. If there was ever any hope for you two,

it'll be gone. He'll hate you, and I'd hate to see that. You're the man's only hope of salvation."

"Yeah. Well, he doesn't see it quite that way."

"He might. The day may come when he'll need a friend, too. Not that he deserves one. Not that he deserves *you*. And it may be that come that time, you won't want him. But if you do, I want you to have him. I'd hate to see you burn that bridge now." She tipped her head. "Which means that you'll be deferring to him again, putting your career second to whatever it is you have or may someday have with him, which is pretty much what you've been doing all your life. It's not right, Hillary."

"I know. So what do I do?"

Pam considered that, finally saying, "You wait. Take things slowly. See what happens over the next few months."

There it was again, that warning. "Will you tell me as soon as there's something to tell?"

Pam nodded. "Will you let me see what you've written before you turn it in?"

Hillary nodded with a sad smile. "We reach agreements so easily, you and I. If only the rest of life were so simple."

Chapter 23

◈◈◈

Boston, 1979

Pam SPENT A WEEK TRYING TO grapple with what John had told her, before finally succumbing and going to see Bob Grossman. He had become a friend over the years, but he was still first and foremost her mother's therapist. Pam had never paid him for therapy time. So, with no more than the briefest of preliminaries, she got to the point of her visit.

"John said that he and my mother had an affair. Is it true?"

Bob's expression showed that he hadn't been expecting that particular bomb. She suspected that he would have made a quip about her pointedness—Bob had that light way about him—if she hadn't looked so sober. Quietly and predictably, he returned the question. "Do you think it is?"

She hesitated for a minute. Saying things out loud somehow gave them legitimacy. But then, that was why she'd come. "It would make sense out of certain things."

"Like?"

"Like how close they were. Like John's possessiveness. Like the way he used to come from her bedroom sometimes. I could never understand what she saw in him. I resented their closeness, but I never gave it a sexual meaning. Then John opened his mouth the other day, and I wanted to believe he was lying." She still did. "But it fits. If Daddy

found them in bed together, he would have been furious enough to storm out of the house. Mom would have been frightened enough of losing him to jump in the car, and he might well have driven recklessly." There was an even stronger argument, though. "If it's true, it helps explain why she retreated into herself after the accident. I used to think it had something to do with me."

"It did, in some respects," Bob said, but gently. "The guilt Patricia felt was compounded when she looked at you. You reminded her of Eugene and of all that could have been if the accident hadn't occurred."

His confirmation was indirect, but there. Pam felt a rush of anger she'd been trying to quash all week. "Why did she have to sleep with him? If she'd wanted to be with a man that badly, she could have gone up to Maine. Daddy was always there. He had the house. It was big and beautiful and comfortable, and we had help. It wasn't like she had to hike up to a rustic cabin somewhere and rough it."

Bob smiled kindly. "Different people see things different ways. You loved Timiny Cove from the first. Patricia never felt quite that way about it."

"But she loved my father. At least, she said she did."

"She did. She still does. It's one of the things she and I have been working on."

Pam wasn't sure she understood. "Working on?"

He turned to more comfortably face her. "After the accident, Patricia put your dad on a pedestal. She idealized everything about him. Correspondingly, she became the fall guy. She took full blame for what had gone wrong with their marriage. In her mind, she was the villain."

"She was. She cheated on him."

"She had reasons for doing what she did. It wasn't a malicious thing, and it wasn't like she did it with lots of men. John was the only one. Your mother was fragile—he took advantage of that. And as for Eugene, he wanted strength in a woman. When he didn't find it in Patricia, he more or less cast her aside."

Pam rushed to her father's defense. "He was faithful."

"Maybe sexually. But emotionally he wasn't there for her."

"He was there for me."

"Because you're basically a strong person. He could accept the downs because there were plenty of ups. With your mother, the downs were predominant. He let her know that, which fed into her insecurities. It became a cyclical thing." He draped an elbow over the sofa back and laced his fingers together. "What I'm trying to do—what I've been trying to do—is to help her see things as they really were. I'm not saying that she was a saint, any more than I'm saying your dad was a sinner. I'm trying to create a balance in Patricia's mind. She has to accept herself. She has to respect herself. She has to put her feelings for Eugene into perspective. She has to learn to love his memory and let go of the man himself if she's ever going to move on in life."

"Will she?"

"Move on? Eventually. She's still a long way from it. This hospital represents security to her. She doesn't feel capable of surviving away from it."

"Maybe she isn't," Pam said, feeling angry again.

Bob was quiet, a sure sign, she knew, that he was waiting for her to go on. She had enough resentment in her—and was comfortable enough with him—to do just that.

"She made a mess of things, having an affair with John. It's bad enough that she cheated on her husband, but John is her stepson. He also happens to be the dregs of the earth."

"Your opinion," Bob said with a raised finger.

"Do you think he's not?"

"I don't know the man well enough to say. He rarely comes here."

Pam snorted. "Rarely?"

"Almost never."

"When was the last time he came? Three, four years ago?"

"Two. But that's fine. Patricia won't see him anyway."

Pam grinned. "Won't see him at all?"

Bob shook his head.

"Good for her."

"Not really," Bob said. "She'll have to come to terms with him at

some point, but she avoids it. Doesn't want to talk about him. Doesn't want to think about him."

Pam found a kind of justice in that. Not that John would be bothered. Patricia was nothing to him. She couldn't help his career.

"He said that if the truth came out, it would destroy her. Do you think it would?"

"Not where she is now. It can't touch her here. Someday, after she leaves, it could hurt her." He thought for a minute. "Destroy? That depends on how strong she is by then."

"What will she feel if she knows I know?"

"Embarrassed. Guilty. Inadequate."

"Then I shouldn't say anything."

He arched a brow. "Depends on what you want to say. If you're angry enough—and you are angry—to yell at her and tell her how wrong she was and how badly she betrayed your dad, then you shouldn't say anything. She already knows those things. Hearing them from you would open up the wound." He paused. "How angry are you?"

"Right now? Not as angry as I was when I walked in here."

He grinned.

"But I was pretty angry when I first found out. It comes and goes. Sometimes it's anger, sometimes disappointment, sometimes pure revulsion. I mean, my stomach actually turns when I think of him—of them. It's sick."

"But it wasn't incest, Pam. Keep that in mind. They were two attractive people, close in age, each lonely in his way."

"If you're asking me to condone it, I can't."

"I'm not asking that. I'm asking you to try to understand what Patricia was feeling. She was frightened and insecure and alone. She fell into something that promised her relief, and when it delivered, she went back for more. She grew dependent on John emotionally, long before anything physical happened. In time, the emotional and the physical became interlocked. She needed one for the sake of the other. It was a package deal, sort of."

Pam sensed a familiar modus operandi. "That sounds like John. He gives with one hand and takes with the other."

"Now you got it."

"But she didn't have to sleep with him."

"She probably wouldn't have, if she'd been thinking clearly, but she wasn't. She is now. And what she needs most is forgiveness." He took a deep breath. "So. In answer to your question about whether to tell her what you know, I say that if you can find it in yourself to forgive her, it might go a long way toward helping her forgive herself."

Pam regarded him sadly. "That sounds pretty and noble and all kinds of other things."

He grinned. "You're pretty and noble and all kinds of other things. You can do it."

It took a while. The first time Pam saw Patricia, knowing what she knew, she felt strange. She brought coffee and sweet rolls—the light, raised kind Patricia liked, with cinnamon and icing, fresh from the doughnut shop—and they ate together. Outwardly, nothing had changed. Inwardly, the question was there. Between sips of coffee, Pam looked at Patricia, trying to imagine her making love with John.

Two attractive people, close in age, each lonely in his way. Bob's words echoed in her mind. She recited them in a silent litany, and kept it up long after she left.

The next time she visited, she brought Patricia a knitted shawl from Bonwit's. It was shot with whispers of pink and green and seemed as delicate as Patricia herself. Pam also brought some pink nail polish to match the shawl and painted her mother's fingernails. When she had finished and was standing back to assess her work, with Patricia darting her quick, self-conscious glances, she had a glimpse of the lovely woman who suffered so inside.

On the third visit, she brought a small cassette player and a tape of Tchaikovsky's *The Nutcracker.* More than once, when Pam was a child, Patricia had taken her to the ballet The music brought back fond memories of a happier, simpler time.

Patricia must have felt it too, because after the tape had clicked off and several quiet minutes had passed, she asked wiih soft but intent curiosity, "Are you happy?"

"Happy? With my life?"

Patricia nodded.

Pam considered her answer carefully. "I've been lucky. I love designing jewelry. It's rewarding."

"But are you happy?"

It was the first time Patricia had pushed. Pam wanted to think it was a good sign. She also wanted to answer honestly and hoped it was the right thing to do. "Yes and no. Some things are great, some aren't."

"Do you love Cutter?"

The question surprised Pam. Of all the times she'd mentioned Cutter, Patricia had never given any response. Apparently, though, she'd been listening. "I've always loved Cutter."

Patricia betrayed nothing of her feelings as she considered that. "Is it an adult love?"

"Very."

"Why aren't you with him?"

Pam was slower in answering this time. She felt a spurt of anger at Patricia for having to ask, for not being around to know. She tempered the anger, drew in a breath, let it out. "John won't have it," she said.

Patricia's face showed no emotion, but her voice was weaker. "It shouldn't be John's decision to make."

"Tell *him* that," Pam blurted out. A second later she wished she hadn't. Patricia's eyes suddenly filled with tears.

"I can't," she whispered. She kept looking at Pam, tears pooling in her eyes without falling.

Helplessness, desperation, sorrow—Pam saw them all. If the suddenness of their appearance stunned her, their intensity was even more gripping. In the past few years Patricia had been a passive entity, seeming almost dim-witted at times. Pam had known the emotions were there—Bob had told her—but she'd never seen evidence of them herself. Now she did. Emotions long buried had suddenly risen to the surface with the most inadvertent of provocations.

Looking at those emotions and the pain behind them, Pam felt a rise of fury. "It isn't right, y'know. It isn't right that you should be

punishing yourself this way, while he goes merrily through life." Without quite saying the words, she had acknowledged that she knew about the affair.

Patricia's response was a frantic shake of her head. "I deserve the punishment."

"But when is it enough? When does it end?"

"When I die."

"No. You deserve more. Daddy would have wanted more for you."

"He hated me."

"He loved you."

"I betrayed him."

Pam tried to remember all the things Bob had said. "You betrayed him when you were feeling weak and unhappy, but you had help. You didn't do it alone. If John hadn't been there luring you on, it wouldn't have happened."

Patricia dropped her eyes to her lap, where her hands lay limply. She stared at them for a long time, although Pam doubted she saw much. Tears were trickling down her cheeks.

"You hate me, too," she whispered finally.

"I love you."

"You hate me."

"If I hated you, would I be coming here to visit this way?"

"You feel you have to."

"I *want* to."

"But I have nothing to offer."

"You're my mother. You gave me life. Isn't that enough?"

"I should have given you more."

"But it's over. You can't go back. Only ahead."

"I can't go ahead," Patricia wailed.

Pam felt utterly helpless. She didn't know what to say or do, since what she had done clearly wasn't right. Acting on nothing more than her own need, she took Patricia's hand and brought it to her cheek. "Someday," she said, pausing to swallow the knot in her throat, "someday you will. Someday you'll leave here and come home where you belong. Someday. You will."

Patricia gave another frantic little shake of her head, from which she went right into a nod. Then, as though the combination of the two gestures had short-circuited her mind, she seemed to wind down, and sank deeper into her chair and grew silent.

Pam continued to hold her hand for a time before kissing it, replacing it in her lap, and standing. "I'll be back in a few days," she said softly.

At the door, she looked back. The image struck her then of the frail, wheelchair-bound woman whose shrunken legs, bowed head, and hollow eyes reeked of the sadness of one living a life of self-inflicted punishment.

In that instant, Pam began to understand the depth of her mother's suffering. In the next instant, forgiveness took root. And in the instant after that, all the anger that might have been channeled toward Patricia was redirected toward John.

One week later, Pam flew to New York. Officially, she was there to meet with a client who wanted to commission several pieces of jewelry. Unofficially—and covertly—she was meeting with Cutter. A single night in Manhattan was all he had between ten days in Texas and a week in Paris, and while she might have preferred to pick a more leisurely time, what she had to discuss with him couldn't wait.

Her client was staying at the Lowell Hotel. Cutter had said that he'd meet her at the Pembroke Room at four for high tea, and Pam appreciated the whimsy. It was Cutter the miner, at his tongue-in-cheek best.

Concluding her meeting early, she reached the Pembroke Room well before him. So she settled into the French period furniture and anticipated his arrival with growing excitement. Even then, she couldn't help but catch her breath when he came into sight. He was wearing a black silk shirt, gray pleated trousers, a loose-fitting tweed jacket, and imported loafers without socks. His immaculately cut hair was sensuously mussed. His face was lightly tanned, his jaw and upper lip lightly shadowed. There was a swagger in his step and a gleam in his eye. He looked spectacular.

"Hi, babe," he whispered, sliding onto the loveseat and kissing her neck. His grin was crooked.

"Hi," she whispered back. She put her fingers to his lips and skimmed their lean planes. "Did you plan that entrance?"

"What entrance?" His eyes took in each of her features.

"The one you just made."

"I just walked in the door." He tipped her head up.

"But beautifully." She took a shaky breath and opened her mouth for his kiss. Her breathing was even shakier when it was finished. "I've missed you," she whispered.

"Me too," he whispered back. He had a hand curved around her neck and was caressing her jaw with his thumb. "You're a sight for sore eyes."

"Bull. You've been looking at gorgeous models all week."

"Six-foot amazons. I like petite women. Women I can look down on."

"What a sexist comment."

"I'm a sexist man. Contrary to the trend. I do believe in the differences between us." His gaze fell to her breasts at the same time as he lowered his hand to her hip. Against her mouth, he asked, "Want me to change?"

"Not on your life."

"Should I order tea?"

"Only if you want to drink it."

"Do you?"

She came forward the fraction of an inch necessary to fuse her mouth with his in a tongue-deep kiss. Cutter was more visibly shaken than she at its end.

His voice was low. "Let's go somewhere, Pam."

"My place or yours?"

"Yours is nicer, but mine is closer."

"Yours, then. I've been waiting for you forever."

Actually, it had been just shy of a month since she'd seen him, but it might have been an eternity for the impatience she felt on the way to his apartment. He led the way, holding her hand as he lengthened his

stride. She half-walked, half-trotted. When traffic lights periodically pinned them to a corner, she pressed as close to him as she could.

Once inside his building, he rushed her into the elevator. The door had no sooner closed than he backed her to the smooth paneling, flattened his body against hers, and began moving. He didn't stop until they'd reached the apartment, stripped off their clothing, and made love.

At last, lying naked on her back beside Cutter, Pam gave a loud moan. "I should have known this would happen. One look at you and I'm not good for much of anything."

"You were real good for a lot of something," he argued, but his lips barely moved. He sounded half-asleep.

"I want to be good at a lot else." She pushed herself up on an elbow. "Marry me, Cutter?"

His eyes remained closed. He didn't move. "Mmmm."

"I want to get married. Now."

"I'm not dressed."

She shook his shoulder. "Cutter, I'm not kidding. I want to get married."

"I can't talk about this now. You've drained me."

"But this was the reason I came. I specifically want to discuss this."

"Then you shouldn't have let me make love to you first."

"I couldn't help it."

Throwing an arm around her, he brought her back down to his side. "Let me hold you for a minute. Then we'll talk."

So he held her. Tipping her head back, Pam studied his face. In total relaxation he looked young and vulnerable. Not that thirty was old. But he hadn't been vulnerable for a long time. He was strong and independent, a man of friends and means. She was the vulnerable one. His world had broadened. She could lose him so easily.

A faint shiver passed through her. His arms tightened, but it was an instinct. The evenness of his breathing told her that he had dozed off. Nestling her cheek in the soft, curling hair on his chest, she closed

her eyes, breathed in the warm, male scent of his skin, and concentrated on the pure heaven of being there with him.

The contentment was a sedative. She dozed, too, awakening to find him perched on an elbow eyeing her appreciatively.

"You look like an angel when you sleep."

"I wasn't sleeping." She stretched, felt the glide of her skin against his, snuggled closer. Then she remembered the point of her visit and flattened a hand on his chest.

He moved it over his nipple, which was already tight, and let a low moan slip from deep inside.

"Oh no you don't!" She snatched back her hand and sat up. Sweeping her hair from her face with her thumb and forefinger, she settled cross-legged facing him.

"I meant what I said before. About marriage."

His eyes were on the juncture of her thighs.

"Cutter?"

He looked up quickly. "Hmm?"

"Let's get married."

"When the time is right, we will."

"Let's do it now. I'm tired of waiting." She had his full attention. He was studying her curiously. "I'm out of school and earning good money. You're earning even better money. You can't give me the argument that I'm going to pass by you in life, because it's more like the other way around. So let's get married."

She watched his curiosity slip into disbelief. "Just like that? Just like we're two people who met last year and fell in love? Just like we haven't been wanting to get married since you were seventeen?"

"Just like that."

His disbelief deepened. "But nothing's changed, Pam. John is still there, still threatening."

"We've changed," she argued. "We're older. Stronger. I'm tired of living my life by John's rules."

Cutter ran a hand over his eyes and left his arm on his forehead. Peering at her from beneath it, he said wearily, "I think we've been through this before."

"And I'm as tired of it as you are. So let's do something. Let's get married."

"No."

"Why not?"

"Because the time isn't right."

"That's what you said before, but it's as right as it'll ever be. John won't just grow old and fade away, and if you think he'll mellow sometime soon, think again. He has this thing about you, Cutter. He'd as soon slash my throat as have me marry you."

"That's why the timing has to be right."

"But I want to get married now."

"Why?"

"Because I love you."

"What else is new?"

Hearing the bitterness in his voice, she felt a sinking inside. She had known that he wouldn't jump at the idea, since they'd discussed it before. Still she wished he would show a little enthusiasm.

"Why now?" he went on in her silence. "It's not like we can spend any more time together. You have your career and I have mine. We're both really busy. I'm hardly ever home. It won't always be that way, but right now it is, and it's no way to start a marriage."

"I want," she repeated, "to get married."

He lowered his arm. "Tell me why, Pam. Why the rush?" She looked him in the eye and spoke through gritted teeth, easy enough to do with John's face hovering in her mind. "Because I want control over my stock and my mother's. I don't want to wait another two years to turn twenty-five. I want that control now."

Cutter came up on an elbow. "Has John done something else?"

"Not directly. Not new." She took a breath and told him about John's affair with Patricia. "Did you know?"

"How would I know? I was up in Maine."

"Then there weren't any rumors flying around?"

"None." He hissed out an angry, "My God, the guy's been in every bed around."

"Not mine," Pam snapped.

"But not for lack of wanting. You know that, don't you?"

She knew it all too well, but her concern was with Patricia. "My mother's nervous breakdown was John's fault. He's the reason she couldn't think, couldn't speak, couldn't act. He's the reason she hasn't been able to face life. He has to be stopped, Cutter. If I can get control of my stock and my mother's, between us we'll have more than he has. I want that control. So I want to get married."

But Cutter shook his head. "If marriage were the answer, we'd have done it years ago. You think I didn't want to? But nothing's changed. Our marrying won't stop John. You may get control of your own stock, but not Patricia's. Do you honestly think John would give it up?"

"I'll get a court order."

"Based on what? You're not a businesswoman, you're an artist."

"What does that have to do with anything?"

He sat up to face her. "John's a businessman. We may hate his guts, but we have to give him that. He's a good businessman. He's built the company, and it's sound."

"It was sound under my father."

"But smaller. John's made something different and larger. He's done well by his stockholders. Given your lack of experience and his wealth of it, no court will shift control of the stock."

"But I'm her daughter."

"And he's her stepson."

"But look what he's done to her!"

"The court won't see that—unless you bring it out."

She brought up her chin. "If need be, I will."

"You will not, because it'll hurt you and it'll hurt Patricia. I'm telling you, Pam, you haven't got a chance of getting those shares. So rushing into marriage is crazy."

"You wouldn't say that if you loved me."

He rolled his eyes. "I do love you. That's not the issue. The issue is whether we let John dictate what we do and when. I want to marry you, Pam. I've wanted it for years, and you know it. But the timing isn't right now. I'm on my way, but I'm not there yet."

"But you have so much!"

"Everything is relative. I've earned a lot and invested a lot. Little by little I'm picking up St. George stock, but I don't have anywhere near enough to be a threat to John, and until I do, I won't have the power to prevent him from carrying out his threats. You can be damn sure that if we get married, he'll lash out at anything and everything. I can't take that risk."

"Risk? Is marrying me such a risk? If you love me, *really* love me, you'd do it."

He took her arms, and for a minute she thought he would shake her. He looked that fierce. But he simply held on tightly. "I do love you, really love you. Years ago I told you that you were the only woman I'd ever consider marrying, and that hasn't changed, but I won't marry you now. Not yet."

"Why not?"

He did shake her then, a short, sharp jostle of frustration. "Because I have pride, dammit! Marrying you may be the most important thing in my life, but I'll do it on my terms. I'll do it when I've come far enough to settle down. I'm not there yet, but I will be someday."

"And if I won't wait?" she was hurt enough to ask.

He looked at her for a minute, then dropped his hands and sat back. "If you won't wait, then it's your loss."

"You pompous ass!" Scrambling off the bed, she reached for her clothes. "It'll be your loss, too, only you're too bullheaded to see it."

"Where are you going?"

"Back to Boston. You need time to think about whether it's me you want, or power."

"It shouldn't be either or."

"Well, it is."

"Don't do that," he warned in a low voice that made her hand falter on a button of her blouse.

"Do what?" She resumed the buttoning.

"Give ultimatums. Either I marry you now, or you're leaving. That's a John kind of move."

She snagged her nylons, swore, felt her eyes water, and knew it had nothing to do with the snag. "No. It's a human kind of move. I

should have made it a while ago. If you loved me, you'd marry me. It's as simple as that."

"It's not simple. Nothing's ever been simple where you and I are concerned."

She stood to stuff her blouse into her skirt. "Maybe there's a message in that."

Heedless of his nudity, Cutter rose from the bed and came around to confront her. "You're sounding like a spoiled kid."

"I'm twenty-three, old enough to get married and more than old enough to have kids." Blazer in hand, she reached for her bag. "I would have had yours, Cutter. Ours. It would have been five years old now, only it never took a breath, because John had it killed."

Cutter was dead silent for an awful moment. "What?"

"You didn't know that?" she asked on her way to the door. Her voice shook. She began to tremble all over. "Hillary didn't tell you?"

He came after her. "What are you talking about?"

She walked faster. "The abortion."

"What abortion?"

"The one John had done while I was drugged." At the front door, she whirled around. "He killed your child, Cutter. Only you never knew it existed, so you never loved it, so you don't grieve like I do. You have your career. You have your money. You have your power." She opened the door. "Well, good! Keep it all. I hope it makes you happy."

Slamming the apartment door, she raced to the elevator. She was too hurt to cry, too angry to think of looking back to see if he would follow. On the street, she hailed a cab and went straight to the airport. She was back in Boston before midnight. Not that there was a great rush. As she saw it, the coach had turned into a pumpkin well before that.

For days she waited, hoping that Cutter would call to say how upset he was, how much he loved her, how badly he wanted to marry her. When no call came, she tried to call him, but all she reached was his answering service. Whether he was out of town or simply not

taking her calls, she didn't know. But she waited and waited, and he didn't call her back.

Convinced that he blamed her for the abortion, she was grief-stricken. She was also angry—angry at Cutter for being so stubborn, angry at John for being so evil. She couldn't do much about Cutter but ache. John was something else.

She wanted to be free of him. She needed control of the stock if she was ever to help her mother. With each day that passed, she felt more certain that she was the only one who could do that. There was no one besides Pam through whom Patricia could finally get back at John.

Marriage was the only answer. Pam was at the right age; many of her friends were getting married. And there was Brendan McGrath, who had asked her more than once, and was so kind.

So she married him. For the sake of herself and her mother, and even Cutter, she married Brendan. It was a quiet ceremony in the living room of his spacious home in Milton. A justice of the peace presided. The only witnesses were Brendan's two grown sons.

Brendan was a banker, better than twice Pam's age, older and even more respected in financial circles than John. His first marriage had been a happy one. His wife had been his best friend until the day she died, five years before. Pam had met him soon after that and found a friend in him, too. He was soft-spoken and low-keyed, interested in what she was doing, respectful of her achievements. He was a strong man, self-confident but not egotistical. At fifty, with his sons in homes of their own, he was looking for companionship over passion.

He was the perfect solution for Pam. He offered her his name, his home, and his affection, and asked little in return but that she be there for him on weekends. In some respects he was the father figure she had missed, and if it struck her as strange that a husband should be that, she reasoned that she could have done a whole lot worse. Brendan McGrath was a good man.

That was, perhaps, why the enormity of her mistake hit her so hard. Well before the honeymoon was over, she felt it the first time Brendan made gentle, almost shy love to her, when Cutter's face was

the one in her mind. He hadn't loved her enough to marry her, but now he was farther from reach than ever, and it was her own fault. She'd been rash. In her rush to defy John, she hadn't thought through her actions. She could blame John, but only to a point. She should have had more sense, more compassion.

Cutter would be furious—more out of pride than anything else, she was sure, and that hurt. Whatever love he still felt for her was sure to be dashed. That hurt. But she hurt, too, when she thought of Brendan. He was an innocent pawn in a game whose rules he barely knew. She had used him, and in that sense she wasn't much better than John.

That thought and others kept her soft-spoken and submissive during the seven days that she and Brendan stayed on Key West. There were times when she was calm and content, times when she despaired, times when she actually started to tremble at the thought of what she had done. By the time they returned home, though, her own pride had kicked into play. She knew that she'd done Brendan a grave injustice. She knew that she would either wallow in guilt or rise to the occasion. She chose to do the latter. Regardless of how badly she missed Cutter, she vowed to make Brendan happy.

Chapter 24

◆◆◆

So CONGRATULATIONS ARE IN ORDER, huh?" Hillary asked.

Cutter bobbled the phone on his shoulder, steadied it, pressed two fingers to his eyes. "Yeah."

"Tell me about it."

"Tell me what you heard."

"Playing coy?"

"Just tired."

"Ahhh. You had a rough night."

He glanced around the apartment. It was a mess, just as it had been for the past two months. Rough night? "You could say that." Every damn night had been rough since he'd learned of Pam's marriage. He hadn't slept well, hadn't eaten well, hadn't been able to concentrate on how badly he'd botched things.

"What I heard," Hillary began, "was that you've been tapped to be the rugged, denim-clad hero in a long-range ad campaign sponsored by the diamond industry. True?"

"Dramatically phrased, but close enough."

"I'm a writer. If I can't phrase things dramatically, what can I do? So tell me about it. Did you have a falling-out with Jondier?"

"No. But my contract is expiring, and I want a change."

"You'll have that. Fancy pants to denim. What about the work? Will it be any less grueling?"

"Yeah. Fewer days. More money."

"Not bad." She paused. "So why don't you sound thrilled?"

He dragged his fingers down his face and dropped his hand to his lap. "I'm just tired."

"And missing her."

He felt a sharp pain. After a time, he said, "Yeah."

"Oh, Cutter."

He squeezed his eyes shut. "Have you talked with her?" he asked.

"Last week. She sounded okay."

"Just okay? Not ecstatic? Not radiant? Isn't that what new brides are supposed to be?"

"Come on, Cutter. Don't be sarcastic."

"Well, how am I supposed to be?" he barked, and then it all poured out. "She's the love of my life—I'm supposedly the love of hers—but when I won't go along with her schemes, she runs off and marries someone else. After fourteen years. *Fourteen years.*"

"Cutter, fourteen years ago she was only nine."

"That was when we first saw each other, and it's been special ever since. So what happened? How could she have considered marrying someone else? How could she have done it? And him. He's as old as the hills, for Christ's sake."

"He's a good man."

"Tell me she loves him. Can you do that?"

"No. But she likes him. And he's good to her."

"I would have been good to her."

"But you wouldn't marry her."

"Because the time wasn't right, and her arguments were dumb. I've been proven right, haven't I?" He gloated. "She couldn't get control of Patricia's stock. The court wouldn't give an inch."

"She got hers."

"It's friggin' little of the whole, so what good does it do?"

"It gives her a seat on the board, and exposure. She's determined to be a vocal presence at meetings. She's also determined to be the best designer *Facets* has."

"Will he give her time for that—the guy she married?"

"His name is Brendan. And yes, he'll let her work. He wants her to. He knows it means a lot to her."

"What about kids? Are they gonna have 'em?" His voice broke up, which was exactly what happened to him inside every time he thought of the baby that wasn't. He grimaced at the pain.

Hillary's voice was quiet. "Let me come over, Cutter."

"No." He cleared his throat. "No. I'm not dressed." He looked down at himself. It was half-true. He was bare-chested and bare-footed. He wore pants, but they were open. There didn't seem much point in doing up the zipper when the only practical thing he'd done in the last twelve hours was pee.

"I'd really like to be there. I think you're upset."

He might have known she would offer; she was giving that way. But he didn't want sympathy. Sympathy wouldn't move him ahead. "Sure, I'm upset, but I'll live. I have a great new contract. I'll have more time to do the things I want."

"If it's any consolation, John isn't—"

"Don't mention that man's name to me! I'm apt to get violent." He fought the pain. "Hillary, did you know about the abortion?"

She was a minute in answering. "Not for a long time."

"But you did find out. Why didn't you tell me."

"It wasn't my place."

"Someone should have. I had a right to know."

"So you could do what? The baby was gone."

Hearing her say it only added to his bitterness. "It was probably just as well. Having a kid at that age would have messed up her life."

"You don't believe that."

"What else am I supposed to believe? She pops this bit about an abortion on me, then walks out the door. How the hell should I know what she was feeling?"

"You could have asked. You could have called her afterward. You could have gone to Boston to see her."

He told himself the same things time and again, and each time he wondered whether it would have made a difference. He guessed it might have. But he had never dreamed she would suddenly marry

someone else just two weeks later. He'd been shortsighted. And bull-headed. "I was angry," was the only excuse he could give.

"You still are. But ease up on Pam, at least about the abortion. She wanted that baby. She wanted it more than anything. I'm not sure she's completely over the loss even now."

"How could he have done that to her?" Cutter exclaimed, then said, "Forget I asked that. It was fully in character. What I don't understand is you. How can you keep seeing a man like that?"

Her voice chilled. "Off limits, Cutter. I tell you what I know about Pam. I even tell you a little about John. But don't criticize me. We all have our quirks. John's mine. Pam's yours."

"Pam isn't a quirk. She isn't evil or cruel. Loving her is as easy as breathing."

"As *easy?* My God, if breathing hurt me as much as loving Pam hurts you, I'd be tempted to turn in my lungs. And you keep going back for more. Fourteen years is a long time. What you feel for her has to be an obsession by now."

"Maybe," Cutter admitted, then his resolve hardened. "But I'll have her someday."

"She's married. You'd better accept that."

"For now. But someday I'll have her. Someday I'll have it all. You watch, Hillary. I'll do it."

That thought, more than any other, kept him going over the months that followed. Leaving Jondier was a good move. By minimizing his work hours and maximizing his income, he was able to deepen his involvement in business. That was his future. Modeling had always been, and still was, simply the means to an end.

Working with the diamond industry opened more doors. He met new people, made new contacts. With some of the top businessmen in the country as his teachers, he took an increasingly active role in his own affairs, and, in so doing, earned their respect. More and more, he was viewed as a professionally shrewd and socially savvy man.

Inevitably, his path crossed Pam's. Although they approached it from different angles, they were in the same field, and when he wasn't

modeling he was doing business. They came to know many of the same people. Their stomping grounds overlapped.

The first time they saw each other was in September in San Francisco. Pam had been married for ten months. Cutter hadn't seen her since the day she had run out of his apartment, and although his initial anger had faded, he was a long way from forgiving her for what she'd done. Then, suddenly, she was there across the room, looking more stunning than ever.

Seeing her was like taking a physical blow. Once he recovered his breath, he felt raw, hurt, and lonely. Mostly, though, he felt hungry. He couldn't look at her enough. She fed his mind and his senses, bringing him alive in ways he hadn't been for ten and a half months.

Then she saw him, and right before his eyes she suffered the same shock as he had, the same rawness, the same loneliness, the same hunger. Unable to deal with it, he turned and left in a fit of fury. She was married; she had no right to look at him that way. But he couldn't forget that she had, which was why, when he saw her at a restaurant in Gstaad the following February, rather than turn away, he excused himself from his friends and approached her table.

"Pam." He tipped his head in greeting. His heart was thudding wildly, but professional training and the heavy knit sweater he wore hid it. "How are you?"

She was paler than she had been moments before. "Fine. And you?"

He nodded his answer. "Are you here skiing?"

"Uh, no. On business." She held his gaze several seconds longer before introducing the four others she was with. Her husband wasn't among them, but Cutter already knew that. He had seen a picture of Pam and Brendan after the wedding and in his mind carried a vivid image of the man.

Pam's eyes were on him again well before the introductions were finished. "How about you?" she asked as soon as she could. Pale pink color had crept in her cheeks. "Business or pleasure?"

"A little of each. It's a great place." But he didn't spare even the

briefest glance around. No ski resort could hold a candle to Pam's face. It was a rare sight, too good to waste for even a second. "This is my first time here."

She nodded and gave a quick once-over to his clothing, but her eyes were drawn right back to his. "You've been skiing." When he confirmed it with a nod, she said, "I'll bet you're good."

He shrugged.

"You were always so physically, uh, so coordinated."

He was having trouble remaining nonchalant. Pam's eyes were rapt with a curiosity that fell just short of longing. It didn't matter that the feelings were forbidden. They reflected everything he felt himself and did nothing to quell his urge to touch her.

For a minute, neither of them spoke. Finally, quietly, he said, "I always tried." Raising his head, he tossed a farewell to her friends. To her, with a lingering look, he said, "Take care."

He returned to his own friends, but he kept glancing across the room. Several times he caught her looking back; each time she averted her gaze. He wasn't sure whether she didn't want him to know she was looking, or whether she simply found the meeting of their eyes too painful. If it was the latter, he knew what she was feeling. Just looking at her reminded him of all he should have had, but didn't. It heightened his determination in ways that might have frightened her if she'd known.

In October, when he saw her at a party at a private country club on the outskirts of Atlanta, he held back. She was with Brendan, and even he had to admit that they made a handsome pair. Silver-haired and trim of build, Brendan was a pleasant-looking man who took an elegance from her. In return, he gave her support in the form of a look, a touch, a smile. Cutter suffered through those until Pam spotted him, when the suffering grew even more intense. After a time, Brendan moved her on through the crowd. Cutter moved in the opposite direction, but the suffering went on.

Needing a break, he wandered onto the veranda. She found him there. "Cutter?"

He looked down at his polished shoes.

She came close and softly repeated his name.

Eyes still low, he said, "Go back inside, Pam."

"Why?"

"This is dangerous."

"John's not here."

"John isn't the danger."

She was silent for a minute, but she didn't leave. Her voice was cautious. "I just wanted to say hello. It's been a long time."

"Eight months."

"Plus one week."

A fractured sound slipped from the back of his throat. He did raise his head then, and what he saw was enough to make him wish he hadn't. Pam's eyes were large, a little frightened, a little desperate. Her skin was smooth and glowing, her lips moist. With her hair draped gracefully behind an ear, her satin dress draped as gracefully around her body, and stunning pieces of tourmaline-spangled gold gracing her ears and her neck, she looked exquisite.

For the longest time he just stood there drinking her in. Finally, in a rusty voice he said, "Married life must be agreeing with you. You're more beautiful than ever."

"So are you."

"And successful."

"You too. The diamond campaign is impressive." She was staring up at him with that same half-frightened, half-desperate look. "I miss you," she whispered.

Something tightened around his heart. "Don't say that."

"It's true."

"But it hurts to hear. And it doesn't help to know."

"It helps me to air it. You were my best friend, Cutter, and I hurt you. If I were to do it again—"

He put two fingers to her lips and shook his head. "Don't say it," he whispered.

Her heart was in her eyes, reaching out with the same longing he'd seen there before, but she heeded his warning this time. Rather

than speak, she formed her lips into a kiss against his fingers, then backed away, turned, and hurried from the veranda.

Cutter left the party soon after, but out of sight wasn't out of mind. He thought about what Pam had said and the way she'd said it, and while he cursed her in one breath, in the next he acknowledged that she'd been more honest than he. He missed her, too, missed her with a soul-deep ache. He should have told her.

Not that it would have made any difference. She was still a married woman.

Somehow, though, when he saw her the following June at a movie premiere in L.A., he had trouble remembering that. Brendan wasn't there. She was with friends. Cutter was with a date, but that didn't stop him from staring at her.

"A friend?" his date asked.

"Uh-huh." He tore his eyes away, but they drifted back after a minute. Pam had seen him by then. She looked stricken. He actually felt guilty at being caught with another woman until he realized the absurdity of that. But the feeling lingered, and when he saw her leave her friends and head for the restroom, he followed. He was waiting, leaning against a nearby wall, out of the line of traffic, when she came out. She didn't pretend that his presence was coincidental. Albeit hesitantly, she came close.

Neither of them spoke. They just looked at each other. When he couldn't bear going without any longer, he raised a hand to her cheek, but it hovered, finally stealing to a more private spot at the back of her neck under her hair. She made a small sound. Seconds later, he felt her hand slip into the one that hung by his side.

Taking a shaky breath, he threw common sense to the winds and whispered, "Meet me later?"

She wanted to. He could see it in her eyes, could feel it in the tightening of her hand. But she resisted. "You were right. It's dangerous."

"Just to talk."

The look she gave him denied that that was possible. Despite everything that had happened, they were too drawn to each other, too

much in love. After staring at him for another minute with a longing that tore him to bits, she wrenched her hand away and left.

The movie was lost on him, as were the charms of his date. Long after he dropped her at her home, he paced his hotel room. He might have called Pam if he'd known where she was staying. It was lucky he didn't. What he had in mind wasn't right. She was married. But he wanted her with a fever that hadn't diminished in two and a half years, and she'd shown him that the fever was shared.

He saw her two months later, at an art show in New York, then three months after that at a gala benefit in Dallas. Both times he exerted the utmost control, but the control steadily eroded until finally, the following March, when he and Pam were attending the same jewelers' conference in New Orleans, the needs that had been gathering for three years broke loose.

Pam didn't tell a soul. She wasn't proud of what she'd done, but somehow the knowledge that she was betraying Brendan didn't hold any weight when she was with Cutter. The sight and the feel of him blotted out everything else. Inevitably, when she returned home she felt remorse; just as inevitably, to compensate, she doted on Brendan. She couldn't keep from dreaming of Cutter, though, and when she began to fear that she might call out the wrong name in her sleep, she knew she had to do something.

She went to see Patricia. She was taking a chance, but Patricia was growing stronger, Bob said. He kept urging her to draw her mother into her life, and to some extent she had. She visited regularly, showed Patricia her jewelry, and talked about the business and her friends. She brought Brendan to visit.

The hospital represented security for Patricia, and since she could afford it, she stayed. But she had moved into the smallest, most private cottage, and had begun to take short outings with Bob. Although she hadn't reached enough confidence to go out with Pam, she was conversing more.

That was what Pam needed. She didn't expect absolution, but

she had to talk, had to tell someone what she'd done, had to have someone say that she wasn't as wicked as she felt at times.

It was a hot and humid July day. The tall elm in the yard behind the cottage offered shade, and a faint breeze stirred from time to time. Pam wheeled Patricia there and went back for two tall glasses of iced tea before sinking down on the creaking wooden swing.

She sipped her tea while she searched for the right way to broach the subject. Inadvertently, Patricia did it for her.

"You're frowning," she said softly. "Are you upset?"

"Upset?" It wasn't that, exactly.

"Angry at me?"

"Oh, no! Not at all!" She took a breath. "It's me."

"Something with Brendan?"

"In a way." She jumped in. "I've been seeing Cutter."

Patricia accepted the statement as though it was perfectly logical. "You love Cutter."

"But I'm married to Brendan. I'm supposed to love Brendan. I *do* love Brendan."

A tiny frown crossed Patricia's brow. "Then everything's fine. Isn't it?"

"Cutter is . . . Cutter and I . . . we fought it but . . ." She took a breath. "I slept with him."

The tiny frown came again. "Before you married Brendan."

Pam wanted to cry. Her mother thought her innocent and good, which was both incredibly wonderful and terribly unfair. She was human, like everyone else. "I slept with Cutter last week. We keep running into each other. All over the country. All over the world. And each time, it's like there's a fire that just—" she motioned with her hands, "explodes. I thought maybe it was just something I had to do so that I could move on, but I still feel it, as strong as ever, and I can't do a thing to stop it. I need him." She ran out of air, dragged in a new breath, and said, "Tell me there are reasons why things like that happen. Tell me there's some justification for it."

Patricia bowed her head, and for an instant Pam wished she'd talked with Bob first. But she hadn't wanted to tell him about her af-

fair with Cutter. And anyway, he was the one who was always telling her to test Patricia's limits.

Eyes down, Patricia said, "My situation was different. I didn't love John. There was no justification for what I did."

"Maybe not in terms of love."

She shook her head. "No justification at all."

"But you needed him." It had taken Pam a long time and many discussions with Bob to accept that.

After a time, Patricia said a quiet, "Yes."

"Was it the kind of thing where you didn't think you'd be able to survive another day without him?"

"No. It was never that desperate." She hesitated, then said even more quietly, "Not the physical part. The other was. He said what I needed to hear. He made me feel better." She sipped her tea, careful to keep her eyes low. "It wasn't that he forced me . . . physically. The attraction was there."

Pam had always wondered about the nature of that attraction, since John didn't turn her on in the least. "Was it the age factor? His being younger than Daddy?"

"It was security. Excitement." She thought for a minute. "Maybe danger. But I always felt so guilty afterward."

Pam knew that feeling all too well. "Did you ever want to tell Daddy about it?"

Patricia's head came up. "I couldn't! It would have destroyed him!" Her voice fell. "It did destroy him."

"No, Mom. His temper was what destroyed him."

"But if I hadn't—"

"You didn't put that car in the middle of that intersection at that particular instant."

"Neither did he. He tried to stop. He stepped on the brake and swore, then there was the crash. He didn't do it on purpose."

"I know." Pam rocked the swing. Its creak was rhythmic, comforting. "And you didn't hurt him on purpose."

"No. I wouldn't have done that. I loved him."

"I know."

Patricia looked up. "Do you?"

"Uh-huh. For a while, I wasn't sure. I didn't understand how you could have been with John if you loved Daddy." She sniffed. "Self-righteous of me, wasn't it?" When Patricia didn't answer, she went on. "I thought that you either loved or you didn't, and if you did, that love was pure and right and all-powerful. That was how things always were with Cutter and me." With her thumb she wiped at the condensation on her glass. "Then Cutter wasn't ready to get married, so I married Brendan." She dared a glance at Patricia. "You never said anything about that."

Patricia gave a slow, one-shouldered shrug.

"I wanted to be married. I wanted to be free of John." When Patricia still didn't speak, Pam nudged the ground with her toe. "I liked Brendan from the first. Once we were married, it was easy to love him. He's a sweet, generous man."

"Yes," Patricia said.

"And I feel bad, because he trusts me. He has no idea that I've seen Cutter." She let the swing carry her to and fro. "What should I do?"

Patricia poked at the ice cubes with her straw. "I'm not the best one to ask."

"I can't ask anyone else."

The ice cubes clinked, then clinked again. "What do you want to do?"

"I want to do the right thing, which means being faithful to Brendan. But then there's all I feel for Cutter. I need him. I can't explain it. Brendan gives me so much, but Cutter is Cutter. When I'm with him, I'm something more than just me. It's like the two of us create something together, something powerful. Brendan is calm and quiet. He's gentle and undemanding. He'd give me the shirt off his back if I asked for it." She smiled helplessly. "With Cutter, I want the back, not the shirt." Her smile faded with the conjuring up of his scars. She figured she knew them better than Cutter did.

"Passion isn't enough. Don't ruin what you have with Brendan."

"But I love Cutter, too."

Patricia shook her head. "It won't work."

"Even if I'm careful?"

"It's not right."

"But I'm a good wife to Brendan. I make him a nice home. I'm there for him whenever he wants. He's the one who gets my time and attention."

"He should. He's your husband."

"But Cutter's alone."

"Cutter had his chance."

"Not a fair one. I was angry. My rushing to marry Brendan was like Daddy jumping in that car and racing down the street on the ice. I didn't think things through. I was being impulsive. I made a mistake."

"We have to live with our mistakes sometimes."

"But all the time? Take you." Pam sat forward on the swing. "You don't have to stay here. You could come live with me. Or get a place of your own."

"No."

"Daddy would have wanted that."

"No!"

Pam wanted to argue more, wanted to extend the argument to her own situation, but instinct told her she'd said enough. So she lapsed into silence, sat back again, and rocked on the swing, alternately sipping her tea and rubbing the glass. The sound of Patricia's voice took her by surprise.

"What you feel for Cutter," she began tentatively, "does it make you warm and light-headed?"

"Very."

Her eyes grew distant. "Does it stay with you . . . like a layer under your skin?"

"Always."

Her fingers curled around the arm of her wheelchair. "When you're with him . . . like that . . . does it make you forget other things that may be all wrong?"

"Oh, yes."

Patricia sighed.

Pam waited for her to speak. Finally, hesitantly, she asked, "Is that what you felt with John?"

Looking straight at her, Patricia shook her head. "No. It's what I felt with your father."

For a minute Pam could only stare. Then she came off the swing and gave Patricia a hug. It wasn't that she had condoned what she was doing or even given her direction. But by equating her feelings for Eugene with Pam's for Cutter, she had taken some of the sting from the act of betrayal. Pam's love for Cutter did the rest.

She didn't see him often, and then only when she was away from Boston and Brendan. Usually they just talked, smiled, held hands. They fought making love, fought it with everything they had, but there were times when the need was simply too great. Such was the case in Paris the following November when, with a single goal in mind, Pam half-walked, half-ran down the Rue Jean-Coujon.

Hoping not to be noticed, she had the collar of her fur raised to overlap the sable turban that covered her hair. She would have worn something more bland if she'd had time to change, but time was of the essence. From the moment she'd spotted Cutter in the opening-night crowd of the Jeu de Paume, she'd thought of nothing but getting closer, and from the moment he'd approached, taken her hand in his and kissed first one cheek, then the other with Gallic grace, his whispered words had rung in her ears.

The San Regis, room twenty-one, twelve-thirty. Be there.

There was never any question but that she would. It had been too long since she'd seen him, too long since she'd lain in his arms and known what it was to be well and truly loved.

At that thought, she quickened her step. When she reached the small hotel, she trotted up the stone steps and slipped through the door. Breezing across the plant-filled lobby with little more than a breathy bonsoir to the clerk behind the desk, she ran lightly up the stairs, down the hall, and around a turn to the door with a 21 marked in small swirls of brass.

She knocked softly. Within seconds the door opened a crack,

then widened, and Cutter drew her inside. In the very next instant, he pressed her back to the door, cupped her chin with a single large hand, and covered her mouth with his.

There was nothing gentle about his kiss. It had the feel of hunger and the taste of need. It was Cutter at his most fierce, his most hungry, and it excited her almost beyond bearing. Closing her fingers around fistfuls of his hair, she returned his kiss until the sheer need for air tore them apart.

Dislodging her turban, he put his forehead to hers. "You're late," he accused in a voice that was deep and ragged. His lower body pinned her to the door while he worked at the buttons of her coat.

"I had trouble getting a taxi," she gasped, trying to catch her breath and open his shirt at the same time. "Then the damned thing got stuck in a jam. Then it kept stalling. Then the driver dropped me at the wrong end of the street."

Cutter had already dispensed with his tuxedo jacket, and his bow tie dangled crookedly from his starched collar. With the impatient release of three diamond studs, Pam spread the shirt wide and put her mouth to his chest. Her lips moved lightly over the fine hair there. Closing her eyes, she inhaled the familiar scent of his skin.

The fur fell from her shoulders to the floor and had barely settled in a heap before Cutter lowered the zipper of her shimmering black sheath. He slipped a hand inside, curved his fingers over her bottom, and pulled her hips against his.

But the satisfaction of that was brief, when the real thing was so near. With a nudge, he sent the sheath whispering to the floor. Pam reached for his pants, but the feel of his hands molding her breasts through the silk of her teddy distracted her. She had to grasp his shoulders for support.

He took over. He unfastened his pants, undid his zipper, pushed the elegant material over his thighs and calves until the satin stripe was an undulating ribbon on the floor by her dress.

Pam touched him then. He was magnificently aroused and grew even more so in the few seconds that he allowed her caress. But patience deserted him. His hand went between her legs, found the

snaps of her teddy, and pulled, baring her for his touch and, with a light boost and a bold thrust, his penetration.

Almost of one voice, they moaned, then laughed at the shared agony of the sound. "God, I've missed you," he muttered into her hair.

She loved hearing the words, loved the ardor behind them, loved the pressure of him inside her. "I know."

"Do you?"

"I feel it, too. I keep thinking the missing will stop."

"It doesn't."

"I know."

He pushed deeper, slowly withdrew, returned deeper still.

"It keeps . . . getting . . . better." She looked up to find his head back, eyes closed, jaw tight against the pain of pleasure. In turn, her own pleasure grew. She tightened her arms around his neck and her legs around his hips, then braced herself when his hands flattened on the door on either side of her head. While he kissed the high-pitched sounds from her lips, he branded her his with long, brash strokes that shook the door on its hinges.

She climaxed first, but only because he'd meant it to be that way. Her body was still racked with sharp spasms when, with a prolonged groan, he rammed into her a final time and found his release.

The pulsing inside her went on and on. At length, he slipped trembling arms around her and slowly sank to his knees, then back on his heels. "Ahhh, babe." His voice was hoarse, his jaw damp against her temple.

She whispered his name, but that was all. She didn't have the strength for more. So she let him hug her, let his closeness be the tonic returning life to her limbs.

He held her tightly, almost compulsively at first, and she didn't mind it a bit. Gradually his hold eased. He nuzzled her cheek, nipped at her earring, fingered its matching choker. The set was of tourmalines and pearls set in broad sterling sweeps. He traced the stones with his fingers, then dipped his head and let the tip of his tongue tell her how beautiful he thought she was.

In that instant, basking in the heady afterglow of love, she believed in the rightness of what they shared. Cutter was special. He was forbidden to her, yet he made her feel safe. He also made her feel whole, and feminine, and sexy. Even then, when she should have been sated, her body was beginning to hum again.

"You're a demon," she teased, shifting on his lap to better feel his growth.

He gave a very smug, very masculine grin. "Old habits die hard. I've been like this for days."

"Hard?"

"Like a rock."

"With no relief?" She knew it was unfair, still she wondered about his women. He was a sex symbol in his own right, and she, more than anyone, knew of his hunger.

"No relief from wanting you," he said without quite answering her question, and Pam didn't pursue it. He was lowering the slim straps of her teddy, baring her breasts. While he rubbed one puckered nipple with his thumb, he took the other into his mouth and drew on it deeply. Swallowing a cry, she arched her back, pushed her fingers into his hair, and clung.

Moments later, her back hit the floor, and this time when they made love, their eyes held. Visually they challenged each other, silent but for a bitten-off cry, a muffled moan, a ground-out grunt. The pace grew wild, their bodies damp and savage, but neither closed his eyes or looked away. And when it was over, when they'd pushed aside the last of their clothing and shifted to the bed, they settled on their sides, face to face, wide awake.

For a time they just lay there, touching gently, breathing softly. They talked, sharing news and thoughts as best friends do but inevitably one word or another conjured intrusive pictures. So they made love again, because that was what most aptly expressed their feelings.

This time it was more gentle, a poignant reunion of the flesh. It was a light hand to a knee, the nudge of a nose near a navel, the brush of knuckles on soft skin joining thigh and hip. It was the scent

of musk, of man and sex and exotic flowers, and the sound of sighs. Inevitably, it was Cutter's tongue circling the delicately fluted gold band on Pam's left hand and her lips sipping her own tears from the pale, puckered scars on his back. Reality always intruded that way, despite their intentions to keep it at bay.

Then the heat rose again, blotting out all else but the moment, and in the fire they blessedly forgot why they had to part. So they kept it stoked, kept forgetfulness high. They loved and loved again, and by the time exhaustion overtook them, it was nearly dawn.

Pam awoke to the pale midmorning sun in a mussed but lonely bed. Clutching the guilt to her breasts, she sat up. "Cutter?" She pushed the hair out of her eyes and tried again, louder this time. "Cutter?" In the silence that followed, she caught sight of the small piece of paper that lay on the pillow by hers. His handwriting was the same barely legible scribble that had helped get him kicked out of school so long ago, but the only difficulty she had in deciphering it was caused by the tears in her eyes.

"Tu tiens mon coeur. C."

For a long time she held the note, moving only to wipe at her nose or her cheeks with the back of her hand. Only when she glanced at the clock and realized that her own time was short did she carefully fold the paper in half, then half again, slip from bed, and tuck it into her purse. It would go, she knew, into her dresser drawer with the others, hidden beneath a cloud of lacy bras, satin camisoles, and silk tap pants. Condemning evidence? Oh, yes, but if those scribbles were the only physical reminders she had of him during the long stretches between trysts, she was willing to take the chance.

She brought another physical reminder of Cutter home with her from Paris that November. By January she knew she was pregnant, and she was ecstatic. She had begun to worry that the abortion had scarred her insides so that she couldn't get pregnant, since four years of marriage to Brendan had produced no children. Now that fear was put to rest. She was being given a second chance. Not only could she make up for the baby she had lost, but she was giving

Brendan a gift, too. He knew how much she wanted to be a mother and was as excited as she about the baby.

In August of 1984, Ariana was born. She was a healthy child, with her mother's delicate nose and mouth and dark eyes that were as familiar to Pam as her own. She was, Pam knew, her father's daughter.

Chapter 25

◈◈◈

Boston, 1988

CUTTER SAT ON A BENCH IN THE Public Garden, his heart swelling as he watched Pam and Ariana approach. They were both beauties—Pam with her dark hair, her elegant features, and her gauzy bohemian look, Ariana with her bow of a mouth, her dark round eyes, and the shiny hair that shimmered on the ruffled shoulders of her tiny peasant dress. Her small hand was in Pam's, and for every step Pam took, she took a skip and a half.

She was the most beautiful child in the whole of Boston, the whole of Massachusetts, the whole of America. Cutter was sure of it, and it wasn't simply that she was his child. He'd spent hours looking at others since Ariana was born, and none could compare.

With a grin for Pam, he leaned forward, propped his elbows on his knees, and, as soon as she was before him, said to Ariana, "Hi, angel."

She gave him a shy smile. "Hi, Cutter."

He didn't think he'd ever get used to hearing her sweet voice say his name. He had Pam to thank for it. Although Ariana's birth had been a death knell for sex between Pam and him, Pam had wanted Ariana to know him, and vice versa. Rather than arrange visits on the sly, she had come right out and introduced him to Brendan as an old friend from Timiny Cove. Brendan knew of Cutter's occupation and

particularly of his involvement with diamonds, and he accepted that Pam and Cutter had a lot in common. So Cutter had been included in things like Christmas parties, Fourth of July cookouts, and even an occasional dinner party. Ariana took to him easily.

Now, sharing his pleasure with Pam in a glance, he looked back at the little girl. "I hear it's a special day," he said softly.

Ariana nodded and grinned.

"How old?"

It was a minute of arranging before she had four fingers standing straight and separate.

"Four? Whoa. Four is really old."

Her eyes grew wide with suppressed excitement and she nodded again.

"Are you having a party?"

She nodded. "Saturday. Wanna come?"

He tapped her tiny nose. "I think the party's for your friends. You don't want me along."

"I do," Ariana insisted, all serious. She looked at Pam. "He can come, can't he, Mommy?"

But before she could answer, Cutter said, "I have to be back in New York. That was why I wanted to see you today." He lowered his voice in a teasing way. "I have something for you."

Ariana was all excited eyes again. "You do?"

"Yup."

"Where is it?"

"Behind me."

Clutching his arm, she climbed up on the bench and peered behind him. A small box was sandwiched there. She tried to pull it out, but couldn't. So she tugged at his arm to move him. He wouldn't budge.

"First a hug," he said.

She reached up for his neck. He helped her, scooping her into his arms and hugging her with a fierce gentleness as he rocked her from side to side. It was a treasured moment. Eyes closed, he savored her warmth, the child smell of her, her delicate feel. He would have held

her longer if she had allowed it. But she drew back, wanting her gift. While he continued to hold her with one arm, he reached back with the other and drew out the box. Settling easily onto his lap, she began to pull at its wrapping.

Cutter caught Pam's eye. "She's precious," he said softly.

Pam nodded. "We're very lucky."

"She has your nose and mouth."

"But the eyes and the hair—" She pointed at him.

He liked that thought. There was something about children as a perpetuation of their parents that he found reassuring. He would have hated to die without leaving something of himself behind in the world. Not that he was planning to die in the immediate future, but he knew that he wouldn't have children with anyone but Pam. Ariana had been unplanned. He didn't regret her birth for a minute, only the circumstances surrounding it.

"Is she a tomboy, like her mommy was?"

Pam blushed. "Nah. She's a lady."

"Like her mommy is. How was day camp?"

Pam waggled a hand. "The part she liked best was coming home."

"Did you mind?"

"Are you kidding? I loved it."

Ariana drew in a loud breath as she lifted a small, intricately carved gold box. "Look, Mommy. It's so pretty."

Cutter smiled. "Open it." He helped. No sooner was the lid up than the music began. Ariana drew in another loud breath when a tiny ballerina started turning on her toe. She stared and stared, her eyes filled with wonder. When she darted him a look, he felt that wonder warm him from head to toe.

"Look, Mommy!" Very carefully, she turned the music box Pam's way.

Pam sat down on the bench to take a closer look. "Oh my. It is beautiful." She listened with a curious smile. "'The Dance of the Sugar Plum Fairy?'"

"I found it in Salzburg when I was there last month."

"It's wonderful." To Ariana she said, "What a lucky girl you are to get such a beautiful gift." She leaned closer to whisper, "Do I hear a thank-you?"

Ariana turned another shy smile on Cutter. "Thank you, Cutter." As an afterthought, but without any coaching from Pam, she craned her neck and planted a kiss on his jaw. Then, holding the music box gingerly in one hand, she maneuvered herself down from his lap with the other. Skipping across the dirt path in front of the bench, she perched on the base of a statue to listen to the music and watch the ballerina turn.

"She loves it," Pam said.

"I'm glad. I wanted something special."

"You found it. Thank you."

"Thank *you.*"

"For what?"

"Bringing her here." He shifted his gaze from Ariana to Pam. "Is it awkward?"

"Not really. I had promised her a ride on the swan boats for her birthday. I told Brendan that you were in town and that we'd probably stop by to say hello. He had no problem with that."

Cutter thought of Brendan, thought of the times he'd welcomed Cutter to his home, thought of the business discussions they'd had, the give and take. He also remembered other, earlier times when he'd begged Pam to leave Brendan. In the last year or two, he'd come to understand why she wouldn't—which made him more frustrated than ever. "He's a nice man. A good man. I wish I could hate him, but I can't."

"He likes you, too."

"He's a good father to her."

"Yes."

Cutter looked at Ariana again. She was holding the music box on her knees, mesmerized by it. In turn, he was mesmerized by her—by little fingers, little shoes, a little nose, a little chin. As he watched, the sun glanced off her hair, giving its light caramel color an even warmer sheen. Pam was right. She had his hair.

"Do you think he suspects anything?" he asked.

Pam, too, was studying Ariana. "I'm not sure. There are times when I think he has to know—but maybe that's my guilty conscience speaking. If he suspects anything, he doesn't let on. He adores Ariana. And she adores him. She's forever climbing all over him."

Cutter felt a stab of jealousy. At about the same time, he caught a look of concern on Pam's face. He shot a fast glance back at Ariana, thinking something had happened to her, but she was sitting just where she'd been. "What is it?"

Pam seemed surprised by his question. "Uh, nothing."

"You looked worried."

After a minute's silence, she said, "Brendan's been more tired lately. He tries not to let me see, but it's there."

"Is he working harder than usual?"

"No. If anything, he's home more. He's president of the bank. He can do it."

"How old is he now?"

"Fifty-nine. He used to have checkups often. I remind him now, but he keeps putting it off." More lightly, she said, "It's probably nothing more than facing sixty."

Cutter stretched out his legs and grunted. "I can identify with that."

Her lips twitched. "Forty? Forty's nothing."

"Fine for you to say. You're not the one turning it soon."

"But look at you. You're doing so well."

He gave a negligent shrug.

"Do you miss modeling?"

"No way." He had officially retired two years before, when his last contract expired. "I got what I wanted from it. It was a vehicle, right from the start. That's all."

"You don't miss the adulation? The attention?"

He gave a firm shake of his head.

"And the business is going well?"

"Uh-huh." He was a partner in an investment banking firm that he had formed with three others shortly before he'd stopped modeling. "My

partners have the degrees, the experience, the technical know-how. I have the contacts."

"You have the charisma," Pam corrected. "You don't talk all the time, but when you do, you have something to say. You don't waste people's time. You give them a feeling of confidence."

He shrugged. "Something works." Then he dropped all show of nonchalance, because nonchalance was the last thing he felt when he thought about John. "We're getting there, Pam. The St. George package is growing." He paused. "John doesn't see it yet, does he?"

"No. He's too arrogant. You'd have to pound him over the head with a takeover before he knew it was happening."

"Good." Cutter sat back and crossed his arms over his chest. Yes, he felt satisfaction. He also—still—felt anger and resentment. "That's exactly how I want it. We're buying small blocks of stock here, small blocks there. Our clients use their own names or those of their businesses. When we finally group together to form a cohesive entity, John will be stunned. Totally outsmarted. Beaten at his own game."

Pam exhaled into a grim smile. "That sounds good."

"How are things on your end?"

She pursed her lips. "I just saw the latest figures. My designs comprise nearly forty percent of *Facets'* sales. Granted, I'm not doing the actual jewelry-making anymore, but I hold copyrights on all of my designs." She tapped her chest with a finger. "Me. Not John. Me. And I've checked and rechecked that with two different lawyers. If I were to suddenly pull out, John would be up shit's creek."

Cutter had to smile at the expression. It wasn't often that Pam swore. She had mellowed with age, as he had, but John was the one thing that could get her riled. "Do you see him much?"

"As little as possible," she said with feeling.

"How much is that?"

"Once a week or so. More when the board meets."

"Is he civil?"

"Oh, yeah. But I don't take chances. I make sure there are people around. He'd never misbehave in public. It wouldn't be good for his image."

"Does he see Ariana much?"

"As little as possible," she repeated with even more feeling than before.

"By his choice or yours?"

"Both. He doesn't like kids. Has no idea what to do with them. That suits me just fine. The less she sees of him, the better. He isn't the kind of role model I want for her." She stopped and considered what she'd said. When she spoke again, he heard an element of doubt. "That goes two ways, I suppose. When I'm with John, I'm not the kind of role model I want for my daughter, either. I feel ugly things. I don't want her seeing that."

Cutter marveled at her sensitivity. "You're a good mother."

"To want to spare her pain?"

"To want her to be a good person."

"Every mother wants that."

"Not every mother takes the care to see that it happens." He hitched his chin toward Ariana. "She's even-tempered, like you."

"No, like you. I'm impulsive."

"Cutter!" Ariana cried.

"Whooops, spoke too soon."

Ariana was rushing toward him, looking crushed. "It broke. Won't go anymore."

Her disappointment made him ache. Reaching for her, he brought her between his legs and arms enveloping her, took hold of the music box. "It wound down," he explained by her ear. "That's all. You have to wind it up to get it going again." Closing the lid, he turned the box over and showed her how to twist the key. Her small fingers were right there trying to help. "It's kind of hard. Maybe you should have your mommy do it."

"I can," she said. Pulling his fingers away, she struggled with the key. In slow, ninety-degree increments, she turned it. After three turns, she stopped.

"More," Cutter prompted.

She worked the key again, then again. What would have been a simple task for Cutter was painstaking—at least, as he had to sit there

and watch Ariana do it. The nice thing was that during her struggles she was close to him again. He suspected that if he ever had her to himself, really to himself, he would carry her everywhere. She was his child. He had helped create her. That she was a human being and growing more human by the day never ceased to amaze him. He only wished he saw her more.

Some of what he was feeling must have shown in his eyes, because when he looked up at Pam, she seemed wistful. As soon as Ariana had scampered off again, she said, "You're so good with her."

"Two of my partners have kids. I get practice."

Pam shook her head. "What you do is natural." She touched her heart. "It comes from here."

"It should. I love her." He sat back on the bench again, but he wasn't as relaxed as he'd been. "There are times when I want to scream. Everything's going my way in business. I've got good money, a respectable occupation, decent partners, and I'm comin' real close to getting back at John for all he did." He let out a breath. "So when that's done, where am I? I don't have you, and I don't have Ariana."

Pam didn't say anything, but he didn't expect her to. He had his chance. He could have married her when she'd asked and bluffed things out with John. But he'd been full of pride then. He wanted to do things his own way. Now, watching Ariana play, he felt the hollowness of that pride. He also felt the same small but niggling fear he did from time to time, the fear that too much time had passed, that too many things had happened for him and Pam ever to be together the way he dreamed.

"There are times," he said quietly, "when I feel like my life has been an endless stream of wanting." His eyes caught Pam's. "Most of the wanting has to do with you." He stretched an arm along the back of the bench so that his fingers could touch her neck. "Since you came along, nothing's been the same. I love you, Pam."

For an instant, she closed her eyes and tipped her head back just the tiniest bit, as though to trap his fingers on her skin. But her eyes opened again soon after to direct a mother's watchful gaze Ariana's way. "It is ironic."

"What?"

"What you were saying before about your success in business. The same is true here. Professionally, things are terrific. I have my team of craftsmen. I design on my own time and get the credit for it without having to put in hours at the shop. I don't have to look at John's face. The people I'm with look to me for direction, not him. It's ideal. I have time for Brendan, time for Ariana, time for my mother," she took a quick breath, "time for you."

"I wish we had it now," he said very quietly.

She made a helpless sound.

"I miss holding you."

"Don't, Cutter."

"And kissing you. Touching you."

She took a shaky breath and whispered, "Stop."

But he only lowered his voice. "If we were alone I wouldn't. I'd keep going until neither of us could move."

"And you're worried about turning forty?" she cried.

"I'll be hard for you till the day I die."

"Shhh."

"She can't hear," he whispered.

"But I can," Pam whispered back, "and it's wrong. You shouldn't be saying those things. You shouldn't be *thinking* those things."

A mocking sound came from deep in his throat, just as two teen-age girls went by with a flash of metal-mouthed smiles. "She's adorable," said one.

"How old is she?" the other asked Cutter.

"Four," he answered, then, because he was a proud father, added, "today."

"It's her birthday?" asked the first, her smile broadening.

"Wow!" said the second and turned to Ariana. "Happy birthday, little sweetie."

Blissfully entranced by her music box, Ariana didn't look up until the girls had swept by. They waved at her, laughed at each other, and were soon turning onto the footbridge and blending into the crowd.

Ariana skipped over to the bench. Setting the music box on it,

she closed the lid, opened it, closed it for a little longer, opened it again. Reassured that the music would keep coming, she gave Cutter a dimpled smile.

His heart turned over.

"Want to come on the swan boats with us?" Pam asked.

It was a minute before he regained his composure enough to say, "Only if I get to hold the birthday girl. Sound fair?" he asked Ariana.

She nodded. "Can I hold my gift?"

"You hold your gift, I'll hold you."

"Who'll hold Mommy?"

Sweeping her up in his arms, he stood. "How about we just keep her real close?" He shifted Ariana to one side and, by the time Pam joined them, had an arm free to throw over her shoulder.

He didn't care who saw them, didn't care if tongues wagged, didn't care even if word got back to Brendan. If people assumed he and Pam were husband and wife out walking with the beautiful child they'd made, it was only a twist of the truth.

He wanted it to be the whole truth, but that was still a distant dream. He'd been waiting all his life for Pam. Now he was waiting for Ariana, too, only having to wait meant that he was missing some of the special times that once gone were gone for good. The worst of it was that he didn't know where it would end. As long as Pam was married to Brendan, he'd be the outsider. No matter how much pleasure he found in stolen moments, they were still stolen.

Pam's concern deepened in the weeks that followed. Brendan looked pale, he wasn't eating well, and he grew short-tempered each time she mentioned his seeing a doctor. The matter was taken out of both their hands one Thursday morning when he collapsed at the bank. Pam was at *Facets*, examining several pieces of tourmaline that had just arrived from Maine, when she got the call. With a sense of dread, she rushed to the hospital.

Brendan was awake and aware enough to reassure Pam that he was fine, but she didn't believe him for a minute. She was relieved

when his doctor ordered a full battery of tests. After the first batch, there were more. Some were done over.

The word wasn't good. Brendan had tumors in his brain and both lungs. Pam was in shock.

"That can't be. He hasn't been sick. Just tired."

At the doctor's request she was meeting with him privately in his office.

"It's an insidious disease, Mrs. McGrath."

She'd heard stories to that effect, but never thought they would concern people she knew and loved, not her own husband. "But no headaches? No cough? Maybe the tests are wrong."

"We've run CAT scans and bone scans. We've done MRIs—magnetic resonance imaging. The results are consistent." He looked troubled, almost annoyed. "I wish your husband had come in sooner. I alerted him to the fact that this could happen. For a while there he saw me every six months, but he hasn't been in for a full physical now in nearly two years. Given his history, that was unwise."

"His history?"

"The melanoma."

Her insides knocked. "What melanoma?"

"The one I removed a while back." The doctor looked at her strangely. "You knew about that, didn't you?"

Her voice was weak. "No."

"Surely he told you."

"No! When was this?"

Pushing his glasses higher on his nose, the doctor shifted a few papers in Brendan's file until he found the right one. "Brendan first came to me in the spring of '76 with a growth on his shoulder. I removed it. It was malignant."

"Malignant," Pam echoed in a whisper. She couldn't believe it.

"At the time, there was mixed sentiment about treatment of that kind of melanoma. Many of my colleagues felt that surgery alone was sufficient. I took the conservative route and followed the surgery up with chemotherapy."

"Chemotherapy," she echoed again. She couldn't believe it.

He put his glasses on the desk and eyed her awkwardly. "Quite frankly, Mrs. McGrath, I was surprised when Brendan told me you'd had a baby. Before I recommended the chemo, I asked whether he thought he'd ever want more children. As a matter of course, chemotherapy usually renders the patient sterile."

He went on to talk about the fact that Brendan was one for the books, that being disease free for twelve years was remarkable, that if only Brendan had had regular checkups things would look brighter.

Stunned, Pam only half-heard him. As soon as she could, she escaped and went to see Brendan. He was sleeping when she stole quietly into the room. She pulled a chair close to the bed and watched him until he woke.

He gave her a tired smile that came and went with lightning speed. Soberly he asked whether she'd talked with the doctor.

She nodded.

For a bit he didn't say anything, just looked at her. When he reached for her hand, she held it tightly.

"I should have told you, Pam." His eyes and voice were tired. "I know that. I should have told you before we married. You were young. You had a right to decide whether you wanted to be saddled with someone who would probably get sick. But I was afraid you'd say no. So I was selfish and kept still. You held such promise for me. I reasoned that if I had to die before my time, I had a right to some good times with you. And they have been good. Pam. You've been wonderful—"

"You talk like it's over!" She couldn't accept that. He was too good a man to die young—and, yes, she'd always thought of him as young. He was a young fifty-nine-year-old, or had been until the cancer had stolen his pep.

"It doesn't look good."

"That's because they haven't started treatment yet. You responded to it last time. You'll respond again."

He blinked in mild rebuke. "Last time it was a preventive measure. This time it's for real. There's a lot to fight."

"Then we'll fight."

He gave her hand a weak squeeze. "You have spirit. That's one of the things I love in you."

He was looking at her, knowing all she didn't. "It's hard, Pam. It's unpleasant, the treatment."

"You did it before, you'll do it again."

"I'm twelve years older now."

"And you have that much more reason to live. Before, you had the boys. They may be grown now, but they still need you. Ariana and I sure do."

She had been talking on pure instinct, saying things straight from the heart. At the mention of Ariana, though, her expression must have betrayed some of the guilt she felt, because Brendan gave her a sad smile.

"It's Cutter, isn't it?"

She didn't answer. She didn't know how much to say, whether to say anything at all, or whether Brendan would fight his illness more if he knew the truth.

He brought her hand to his mouth, kissed it lightly, anchored it on his chest. "It's time," he admonished softly.

"Don't Bren. Don't say it like that. You're not dying on me today or tomorrow or next week. The doctor said that even without treatment, you could have years."

"The doctor doesn't know. None of them do. There's no set pattern to the illness. Every case is different. It may be that I have years. The question is what the quality of those years will be. I could go downhill pretty fast."

He seemed calm. She felt near panic. "How can you accept that?"

"I've had years to accept it."

"You should have shared the worry."

"I couldn't."

"You should have gone to the doctor sooner."

"I was tired of tests. I was tired of thinking of tests. At some point—soon after Ariana's birth—I made a conscious decision that I wanted to enjoy you and her without the specter of illness. I had already accepted that it would probably get me one day."

"But when you began to feel tired—"

"I didn't want to know. I figured I either had it or I didn't. I knew that if there was a recurrence, the odds weren't good. So I decided to ignore it and go on with my life. And I'm not sorry. I'd make the same decision again. You've brought me so much happiness." There was a split second's hesitation. "Both of you."

Pam saw it again in his eyes, the knowledge that Ariana wasn't his. This time, she couldn't ignore it. "Do you hate me?" she whispered.

"Hate you? I love you."

"But I . . . she . . ."

"From the start I guessed there was someone else. You didn't love me back then."

"I love you now."

"I know that. You've been a very good wife to me."

Pam wanted to cry. "But I betrayed you."

"You've given me eight wonderful years and a beautiful daughter. I never had a daughter."

"But she isn't—"

"Mine? Biologically true, but that's all. I love her like my own. She loves *me* like my own. Is that any different from what people feel who adopt babies?"

Pam started to cry. She wished he'd get angry, yell, call her names. She deserved all of that for having deceived him so. "How can you be so forgiving?"

"How can you?" he returned, for the first time growing upset. "I couldn't have children. I knew that before I married you. You were young. You wanted children. You never used birth control. You kept thinking you might conceive, and all the time I knew there wasn't a chance of it happening. Still I didn't tell you the truth. Even after I felt you loved me, I didn't tell you." He glowered at the sheets. "Sure, I can say that I was afraid you'd leave me, but that wasn't my main worry. My main worry was that you'd think me less of a man if you knew." He couldn't quite look at her. "Vanity. Pride. Male egotism. Whatever, I didn't tell you the truth."

He did look at her then. "I was thrilled when you got pregnant.

Really thrilled. Oh, I knew that I hadn't fathered the baby, but no one else knew it. Chemotherapy may cause sterility, but there are rare exceptions."

For a split second, Pam's eyes widened.

But he rushed on. "I wasn't one. I had myself tested when I thought of asking you to marry me. It was conclusive."

He took a breath that seemed to echo in his lungs, reminding Pam how ill he was. "You shouldn't be talking so much. You should rest."

But once started, he wouldn't. "See? You're concerned about me. And that's what I'm trying to say. How can I be angry at you when you care so much? When you give so much?"

"I was wrong."

"So was I, so we've canceled each other out. And there is something to that, Pam. When we learned you were pregnant, I was actually relieved. Right from the first, you were excited, and it was clear that you had no intention of leaving me to be with the baby's father. So I was excited that you were excited, and I was excited for myself, because I love you and I love children. I figured that if you were giving me this chance to be a father again, I wasn't going to throw it back in your face. How could I do that, when I'd been dishonest about something so important? I didn't tell you that I might not live to see you hit middle age. I knew I'd be leaving you well-to-do if I died, and that was something."

Seeming to run out of strength, he grew quiet. After a minute, he lifted her hand and lightly rapped it against his chest. After several more minutes, he murmured, "Are we even?"

Pam couldn't begin to answer that. She couldn't begin to tally the sides. She was overwhelmed by all she'd learned that day.

"We'll fight this, Brendan. We'll do what the doctor suggests. He's bringing in a whole team. They'll decide on a protocol, and we'll follow it."

He remained silent, eyes closed. Then his voice came reed-thin. "Once I'm gone, you can be with him."

"Don't say that! Don't even think it! I want to be with you!" And

at that moment she did. The thought of wishing Brendan dead so that she could be with Cutter was abhorrent to her.

Brendan rested for a while before opening his eyes again. "Is it Cutter?"

She carried his hand to her lips, kissed it, gave a short nod.

Seeming content with that, he closed his eyes again. After a time, he sighed. "Ahhhh, Pam. There's a hard road ahead. I hate to drag you down it."

"I wouldn't be anywhere else, Bren."

She was as good as her word. Just as years before she had vowed to be a good wife to Brendan, so now she decided to make his remaining time—however long—as happy as possible. That meant special times spent with him alone doing his favorite things, and with Ariana, just the three of them as a family. It meant planning weekends away with his sons and their families, and arranging dinners with the best of Brendan's friends. She worked around his treatment schedule and around the few hours each day that he tried to spend at the bank. Her own work was limited to the times when he rested, which came more often and lasted longer as the treatment zapped his strength.

Devoting herself to Brendan was satisfying in its way. She did love him. She worried about him. She was happiest when she could do small things to please him, to make him smile.

She also found satisfaction in Ariana and in her work. Although she dramatically decreased her hours, her name continued to grow. When *Facets* London opened, she was there for the festivities. Her reception was better than she had dared hope, her following even larger than she'd been led to believe by the British clients she already serviced.

That made John nervous, which pleased Pam no end. He wasn't used to being upstaged, and although the British upper crust was far too well mannered to make it obvious, he was sensitive enough to the subtleties of power to catch on. As the party progressed, he moved close to Pam's side, but if he thought he might fool her into thinking that he was the one attracting the crowd, he was wrong. She was

in her element, feeling self-confident and sharp. She knew who was drawing the attention, and for the space of those few hours she basked in it.

Buoyed, she returned to Boston, where she concentrated on keeping her wits and some small measure of good humor while Brendan's condition wavered.

Chapter 26

New York, July 1990

Want to stop by here when you get a minute?" Arlan asked without preamble. His terseness made Hillary wary.

"Is there a problem?"

"Just need to talk."

She was trying to imagine what was wrong when a suspicious sound made her frown. "Arlan? Are you smoking?"

He didn't answer.

"Arlan?"

"Just one."

"One, my foot. Oh, Arlan, you were doing so well."

"It's been a rough day."

"But this is your *life*."

"Look. I don't tell you how to live. Don't tell me how to live. When can you stop by?"

He sounded truly annoyed, which was a first for him with her. "Uh, if it's urgent, in an hour."

"Good. I'll see you then."

An hour later she walked into his office. He had a cigarette in his hand and was regarding her in defiance, daring her to comment on it. She didn't. Instead, she slid into a chair, propped an elbow on its arm,

and put her fingers under her nose. In response, he took a long drag of the cigarette and exhaled an even longer stream of smoke.

"See?" she said, unable to resist. "By not smoking, you've improved your lungs' capacity so that you can now smoke even more deeply than before."

"I'm quitting."

"You did that before."

"No. Not smoking. I'm quitting this job."

She blinked. "What?"

"Quitting this job. Your contract has been nixed."

There was no blink this time. Everything inside her went still. "What?"

"You heard."

"But I signed it."

"It hasn't been countersigned. Now I'm told it won't be."

"What do you mean, it won't be?" She didn't understand. A contract was a contract. "We had an agreement. The house can't pull out now."

"The house," he said with distaste, "can pull out at any point before signing."

"No. A verbal agreement implies intent." But that wasn't even the primary issue. "My book is good. You love it. Your editor-in-chief loved it. Your publisher loved it."

"My chairman of the board thought it was too risky."

"Too risky? What are you talking about?"

Arlan kept her waiting while he took another drag on his cigarette, but this time he didn't do it out of defiance so much as raw need. With the last of the smoke curling from his lips, he said, "John St. George got to Templar."

"What?"

"John threatened a libel suit if the house goes ahead with the contract."

Hillary came out of her chair. "But he has no grounds for libel. There's nothing I planned to say in my book that isn't true. I can prove it all. He doesn't have a case."

"Templar thinks he might, and that's all that counts."

For a minute, she could only stare at him. She didn't know which one to be most furious with, John or Simon Templar. But neither of them was there just then, so Arlan took the brunt of her rage. Planting her fists on his desk, she cried, "Dammit, Arlan, you can't let them do this to me!"

"I spent the whole morning arguing, but it didn't do much good."

"Then you weren't arguing the right things. Talk to Templar again. Tell him that he can't pull out now. Tell him I'll take him to court myself. Make him change his mind."

"He won't. He's already put through orders to have the paperwork destroyed."

"He can't do that!"

"He's doing it."

"You can't let him!"

"For God's sake," Arlan snapped, "I've done all I can. What do you want from me?"

Hillary forced herself to calm down. It wasn't Arlan's fault. She believed him when he said he'd tried. And she did know that he loved her book. With a deliberate effort, she sat down.

"Look," he said in a more measured way, "we'll both leave. We'll take your story to another house. It'll be snapped up in a minute."

"That's not the point." He voice trembled under the force of restraint. "It's a matter of principle."

"So you'll take the house to court? What will you accomplish? If you win, if the house is forced to publish your book, it won't be published well. They'll let it die on the shelves. Correct that—they'll let it die in the warehouse. Is that what you want?"

It certainly wasn't. She wanted sales and PR behind her. She wanted every bookstore in the country pushing her book. She wanted it on every bestseller list. None of that would happen if the house wasn't with her.

Feeling frustrated beyond belief, she cried, "Dammit, it's not fair! Templar can't screw around with his writers that way! And John can't screw around with me!"

"Tell him that."

"I just might." She pictured it, and the picture looked good. "I will." Reaching for Arlan's phone, she punched out John's number.

"Hey, that's long distance."

"Tough." She listened to several rings, then listened to Christian telling her that she'd reached the St. George residence. "Hi, Christian," she said with utter nonchalance. "It's Hillary Cox. I have a quick question for John. Is he around?"

"I'm sorry, Miss Cox, but he's still at the office."

"What time do you expect him home?"

"He said he'd be back by four. He's going out again at six. Would you like me to leave a message that you called?"

"Uh, you could. Then again, I'll probably be out when he gets home. Why don't I just try him another time?"

"That sounds fine, Miss Cox."

"Thanks, Christian."

Wearing a tight smile, she hung up the phone, rose from her chair, and made for the door. "I'm on my way."

"Now?"

She checked her watch. It was nearly two. "If I can make the two-thirty shuttle, I'll be on John's front step when he gets home."

"Wait, Hillie." He stood. "Maybe you ought to think about this. Bearding the lion in his den may not be the wisest move. Maybe—"

"Save it, Arlan." She knew what she wanted to do. "I'm on my way."

The traffic to LaGuardia was heavy. She missed the two-thirty shuttle, but made the three o'clock. So instead of sitting on John's front steps, she walked right up and rang the bell.

Christian's brows rose at the sight of her. "Weren't you calling from New York?" he asked politely.

"Uh-huh." She slipped past him into the house. "Is he upstairs?"

"Perhaps you ought to have a seat in the parlor while I—"

"He is home, isn't he? When John says four, he means four. He's never late."

"If you would make yourself comfortable in the—"

"And give him a chance to sneak out the back? No way." She went to the foot of the stairs and gave a loud call. "John?" She was starting up when John's level voice came from behind her.

"Here, Hillary." To Christian he said, "I'll see her in the library." He turned and walked off.

At first sight of him, she was hit by the same visceral tingle as always. But the tingle fell prey to the hurt his rudeness caused, then to anger. Holding her head high, she went after him. In the short time that it took to walk through the living room to the library, her anger mushroomed. If his good looks registered in the back of her mind, she was unaware of it.

"I just came from my editor's office. He told me what you did."

"You didn't tell me you were writing a book. That wasn't very honest of you, Hillary."

"How dare you threaten Simon Templar."

"I didn't threaten anyone. I simply explained what I'd have to do if his company went ahead with plans to publish your book."

"You call it an explanation, I call it a threat. You're trying to manipulate me by manipulating Templar. Where do you get off doing that? Who do you think you are?"

"I'm a man who doesn't want the intimate details of his life printed for all the world to see," he said calmly, which infuriated her all the more.

"Why not? You're a big deal—public property now."

"No. If I were a politician, I'd be fair game. But I'm not."

"You're famous. Surely you can take a little jabbing. Don't you think people are wondering anyway? Don't you think there were people who saw that *20/20* piece and said to themselves, he must sweat just like the rest of us?"

"I'm respected. I won't have that respect tarnished."

He sounded so pompous that she wanted to scream. It was all she could do to keep her temper in check. "If you didn't want it tarnished, you shouldn't have been such a sleaze. Did you honestly think you could get away with it forever? Did you think that just because you

donate ten grand to this or ten grand to that you guarantee yourself a good name?"

His dark eyes flashed. "I have a good name. I won't have it ruined."

"So you'd ruin my career instead? You can't do that, John. It's a free world. The Constitution protects my right of free speech, and my book is an exercise of that right."

"Well said, but worthless," he sneered. "I don't give a damn what the Constitution says. Given the choice between your right to free speech and my right to self-protection, I'll opt for myself any day."

"The courts won't agree. And I will go to court, if I don't get my contract as it was agreed on two months ago. I'll sue the publishing house, and I'll sue you."

"You won't have a chance of winning. I'll smear you to kingdom come."

"Based on what? What can you smear me for? Have I ever had someone beaten? Have I ever illicitly changed someone else's will? You don't have a thing on me."

"I'll find something."

She shook her head. "The only really stupid thing I've done in my life is to come when you call. But that's over, John. *Over.*"

His mouth twitched. Softly, he said, "Is it?"

"Definitely."

"Now that would be a stupid thing." He started toward her with the slow walk she found so attractive. "We're good together, Hillary. We may have a few philosophical differences—"

"A few? We have so many it's a miracle we could ever stand being in the same room together! We're miles apart on just about everything that matters."

"We're not miles apart on this." He reached out to touch her but she swatted his hand away.

"No, John. I didn't come here for that."

"No?"

"No."

"Then it's a pity. You do it like no one else does. I could use some of your fire."

Immune to the seduction in his voice, she glared at him. "Talk all you want. It won't make any difference. You've pushed me too far this time."

"I haven't pushed you anywhere. Give me the chance, and I will." This time he caught her around the waist and hauled her against him before she could duck away.

She pushed at his chest. "Let me go, John."

"I like the feel of you against me."

She pushed harder. "Let . . . me . . . go."

"Or what?" he tossed off.

"I'll cry rape."

"You'll never prove it."

"I'll make enough noise to do the damage."

He grinned. "You're a minx." He shook his head and murmured, "Rape." He chuckled. "Kiss me, Hillary. I've missed you."

When his mouth sought hers, she turned her head away. He turned it back with a firm hand and covered her lips before she could utter a protest. She did make sounds in her throat, though, and struggled to free herself. Finally, she gave him a swift kick in the shin.

Abruptly he released her and bent to rub his leg. "What's the matter with you?"

With an arm at her mouth, she took a step back. "What's the matter?" She couldn't believe he was asking. "What's the *matter*? I don't want you to kiss me. That's what's the matter. Didn't you hear me telling you that? Are you deaf?"

"I heard you say it, but you didn't mean it. You want me."

"Right now, I want you drawn and quartered. You're beyond salvation."

"I never asked for salvation."

Her nod was slow and held equal parts acknowledgment and confession. "You're right. You never did. Only I guess I thought that maybe, somehow, sometime, I could make a difference in your life. I was wrong."

She whirled around and started for the door, only to be caught by the arm and whirled back. "Where are you going?"

"Out. Away. Back to New York. You're a waste of my time."

"What's that supposed to mean?" he demanded.

She glared up at him. "I walk in here absolutely furious because you're sabotaging my career, and all you can say is 'you want me.' You think sex is the answer to every little worry?"

"Between us it is."

"No more!" She threw up her hands. "I've had it."

"It always worked before," he had the gall to say.

She gave another exaggerated nod. "You're right. It did work before, and that was my fault. My weakness. One look at you, and I started to tremble. You came near me, and I melted. It didn't matter that I knew all the hideous things you were doing to the people around you. The sex was good, so I took it while I could get it. I was an easy lay." Her head jerked. "But no more. I'm not melting, and if I'm trembling, it's from anger—anger at you for being a bastard and at myself for having been taken in all these years. I've been defending you. Do you know that? At the slightest negative word, I've always come to your defense. So what do you do to repay me for that? You go to the chairman of the board of my publishing house and have my contract rescinded."

"Be grateful. That book would have been a piece of shit."

She pounded her chest with a fist. "That book was my work. I had a right to get it published whether it was a piece of shit or not." She waved a hand. "But forget that. I can go to another publisher. There's always someone who'll publish shit. And you won't be able to stop me. Unless you kill me. You've committed murder before, if you consider Pam's abortion, and you nearly beat Cutter to death. So I suppose you could kill me. Only I've got my story locked up somewhere safe. If something happens to me, the finger will point straight at you. Won't do much for the respect you want, will it?"

He was looking disgusted. "I'm not a murderer, for God's sake. You're talking ragtime."

"I'm talking reality, and the reality is that you're an evil man."

He rolled his eyes.

"You're frightening, John. You have a warped idea of what's right and what isn't. What's right is what serves your purposes. Whoever gets in the way is out of luck. You barge ahead full steam, rolling over anyone in your path."

"Every successful businessman does that to some extent."

"I don't know about every successful businessman. I only know about you."

"I'm successful."

"You're pathetic and sad and lonely. You've hit middle age. You have money and a business to show for it, but nothing else. No family. No close friends."

"I have friends—"

"Not close ones. You won't let any come close. And I doubt they'd want to. You have a dark side that's off-putting. So you're alone."

"I choose to be alone."

"Because to this day you're insecure. Despite everything you've done and been, deep down inside you're still insecure."

"That's crap."

She shook her head. "I'll bet you have nightmares about being little again, up in Timiny Cove, trying to please your father and failing. You never got over that, did you? You never got over the fact that you didn't measure up to the standards he set." She gave a bitter laugh that helped ease the knot slowly forming in her throat. "God, it's ironic. If he'd lived, if he'd seen half of what you've done, he'd have been in awe."

"If he'd lived," John said in a stony way, "he wouldn't have allowed me to do any of what I've done. I told him my ideas. He said it was all wrong."

"He was conservative. He was frightened about taking as big a step as you wanted. He wasn't sophisticated like you are. He didn't have the vision, and when you tried to give it to him, he couldn't see it. That was his limitation, John, not yours. In so many ways, you're so much more than Eugene ever was—" She caught herself, stared at him, shook her head. "Do you hear me?" she asked in astonishment. "I'm defending you still." The knot tightened in her throat. "I guess I'll

always do that. Just like you'll always feel second best. It's so much a part of you that you can't give it up. You've lived so long with jealousy and hatred that you'd feel empty without it."

She felt the first prick of tears in her eyes. She tried to will them away but she failed. "They're the evil things, John, the jealousy and hatred. Not you. You're not an inherently evil person, but you've let yourself be taken over. You've let yourself be emotionally stunted. And it's made you miss out on so much."

John stood with his legs apart and his features tight. "I'm not missing out on a thing. I have everything I want in life."

"You do not. It's sad."

His eyes flashed. "There's nothing sad about me. I have more than most people ever hope for."

"You have nothing! You go to work. You come home, change your clothes, go out and come home again, and through it all you're alone."

"Look who's talking. Are you any better? You're not involved with anyone. You never have been. You work, go out, come home, and you're alone. So who are you to criticize me?"

"But I don't want to be alone! I never have, and I freely admit it!"

"So why do you do it?"

"Because I've been loving you all these years, waiting for you to love me back, only you can't! You can't love anyone! You're too busy loving yourself, because you think that if you don't, no one else will and you'll have to go without. That's the sad part." Tears gathered on her lids, and her voice shrank. "But I can't go on like this, John. I want more. I want someone to love me. I'm too old to have children. I blew that on you, too—not that you'd want children, because you'd see them as competition for your wife's affections—and it may be that I'm too old to find someone to love me the way I want. But I can't go on waiting for you this way, wondering when you're going to come, holding my breath and praying." In a splintered voice, she said, "It hurts too much. Loving you is too painful."

His face blurred. She tossed a limp hand in the air and whispered, "I'm done with it." Feeling drained and defeated, she turned and left.

John didn't follow her. She wandered aimlessly through downtown Boston for a while before taking a cab to Logan and returning to New York. Rather than go straight to her apartment, she walked some, even stopped for dinner, since it was well past the hour. But she wasn't hungry, and the loneliness of sharing a table with herself got to her. So she left without doing much more than picking at her food.

There were four messages on her answering machine. None of them was from John.

She grappled with her dilemma for hours and hours over the next few days. She didn't answer her phone. If Arlan called with good news—either that John had relented and Templar wanted to go ahead with her book, or that Arlan was moving to another house and was taking the book with him as part of the deal—he would leave a message. But he didn't call.

Nor did John.

Her loneliness had been bad before, but it was even worse now. Things were over with John. Really over. The emptiness she felt was just like the one she predicted John would feel if he ever let go of his jealousy and hatred. If he'd done that, she would have gladly filled the void in his life. He wasn't doing it, though, and now she had a void in her own.

To fill it, she turned her attention back to her book. The only emotional energy she had seemed tied to it, and although she had neither a publisher nor a contract, she couldn't just stop. She had to finish. She had to work John out of her life.

For several weeks, she wrote without a break. It was summertime in New York. Most of her friends were away, and the heat was oppressive enough to keep her indoors. She edited and polished, made calls to check her facts. If she planned to take her book to a new publisher, it had to be *supergood*. Everything had to be backed up so that John wouldn't be able to pull the stunt he'd pulled with Templar.

Then the unexpected happened. She managed to track down Joe Grogan, the lawyer who had written Eugene's will. She had assumed he had died, but in her effort to leave no stone unturned she followed a lead and found him retired and living in northern Arizona. On the

phone, he was cordial and seemed perfectly lucid. He remembered Eugene well.

The next morning, she flew to Arizona. Grogan, not being an executor of Eugene's estate, had had no way of knowing that Cutter had never received his bequest. He did remember the codicil, though, and made a sworn statement to that effect, witnessed by his ranch foreman and a local law officer.

Hillary returned to New York feeling both ebullient and terrified. She added Grogan's statement to her book, but she was uneasy about it. It was disconcertingly real, evidence of a breach of the law. It was a potential firecracker.

For that matter, so was much of what she'd written. John had been right to want her to stop. She wasn't just telling secrets; she was backing them up several times over. Perhaps because of her connection with Timiny Cove, she found people there who were willing to talk to her. Because of her connection with John, she likewise found people in his circle who opened up. She saw him more clearly than she ever had, and that picture emerged in her book.

Gradually she began to grasp what was in her hands. She had power. For the first time in her life, she had the means to move John in some way, shape, or fashion. It was a daunting realization.

That realization took on even greater meaning in the course of the next few weeks. Summer ended, Labor Day came and went, and business in the city picked up where it had left off. Hillary had dinner with Cutter one night. A week after that, she had lunch with Pam. In both of them she found an air of expectancy. At her prodding, both admitted that it had to do with the company.

One part of her—the part that had loved him for years—wanted to warn John. In her mind's eye, he stood alone, arrogant and, therefore, defenseless. He had been wrong about the legacy, the beating, and the abortion. He had been wrong about a slew of other things. But he was in for a fall. She felt it in her gut. He was in for a fall, and a part of her still wanted to help him.

She didn't see how she could warn him. She couldn't betray Cutter and Pam, after the way they had trusted her. Besides, she hadn't been

in contact with John since the night she had told him off. She thought of calling him now, just to reestablish some sort of contact. But she feared he would hang up on her, and that would hurt.

In truth, she still loved him. She hated him for not loving her back, but she did love him. Her love was insane. Cutter told her so, Pam did, and Arlan did, and she knew they were right. But she couldn't help what she felt. It was visceral, not rational. She couldn't turn it off with a snap of her fingers. It was buried deep inside her and had been for twenty-seven long years.

John was part of her. He was the one person who had shaped her more than any other. She had learned that over the past few months. Revenge may have spurred her to write the book, but John was a force behind it in more ways than that. If she had become a dedicated writer over the years, it was to win his praise, far more than to distinguish herself from her family. If she wrote to exorcise her personal frustration, he was at the root of that frustration.

She wished it weren't so. She wished she didn't care what happened to him. She wished she hated him more than she loved him. But she didn't. Whatever his fate, it would touch her.

That was why, when Pam called her on a cloudy Sunday in late September with the news that she and Cutter were meeting with John in the library of the Beacon Hill townhouse the following morning, she asked if she could come.

Chapter 27

❖ ❖ ❖

For years Cutter had imagined setting foot inside the town-house on Beacon Hill. He had imagined what it would look like, and imagined the sense of triumph he would feel. He hadn't counted on the sense of disappointment he felt as he followed Christian toward the library. The townhouse looked well kept and attractive. It was traditional in decor, although it had recently been redecorated. It was perfect in the same way as dozens of other houses he'd seen were perfect. It had no distinctive character whatsoever.

He didn't have time to dwell on the sadness of that, or on how different things might have looked had Eugene lived there. Christian opened the double doors and gestured him in with the aristocratic tip of his head. Feeling a sense of anticipation, Cutter went forward. The moment had been a long, long time in coming.

Pam was sitting on a leather sofa looking beautiful. The sight of her enhanced the anticipation he felt. Brendan was by her side, looking twenty years older than he had when Cutter had seen him last. He immediately went over and offered his hand.

"Good to see you Brendan," he said quietly, meaning it. "How are you feeling?"

Brendan gave a dubious shrug with one brow, then relented, smiled, and nodded.

"Cutter, do you remember my mother?" Pam asked.

He heard tension in her voice along with excitement, and tried

to encourage her with a look before he turned to the other side of the room, where Patricia sat in a wheelchair. He had known she would be there. He had also known what she would look like, since Pam had described her to him more than once. It had been years since he'd seen her himself. She looked older now, but lovely in a fragile sort of way. She also looked extremely nervous and vulnerable, both of which he could understand. She hadn't been in the townhouse since the day of the accident.

He held out a hand, and, out of gut protectiveness, when she put hers in it, he covered it with his free one. Softly he said, "It's good to see you again, Mrs. St. George. I'm glad you're here."

"I'm not sure I am," Patricia whispered.

He smiled and gave her hand a gentle squeeze before releasing it to greet the man standing nearby. "It's a pleasure, Dr. Grossman."

"Same here."

Cutter had never met Bob before, but he liked him on sight. Pam said he was good to Patricia, even in love with her. Aside from that, Cutter was grateful for the support Bob had given Pam over the years.

He hoped some of that gratitude showed in his look, because in the next instant anything remotely relating to pleasure or gratitude vanished from his face. With no one else present in the room to divert him, he turned at last to John.

He had seen the man over the years from time to time, but always from a distance and with people between them. The distance now was no more than ten feet, and there were no people between them, just the venerable mahogany desk behind which John sat.

The last time Cutter had looked directly into John's eyes was on a cold night in December seventeen years before. He had been a miner then, poor, uneducated, feeling hatred and pain. There was no pain now, but the hatred flooded back, and for a split second it was as strong as ever. In that split second Cutter remembered the threats that had kept him from Pam. He remembered the big brick house in Timiny Cove that had been sold, the baby that had been aborted, the five rows of metal studs that had torn up his back.

Then the split second was over, and the hatred was muted by the civility of the setting, the presence of Patricia and Pam, and his own hard-earned dignity.

He didn't greet John. John didn't greet him. They stared at each other in silent challenge, until John finally announced, "If you're done with the social niceties, perhaps we could get on with this. I have a meeting across town at eleven."

That left them an hour, which was more than enough as far as Cutter was concerned. He nodded, but before he could speak the door opened again and Hillary slipped in. She looked slightly breathless and more than a little frazzled. After a quick glance around, her gaze settled on John.

"What are you doing here?" he asked in a tone that made Cutter hurt for her.

"I wanted to come."

"This is business."

"I know."

"You haven't any part in it."

Pam broke in. "I asked her to come. She has a vested interest in all of us."

John's features went even more rigid. "Is she taking notes?"

"No," Hillary answered for herself. "I'm here as a friend."

"Whose friend?"

"Yours."

"And Pam's, and his." He jutted his chin toward Cutter. "I sense a confrontation here, Hillary. Better decide whose side you're on."

Again Pam spoke, less patiently this time. "There's no need to take sides." She glanced at her watch. "Since we have limited time, I think we should start."

John sat back in his chair and leveled Cutter an icy stare. "I assume you're here because you own company stock. That's the only reason I'd allow you in my home. Do you understand that?"

"It is not your home," came Patricia's frail voice, drawing every eye in the room her way. "It's mine. It was left to me as part of my

husband's estate. You live here because I let you. When I decide that you leave, you leave."

The swell of triumph in the air was nearly tangible. It came from everyone present but John. Incredibly, he maintained his poise. He didn't even blink. Ignoring Patricia, he said to Cutter, "If you have something to say, spit it out. I don't have all day."

If Cutter had been holding a gun to John's head—a regular fantasy of his—and John had told him to shoot, he would have done just that. In the absence of a gun, he said in a clear voice, "We're taking you over."

John nodded. "Uh-huh."

"It's true," Pam assured him, but Cutter held up a hand to still her before she said more. This was his baby. It had been years in the planning and years in the carrying out. He wanted the pleasure all to himself.

"A while back, I started an investment banking firm. My partners and I have done well. Our client list has quadrupled in the last few years, and in that time, many of those clients have picked up St. George Company common stock. We have enough now to take you over."

"That's impossible," John said. He was still sitting back in his chair with his fingers laced over his middle and would have looked complacent had his knuckles not been white. "You'd need a majority for that, but I can personally account for better than fifty-five percent of the company stock. Forty-five percent is held by the family, another ten percent by close friends."

"Forty-five percent may be held by family," Cutter informed him, "but thirty of that forty-five percent agree with this takeover."

John's reaction was subtle. Cutter had to hand it to the man; his self-control was like iron. Other than the faint paling of his skin, there was nothing.

"Thirty percent? How do you figure that?"

"Pam will vote for a change in company leadership. So will Patricia."

"Patricia doesn't control her stock," John replied. "I do."

"Not for long," Patricia put in. Her voice was shaky, but her words were clear. "I've already asked my lawyer to see about returning control to me."

Unable to ignore her a second time, John gave a negligent shake of his head. "He won't succeed. You've been in a mental hospital for more than twenty years. No judge is going to suddenly decide that you're competent."

Bob Grossman straightened and said more forcefully than Patricia, "She's competent. I'll testify to it. She's been competent for years."

"Then why has she been hospitalized?"

"Because she chose to live in a defined environment."

"If that isn't crazy," John tossed off, "I don't know what is."

Pam had stiffened and was about to come to her mother's defense when Bob beat her to it. "It's not crazy. Most people have the need to build walls around themselves. Some do it in the form of a close group of friends, others in the form of a business, others in the form of where they live. No, there's nothing crazy about Patricia, and believe me, I know what crazy is."

"That's right. You're a psychiatrist. You've been treating her all these years, yet you claim she's competent. Quite frankly, that sounds like fraud."

Bob was unfazed. "The majority of people in therapy are competent. One has little to do with the other. And as for Patricia, she'll be leaving the hospital soon. We're getting married."

Cutter hadn't known that. He was happy for Patricia, and glancing at Pam, he read the same on her face. John, too, looked pleased, but in an ugly way.

"Ahhh," he said. "Now it makes sense. You were taken with the woman, so you kept her at the hospital all this time. You accepted the hefty fees she paid for room and board, and the even heftier fees she paid for your services. Suddenly, when you sense fresh money in the pot, you say that she's competent, that she should be discharged, that she can marry you. I'd think the medical board would like to hear this story."

Pam flew to her feet. "Oh no you don't, *no-oo* you don't. You've

pulled that trick one too many times. Threatening to blackmail Bob won't work. He hasn't done a thing wrong."

"He took advantage of a helpless woman who depended on him."

"I'm not helpless," Patricia said in a huff. "I let myself be helpless when I was younger. That was when you took advantage of me. Bob has never done that."

"I'm aware of the ethical considerations here, Mr. St. George," Bob said. "At no time during Patricia's stay at my hospital have I taken advantage of her. I haven't touched her physically. She pays the same fees as every other patient. And she has been seeing another therapist, not me, for a year now. Besides, when we get married, we'll be living in my house, a house that I bought twelve years ago and have been paying off ever since. I won't take her money. I've already told her that, and I'll be putting it in writing—at my insistence, not hers." He took a quick breath. "Sorry, chum, but you're barking up the wrong tree."

"I'm not your chum," John ground out.

"Thank God for it," was Bob's response, and for a minute there was utter silence.

Cutter ended it by clearing his throat. "I'd suggest we move on." He waited only until Pam was seated before saying to John, "You're outvoted. Pam favors a change, Patricia favors a change, I favor a change, and so do my clients."

John's voice came more sharply. "Your clients only know what you feed them. If they took the time to read the company reports—"

"They've taken the time—"

"—they'd see that the business is thriving under my leadership. There's no cause for a change."

"They feel there is."

"Only because you tell them that."

Cutter shrugged. He was feeling pretty good, pretty confident, pretty satisfied with the way things were going. John was starting to worry. He was starting to look a little pinched around the mouth. His hands weren't linked anymore, and he was sitting straighter.

"I made *Facets*," he said in a commanding voice. "Those stores are

mine. Neither you nor anyone else in this room is going to take them away from me."

Cutter turned first toward Pam and Brendan, then Patricia and Bob. When he caught sight of Hillary, who was pressed back against one of the library doors with her arms wrapped around her middle, staring at John, he felt a moment's compassion. At the same time, he wanted to shake her into realizing that what was happening was for the best. He couldn't believe that she still loved the man—couldn't believe that she'd ever loved him.

Slowly he turned back to John. "It seems," he said in a quiet and dignified tone that, given his modest beginnings, mocked John, "that you won't have much choice. We have the votes." He reached into his blazer and pulled a thick envelope from its inner pocket. "I have the proxies necessary should we decide to call an emergency meeting of the board."

"You're not calling a meeting of my board."

"It's my board, too," Cutter took pleasure in reminding him. "I'm a stockholder."

"An insignificant one."

"Alone, perhaps. But I'm not alone. I have all these other people just dying to get you booted out."

"You've brainwashed them."

"I didn't have to do anything as drastic as that." As business associates of Cutter's, they were more than ready to follow his lead.

"You have no legitimate reason to have me removed."

"Do I need one?"

John came to his feet then and set his shoulders back. "You sure as hell do. I made this company. My record is impeccable. Our profits have grown every year. The stockholders have received healthy dividends."

"That's not the point," Cutter replied calmly. "The point is that you serve at the will of the board of directors, which serves at the will of the general stockholding population."

"The board is on my side."

"Maybe the old board. The new board won't be." He waved the

envelope that was still in his hand. "I have a proposed slate of officers here. It's an interesting group. I think they'll want their own man as head of the company." No longer pale but slightly red-faced now, John looked as though steam were building inside him. "And that man is you?"

"Me? God, no. I have my own business. I don't want to be head of the St. George Company. But I do have some people in mind for the job. All of them have experience with international corporations."

"None of them are part of this family. My father conceived of the St. George Company as a family business."

"Your father," Cutter spat back, losing it for a minute, "would have kicked you out long ago if he'd known all you did to Pam and Patricia. And to me." He took a steadying breath. "You don't have to worry that the company will go to pot. It'll thrive, even expand."

"It's my company."

"You'll certainly still own your stock—"

"I *am* the company."

"Not for much longer. As I started to say before," he held up the proxies one last time before slipping them back into his pocket, "we can either call an emergency meeting or wait for the annual meeting in November. If you resign now—"

"I'm not resigning!" John bellowed, sounding so much like Eugene that Cutter had a moment's pause, but only a moment's. That fiery temperament was about all the two men shared. Remembering Eugene, remembering how much heart and soul the man had, how much he would have wanted for Patricia and Pam that they hadn't had, Cutter was hardened.

"You have a choice," he told John coolly, curtly. He was finished with toying. It was time for the belt with the five rows of metal studs. "You can resign now, in which case an acting president will be chosen until the annual meeting. Or you can fight us. If you decide to do that, we'll call an emergency meeting and push things through sooner. We have enough votes, John. *More* than enough votes. You don't have a chance of winning. It's just a question of how hard you fall." He barely paused for a breath before hauling back and swinging the belt

again. "If you fight us, we'll get dirty. You'll go down anyway, but we'll bad-mouth you all the way. On the other hand, if you submit your resignation and get out of the picture, we'll be quiet. You can pack up your things and take your expertise somewhere else. You'll get a job in a minute. They'll fight over you, and the only explanation you'll have to give for leaving the St. George Company is that you wanted a change. Or you can sell your interest in St. George and start a new business. Or you can retire. You can move down south or out west. In any case, you'll have your reputation intact. If you resign. Within the week."

John stood frozen. "That's blackmail."

"You should know. You've used it often enough."

"You can't do this."

"It's done. I have Pam's support and Patricia's support and," he patted his breast pocket, "the support of a majority of the remaining stockholders. Face it, John. You're beaten."

"No. I've worked too hard to get where I am. I'm the force behind the company—"

"I'm the force behind *Facets*," Pam interrupted. "My designs are the backbone of our business. So it won't really matter if you're gone. The merchandise will be every bit as good, if not better."

John's eyes narrowed on her. "You've been dying for this. You've been working up to it since the day you came to work for me."

"Since long before that," she corrected, "and I work with you, not for you."

"You've been just waiting to get your claws into me."

She grinned. "Got them in good now, don't I?"

To Brendan, John said, "She's making a mistake. They all are. You don't fix something that's not broken. You're a businessman. You know that."

Brendan answered in a voice that was raspy but firm. "I know that change is good sometimes. It puts a fresh perspective on things. Like the airing of dirty laundry. It makes the room smell a whole lot better."

Pam chuckled.

John glared at her. "Think that's funny? You won't be laughing when the figures start falling."

"They won't. I have faith in Cutter. He knows what he's doing." She grew puzzled. "Didn't you have any inkling of it? Didn't you see it at all? Didn't you have any idea that he was becoming a force to be reckoned with? Where have you been all these years?"

"I've been working my tail off making *Facets* a success."

"You've been hobnobbing with the rich and famous."

"I am the rich and famous."

"Maybe," she conceded, "and there's nothing we can do to change that. But you won't be entertaining your friends on *Facets'* expense account anymore. You'll be on your own."

He considered that for a minute. He looked from her face to Cutter's, to Patricia's. In the process, some of the steam seemed to leave him. "It's revenge, then?" Again he looked around. "Is that it? Revenge?"

"You could say," Cutter replied, but with the loss of John's steam he too was feeling less anger. "I prefer to call it poetic justice."

"There's no poetic justice in this, not after all the years I've worked to build the company."

"While you were working to build the company, the rest of us were working to find firm footing after you'd knocked the ground out from under us. We've worked just as hard as you have, each in our own way." He nodded. "This is poetic justice."

John remained quiet. He stared at Cutter for a bit, then frowned down at the desk. When he looked back up, his chin was cocked at an arrogant angle. "I won't do a thing until I see the paperwork backing up what you've said. As far as I'm concerned, you're bluffing."

"I'm not."

"I'll see that paperwork. Then I'll decide for myself."

Despite John's command, Cutter was in the driver's seat, and he knew it. He was the one calling the shots. "I'll have my lawyer contact you later today to arrange a meeting."

"I won't be in later today." John glanced at his watch. There was a faint tremor in his hand when he braced his fingertips on the desk. "I

have one meeting at eleven and another at two. I won't be returning to the office today."

"Then he'll contact you in the morning. You have until Friday to make a decision. That should be enough time."

Without acknowledging the statement one way or the other, John lifted his briefcase from the side of the desk and started for the door.

Cutter had never been one to kick a dog when it was down, but John wasn't any ordinary dog. "If you're hoping to stall long enough to put a counterattack together, don't," he advised. "The smear starts at the first hint of a fight. Once it starts, you'll have trouble finding another position."

John stopped at the door with his hand on the knob.

To his back, Cutter said, "And don't think that you'll be able to set up shop somewhere else and then force a hostile takeover of the St. George Company. We'll be putting through some stringent anti-takeover clauses. You won't have a chance."

John turned the handle, opened the door, went through, closed the door behind him. He walked at an even pace, one impeccably shod foot following the other with mechanical ease. He was aware of an odd, almost distant shaking inside him, but his mind couldn't seem to focus in on it. Although he held his briefcase, his hand felt empty. That was pretty much what he felt all over. Empty. Stunned. Alone.

He looked for the anger in him, looked hard and deep, and it was there, he supposed, but he didn't have the strength to drag it up to the surface. The same thing went for his cockiness. He was tired of fighting silent ghosts. It seemed he'd been doing that all his life, trying to find the spot that was just right for him. He thought he'd found it. He thought he'd made it. Being at the helm of the St. George Company filled most of his needs.

Now he was going to lose it. Cutter had it all worked out. John knew enough about business—he'd been the one to take the company public in the first place—to know that it would happen just as Cutter had said. Without Patricia and Pam, he'd lose it. He had counted on them. Assumed. He didn't know why. But he had.

The front door was before him, but he saw the faces back in the library as they had just looked at him. There had been no warmth, no support, no understanding. Except in Hillary. She had had tears in her eyes and a fist pressed to her mouth. She was the only one of the bunch who felt anything for him, anything at all.

Was it pity, or compassion? He didn't know. Pity, he didn't want. He still had his name. He still had his pride. He still had a future.

Compassion was something else. He could deal with compassion, he supposed.

But not right now. Taking a long, hard breath, he closed his eyes for a minute and dug down deep for composure. He had a meeting to make, and he didn't want to be late. He was known for punctuality. It was part of the executive image—on time for one meeting, so that he would be on time for the one after it, and the next, and the next. He was a busy man. He was important. He was in demand. It was time to get going.

Hillary heard the sharp close of the front door. It echoed through the silence that had filled the library since John's exit. Blinking back her tears, she looked around at the others in the room. They didn't look triumphant. She wished they would. Then she could be angry. She could tell them what hypocrites they were for having criticized John over the years, when they'd just done to him what he'd done to them.

No, they didn't look triumphant. But that didn't mean they were going to change their minds. She couldn't ask them to, and even if she did, they wouldn't. They had worked too long and hard to get where they were. And she had to admit that Cutter was right about the poetic justice in what had happened.

Through it all, John had kept his dignity. She was proud of him. He hadn't embarrassed himself or her by resorting to tantrums or yelling matches. He had known he was beaten. His final words were simply a way of saving face.

Lord, she felt for him. And he had looked so alone as he walked out that door.

Whirling around, she pulled open the door and started after him. But by the time she reached the front steps there was no sign of him at all.

Cutter was behind her. After a minute, he took her hand. "What now, Hillary?"

She looked up the street again, thinking that maybe John would somehow reappear. But he didn't. "I don't know," she said, sounding just as she felt, on the near side of panic. "I think I'll try to call him later."

"What if he hangs up on you?"

"Then he hangs up. He's done it before. I'll wait a little while, then try again."

Cutter squeezed her hand. "You deserve more."

"I know. I know, Cutter. But he's all I ever wanted."

"You wanted a career."

"Because I couldn't have him."

"You still have your book."

She thought about that for a minute, thought about why she'd written it, what she had hoped to get out of it. Then she shook her head. "I'm not finishing it."

"Not finishing it at all?"

She shook her head again.

"Why?"

She shrugged. "Too close. Too hot. Too painful." She took a shaky breath. "I thought I wanted revenge. But revenge hurts. Besides," she tried for a smile and failed, "I don't know how it will end. How's that for a reason?"

"As good as any for now," he said so kindly that she fought back a moan. In the next breath, she slipped an arm around his neck and gave him a tight hug.

"You're my friend. Can I call you sometimes?"

"I'll be mad if you don't."

Drawing back, she patted his lapel. "Mad is for dogs. But you're a man. A good man." She sent him a timid look. "Will you be angry if I stick with him?"

"Angry as hell. You deserve better than what he'll give."

"But I love him."

"Which is something I'll never understand."

She paused, swallowed, shrugged. "Me neither. But that's the way it is."

He seemed about to say more, then thought better of it and simply said, "I want the world for you, Hillary."

There were tears behind her smile. "Same here," she whispered. After giving his lapel a final pat, she trotted down the steps and went off up the street.

Cutter watched her until he heard Pam's voice. "Will she be all right?"

He turned, smiled, put a hand to her neck because he badly needed to touch her. "I don't know. It's such a crazy thing, what she feels for John."

"It always has been. I've never understood it. He's been so cruel to her, yet she keeps going back for more."

"Some women do that."

"But I want her happy."

"Maybe she will be." He swore softly. "All these years she's been on his side, and the bastard never saw it. He has a gold mine in her. If he doesn't see that now, he deserves to go right down the tubes."

Pam slipped an arm under his jacket and around his waist. She was feeling strangely deflated. "I thought it would feel so good," she said quietly. "I thought there would be this tremendous high, this fantastic sense of victory, this . . . glee. But there isn't."

Cutter knew just what she meant. "That's the difference between us and him. He would have felt it."

"What do you think he'll do?"

"Resign. He'll go elsewhere. He'll do fine."

She tipped her face up against his shoulder. "Does that bother you?"

He met her gaze. "No. He can do what he wants. I just want him out of my hair. Out of your hair. Away from this company. Once that's done, he's lost the power to hurt us."

They looked at each other in silence for several minutes.

"It's been a long time in the coming," she whispered.

"I'll say," he whispered back.

"There's so much we've lost."

"But so much we've gained. We both have names and careers. We have an incredibly beautiful daughter. And we have time, lots of time down the road."

Pam felt a pang of sorrow. "Brendan doesn't. We're starting a new treatment program next week, but it may buy a few months at most. Things don't look good, Cutter."

He wrapped an arm around her shoulder and drew her close.

"Will you be there for me when it happens?" she asked.

"You know I will."

"Even when I'm sad and grieving? I do love him. It's very different from how I love you, but I'll miss him when he's gone. Can you live with that?"

"It's what makes you you."

His comment was what made Cutter Cutter, and she loved him all the more for it. Slipping her arms around him, she took strength from the sound of his heartbeat for a poignant moment, before kissing him lightly and going back inside.